BISON FRONTIERS OF IMAGINATION

WHEN WORLDS COLLIDE

PHILIP WYLIE AND EDWIN BALMER

INTRODUCTION TO THE BISON BOOKS EDITION BY
John Varley

UNIVERSITY OF NEBRASKA PRESS
LINCOLN AND LONDON

When Worlds Collide copyright © 1932, 1933 by Edwin Balmer and
Philip Wylie
After Worlds Collide copyright © 1933, 1934 by Edwin Balmer and
Philip Wylie
Introduction © 1999 by the University of Nebraska Press
All rights reserved
Manufactured in the United States of America

∞

First Bison Books printing: 1999

Library of Congress Cataloging-in-Publication Data
Wylie, Philip, 1902–1971.
[When worlds collide]
When worlds collide / Philip Wylie and Edwin Balmer; introduction to
the Bison Books edition John Varley.
p.   cm.—(Bison frontiers of imagination)
ISBN 0-8032-9814-5 (pbk.: alk. paper)
1. Science fiction, American.   I. Balmer, Edwin, 1883–1959.
II. Wylie, Philip, 1902–1971. After worlds collide.   III. Title.
IV. Title: After worlds collide.   V. Series.
PS3545.Y46W48   1999
813′.52—dc21
99-35221   CIP

This Bison Books edition follows the original in beginning both books
on arabic page 5; no material has been omitted.

INTRODUCTION

John Varley

When I was first asked to do an introduction to this new edition of *When Worlds Collide* and *After Worlds Collide*, the letter I received mentioned five other science fiction books recently published by the University of Nebraska Press. All of them were what I'd call sterling examples of Classic Science Fiction. I had never read any of them. I'm putting that here, right up front, to establish my credentials, or lack of them. I am not any kind of science fiction historian. I've read *20,000 Leagues under the Sea* and *The Time Machine*, and that's about it for works published before 1930. This will not, then, be a treatise on how these two novels fit into the grand scheme of the development of science fiction as a genre.

What I intend to speak of here is how much I loved these books when I first read them, and what they have to offer for today's reader.

Oh, I do know a few things about the authors, most of which I learned in the last few days—though I'm embarrassed to admit that I had completely forgotten the books were a collaboration.

Philip Wylie lived from 1902 to 1971. He wrote around a dozen novels and many essays, gaining a reputation as a social critic. He was an early advocate of conservation, what we today call ecology. He's probably best known for his 1942 book *Generation of Vipers*, which describes "the tyranny American women exercise over the male spirit" and introduced the word "Momism" into the language—where it apparently didn't stick. I've never read it and probably never will. That strikes me as a political issue more safely left alone, almost sixty years later.

He wrote two novels of nuclear war, *Tomorrow!* in 1954 and *Triumph* in 1963. I read *Triumph* only last week, and it is a hair-raising tale. It is somewhat shocking today to read a novel written in the darkest depths of the cold war, wherein it is postulated that the Soviets would be willing to absolutely sterilize the entire northern hemisphere so that a small, chosen cadre of commissars could emerge from their deep shelters several years later and, with their remaining nuclear weapons, establish dominance over the remnants of humanity in Africa and Australia. Were the Russians ever fanatical enough to actually do that? I don't know. But Wylie is ingenious at using nuclear weapons, already intrinsically terrifying, in ways that are even more horrific.

Edwin Balmer was born in 1883 and died in 1959. He wrote mainly in the mystery field, publishing a dozen novels and numerous short stories, many with William MacHarg. He edited *Red Book* magazine for over twenty years. In addition to the two novels printed here, he co-wrote three mysteries with Philip Wylie.

Who handled which part of what book is a complete mystery to me.

Wylie shows a good grasp of the scientific and engineering side of his nuclear war story—good enough to convince me, anyway. Most of the science in *When Worlds Collide* is plausible enough, too . . . except the way gravity works. The authors inexplicably don't understand the nature of gravity and acceleration, having their space travelers experience weightlessness at the point midway between the Earth and Bronson Beta, when the gravity "balances." This despite being under acceleration for the entire journey. This is completely wrong. Look it up if you don't believe me.

An even stranger misconception leads Wylie and Balmer to design their spaceship with identical engines on each end of the vessel. Surely it would be easier to turn the ship around when it comes time to slow down.

It was 1960, I was in the seventh grade, thirteen years old—the golden age of science fiction. Mr. Green, the librarian at C.O. Wilson Junior High in Nederland, Texas, had noticed I was reading all those odd books by people like Robert A. Heinlein, Isaac Asimov, Andre Norton, Theodore Sturgeon, and Lester del Rey. I already had a sci-fi monkey on my back as big as the Mighty Joe Young. So Mr. Green handed me this *huge* book (and by the way, Thanks, Mr. Green) that had been read so hard it was just about ready for pulping. It was called *When Worlds Collide and After Worlds Collide*. (Hereinafter to be referred to as one book called *WWC/AWC* because, let's face it, though *WWC* could be read and enjoyed alone so long as you don't know there's a sequel, *AWC* cannot. You wouldn't know who these people were.)

I *loved* this book. I can't describe how much I loved it except to say that, for the first and only time I can recall, I finished the last page and went immediately back to page one and read it though again.

And something else happened. I had read dozens of science fiction novels by then and was in awe of the (mostly) men who wrote them. Never for one second did I think I could do that. But after reading *WWC/AWC* for the *third* time, I picked up a ballpoint pen and a big pad of paper and I started to write. I must have written a hundred stories. Some of them were five pages long; some went on for several hundred pages. None of them had what you'd call an end; at some point I just got tired of them or had a better idea and started writing on that instead.

All these stories had something in common. They were all what I now call after-the-apocalypse stories. Or shipwreck stories, like *Robinson Crusoe* or *The Swiss Family Robinson*, which I also read around this time. Each story started with the destruction of 99.999 percent of humanity or the stranding of a small band of brave men and women on an alien planet. From then on they were all about how one survived in the ruins or what one found in this strange new environment. Believe me, I wrote "Lost in Space" *years* before television writers ever thought of it.

WWC/AWC is the only novel I can think of that uses *both* these plots.

It wasn't until many years later, after many discussions with many other readers and writers, that I realized what may be a dirty little secret about after-the-apocalypse stories: They are fun. Billions of people have died of plague or nuclear war or planetary catastrophe of one sort or another . . . and they're fun.

I think most of us, from time to time, get to feeling a little crowded. Maybe you're stuck in traffic. Maybe you're driving by a place that, two years ago, was a cow pasture, and now it's a shopping center. Maybe you're being jostled in a jammed department store trying to finish your Christmas shopping. And you think, "Wouldn't it be nice to be stranded on a desert island?" You've just put your finger on why Daniel Defoe still sells books after all these years.

Yes . . . but that's a desert island. What about the huge disaster?

I felt guilty about that for a long time. Then I got over it. I mean, it's not as if I'm wishing something terrible would happen to six billion people. All I'm fantasizing about is the opportunity to shop for canned goods in a deserted Safeway and not wait in a check-out line. Or drive my borrowed Rolls-Royce around the abandoned cars on the Hollywood Freeway. Is that so bad?

Whether it is or not, it's a story line that hasn't lost its appeal, from Noah's Ark to Stephen King's *The Stand*. *WWC/AWC* is the *Gone With the Wind* of after-the-apocalypse stories.

So here I am, nearly forty years later. My copy of the book arrives in the mail. I eagerly tear it open and begin reading . . .

If you have read William Goldman's wonderful book *The Princess Bride* you may have an idea of what happened next. (If you haven't read it, run right out and buy a copy, just as soon as you finish reading *this* book. The new twenty-fifth anniversary edition is just out.) In his introduction, Goldman describes how he tried to interest his son in what he believed was the best book ever written. The son didn't see it that way, so Goldman began to re-read it . . . and it stunk. It was long-winded and verbose and chock full of things no one in the twentieth century could possibly care about. Goldman's father had been reading only the good parts, leaving out whole chapters of politics and such.

And me . . . along about chapter two I was in a cold sweat. I was starting to fear it would be tough to find good things to say about this book. Let me cite a few examples of what had me worried:

The nicest word I can think of to describe most of the dialogue is "Shakespearean." These people orate a lot, in Byzantine sentences full of, to me, overly poetic imagery. This is fine, in Shakespeare. Modern readers are used to more realistic prose.

When it is revealed that a few humans might make a trip through space and avoid the total destruction of the Earth, they quickly set out to find the absolute best crew of white Park Avenue Episcopalians possible. Being on the social register doesn't hurt. Ethnic diversity is an idea that had not arrived in 1932.

The one "person of color" who *does* make it aboard was *not* included in the original passenger list. He is Tony's "Jap servant," Kyto, as inscrutable an oriental as you'll find anywhere in fiction. One other "ordinary" person sneaks aboard at the last minute, and she is consistently referred to as a "moron," apparently because she didn't finish high school and works as an "acrobatic dancer."

Even eugenics rears its nasty head. At first it is agreed that our "primitive" notions of love and marriage must be jettisoned, and a new, "modern" man should be produced by matching men and women according to scientific principles. I can't think of a better recipe for disaster, myself. Luckily, this idea is abandoned before people begin killing each other out of jealousy.

You may be wondering by now if I hated the book. Stop worrying. You didn't really think I'd introduce a book by saying it's not worth reading, did you?

Something happened around chapter three. Actually, I think it had been happening in the first two chapters, too, but I hadn't noticed it yet. First, I stopped being jarred by the politically incorrect things I was coming across. You can find things like this in *any* book or movie from 1932. Second, I stopped worrying about the Shakespearean dialogue. It was good enough for Shakespeare, wasn't it? And third, I began to enjoy it for what it is: one great big, wildly enjoyable, and hugely horrifying story of the end of everything. This is a story that will take you back to 1960, even if you weren't even born in 1960. It will take you back to the age of thirteen, to *your* golden age of science fiction. To the time when you first realized that this spaceship stuff that your teachers and parents didn't really approve of could paint on a canvas a billion times larger than *Silas Marner* or *The Red Badge of Courage*—the stuff they wanted you to read.

I'm not here to knock the classics. *The Red Badge of Courage* is a great book. It will take you places you've never been before. But *WWC/AWC* will take you to a place where these two sentences are possible:

The two planets struck.
Decillions of tons of mass colliding in cosmic catastrophe.

(Please don't accuse me of letting the cat out of the bag. Did you think that, in a book titled *When Worlds Collide*, they were going to *miss*?)

I remember trying to imagine a decillion. I was just coming to terms with one trillion as a million million. One decillion is a billion trillion *trillion*! I remember trying to imagine what it would look like—and with all our cinema magic, this is an effect we still haven't put convincingly on the screen. (Maybe someone will remake the film of *When Worlds Collide* one of these days. The less said about the original, the better.)

Well, *I've* seen two planets collide, playing on the super CinemaScope screen in my head. Let me assure you, it's an awesome sight to see. And I have stood on the alien soil of Bronson Beta, looked up in the sky, and seen the remains of Earth and all mankind's works come flaming through the night sky as meteors. And then, I have rolled up my sleeves with all my brave shipmates, because there's a lot of work to be done and an entire planet to explore.

Now it's your turn.

WHEN WORLDS COLLIDE

THE secret itself was still safe. It was clear that the public not yet could have learned it. No; the nature of the tremendous and terrific Discovery remained locked in the breasts of the men who had made it. No one had broken so badly under the burden of it that he had let slip any actual details of what had been learned.

But the fact that there was a secret, of incomparable importance, was out.

David Ransdell received plenty of proof of it, as he stood at the liner's rail, and the radiograms from shore were brought to him. He had had seven, all of the same sort, within the hour; and here was another.

He held it without opening it while he gazed across the sparkling water at the nearing shores of Long Island beyond which lay New York. Strange that, in a city which he could not yet see, men could be so excited about his errand, while the fellow-passengers, at his elbow, glanced at him with only mild curiosity at the sudden frequency of radiograms for him.

They would be far less indifferent, if they had read them.

The first, arriving less than an hour ago, offered him one thousand dollars for first and exclusive information—to be withheld from all others for twelve hours—of what he carried in his black box. It was signed by the most famous newspaper in New York.

Hardly had the messenger started back to the radio station when a second boy appeared with a message from another newspaper: "Two thousand dollars for first information of your business in New York."

Within ten minutes the offer had jumped to five thousand dollars, made by another paper. Plainly, the knowledge that there was a secret of utmost importance had spread swiftly!

The offer remained at five thousand for twenty minutes; indeed, it dipped once to twenty-five hundred dollars as some timid soul, on a more economical newspaper, ventured to put in his bid; but quickly it jumped again and doubled. It was ten thousand dollars, in the last radiogram which Dave had opened. Ten thousand dollars cash for first information, which now needed to be withheld from others only for six hours, regarding what he was bringing to New York.

The thrilling and all-absorbing fact of it was that David Ransdell himself did not know what he carried which could become of such amazing concern. He was merely the courier who transported and guarded the secret.

He could look in his box, of course; he possessed the key. But he had the key, as also he had custody of the heavy black box, because those who had entrusted it to him knew that he would never violate his word. Least of all, would he sell out to others. Moreover (if curiosity tried him beyond his strength) he had Professor Bronson's word for it that the contents of the box would be utterly meaningless to him. Only a few men, with very special training, could make out the meaning.

Cole Hendron in New York—Dr. Cole Hendron, the physicist—could make it out. Indeed, he could determine it more completely than any other man alive. That was why Dave Ransdell, from South Africa, was bound for New York; he was bringing the box to Cole Hendron, who, after he had satisfied himself of the significance of its contents, would take the courier into his confidence.

Dave gripped the rail with his aggravated impatience for arrival in the city. He wondered, but with secondary interest only, under the circumstances, what it would be like in America. It was the native land of his mother; but David had never so much as seen its shores before. For he was a South African—his father an Englishman who had once ranched in Montana, had married a Montana girl and had taken her to the Transvaal. Dave had been born at Pretoria, schooled there, and had run away from school to go to war.

The war had made him a flyer. He had stayed in the air afterward, and he was flying the mails when, suddenly, at the request of Capetown,—and he did not yet know from how high an official source,—he had been granted a special leave to fly a certain shipment of scientific material to America. That is, he was instructed to fly it not only the length of his ordinary route, but to continue with it the length of Africa and across to France, where he was to make connection with the first and fastest ship for New York.

Of course, the commission intrigued him. He had been summoned at night to the great mansion of Lord Rhondin, near Capetown.

Lord Rhondin himself, a big, calm, practical-minded man, received him; and with Lord Rhondin was a tall, wiry man of forty-odd, with a quick and nervous manner.

"Professor Bronson," Lord Rhondin said, introducing Ransdell.

"The astronomer?" Dave asked as they shook hands.

"Exactly," said Lord Rhondin. Bronson did not speak at all then, or for several minutes. He merely grasped Dave's hand with nervous tightness and stared at him while he was thinking, patently, of something else—something, Dave guessed, which recently had allowed him too little sleep.

"Sit down," Lord Rhondin bade; and the three of them seated themselves; but no one spoke.

They were in a big, secluded room given to trophies of the

hunt. Animal skins covered the floor; and lion and buffalo and elephant heads looked down from the walls, their glass eyes glinting in the light which was reflected, also, by festoons of shining knives and spears.

"We sent for you, Ransdell," said Lord Rhondin, "because a very strange discovery has been made—a discovery which, if confirmed in all details, is of incomparable consequence. Nothing conceivable can be of greater importance. I tell you that at the outset, Ransdell, because I must refrain for the present from telling you anything else about it."

Dave felt his skin prickling with a strange, excited awe. There was no doubt that this man—Lord Rhondin, industrialist, financier and conspicuous patron of science—thoroughly believed what he said; behind the eyes which looked at David Ransdell was awe at knowledge which he dared not reveal. But Dave asked boldly:

"Why?"

"Why can't I tell you?" Lord Rhondin repeated, and looked at Bronson.

Professor Bronson nervously jumped up. He stared at Lord Rhondin and then at Ransdell, and looked up from him at a lion's head.

"Strange to think of no more lions!" Bronson finally muttered. The words seemed to escape him involuntarily.

Lord Rhondin made no remark at this apparent irrelevance. Ransdell, inwardly more excited by this queerly oppressive silence, at last demanded:

"Why will there be no more lions?"

"Why not tell him?" Bronson asked.

But Rhondin went abruptly to business: "We asked leave for you, Ransdell, because I have heard that you are a particularly reliable man. It is essential that material connected with the discovery be delivered in New York City at the earliest practicable moment. You are both an expert pilot who can make the best speed, and you are dependable. If you will take it, I will put the material in your care; and—can you start to-night?"

"Yes sir. But—what sort of material, I must ask, if I am to fly with it?"

"Chiefly glass."

"Glass?" Dave repeated.

"Yes—photographic plates."

"Oh. How many of them?"

Lord Rhondin threw back a leopard-skin which had covered a large black traveling-case.

"They are packed, carefully, in this. I will tell you this much more, which you may guess, from Professor Bronson's presence. They are photographic plates taken by the greatest telescopes in South Africa, of regions of the southern sky

7

which are never visible in the Northern Hemisphere. You are to take them to Dr. Cole Hendron in New York City, and deliver them personally to him and to no one else. I would tell you more about this unusual errand, Ransdell, if the—the implications of these plates were absolutely certain."

At this, Professor Bronson started, but again checked himself before speaking; and Lord Rhondin went on:

"The implications, I may say, are probably true; but so very much is involved that it would be most disastrous if even a rumor of what we believe we have discovered, were given out. For that reason, among others, we cannot confide it even to you; but we must charge you personally to convey this box to Dr. Hendron, who is the scientific consultant of the Universal Electric and Power Corporation in New York City. He is now in Pasadena, but will be in New York upon your arrival. Time is vital—the greatest speed, that is, consistent with reasonable safety. We are asking you, therefore, to fly the length of Africa along the established routes, with which you are familiar, and to fly, then, across the Mediterranean to France, where you will board a fast liner. You should reach Dr. Hendron not later than a week from Monday. You may return, then, if you wish. On the other hand"—he paused as crowded considerations heaped in his mind,—"you may be indifferent as to where you are."

"On the earth," added Professor Bronson.

"Of course—on the earth," Lord Rhondin accepted.

"I would go myself, Ransdell, you understand," Bronson then proceeded. "But my place, for the present, certainly is here. I mean, of course, at the observatory. . . . It is possible, Ransdell, in spite of precautions which have been taken, that some word of the Bronson discovery may get out. Your errand may be suspected. If it is, you know nothing— nothing you understand? You must answer no inquiry from any source. None—none whatever!"

At the landings during the fast flight north along the length of Africa, and in France, and during the first four days aboard the transatlantic vessel, nothing had happened to recall these emphatic cautions; but now, something was out. A boy was approaching with another radiogram; and so Ransdell swiftly tore open the one he had been holding:

"Twenty thousand dollars in cash paid to you if you grant first and exclusive interview regarding the Bronson discovery to this paper."

It was signed by the man, who, an hour ago, had opened the bidding with one thousand dollars.

Dave crumpled it and tossed it overboard. If the man who had sent it had been in that trophy-room with Bronson and Lord Rhondin, he would have realized that the matter on their minds completely transcended any monetary consideration.

The evening in New York was warm. It pressed back the confused uproar of the street; and the sound which ascended to the high terrace of the Hendron apartment seemed to contain heat as well as noise. Eve found that her search for a breath of fresh air was fruitless. For a moment she gazed into the mist and monotone that was Manhattan, and then stared over the city toward the channels to the sea.

"Suppose those lights are the ship's?" she asked Tony.

"It left quarantine before seven; it's somewhere there," Tony said patiently. "Let's not go back in."

His cigarette-case clicked open. The light of his match made a brief Rubens: buff satin of her bare shoulders, green of her evening dress, stark white of his shirt-bosom, and heads bent together. Some one inside the apartment danced past the French windows, touched the door-handle, perceived that the terrace was occupied, and danced away to the accompaniment of music that came from the radio.

"Guests take possession these days," Eve continued. "If you suggest bridge, they tear up the rugs and dance. If I'd asked them to dance,—and had an orchestra,—they'd have played bridge—or made fudge—"

"Or played District Attorney. Why have guests at all, Eve? Especially to-night?"

"Sorry, Tony."

"Are you, really? Then why did you have them, when for the first night in weeks the three thousand miles of this dreary continent aren't between us?"

"I didn't have them, Tony. They just heard we were home; and they came."

"You could have had a headache—for them."

"I almost did, with the reporters this afternoon. This is really a rest; let's enjoy it, Tony."

She leaned against the balustrade and looked down at the lights; and he, desirous of much more, bent jealously beside her. Inside the apartment, the dancing continued, making itself sensible as a procession of silhouettes that passed the window. Tony laid his hand possessively on Eve's. She turned her hand, lessening subtly the possessiveness of his, and said:

"You can kiss me. I like to be kissed. But don't propose."

"Why not? . . . See here, Eve, I'm through with Christmas kisses with you."

"Christmas kisses?"

"You know what I mean. I've been kissing you, Christmases, for three years; and what's it got me?"

"Cad!"

9

He put his hand on her shoulder, and turned her away from the panorama of the city.

"Is there some real trouble, Eve?" he inquired gently.

"Trouble?"

"I mean that's on your mind, and that stops making to-night what it might be for us."

"No; there's no trouble, Tony."

"Then there's somebody else ahead of me—is there? Somebody perhaps in Pasadena?"

"Nobody in Pasadena—or anywhere else, Tony."

"Then what is it, to-night? What's changed you?"

"How am I changed?"

"You drive me mad, Eve; you know it. You're lovely in face, and beautiful in body; and besides, with a brain that your father's trained so that you're beyond any other girl—and most men too. You're way beyond me, but I love you; and you don't listen to me."

"I do!"

"You're not listening to me even now. You're thinking instead."

"What do you want me to do?"

"Feel!"

"Oh, I can do that, too."

"I know; then why don't you—and stop thinking?"

"Wait! Not now, Tony. . . . Do you suppose that's the ship?"

"Why do you care? See here, Eve, *is* there anything in that newspaper story your father and you have been denying all afternoon?"

"What story?"

"That something unusual is up between all the big scientific leaders."

"There's always something up in science," Eve evaded. . . .

The doors were flung wide open. Music blared from the radio. In the drawing-room a half-dozen people continued to dance. Another group surrounded the punch-bowl. The butler was passing a tray of sandwiches. Some one stepped out and asked Eve to dance, and she went in with him.

Tony wandered in from the terrace.

The butler stopped before him. "Sandwich, Mr. Drake?"

"Keep three of the tongue for me, Leighton," Tony said solemnly. "I want to take them home to eat in bed."

The butler nodded indulgently. "Certainly, Mr. Drake. Anything else?"

"Possibly an anchovy."

"Very good, Mr. Drake."

An arm encircled Tony's broad shoulders. "Hello, Tony. Say—give me the low-down on what shot the market to hell's basement to-day."

Tony frowned; his eyes were following Eve. "Why do you compliment me with thinking I may know?"

"It's something happened in Africa, I hear. Anyway, the African cables were carrying it. But what could happen down there to shoot hell out of us this way? Another discovery of gold? A mountain of gold that would make gold so cheap it would unsettle everything?"

"Cheap gold would make stocks dear—not send them down," Tony objected.

"Sure; it can't be that. But what could happen in South Africa that—"

Tony returned alone to the terrace. His senses were swept by intimate thoughts of Eve: A perfume called Nuit Douce. Gold lights in her red-brown hair. Dark eyes. The sweep of a forehead behind which, in rare company, a woman's instincts and tenderness dwelt with a mind ordinarily as honest and unevasive as a man's. All the tremendous insignificances that have meaning to a man possessed by the woman he loves.

He stood spellbound, staring through the night. . . . Anthony Drake was an athlete—that would have been the second observation another man would have made of him. The first, that he owned that uncounterfeitable trait which goes with what we call good birth and breeding, and generations of the like before him.

With this he had the physical sureness and the gestures of suppressed power which are the result of training in sports. He had the slender waist of a boxer, with the shoulders of a discus thrower. His clothes always seemed frail in comparison with his physique.

He also had intelligence. His university companions considered it a trivial side-issue when he was graduated from Harvard with a *magna cum laude;* but the conservative investment-house with which he afterward became affiliated appreciated the adjunct of brains to a personality so compelling. His head was large and square, and it required his big physique to give that head proportion. He was blue-eyed, sandy-haired. He possessed a remarkably deep voice.

He was entirely normal. His attainments beyond the average were not unusual. He belonged more or less to that type of young American business man upon whom the older generation places its hope and trust. Eve was really a much more remarkable human being—not on account of her beauty, but because of her intellectual brilliance, and her unique training from her father.

Yet Eve was not the sort who preferred "intellectual" men; intellectualism, as such, immensely bored her. She liked the outright and vigorous and "normal." She liked Tony Drake; and Tony, knowing this, was more than baffled by her attitude to-night. An emotional net seemed to have been stretched between them, through which he could not quite reach her; what the substance of the net was, he could not determine; but it balked him when, as never before, he wanted nearness to her. He believed her when she told him that her tantalizing abstraction was not because of another man. Then, what was its cause?

Tony was drawn from his reverie by the appearance of Douglas Balcom, senior partner of his firm. His presence here surprised Tony. No reason why old Balcom should not drop in, if he pleased; but the rest of the guests were much younger.

Balcom, halting beside Tony, reflected the general discontent of the day by waving at the city and murmuring: "In the soup. Everything's in the soup; and now nobody cares. Why does nobody care?"

Tony disagreed, but he deferred to Balcom by saying: "It seems to me, a lot of people care."

"I mean nobody who's in the know cares. I mean the four or five men who *know* what's going on—underneath. I mean," particularized old Balcom, "John Borgan doesn't care. Did you see him to-day?"

"Borgan? No."

"Did you hear of his buying anything?"

"No."

"Selling anything?"

"No."

"That's it." Balcom thought out loud for a while. Tony listened. "Borgan's the fourth richest man in America; and normally the most active, personally. He'll be the richest, if he keeps up. He wants to be the richest. Oil—mines—rails—steel—shipping—he's in everything. He's only fifty-one. To my way of thinking, he's smarter than anyone else; and this looks like a market—superficially—which was made for Borgan. But for two weeks he's gone dead. Won't do a thing, either way; takes no position. Paralyzed. Why?"

"He may be resting on his oars."

"You know damn' well he isn't. Not Borgan—now. There's only one way I can explain; he knows something damned important that the rest of us don't. There's an undertone—don't you feel it?—that's different. I met Borgan to-day, face to face; we shook hands. I don't like the look of him. I tell you he knows something he's afraid of. He did a funny thing, by the way, Tony. He asked me: 'How well do you know Cole Hendron?'

"I said, 'Pretty well.' I said: 'Tony Drake knows him damn' well.' He said: 'You tell Hendron, or have Drake tell Hendron, he can trust me.' That's exactly what he said, Tony—

12

tell Hendron that he can trust N. J. Borgan. Now, what the hell is that all about?"

"I don't know," said Tony, and almost added, in his feeling of the moment: "I don't care." For Eve was returning.

She slipped away from her partner and signaled to Tony to see her alone. Together they sought the solitude of the end of the terrace.

"Tony, can you start these people home?"

"Gladly," rejoiced Tony. "But I can stay?"

"I'm afraid not. I've got to work."

"Now? To-night?"

"As soon as I possibly can. Tony, I'll tell you. The ship is in, and Ransdell was taken off at quarantine and brought here. He's in Father's study now."

"Who's Ransdell?"

"Nobody I know. I haven't set eyes on him yet, Tony. He's just the messenger from Africa. You see, Tony, some—some things were being sent rush, by airplane and by messenger, to Father from Africa. Well, they've arrived; and I do his measuring for him, you know."

"What measuring?"

"The delicate measuring, like—like the position and amount of movement shown by stars and other bodies on astronomical plates. For weeks—for months, in fact, Tony—the astronomers in the Southern Hemisphere have been watching something."

"What sort of a something, Eve?"

"Something of a sort never seen before, Tony. A sort of body that they knew existed by the millions, probably, all through the universe—something they were sure must be, but the general existence of which has never been actually proved. It—it may be the most sensational fact for us, from the beginning to the end of time. I can't tell you more than that to-night, Tony; yet by to-morrow we may be telling it to all the world. Rumors are getting out; and so some scientist, who will be believed, must make an authoritative announcement. And the scientists of the world have selected Father to make it.

"Now, help me, Tony. You clear these people out; and then you run along. For I've measurements to make and report to Father; and he has to check over calculations made by the best men in the southern half of the world. Then, by to-morrow, we may know, for certain, what is going to happen to us all."

Tony had his arm about her; he felt her suddenly trembling. He swept her up and held her against him; and kissing her, he met on her lips, a new, impetuous passion which exalted and amazed him. Then some one came out and he released her.

13

"I—I didn't mean that, Tony," she whispered.

"You must have."

"I didn't! Not all of it, Tony. It was just for that moment."

"We'll have a thousand more like it—thousands—thousands!"

They both were whispering; and now, though he had let her go, his hand was over hers, and he could feel her quivering again. "You don't know, Tony. Nobody really knows yet. Come, help me send them all away."

He helped her; and when the guests had gone, he met, at last, the man who had come from South Africa. They shook hands, and for a few moments the three of them—Eve Hendron and Tony Drake and Ransdell, the mail-flyer from under the Southern Cross—stood and chatted together.

There must be presentiments; otherwise, how could the three of them always have carried, thereafter, a photographic memory of that moment of their meeting? Yet no one of the three—and least of all Eve, who on that night knew most of what was to come—could possibly have suspected the strange relation in which each was to stand to the others. None of them could have suspected, because such a relationship was, at that moment, inconceivable to them—a relationship between civilized men and women for which there then existed, indeed, no word in the language.

Chapter 2—The League of the Last Days

THE lobby of Tony's favorite club was carpeted in red. Beyond the red carpet was a vast room paneled in oak. It usually was filled with leisurely men playing backgammon or bridge or chess, smoking and reading newspapers. Behind it, thick with gloom, was a library; and in a wing on the left, the dining-room where uniformed waiters moved swiftly between rows of small tables.

As Tony entered the club, however, he felt that it had emerged from its slumbers, its routine, its dull masculine quietude. There were only two games in progress. Few men were idling over their cigars, studying their newspapers; many were gathered around the bar.

The lights seemed brighter. Voices were staccato. Men stood in groups and talked; a few even gesticulated. The surface of snobbish solitude had been dissipated.

Tony knew at once why the club was alive. The rumors, spreading on the streets, had eddied in through these doors too.

Some one hailed him. "Hi! Tony!"

"Hello, Jack! What's up?"

"You tell us!"

"How could I tell you?"

"Don't you know Hendron? Haven't you seen him?"

Jack Little—a young man whose name was misleading—stepped away from a cluster of friends, who, however, soon followed him; and Tony found himself surrounded. One of the men had been one of the guests whom Tony, half an hour before, had helped clear from the Hendrons'; and so he could not deny having seen Hendron, even if he had wanted to.

"What in hell have the scientists under their hats, Tony?"

"I don't know. Honest," Tony denied.

"Then what the devil is the League of the Last Days?"

"What?"

"The League of the Last Days—an organization of all the leading scientists in the world, as far as I can make out," Little informed him.

"Never heard of it," said Tony.

"I just did," Little confessed; "but it appears to have been in existence some time. Several months, that is. They began to organize it suddenly, all over the world, in the winter."

"All over the world?" asked Tony.

"In strictest and absolutely the highest scientific circles. They've been organized and communicating for half a year; and it's just leaking out."

"The League of the Last Days?" repeated Tony.

"That's it."

"What does it mean?"

"That's what I thought you might tell us. Hendron's a member, of course."

"The head of it, I hear," somebody else put in.

"I don't know anything about it," Tony protested, and tried to move away. Actually, he did not know; but this talk fitted in too well with what Eve had told him. Her father had been chosen by the scientists of the world to make some extraordinary announcement. But—the League of the Last Days! She had not mentioned that to him.

League of the Last Days! It sent a strange tingle under his skin.

"How did you hear about it?" Tony now demanded of Jack Little.

"From him," said Jack, jerking toward the man who had heard that Cole Hendron headed the League.

"I got it this afternoon," this fellow said importantly. "I know the city editor of the *Standard*. He had a reporter—a smart kid named Davis—on it. I was there when the kid came back. It seems that some months ago, the scientists—the top men like Hendron—stumbled on something big. So big that it seems to have scared them. They've been having meetings about it for months.

"Nobody thought much about the meetings at first. Scientists are always barging around visiting each other and having conventions. But these were different. Very few men—and all big ones; and no real reports coming out. Only camouflage stuff—like about progress in smashing the atom. But the real business that was exciting them wasn't given out.

"Nobody knows yet what it is; but we do know there is something mighty big and mighty secret. It's so big and so secret that they only refer to it, when writing to each other, by a code.

"That's one thing definitely known. They write to each other and cable to each other about it in a code that's so damned good that the newspapers, which have got hold of some of the messages, can't break the cipher and figure it out."

"What's the League of the Last Days got to do with that?" Tony asked.

"It's the League of the Last Days that's doing it all. It's the League of the Last Days that communicates with its members by the code."

That was all any one knew; and soon Tony left the circle. He did not want to talk to men who knew even less than himself. He wanted to return to Eve; and that being impossible, he wanted to be alone. "I need," he said to nobody in particular, "a shower and a drink." And he pushed out of the club and started home.

His cab lurched through traffic. When the vehicle stopped for a red light, he was roused from his abstractions by the hawking of an extra. He leaned out and bought one from the bawling newsboy. The headline disappointed him.

SCIENTISTS FORM SECRET
"LEAGUE OF THE LAST DAYS."

A second paper—a tabloid—told no more.

SENSATIONAL SECRET DISCOVERY
World Scientists Communicating in Code.

When he reached his apartment, he thrust the papers under his arm. The doorman and the elevator boy spoke to him, and he did not answer. His Jap servant smiled at him. He surrendered his derby, threw himself in a deep chair, had a telephone brought, and called Eve.

The telephone-company informed him that service on that number had been discontinued for the night.

16

"Bring me a highball, Kyto," Tony said. "And hand me that damn' newspaper." And Tony read:

"A secret discovery of startling importance is exciting the whole world of science.

"Though denied both by American and foreign scientists, the *Standard* has come into possession of copies of more than a score of cablegrams in code exchanged between various physicists and astronomers in America, and Professor Ernest Heim of Heidelberg, Germany.

"This newspaper has sought out the American senders or receivers of the mysterious code messages, who include Professor Yerksen Leeming at Yale, Doctor K. Belditz of Columbit, Cole Hendron of the Universal Electric and Power Corp., and Professor Eugene Taylor at Princeton. Some of these scientists at first denied that a secret code communication was being carried on; but others, confronted with copies of messages, admitted it, but claimed that they referred to a purely scientific investigation which was being conducted by several groups in coöperation. They denied that the subjects under investigation were of public importance.

"Challenged to describe, even in general terms, the nature of the secret, each man refused.

"But matters are coming to a head. To-day it was discovered that a special courier from South Africa, sent by Lord Rhondin and Professor Bronson of Capetown, had flown the length of the Dark Continent with a mysterious black box; at Cherbourg he took the first ship for New York and upon his arrival, was taken off at quarantine and hurried to Cole Hendron's apartment.

"Dr. Cole Hendron, chief consultant of the Universal Electric and Power Corp., only to-day returned to New York from Pasadena, where he has been working with the scientists of the observatory on Mt. Wilson. . . .

"To add to the disturbing and spectacular features of this strange scientific mystery, it is learned that the scientists associated in this secret and yet world-spanning investigation are in a group which is called the League of the Last Days. What this may mean . . ."

There was nothing more but speculation and wild guesses. Tony tossed aside the newspapers and lay back in his chair; he could speculate for himself. The League of the Last Days! It might, of course, have been manufactured by one of the tabloids itself, and thus spread about the city. But Tony too vividly recollected Eve Hendron.

Kyto appeared with his highball; and Tony sipped slowly and thoughtfully. If this which he had just read, and that which he previously had encountered to-day, had meaning, it must be that some amazing and unique menace threatened human society. And it was at a moment when, more than

17

ever before in his life or in his dreams, Tony Drake wanted human society, with him in it—with him and Eve in it—to go on as it was. Or rather, as it would be, if things simply took their natural course.

Eve in his arms; her lips on his again, as he had had them to-day! To possess her, to own her completely! He could dream of no human delight beyond her! And he would have her! Damn this League of the Last Days! What were the scientists hiding among themselves?

Tony sat up vehemently. "A hell of a thing," he said aloud. "The whole world is haywire. Haywire! By the way, Kyto, you aren't a Japanese scientist, are you?"

"How?"

"Never mind. You don't happen to send code messages to Einstein, do you?"

"Cold messages?"

"Let it pass. I'm going to bed. If my mother calls from the country, Kyto, tell her I'm being a good boy and still wearing woolen socks against a cold snap. I must have sleep, to be in shape for work to-morrow. Maybe I'll sell five shares of stock in the morning, or possibly ten. It's wearing me down. I can't stand the strain."

He drained his glass and arose. Four hours later, after twice again having attempted to phone Eve Hendron, and twice again having been informed that service for the night was discontinued, Tony got to sleep.

CHAPTER 3—THE STRANGERS FROM SPACE

IT was no tabloid but the *Times*—the staid, accurate, ultra-responsible New York *Times*—which spread the sensation before him in the morning.

The headines lay black upon the page:

"SCIENTISTS SAY WORLDS FROM ANOTHER STAR APPROACH THE EARTH

DR. COLE HENDRON MAKES ASTONISHING STATEMENT IN WHICH SIXTY OF THE GREATEST PHYSICISTS AND ASTRONOMERS CONCUR."

Tony was scarcely awake when Kyto had brought him the paper.

Kyto himself, it was plain, had been puzzling over the news, and did not understand it. Kyto, however, had comprehended enough to know that something was very different to-day; so he had carried in the coffee and the newspaper a bit earlier than customary; and he delayed, busying himself with the black, clear coffee, while Tony started up and stared.

"Dr. Cole Hendron, generally acknowledged to be the leading astro-physicist of America," Tony read, "early this morning gave to the press the following statement, on behalf of the sixty scientists named in an accompanying column."

Tony's eyes flashed to the column which carried the list of distinguished names, English, German, French, Italian, Swiss, American, South African, Australian and Japanese.

"Similar statements are being given to the press of all peoples at this same time.

" 'In order to allay alarms likely to rise from the increase of rumors based upon incorrect or misunderstood reports of the discovery made by Professor Bronson, of Capetown, South Africa, and in order to acquaint all people with the actual situation, as it is now viewed, we offer these facts.

" 'Eleven months ago, when examining a photographic plate of the region 15 (Eridanus) in the southern skies, Professor Bronson noticed the presence of two bodies then near the star Achernar, which had not been observed before.

" 'Both were exceedingly faint, and lying in the constellation Eridanus, which is one of the largest constellations in the sky, they were at first put down as probably long-period variable stars which had recently increased in brightness after having been too faint to affect the photographic plate.

" 'A month later, after photographing again the same locality, Professor Bronson looked for the two new stars and found that they had moved. No object of stellar distance could show displacement in so short a space of time. It was certain, therefore, that the newly observed bodies were not stars. They must be previously unobserved and unsuspected members of our solar system, or else objects, from outside our system, now approaching us.

"They must be new planets or comets—or strangers from space.

" 'All planets known to be associated with our sun move approximately in the plane described by the earth's orbit. This is true, whatever the size or distance of the planets, from Mercury to Pluto. The two Bronson bodies were moving almost at right angles to the plane of the planetary orbits.

" 'Comets appear from all directions; but these two bodies did not resemble comets when viewed through the greater telescope. One of them, at the time of the second observation, showed a small but perceptible disk. Its spectrum exhibited the characteristic lines of reflected sunlight. Meanwhile, several observations of position and movement were made which made it plain that the two Bronson bodies were objects of planetary dimensions and characteristics, approaching us from out of stellar distances—that is, from space.

" 'The two bodies have remained associated, approaching

us together and at the same speed. Both now show disks which can be measured. It can now be estimated that, when first observed, they had approached within the distance from the sun of the planet Neptune. It must be remembered, however, that they lie in an entirely different direction.

"'Since coming under observation, they have moved within the distance of the orbit of our planet Uranus, and are approaching the distance of Saturn.

"'Bronson Alpha—which is the name temporarily assigned to the larger of the two new bodies—appears in the telescope similar in size to Uranus. That is, its estimated diameter is something over forty thousand miles. Bronson Beta, which is the smaller of the two bodies, has an estimated diameter of eight thousand miles. It is similar in size, therefore, to the earth.

"'Bronson Beta at present is in advance of Alpha in their approach toward the solar system; but they do not move in parallel lines; Beta, which is the smaller, revolves about Alpha so that their positions constantly change.

"'They have both come definitely within the sphere of gravitational influence of the sun; but having arrived from interstellar space, their speeds of approach greatly exceed the velocities of our familiar planets in their orbits around the sun.

"'Such are the observed phenomena. The following is necessarily highly speculative, but it is offered as a possible explanation of the origin of the two Bronson bodies.

"'It has long been supposed that about other stars than ours—for of course our sun is only a star—are other planets like the earth and Mars and Jupiter. It is not presumed that all stars are surrounded by planets; but it has been estimated that probably at least one star in one hundred thousand has developed a planetary system. Among the many billions of stars, there are probably millions of suns with planets. It is always possible that some catastrophe would tear the planets away. It would require nothing more than the approach of another star toward the sun to destroy the gravitational control of the sun over the earth and Venus and Mars and Jupiter and other planets, and to send them all spinning into space on cold and dark careers of their own.

"'This world of ours, and Venus and Mars and Jupiter and Saturn, would then wander throughout indefinite ages—some of them perhaps eternally doomed to cold and darkness; others might, after incalculable ages, find another sun.

"'It might be assumed, for purposes of explanation of the Bronson Bodies, that they once were planets like our earth and Uranus, circling about some life-giving sun. A catastrophe tore them away, together with whatever other of her planets there might have been, and sent them into the dark-

20

ness of interstellar space. These two—Bronson Alpha and Bronson Beta—either were associated originally, or else established a gravitational influence upon each other in the journey through space, and probably have traveled together through an incalculable time until they arrived in a region of the heavens which brought them at last under the attraction of the sun. Their previous course, consequently, has been greatly modified by the sun, and as a result, they are now approaching us.'"

At this point, the prepared statement of Cole Hendron terminated.

Tony Drake was sitting up straight in bed, holding the paper before him and trying, with his left hand and without looking away, to strike a match for the cigarette between his lips. He did not succeed, but he kept on trying while his eyes searched down the column of questions put by the reporters to Dr. Hendron—and his answers.

"'What will be the effect of this approach upon the earth?'

"'It is impossible yet to tell.'

"'But there will be effects?'

"'Certainly there will be effects.'

"'How serious?'"

Again Cole Hendron refused to answer.

"'It is impossible yet to say.'

"'Will the earth be endangered?'

"Answer: 'There will undoubtedly be considerable alterations of conditions of life here.'

"'What sort of alterations?'

"'That will be the subject of a later statement,' Dr. Hendron replied. 'The character and degree of the disturbance which we are to undergo is now the subject of study by a responsible group. We will attempt to describe the conditions likely to confront all of us on the world as soon as they clearly define themselves.'

"'When will this supplementary statement be made?'

"'As soon as possible.'

"'To-morrow?'

"'No; by no means as soon as to-morrow.'

"'Within a week? Within a month?'

"'I would say that it might be made within a month.'"

Tony was on his feet, and in spite of himself, trembling. There was no possible mistaking of the undertone of this astonishing announcement. It spelled doom, or some enormous alteration of all conditions of life on the world equivalent to complete disaster.

The League of the Last Days! There was some reference to it in another column, but Tony scarcely caught its coherence.

Where was Eve; and what, upon this morning, was she

doing? How was she feeling? What was she thinking? Might she, at last, be sleeping?

She had been up all night, and at work assisting her father. The statement had been released at one o'clock in the morning. There was no mention in the paper of her presence with her father; Cole Hendron apparently had received the reporters alone.

How much more than this which had been told, did Eve now know? Plainly, manifestly the scientists knew more—much, much more, which they dared not yet tell the public. Dared not! That was the fact. They dared, to-day, only to issue the preliminary announcement.

Chapter 4—Dawn After Doomsday?

KYTO, who usually effaced himself, did not do so this morning. Kyto, having the untasted coffee for an excuse, called attention to himself and ventured:

"Mister, of course, comprehends the news?"

"Yes, Kyto; I understand it—partly, at any rate."

"I may inquire, please, perhaps the significance?"

Tony stared at the little Jap. He had always liked him; but suddenly he was assailed with a surge of fellow-feeling for this small brown man trapped like himself on the rim of the world.

Trapped! That was it. *Trapped* was the word for this strange feeling.

"Kyto, we're in for something."

"What?"

"Something rather—extensive, Kyto. One thing is sure, we're all in for it together."

"General—destruction?" Kyto asked.

Tony shook his head, and his reply surprised himself. "No; if it were just that, they'd say it. It would be easy to say—general destruction, the end of everything. People after all in a way are prepared for that, Kyto." Tony was reasoning to himself as much as talking to Kyto. "No; this can't be just—destruction. It doesn't *feel* like it, Kyto."

"What else could it be?" questioned the Jap practically.

Tony, having no ansyer, gulped his coffee; and Kyto had to attend to the telephone, which was ringing.

It was Balcom.

"Hey! Tony! Tony, have you seen the paper? I told you Hendron had something, but I admit this runs considerably beyond expectations. . . . Staggers one, doesn't it, Tony? . . . Now, see here, it's perfectly plain that Hendron knows much more than he's giving out. . . . Tony, he probably knows it *all* now! . . . I want you to get to him as soon as you can."

As soon as possible, Tony got rid of Balcom—another rider on the rim of the world, trapped with Tony and Kyto and all the rest of these people who could be heard, if you went to the open window, ringing one another to talk over this consternation.

Tony commanded, from before the bathroom mirror, where he was hastily shaving: "Kyto, make sure that anybody else that calls up isn't Miss Hendron, and then say I'm out."

Within five minutes Kyto was telling the truth. Tony, in less than five more, was at the Hendrons'. The place was policed. Men, women and children from Park Avenue, from Third and Second avenues crowded the sidewalks; sound-film trucks and photographers obstructed the street. Radio people and reporters, refused admittance, picked up what they could from the throng. Tony, at last, made contact with a police officer, and he did not make the mistake of asserting his right to pass the police-lines or of claiming, too publicly, that he was a personal friend of the family.

"There is a possibility that Dr. Hendron or perhaps Miss Hendron might have left word that I might see them," Tony said. "My name is Tony Drake."

The officer escorted him in. The elevator lifted him high to the penthouse on the roof, where the street noises were vague and far away, where the sun was shining, and blossoms, in their boxes, were red and yellow and blue.

No one was about but the servants. Impassive people! Did they know and understand? Or were they dulled to it?

Miss Eve, they said, was in the breakfast-room; Dr. Hendron still was asleep.

"Hello, Tony! Come in!"

Eve rose from the pretty little green table in the gay chintz-curtained nook which they called the breakfast-room.

Her eyes were bright, her face flushed the slightest bit with her excitement. Her hands grasped his tightly.

Lovely hands, she had, slender and soft and strong. How gentle she was to hold, but also how strong! Longing for her leaped in Tony. Damn everything else!

He pulled her within his arms and kissed her; and her lips, as they had last night, clung to his. They both drew breath, deeply, as they parted—stared into each other's eyes. Their hands held to each other a moment more; then Tony stepped back.

She had dressed but for her frock itself; she was in negligée, with her slim lovely arms in loose lace-decked silk, her white neck and bosom half exposed.

He bent and kissed her neck.

"You've breakfasted, Tony?"

"Yes—no. Can I sit with you here? I scarcely dreamed you'd be up, Eve, after your night."

"You've seen the papers? We were through with them before three. That is, Father then absolutely refused to say any more or see any one else. He went to sleep."

"You didn't."

"No; I kept thinking—thinking—"

"Of the end of everything, Eve?"

"Part of the time, I did; of course I did; but more of the time of you."

"Of me—last night?"

"I hoped you'd come first thing to-day. I thought you would. . . . It's funny what difference the formal announcement of it makes. I knew it all last night, Tony. I've known the general truth of it for weeks. But when it was a secret thing—something shared just with my father and his friends —it wasn't the same as now. One knew it but still didn't admit it, even to one's self. It was theoretical—in one's head, like a dream, not reality. We didn't really *do* much, Father and I, last night. I mean do much in proving up the facts and figures. Father had them all before from other men. Professor Bronson's plates and calculations simply confirmed what really was certain; Father checked them over. Then we gave it out."

"That's what's made everything so changed."

"Yet you didn't give out everything you know, Eve."

"No, not everything, Tony."

"You know exactly what's going to happen, don't you, Eve?"

"Yes. We know—we think we know, that is, exactly what's going to happen."

"It's going to be doomsday, isn't it?"

"No, Tony—more than doomsday."

"What can be more than that?"

"Dawn after doomsday, Tony. The world is going to be destroyed. Tony, oh, Tony, the world is going to be most thoroughly destroyed; yet some of us here on this world, which most surely will come to an end, some of us will not die! Or we need not die—if we accept the strange challenge that God is casting at us from the skies!"

"The challenge that God casts at us—what challenge? What do you mean? Exactly what is it that is going to happen, Eve—and how?"

"I'll try to tell you, Tony: There are two worlds coming toward us—two worlds torn, millions of years ago perhaps, from another star. For millions of years, probably, they've been wandering, utterly dark and utterly frozen, through space; and now they've found our sun; and they're going to attach themselves to it—at our expense. For they are coming into the solar system on a course which will carry them close—oh, very close indeed, Tony, to the orbit of the earth.

24

They're not cutting in out on the edge where Neptune and Uranus are, or inside near Venus and Mercury. No; they're going to join up at the same distance from the sun as we are. Do you understand?"

In spite of himself, Tony blanched. "They're going to hit the earth, you mean? I thought so."

"They're not going to hit the earth, Tony, the first time around. The first time they circle the sun, they're going to pass us close, to be sure; but they're going to pass us—both of them. But the second time they pass us—well, one of them is going to pass us a second time too, but the other one isn't, Tony. The smaller one—Bronson Beta, the one about the same size as the earth and, so far as we can tell, very much like the earth—is going to pass us safely; but the big one, Bronson Alpha, is going to take out the world!"

"You know that, Eve?"

"We know it! There must be a margin of error, we know. There may not be a direct head-on collision, Tony; but any sort of encounter—even a glancing blow—would be enough and much more than enough to finish this globe. And an encounter is certain. Every single calculation that has been made shows it.

"You know what an exact thing astronomy is to-day, Tony. If we have three different observations of a moving body, we can plot its path; and we've hundreds of determinations of these bodies. More than a thousand altogether! We know now what they are; we know their dimensions and the speed with which they are traveling. We know, of course, almost precisely the forces and attractions which will influence them—the gravitational power of the sun. Tony, you remember how precise the forecast was in the last eclipse that darkened New England. The astronomers not only foretold to a second when it would begin and end, but they described the blocks and even the sides of the streets in towns that would be in shadow. And their error was less than twenty feet.

"It's the same with these Bronson bodies, Tony. They're falling toward the sun, and their path can be plotted like the path of Newton's apple dropping from the bough. Gravity is the surest and most constant force in all creation. One of those worlds, which is seeking our sun, is going to wipe us out, Tony—all of us, every soul of us that remains on the world when it collides. But the other world—the world so much like this—will pass us close and go on, safe and sound, around the sun again. . . .

"Tony do you believe in God?"

"What's that to do with this?"

"So much that this has got me thinking about God again, Tony. God—the God of our fathers—the God of the Old Testament, Tony; the God who did things and meant something, the God of wrath and vengeance, but the God who also could be merciful to men. For He's sending two worlds to us, Tony, not one—not just the one that will destroy us. He's sending the world that may save us, too!"

"Save us? What do you mean?"

"That's what the League of the Last Days is working on, Tony—the chance of escape that's offered by the world like ours, which will pass so close and go on. We may transfer to it, Tony, if we have the will and the skill and the nerve! We could send a rocket to the moon to-day, if it would do us any good, if any one could possibly live on the moon after he got there. Well, Bronson Beta will pass us closer than the moon. Bronson Beta is the size of the earth, and therefore can have an atmosphere. It is perfectly possible that people—who are able to reach it—can live there.

"It's a world, perhaps very like ours, which has been in immutable cold and dark for millions of years, probably, and which now will be coming to life again.

"Think of it, Tony! The tremendous, magnificent adventure of making a try for it! It was a world once like ours, circling around some sun. People lived on it; and animals and plants and trees. Evolution had occurred there too, and progress. Civilization had come. Thousands of years of it, maybe. Tens of thousands of years—perhaps much more than we have yet known. Perhaps, also, much less. It's the purest speculation to guess in what stage that world was when it was torn from its sun and sent spinning into space.

"But in whatever stage it was in, you may be sure it is in exactly that stage now; for when it left its sun, life became extinct. The rivers, the lakes, the seas, the very air, froze and became solid, encasing and keeping everything just as it was, though it wandered through space for ten million years.

"But as it approaches the sun, the air and then the seas will thaw. The people cannot possibly come to life, nor the animals or birds or other things; but the cities will stand there unchanged, the implements, the monuments, their homes—all will remain and be uncovered again.

"If this world were not doomed, what an adventure to try for that one, Tony! And a possible adventure—a perfectly possible adventure, with the powers at our disposal to-day!"

Tony recollected, after a while, that Balcom had bid him to learn from Hendron, as definitely as possible, the date and nature of the next announcement. How would it affect stocks? Would the Stock Exchange open at all?

He remembered, at last, it was a business day; downtown he had duties—contracts to buy and orders to sell stocks, which he must execute, if the Exchange opened to-day. He did not venture to ask to have Hendron awakened to speak to him but, before ten o'clock, he did leave Eve.

26

He walked to the subway. His eyes stared at the myriad faces passing him. His body was jolted by innumerable brief contacts.

"Gimme five cents for a cup of coffee?"

Tony stopped, stared. This panhandler too was trapped, with him and Kyto and Eve and all the rest, on the rim of the world which was coming to its end. Did he have an inkling of it? Whether or not, obviously to-day he must eat. Tony's hand went into his pocket.

Speculation about the masses assailed him. What did they think this morning? What did they want? How differently would they do to-day?

Near the subway, the newsboys were having a sell-out; a truck was dumping on the walk fresh piles of papers. Everybody had a paper; everybody was reading to himself or talking to somebody else. The man with the half inch of cigar-stub, the boy without a hat, the fat woman with packages under her arm, the slim stenographer in green, the actor with the beaver collar; they all read, stared, feared, planned, hoped, denied.

Some of them smirked or giggled, almost childishly delighted at something different even if it suggested destruction. It was something novel, exciting. Some of them seemed to be scheming.

CHAPTER 5—A WORLD CAN END

AT ten o'clock the gong rang and the market opened. There had been no addition to public knowledge in the newspapers. The news-ticker carried, as additional information, only the effect of the announcement on the markets in Europe, which already had been open for hours.

It was plain that the wild eyes of terror looked across the oceans and the land—across rice-fields and prairies, out of the smoke of cities everywhere.

The stock market opened promptly at ten with the familiar resonant clang of the big gong. One man dropped dead at his first glance upon the racing ticker.

On the floor of the Exchange itself, there was relative quiet. When the market is most busy, it is most silent. Phones were choked with regular, crowded speech. Boys ran. The men stood and spoke in careful tones at the posts. Millions of shares began to change hands at prices—down. The ticker lagged as never in the wildest days of the boom. And at noon, in patent admission of the obvious necessity, New York followed the example already set by London, Paris and Berlin. The great metals doors boomed shut. There would be no more trading for an indeterminate time. Until "the scientific situation became cleared up."

Cleared up! What a phrase for the situation! But the Street had to have one. It always had one.

Tony hung on the telephone for half an hour after the shutting of the mighty doors. His empire—the kingdom of his accustomed beliefs, his job—lay at his feet. When he hung up, he thought vaguely that only foresight during the depression had placed his and his mother's funds where they were still comparatively safe in spite of this threat of world-cataclysm.

Comparatively safe—what did that mean? What did anything mean, to-day?

Balcom came into his office; he put his head on Tony's desk and sobbed. Tony opened a drawer, took out a whisky-bottle which had reposed in it unopened for a year, and poured a stiff dose into a drinking-cup. Balcom swallowed it as if it were milk, took another, and walked out dazedly.

Tony went out in the customers' room. He was in time to see the removal of one of the firm's clients—a shaky old miser who had boasted that he had beaten the depression without a loss—on a stretcher. The telephone-girl sat at her desk in the empty anteroom. Clerks still stayed at their places, furiously struggling with the abnormal mass of figures.

Tony procured his hat and walked out. Everyone else was on the street—people in herds and throngs never seen on Wall Street or Broad Street or on this stretch of Broadway, but who now were sucked in by this unparalleled excitement from the East Side, the river front, the Bowery and likewise down from upper Fifth and from Park Avenues. Women with babies, peddlers, elderly gentlemen, dowagers, proud mistresses, wives, schoolchildren and working-people, clerks, stenographers—everywhere.

All trapped—thought Tony—all trapped together on the rim of the world. Did they know it? Did they feel it?

No parade ever produced such a crowd. The buildings had drained themselves into the streets; and avenues and alleys alike had added to the throng.

The deluge of humanity was possessed of a single insatiable passion for newspapers. A boy with an armful of papers would not move from where he appeared before he sold his load. News-trucks, which might have the very latest word, were almost mobbed.

But the newspapers told nothing more. Their contents, following the repetition of the announcement of the morning, were of a wholly secondary nature, reflecting only the effect of the statement itself. A hundred cranks found their opinions in big type as fast as they were uttered—absurd opinions, pitiful opinions; but they were seized upon. There were religious revivals starting in the land. But the scientists—those banded together who had worked faithfully first to learn the nature of the discovery and then to keep it secret until to-day—they had nothing more to say.

Tony dropped into a restaurant, where, though it was only afternoon, an evening hilarity already had arrived. The Exchange was closed! No one knew exactly why or what was to happen. Why care? That was the air here.

Two men of Tony's age, acquaintances in school and friends in Wall Street, stopped at his table. "We're going the rounds. Come along."

Tony returned with them to the warm, sunlit street where the exhilaration of night—the irresponsibility of after-hours with offices closed and work done—denied the day. . . . Their taxi squeezed through Broadway in which frantic policemen wrestled vainly with overwhelming crowds. It stopped at a brownstone house in the West Forties.

A night-club, and it was crowded, though the sun was still shining. The three floors of the house were filled with people in business clothes drinking and dancing. On the top floor two roulette-wheels were surrounded by players. Tony saw heaps of chips, the piles of bills. He looked at the faces of the players and recognized two or three of them. They were hectic faces. The market had closed. This was a real smash,—not merely a money smash,—a smash of the whole world ahead. Naturally money was losing its value, but men played for it—cheered when they won, groaned when they lost, and staked again. The limit had been taken off the game.

Downstairs, at the bar, were three girls to whom Tony's two friends immediately attached themselves. They were pretty girls of the kind that Broadway produces by an over-night incubation: Girls who had been born far from the Great White Way. Girls whose country and small-town attitudes had vanished. All of them had hair transformed from its original shade to ashen blonde. Around their eyes were beaded lashes; their voices were high; their silk clothes adhered to their bodies. They drank and laughed.

"Here's to old Bronson!" they toasted. "Here's to the ol' world coming to an end!"

Tony sat with them: Clarissa, Jacqueline, Bettina. He gazed at them, laughed with them, drank with them; but he thought of Eve, asleep at last, he hoped. Eve, slender as they, young as they, far, far lovelier than they; and bearing within her mind and soul the frightful burden of the full knowledge of this day.

The room was hazy with smoke. People moved through it incessantly. After a while Tony looked again at the motley crowd; and across the room he saw a friend sitting alone in a booth. Tony rose and went toward the man. He was a person—a personage—worthy of notice. He was lean, gray-haired, immaculate, smooth. His dark eyes were remote and unseeing. First nights knew him. Mothers of very rich daughters, mothers of daughters of impeccable lineage, sought him. Wherever the gayest of the gay world went, he could be found. Southampton, Newport, Biarritz, Cannes, Nice, Deauville, Palm Beach. He was like old silver—yet he was not old. Forty, perhaps. A bachelor. He would have liked it if some one of authority had called him a connoisseur of life and living—an *arbiter elegantiæ*, a Petronius transferred from Nero's Rome to our day. He would have been pleased, but he would not have revealed his pleasure. His name was Peter Vanderbilt. And he was trapped too,—Tony was thinking as he saw him,—trapped with him and Eve and Kyto and the panhandler and Bettina and Jacqueline and all the rest on the rim of the world which was going to collide with another world sent from space for that errand; but a world with still another spinning before it, which would pass close to our world —close and spin on, safe.

Tony cleared his brain. "Hello," he said to Peter Vanderbilt.

Vanderbilt looked up and his face showed welcome. *"Tony! Jove!* Of all people. Glad to see you. Sit. Sit and contemplate." He beckoned a waiter and ordered. "You're a bit on the inside, I take it."

"Inside?"

"Friend of the Hendrons, I remember. You know a bit more of what's going on."

"Yes," admitted Tony; it was senseless to deny it to this man.

"Don't tell me. Don't break confidences for my sake. I'm not one that has to have details ahead of others. The general trend of events is clear enough. Funny. Delicious, isn't it, to think of the end of all this? I feel stimulated, don't you? All of it—going to pieces! I feel like saying, 'Thank God!' I was sick of it. Every one was. Civilization's a wretched parody. Evidently there was a just and judging God, after all.

"Democracy! Look at it, lad. Here are the best people, breaking the newest laws they made themselves. Imagine the fool who invented democracy! But what's better on this world anywhere? So there is a God after all, and He's taking us in hand again—the way He did in Noah's time. . . . Good thing, I say.

"But Hendron and his scientists aren't doing so well. They're making a big mistake. They've done splendidly—hardly could have done better up to to-day. I mean, keeping it under cover and not letting it out at all until they had some real information. They had luck in the fact that these

Bronson bodies were sighted in the south, and have been only visible from the Southern Hemisphere. Not many observatories down there—just South Africa, South America and Australia. That was a break—gave them much more of a chance to keep it to themselves; and I say, they did well up to now. But they're not well advised if they hold anything back much longer; they'd better tell anything—no matter how bad it is. They'll have to, as they'll soon see. Nothing can be as bad as uncertainty.

"It proves that all those names signed to this morning's manifesto are top-notch scientists. The human element is the one thing they can't analyze and reduce to figures. What they need is a counsel in public relations. Tell Cole Hendron I recommend Ivy Lee."

Rising, he left Tony and vanished in the throng. Tony started to pay the check, and saw Vanderbilt's ten-dollar bill on the table. He rose, secured his hat and went out.

The latest newspaper contained a statement from the White House. The President requested that on the morrow every one return to work. It promised that the Government would maintain stability in the country, and inveighed violently against the exaggerated reaction of the American people to the scientists' statement.

Tony smiled. "Business as usual! Business going on, as usual, during alterations," he thought. He realized more than ever how much his countrymen lived for and believed in business.

He wondered how much of the entire truth had been told to the President, and what the political angle on it would be. Amusing to think of the end of the world having a political angle; but of course, it had. Everything had.

He took a taxi to the Hendrons' apartment. More than a block away from the building, he had to abandon the cab. The crowd and the police cordon about the apartment both had increased; but certain persons could pass; and Tony learned that he still was one of them.

Several men, whose voices he could overhear in loud argument, were with Cole Hendron behind the closed doors of the big study on the roof. No one was with Eve. She awaited him, alone.

She was dressed carefully, charmingly, as she always was, her lovely hair brushed back, her lips cool to look at, but so warm upon his own!

He pressed her to him for a moment; and for that instant when he kissed her and held her close, all wonder and terror was sent away. What matter the end of everything, if first he had her! He had never dreamed of such delight in possession as he felt, holding her; he had never dared dream of such response from her—or from any one. He had won her, and she

31

him, utterly. As he thought of the cataclysm destroying them, he thought of it coming to them together, in each other's arms; and he could not care.

She felt it, fully as he. Her fingers touched his face with a passionate tenderness which tore him.

"What's done it for us so suddenly and so completely, Tony?"

" 'The shadow of the sword,' I suppose, my dear—oh, my dear! I remember reading it in Kipling when I was a boy, but never understanding it. Remember the two in love when they knew that one would surely die? 'There is no happiness like that snatched under the shadow of the sword.' "

"But we both shall die, if either does, Tony. That's so much better."

The voices beyond the closed door shouted louder, and Tony released her. "Who's here?"

"Six men: the Secretary of State, the Governor, Mr. Borgan, the chief of a newspaper chain, two more." She was not thinking about them. "Sit down, but don't sit near me, Tony; we've got to think things out."

"Your father's told them?" he asked.

"He's told them what will happen first. I mean, when the Bronson bodies—both of them—just pass close to the world and go on around the sun. That's more than enough for them now. It's not time yet to tell them of the encounter. You see, the mere passing close will be terrible enough."

"Why?"

"Because of the tides, for one thing. You know the tides, Tony; you know the moon makes them. The moon, which is hardly an eightieth of the world in mass; but it raises tides that run forty to sixty feet, in places like the Bay of Fundy."

"Of course—the tides," Tony realized aloud.

"Bronson Beta is the size of the earth, Tony; Bronson Alpha is estimated to have eleven or twelve times that mass. That sphere will pass, the first time, within the orbit of the moon. Bronson Beta will raise tides many times as high; and Bronson Alpha—you can't express it by mere multiplication, Tony. New York will be under water to the tops of its towers—a tidal wave beyond all imaginations! The seacoasts of all the world will be swept by the seas, sucked up toward the sky and washed back and forth. The waves will wash back to the Appalachians; and it will be the same in Europe and Asia. Holland, Belgium, half of France and Germany, half of India and China, will be under the wave of water. There'll be an earth tide, too."

"Earth tide?"

"Earthquakes from the pull on the crust of the earth. Some of the men writing to Father think that the earth will be torn

32

to pieces just by the first passing of Bronson Alpha; but some of them think it will survive that strain."

"What does your father think?"

"He thinks the earth will survive the first stress—and that it is possible that a fifth of the population may live through it, too. Of course that's only a guess."

"A fifth," repeated Tony. "A fifth of all on the earth."

He gazed at her, sober, painless, without a sense of time.

Here he was in a penthouse drawing-room on the top of a New York apartment, with a lovely girl whose father believed, and had told her, that four-fifths of all beings alive on the earth would be slain by the passing of the planets seen in the sky. A few months more, and all the rest—unless they could escape from the earth and live—would be obliterated.

Such words could stir no adequate feeling; they were beyond ordinary meanings, like statements of distance expressed in light years. They were beyond conscious conception; yet what they told could occur. His mind warned him of this. What was coming was a cosmic process, common enough, undoubtedly, if one considered the billions of stars with their worlds scattered through all space, and if one counted in eternities of endless time. Common enough, this encounter which was coming.

What egotism, what stupid vanity, to suppose that a thing could not happen because you could not conceive it!

Eve was watching him. Through the years of their friendship and fondness, she had seen Tony as a normal man, to whom everything that happened was happy, felicitous and unbizarre. The only crises in which she observed him were emergencies on the football-field, and alarms in the stock-market, which in the first case represented mere sport, and in the second, money which he did not properly understand, because all his life he had possessed money enough, and more.

Now, as she watched him, she thought that she would meet with him—and she exulted that it would be with him— the most terrific reality that man had ever faced. So far as he had yet been called upon, he had met it without attempting to evade it; his effort had been solely for more complete understanding.

A contrast to some of those men—among them men who were called the greatest in the nation—whose voices rose loud again behind the closed doors.

Some one—she could not identify him from his voice, which ranted in a strange, shrill rage—evidently was battling her father, shouting him down, denying what had been laid before them all. Eve did not hear her father's reply. Probably he made none; he had no knack for argument or dialectics.

But the ranting and shouting offended her; she knew how

33

helpless her father was before it. She wanted to go to him; not being able to, she went to Tony.

"Somebody," said Tony, "seems not to like what he has to hear."

"Who is he, Tony?"

"Somebody who isn't very used to hearing what he doesn't like. . . . Oh, Eve, Eve! My dear, my dear! For the first time in my life, I'd like to be a poet; I wish for words to say what I feel. I can't make a poem, but at least I can change one:

"Yesterday this day's madness did prepare;
To-morrow's silence, triumph, or despair;
Love! For you know not whence you came, nor why;
Love! For you know not why you go, nor where."

The sudden unmuffling of the voices warned them that a door from the study had opened. Instantly the voices were dulled again; but they turned, aware that some one had come out.

It was her father.

For a few moments he stood regarding them, debating what he should say. Beyond the closed door behind him, the men whom he had left increased their quarrel among themselves. He succeeded in clearing his mind of it.

"Father," Eve said, "Tony and I—Tony and I—"

Her father nodded. "I saw you for a few seconds before you realized I was here, Eve—and Tony."

Tony flushed. "We mean what you saw, sir," he said. "We more than mean it. We're going to be married as soon as we can—aren't we, Eve?"

"Can we, Father?"

Cole Hendron shook his head. "There can't be marrying or love for either of you. No time to tell you why now; only—there can't."

"Why can't there be, sir?"

"There's going to be altogether too much else. In a few months, you'll know. Meanwhile, don't spoil my plans for you by eloping or marrying in the Church Around the Corner. And don't go on doing—what I just saw. It'll only make it harder for both of you—as you'll see when you figure out what's before you. Tony, there's nothing personal in that. I like you, and you know it. If the world were going to remain, I'd not say a word; but the world cannot possibly remain. We can talk of this later."

The study door again opened; some one called him, and he returned to the argument in the next room.

"Now," demanded Tony of Eve, "what in the world, which cannot possibly remain, does he mean by that? That we shouldn't love and marry because we're going to die? All the more reason for it—and quicker, too."

"Neither of us can possibly guess what he means, Tony; we'd be months behind him in thinking; for he's done nothing else, really, for half a year but plan what we—what all the human race—will have to do. He means, I think, that he's put us in some scheme of things that won't let us marry."

The argument in the room broke up and the arguers emerged. In a few minutes they all were gone; and Tony sought Cole Hendron in his big study, where the plates which had come from South Africa were spread upon the table.

There were squares of stars, usually the same square of stars repeated over and over again. There seemed to be a score of exposures of the identical plate of close-clustered stars.

"You were downtown to-day, Tony?"

"Yes."

"To-day they took it, didn't they? They took it and closed the Exchange, I hear; and half the businesses in town had a holiday. For they've known for quite some time that something has been hanging over them, hanging over the market. This morning we half told them what it is; and they thought they believed it. Just now I told six men the other half—or most of it—and—and you heard them, Tony; didn't you?"

"Yes; I heard them."

"They won't have it. The world won't come to an end; it can't possibly collide with another world, because—well, for one thing, it never has done such a thing before, and for another, they won't have it. Not when you dwell upon the details. They won't have it. To-morrow there'll be a great swing-back in feeling, Tony. The Exchange will open again; business is going on. That's a good thing; I'm glad of it. But there are certain drawbacks.

"The trouble is, men aren't really educated up to the telescope yet, as they are to the microscope. Every one of those men who were just here would believe what the microscope tells them, whether or not they could see it or understand it for themselves. I mean, if a doctor took a bit of cell-tissue from any one of them, and put it under the microscope, and said, 'Sorry, but that means you will die,' there isn't a man of them who wouldn't promptly put his affairs in shape.

"None of them would ask to look through the microscope himself; he'd know it would mean nothing to him.

"But they asked for Bronson's plates. I showed them; here they are, Tony. Look here. See this field of stars. All those fixed points, those round specks, every single one of them are stars. But see here; there is a slight—a very slight—streak, but still a streak. There, right beside it, is another one. Some-

35

thing has moved, Tony! Two points of light have moved in a star-field where nothing ought to move! A mistake, perhaps? A flaw in the coating of the plate? Bronson considered this, and other possibilities. He photographed the star-field again and again, night after night; and each time, you see, Tony, the same two points of light make a bit of streak. No chance of mistake; down there, where nothing ought to be moving, two objects have moved. But all we have to show for it are two tiny streaks on a photographic plate.

"What do they mean? 'Gentlemen, the time has come to put your affairs in order!' The affairs of all the world, the affairs of every one living in the world— Naturally, they can't really believe it.

"Bronson himself, though he watched those planets himself night after night for months, couldn't really believe it; nor could the other men who watched, in other observatories south of the equator.

"But they searched back over old plates of the same patch of sky; and they found, in that same star-field, what they had missed before—those same two specks always making tiny streaks. Two objects that weren't stars where only stars ought to be; two strange objects that always were moving, where nothing 'ought' to move.

"We need only three good observations of an object to plot the course of a moving body; and already Bronson succeeded in obtaining a score of observations of these. He worked out the result, and it was so senational, that from the very first, he swore to secrecy every one who worked with him and with whom he corresponded. They obtained, altogether, hundreds of observations; and the result always worked out the same. They all checked. . . .

"Eve says she has told you what that result is to be."

"Yes," said Tony, "she told me."

"And I told these men who demanded—ordered me—to explain to them everything we had. I told them that those specks were moving so that they would enter our solar system, and one of them would then come into collision with our world. They said, all right.

"You see, it really meant nothing to them originally; it stirred only a sort of excitement to close the Exchange and give everybody a hilarious holiday.

"Then I told them that, before the encounter, both of these moving bodies—Bronson Alpha and Bronson Beta—would first pass us close by and cause tides that would rise six hundred feet over us, from New York to San Francisco—and, of course, London and Paris and all sea-coasts everywhere.

"They began to oppose that, because they could understand it. I told them that the passing of the Bronson bodies would cause earthquakes on a scale unimaginable; half the inland cities would be shaken down, and the effect below the crust would set volcanoes into activity everywhere, and as never since the world began. I said, perhaps a fifth of the people would survive the first passing of the Bronson bodies. I tried to point out some of the areas on the surface of the earth which would be completely safe.

"I could not designate New York or Philadelphia or Boston. . . . They told me that to-morrow I must make a more reassuring statement."

Cole Hendron gazed down again at his plates.

"I suppose, after all, it doesn't make much difference whether or not we succeed in moving a few million more people into the safer areas. They will be safe for only eight months more, in any case. For eight months later, we meet Bronson Alpha on the other side of the sun. And no one on earth will escape.

"But there is a chance that a few individuals may leave the earth and live. I am not a religious man, as you know, Tony; but as Eve said to you, it seems that it cannot be mere chance that there comes to us, out of space, not merely the sphere that will destroy us, but that ahead of it there spins a world like our own which some of us—some of us—may reach and be safe."

Chapter 6—First Effects

TONY took Dave Ransdell home with him. The South African wanted to "see" New York.

They awoke late; or at least Tony did, and for a few moments lay contentedly lazy, without recollection of the amazing developments of the day that was past.

Only a vague uneasiness warned him that, when he finally roused, it would be to some sort of trouble. Tony, being a healthy and highly vigorous young man, had drowsed through such semirecollections before. . . . He had fought with and "put out" another policeman, perhaps? Tony became able to recollect "showing" some one the city; but who?

Now Tony could visualize him—a tanned, quiet-humored, solid chap who could look out for himself anywhere. And girls liked him; but he was wary, even if he hadn't been to New York before. Even if he did come from South Africa!

There, Tony had it! Dave Ransdell, the Pretoria flyer, who had brought the plates of the sky from Capetown to New York. Why? Because there were two little specks on those plates of the southern skies, which meant that two strange planetary bodies were approaching the earth—to wipe it out!

That was the trouble Tony had to remember when he fully

awoke. It wasn't that he'd knocked another policeman for a goal. It was that—that this room, and the bed, and the chair, everything outside, everywhere and every one, including you yourself, were simply going to cease to exist after a while. After a very definite and limited time, indeed, though the exact period he did not know.

Eve had refused to tell him; and so had Dr. Hendron. No; the exact amount of time left for every one on the world, the members of the League of the Last Days would not yet impart.

Tony stirred; and Kyto, hearing him, came in and began to draw his bath.

"All right, Kyto; never mind," Tony greeted him. "I'll take a shower this morning. Is Mr. Ransdell up?"

"Oh, entirely!"

"Has he had breakfast yet, Kyto?"

"Only one."

"You mean?"

"He said he would have a little now—that was an hour ago—and finish breakfast with you."

"Oh. All right. I'll hurry." And Tony did so, but forgetting Ransdell, mostly, for his thinking of Eve.

To have held her close to him, to have caught her against him while she clung to him, her lips on his—and then to be forbidden her! To be finally and completely forbidden to love her!

Tony arose defiantly. Last night he had been rebellious; this morning he was only more so. Never had he known or dreamed of such dear delight as when he had claimed her lithe body with his arms, and she had clung to him; the two of them together against all the world—even against the end of all the world, against the utter annihilation!

It was, he realized now, the terror of the approaching destruction which had thrown her so unquestioningly into his arms. Who could stand alone and look at doom? All nature, every instinct and impulse, opposed loneliness in danger. The first law of living things is self-perpetuation. Save yourself; and when you cannot, preserve your kind! Mate and beget—or give birth—before you die!

Nothing less elemental, less overwhelming, than this threw Eve Hendron and Tony Drake together; and no joy compared with the result. What had he heard said, that he understood now: "There is no happiness like that snatched under the shadow of the sword!"

But her father forbade that joy. He not only forbade it, but denied its further possibility for them. And her father controlled her, not merely as her father, but as a leader of this strange society, the uncanny power of which Tony Drake was just beginning to feel: The League of the Last Days!

38

A pledged and sworn circle of men, first in science all over the world, who devoted themselves to their purposes with a sternness and a discipline that recalled the steadfastness of the early Christians, who submitted to any martyrdom to found the Church. They demanded and commanded a complete allegiance. To this tyrannical society Eve was sworn; and when Cole Hendron had spoken to her, he commanded her and forbade not only as her father but as her captian in the League of the Last Days. . . .

Tony found Ransdell at a window of the living-room. The morning paper was spread over a table.

"Hello," said Tony. "Hear you've been up awhile. You've altogether too many good habits."

The South African smiled pleasantly. "I'll need more than I have for a starter, if I'm joining the League of the Last Days," he observed.

"Then you've decided to?" asked Tony. It was one of the topics they'd discussed last night.

"Yes. The New York chapter, for choice."

"You're not going back to Capetown?"

"No. Headquarters will be here—or wherever Dr. Hendron is."

"That's good," said Tony, and glanced toward the paper, but did not pick it up. "Any special developments anywhere?"

"Apparently a rather unanimous opinion that yesterday's announcement may be wrong."

"Hendron said there'd be general reaction. When you think of yesterday, you'd see there'd have to be."

And Tony took the paper to the breakfast-table, where Ransdell joined him for another cup of coffee.

The two young men, of widely differing natures and background and training, sipped their coffee and glanced at each other across the table.

"Well," questioned Tony at last, "want to tell me how you really feel?"

"Funny," confessed the South African. "I bring up the final proof that the world's going to end; and on the trip find the dear old footstool a pleasanter place for me than I ever figured before it might be. . . .

"To mention the minor matters first," Ransdell continued in his engagingly frank and outright way, "I've never lived like this even for a day. I've never been valeted before."

Tony smiled. "That reminds me; wonder if they'll let Kyto into the League?"

"Not as our valet, I'm afraid," the South African said. "I hope you permit me the 'our' for the duration of my stay. I do fancy living like this, I must admit. I'll also tell you that I appreciate very much just being around where Miss Hendron is. I didn't know there really was a girl like her anywhere in the world."

"Which is going to end, we must remember," Tony warned him. "Every time we mention the world, we must remember it is going to end."

"Will you permit me, then, a particularly personal remark?" inquired the South African.

"Shoot," said Tony.

"It is—that if I were in your place, I wouldn't particularly care what happened."

"My place, you mean, with—"

"With Miss Hendron. In other words, I heartily congratulate you."

"You don't know what you're talking about," said Tony—too brusquely, and realized it. "I beg your pardon. I mean, I thank you. . . . The Stock Exchange, I see, is going to be open to-day. In fact, it undoubtedly is open now; and I am not at my office watching the ticker and buying A. T. and T. on a scale down, and selling X—that's United States Steel—whenever it rises half a point, for somebody who wants to go short from lack of faith in the future. What am I talking about? Where is the future? What's happened to it?"

"It seems to have regained its feet a bit to-day."

"Yes. The stock market is open. . . . There's the phone—probably my office. Mr. Balcom wants my personal advice after my last talk with Cole Hendron. I'm out or asleep, and you won't disturb me. You have my permission to put me into a coma—anything. . . . I ought to have said to you, Ransdell, I'm glad you're staying on. Stay on right here with me, if you like.

"There's no sense in my going to the office. There's no sense in anything on the world, now, but preparing and perfecting the Space Ship which—besides watching the stars—has been the business of the best brains in the League of the Last Days."

"How far have they got?"

"Not far enough; but of course there's no mother to invention like necessity. And necessity seems to be distinctly visible —at least through a telescope—now."

Tony went downtown; he visited his office. Habit held him, as it was holding most of the hundreds of millions of humans in the world this day. Habit—and reaction.

What was threatened, could not be! If Cole Hendron and his brother-scientists refused, there were plenty of other people to put out reassuring statements; and the dwellers on the rim of the world regained much of their assurance. The President of the United States pointed out that, at worst, the sixty scientists had merely suggested disturbances of importance; and he predicted that if they occurred, they would be less than was now feared.

Professor Copley, known to Tony as a friend of Cole Hendron's, called at the office.

"I've some things to sell," he said, plucking the *pince-nez* from the center of his ruddy, cheerful face. "When do you think you can get me the most for them?"

And he laid down upon Tony's desk an envelope full of stock certificates. "I'm just back from Peru," he explained, "where I have been watching the progress of the Bronson bodies. Hendron tells me that you know the whole truth about them."

"It is the truth, then?" asked Tony.

"Do you mean, do I agree? Do you agree that the sun will rise to-morrow morning?" Professor Copley returned. "My dear friend, the Bronson bodies move from the effect of the same forces."

"But," pursued Tony, "exactly what do you think will happen to us?"

"What will happen," retorted Professor Copley, cheerfully enough, "if you toss a walnut in front of an eighteen-inch gun at the instant the shell comes out? The result, I should say, would be quite decisive and entirely final. So, I say, sell my stocks. My family, and my personal responsibilities, consist of only my wife and myself; there are many things we have desired to do which we have sacrificed in exchange for a certain security in the future. There being no future, why not start doing what we want immediately?—if now is the day to sell."

"Your guess on that," said Tony, "will be as good as mine. To-day is better than yesterday; to-morrow the market may be nearer normal again—or there may be none at all. How do you find that people are taking it?"

"Superficially, to-day they deny; but they have had a terrible shock. Shock—that's the first effect. Bound to be. Afterward—they'll behave according to their separate natures. But now they react in denials, because they cannot bear the shock.

"All over the world! Some are standing in the Place de l'Opéra in Paris, hour after hour, I hear, silent for the most part, incredulous, numb. These are the few that are too intelligent merely to deny and reject, too stunned to substitute a sudden end of everything for the prospect of years ahead for which they scrimped and saved.

"In Berlin there are similar groups. And imagine the reaction in Red Square, my friend! Imagine the Russians trying to realize that their revolution, their savage effort to remodel themselves and their inner nature, has gone for nothing. All wasted! It will be knocked aside by a mere pebble—a grain of sand sifting through the cosmos on an errand of its own. Knocked aside and annihilated, as if no Russian had ever lived! It is stupendous! Imagine being Stalin to-night, my friend. What horror! What humor! What merciless depths of tragedy!

"Imagine the haughty Mussolini, when he finds that the secret he could not exhort from his iron-souled men of learning is the secret of Fascism's vanity. Vanity of vanities! All, in the end, is vanity! Dust!

"He has jutted out his chin and lifted his hand in salute to his Black Shirts, mouthed his ringing sentences, and defied any one or anything to stay him; and behold! Ten billion, billion, billion miles away some trifling approach of stars made unstable the orbits of a couple of planets and sent them out into space so long ago that Mussolini's ancestors were not yet hairy apes—and now they appear to confound him. Imagine our President trying to decry, now, this! Ah, I could weep. But I do not. Instead—I laugh. I laugh because few men—but some—some—some, my friend—even in the face of this colossal ignominy of fate, go on and on through the night, burning out their brains yet in the endeavor to guide their own destinies. What a gesture! But to-day—what appalling shock! And afterward—what a scene! When the world—the fifteen hundred millions of human beings realize, all of them, that nothing can save them, and they cannot possibly save themselves. What a scene! I hope to be spared for it. Meanwhile, sell my stocks for the best prices you can obtain, please; for my wife and I—we have saved for a long time, and denied ourselves too much."

In a taxi later in the day, Tony found the street suddenly blocked by a delirious group of men with locked arms, who charged out of a door, singing—drunk, senseless.

Tony was on his way to the Newark Airport, where a certain pilot, for whom he was to inquire, would fly him to the estate in the Adirondacks which had been turned over to Cole Hendron.

CHAPTER 7—SOME DEMANDS OF DESTINY

EVE awaited him in a garden surrounded by trees. In the air was the scent of blossoms, the fragrance of the forest, the song of birds. It bore new qualities, a new interpretation of the external world, distinct from the tumultuous cacophony of the city.

She was in white, with her shoulders and arms bare, her slender body sheathed close in silk. All feminine, she was, too feminine, indeed, in her feeling for the task she set for herself. Would she succeed better at it if she had garbed herself like a nun.

An airplane droned in the twilight sky and dropped to its cleared and clipped landing-field. Eve arose from the bench beside the little pool, which was beginning to glint with the reflection of Venus, the evening star. She trembled, impatient; she circled the pool and sat down again.

Here he came at last and alone, as she hoped.

"Hello, Tony!" She tried to make it cool.

"Eve, my dear!"

"We mustn't say even that! No—don't kiss me or hold me so!"

"Why? . . . I know your father said not to. It's discipline of the League of the Last Days. But why is it? Why must they ask it? And why must you obey?"

"There, Tony. Just touch my hands, like this—and I'll try to explain to you. But first, how was it in the city to-day?"

Tony told her.

"I see. Now, Tony, let's sit here side by side—but not your arm around me. I want it so much, I can't have it. That's why, don't you see?

"We're in a very solemn time, Tony. I spent a lot of to-day doing a queer thing—for me. I got to reading the Book of Daniel again—especially Belshazzar's feast. I read that over and over. I can remember it, Tony.

" 'Belshazzar the king made a great feast to a thousand of his lords, and drank wine before the thousand.

" 'They brought the golden vessels that were taken out of the temple of the house of God; and the king, and his princes, his wives and his concubines, drank in them.

" 'They drank wine, and praised the gods of gold, and of silver, of brass, of iron, of wood, and of stone.'

"Isn't that a good deal like what we've—most of us—been doing, Tony?"

" 'Now in the same hour came forth fingers of a man's hand, and wrote over against the candlestick upon the plaster of the wall of the king's palace; and the king saw the part of the hand that wrote.

" 'Then the king's countenance was changed; his knees smote together. The king cried aloud to bring in the astrologers, the Chaldeans and the soothsayers.'

"And Daniel, you may remember, interpreted the writing on the wall. '*Mene, Mene, Tekel, Upharsin.* God hath numbered thy kingdom and finished it. Thou art weighed in the balances and art found wanting. And in that night was Belshazzar, the king of the Chaldeans, slain.'

"It is something very like that which is happening to us now, Tony; only the Finger, instead of writing again on the wall, this time has taken to writing in the sky—over our heads. The Finger of God, Tony, has traced two little streaks in the sky—two objects moving toward us, where nothing

43

ought to move; and the message of one of them is perfectly plain.

"'Thou art weighed in the balances and art found wanting,' that one says to us on this world. 'God hath numbered thy kingdom and finished it.' But what does the other streak say?

"That is the strange one, Tony—the one that gives you the creeps and the thrills when you think of it. For that is the afterthought of God—the chance He is sending us!

"Remember how the Old Testament showed God to us, stern and merciless. 'God saw that the wickedness of man was great in the earth!' it said. 'And it repented the Lord that he had made man on the earth. And the Lord said, I will destroy man, whom I have created, from the face of the earth; both man, and beast and the creeping things, and the fowls of the air; for it repenteth me that I have made them. And then, God thought it over and softened a little; and He warned Noah to build the ark to save himself and some of the beasts, so that they could start all over again.

"Well, Tony, it seemed to me the second streak in the sky says that God is doing the same thing once more. He hasn't changed His nature since Genesis; not in that short time. Why should He? It seemed to me, Tony, He looked us all over again and got disgusted.

"Evolution, you know, has been going on upon this world for maybe five hundred million years; and I guess God thought that, if all we'd reached in all that time was what we have now, He'd wipe us out forever. So He started that streak toward us to meet us, and destroy us utterly. That's Bronson Alpha. But before He sent it too far on its way, maybe He thought it all over again and decided to send Bronson Beta along too.

"You see, after all, God had been working on the world for five hundred millions of years; and that must be an appreciable time, even to God. So I think He said, 'I'll wipe them out; but I'll give some of them a chance. If they're good enough to take the chance and transfer to the other world I'm sending them, maybe they're worth another trial. And I'll save five hundred millions of years.' For we'll start on the other world, Tony, where we left off here."

"I see that," Tony said. "What's in that to forbid my loving you now, my taking you in my arms, my——"

"I wish we could, Tony!"

"Then why not?"

"No reason not, if we were surely to die here, Tony—with all the rest of the world; but every reason not to, if we go on the Space Ship."

"I don't see that!"

"Don't you? Do you suppose, Tony, that the second streak

44

in the sky—the streak that we call Bronson Beta which will come close to this world, and possibly receive us safe, before Bronson Alpha wipes out all the rest—do you suppose, Tony, that it was sent just for you and me?"

"I don't suppose it was sent at all," objected Tony impatiently. "I don't believe in a God Who plans and repents and wipes out worlds He made."

"I do. A few months ago, I wouldn't have believed in Him; but since this has happened, I do. What is coming is altogether too precise and exact to be unplanned by Intelligence somewhere, or to be purposeless. For those two streaks—the Bronson bodies—aren't cutting in on our little system out by Neptune or Jupiter, where they'd find no living thing. They've chosen, out of all space near us, the single sphere that's inhabited—they're directed for us. Directed—*sent*, that is, Tony. And if the big one is sent to wipe out the world, I don't believe the other is sent just to let me go on loving you and you go on loving me."

"What is your idea, then?"

"It's sent to save, perhaps, some of the results of five hundred million years of life on this world; but not you and me, Tony."

"Why not? What are we?"

Eve smiled faintly. "We're some of the results, of course. As such, we may go on the Space Ship. But if we go, we cease to be ourselves, don't you see?"

"I don't," persisted Tony stubbornly.

"I mean, when we arrive on that strange empty world,—if we do,—we can't possibly arrive as Tony Drake and Eve Hendron, to continue a love and a marriage started here. How insane that would be!"

"Insane?"

"Yes. Suppose one Space Ship got across with, say, thirty in its crew. We land and begin to live—thirty alone on an empty world as large as this. What, on that world, would we be? Individuals paired and set off, each from the others, as here? No; we become bits of biology, bearing within us seeds far more important than ourselves—far more important than our prejudices and loves and hates. We cannot then think of ourselves, only to preserve ourselves while we establish our kind."

"Exactly what do you mean by that, Eve?"

"I mean that marriage on Bronson Beta—if we reach it— cannot possibly be what it is here, especially if only a few, a very few of us, reach it. It will be all-important then—it will be essential to take whatever action the circumstances may require to establish the race."

"You mean," said Tony savagely, remembering the remarks at breakfast, "if that flyer from South Africa—Rans-

45

dell—also made the passage on that Space Ship, and we all live, I may have to give you up to him—when circumstances seem to require it?"

"I don't know, Tony. We can't possibly describe it now; we can't imagine the circumstances when we're starting all over again. But one thing we can know—we must not first fix relations between us here which may only give trouble."

"Relations like love and marriage!"

"They might not do at all, over there."

"You're mad, Eve. Your father's been talking to you."

"Of course he has; but there's only sanity in what he says. He has thought so much more about it, he can look so calmly beyond the end of the world to what may be next that—that he won't have us carry into the next world sentiments and attachments that may only bring us trouble and cause quarrels or rivalry and death. How frightful to fight and kill each other on that empty world! So we have to start freeing ourselves from such things here."

"I'll be no freer pretending I don't want you more than anything else. What sort of thing does your father see for us —on Bronson Beta?"

She evaded him. "Why bother about it, Tony, when there's ten thousand chances to one we'll never get there? But we'll try for it—won't we?"

"I certainly will, if you're going to."

"Then you'll have to submit to the discipline."

His arms hungered for her, and his lips ached for hers, but he turned away.

Inside the house, he found her father, Cole Hendron.

"Glad to see you, Tony. We're going ahead with our plans. I suppose you knew I had been counting on you."

"For what?" Tony inquired brusquely.

"For one of my crew. You've the health and the mind and the nerve, I think. It's going to take more courage, in the end, than staying here on the world. For we will all leave— we will shoot ourselves up into the sky while the world still seems safe. We leave, of course, before the end; and the end of the world will never be really believed till it comes. So I need men of your steadiness and quality. Can I count on you?"

Tony looked him over. "You can count on me, Mr. Hendron."

"Good. . . . I can guess that Eve has acquainted you with some features of the discipline of the League. I will tell you, in proper time, of others; nothing will be asked of you which will not be actually reasonable and necessary. But now I should advise you to learn something useful. Investment experience, and skill in trading, will scarcely be an asset on Bronson Beta, whereas knowledge of agriculture and proficiency in manual arts and elementary mechanics may be invaluable. You have time to learn the simple, primary processes by which life is maintained. You will have, I might say, approximately two years to prepare, before affairs here become acute with the approach of the planets on their first passage."

Chapter 8—Marching Orders for the Human Race

NO record could picture a thousandth part of the changes that came in those two years. No single aspect of human enterprise was left undisturbed.

It was on the half of the world which we call the Northern Hemisphere that the effect of the approach of the planets proved most disastrous. Of course, it was the north that possessed the continents teeming with people—Asia, Europe, North Africa, North America. The Southern Hemisphere, in comparison, was sparsely settled; and the South, moreover, had the advantage of seeing the strange stars slowly become visible and slowly, thereafter, brighten. The South became accustomed to their shining in the sky.

But at the end of the first year after the announcement of their approach, they stood for the first time in the northern sky. Partly this was due to their actual approach, which was bringing them not only closer but higher in the heavens; but chiefly it was due to the seasonal shifts of the earth which in spring showed more and more of the southern skies.

So there they stood, not high above the horizon as seen from New York or Chicago or San Francisco, but quite distinct and strange—two new stars clearly connected, one much brighter than the other. Even in a good field-glass, the brighter showed a round, gleaming disk, and the dimmer one appeared more than a point.

It was yet more than a year before the first serious physical manifestations were expected; so the statement that Hendron signed merely read:

"It is still impossible to forecast the entire effect of the approach of the Bronson bodies. Unquestionably they will disturb us greatly. We may anticipate, *as a minimum,* the following phenomena: tides which will destroy or render uninhabitable all coastal cities and all inland cities within five hundred or more feet of sea-level. We have no terrestrial precedent for such tides. The existing sixty-foot rise and fall in the Bay of Fundy will certainly be trifling in comparison. The tides we anticipate will be perhaps several hundreds of feet high, and will sweep overland with a violence difficult to anticipate.

"The second manifestation, which will be simultaneous, will consist of volcanic activity and earthquakes of unpredictable extent and violence.

47

"The Bronson bodies, if they pass on a parabola, will approach the earth twice. If, however, their course becomes modified into an ellipse, the earth will meet them again in its journey around the sun. Direct collision with one or another of the bodies, or grazing collision due to mutual attraction when in proximity, cannot be regarded as impossible. The succession of tides and earthquakes caused by gravity and resultant stresses may instantly or in time render the surface of this globe wholly uninhabitable; but we cannot say that there is no hope.

"Certain steps must be taken. All coastal cities in all parts of the world must be evacuated. Populaces must be moved to high, non-volcanic regions. Provision for feeding, clothing and domiciling migrated peoples must be made.

"There remains considerable doubt concerning the origin and nature of the Bronson bodies. Efforts are being made to determine their composition, but determinations are difficult, as they are non-luminous.

"The scientists of the world are in agreement that the course outlined above is the only logical one to pursue. Since the first approach of the Bronson bodies may be expected to take place with effect upon the tides and seaboard on and about the end of next summer, general migration should begin at once."

On the morning succeeding the spread of this statement, Tony stood in the vast, populous waiting-room of the Grand Central Station. Yesterday there had been issued marching orders for fifteen hundred millions of human beings. If they did not now know that it was to be the end of the world, at least they were told that it was the end of the world as it had been.

He listened to fragments of the conversations in progress in his vicinity:

"I tell you, Henry, it's silly, that's all. If anybody expects me to give up my apartment and pack up my duds and move off one Hundred and Eighty-first Street just because a few gray-headed school-teachers happen to think there's a comet coming, then they're crazy. . . ."

"It's the end, that's what it is; and I for one am glad to see it. When the sea starts to rise and the earth starts to split open, I'm going to stand there and laugh. I'm going to say: 'Now what's the good of the Farm Relief? Now who's going to collect my income-tax? Now what does it matter whether we have Prohibition or not? Now who's going to stop your car and bawl you out because you drove on the wrong side of the street? Good-by, world.' That's what I'm going to say. 'Good-by! Good riddance!' I hope it wipes the whole damn' thing as clean as a billiard ball. . . ."

"Don't hold my hand so tight, Daddy. You hurt me. . . ."

"It's ridiculous. They've been fighting about their fool figures for generations. They can't even tell whether it's going to rain or not to-morrow. How in the hell can they say this is going to happen? Give a scientist one idea, and a lot of trick figures, and he goes hay-wire, that's all. . . ."

"So I says to him, the big oaf: 'I'm a working-girl, and I'm gonna be a working-girl all my life, and you can tell me it doesn't matter on account of the world's coming to an end, and you can tell me the better I know you the better I'll like you, till you're blue in the face; but I'm gonna get out of this car right here and now, end of the world or no end of the world.' . . ."

"Laugh that off. Go ahead. Let me see you laugh that off. You've been laughing everything off ever since we were married. You laugh off the unpaid bills. You laugh off my ratty fur coat. You laugh off not being able to buy an automobile. Now let me see if you can laugh off an earthquake. . . ."

"I drew it all out and bought gold. I got two revolvers. I filled the house with canned goods. I said: 'Here you are, Sarah. You've been telling me all your life how well you can run things. Take the money. Take the house. Take these two guns. I'm leaving. If we've only got a couple of months left, I'm going to see to it that I have a little fun, anyway.' That's what I said to her; and, by God, here I am. . . ."

Tony shook his head. Every word to which he had listened surfeited him with a sense of the immobility of humanity. Each individual related a cosmic circumstance to his particular case. Each individual planned to act independently not only of the rest of his fellows but of all signs and portents in the sky. Tony's mind conceived a picture of huge cities on the verge of inundation—cities in which thousands and even millions refused to budge and went about the infinitesimal affairs of their little lives selfishly, with nothing but resentment for the facts which wiser men were futilely attempting to impress upon them. He heard his train announced, and walked to the gate.

He rode through a long dark tunnel and then out to the station at One Hundred and Twenty-fifth Street. His eyes rested uncomfortably on the close-pressed accumulation of ugly houses. It had been taken for granted too long; and upon the spawn who inhabited it, the best thoughts and dreams of the race fell unheeded. They lived and died and did not matter. A pollution ate steadily upward in every body of society from these far-reaching honeycombs of disease, dirt, stupidity, these world-wide remainders from the Middle Ages.

Tony, who had never been religious in any conventional sense, had begun to share the feeling of Eve about what was going to happen. She had not been religious; but emotionally, at least, she accepted the idea that God Himself had sickened with our selfishness, stupidity and squalor, and in disgust had tossed two pebbles through the sky on their errand which, night by night now, was becoming more apparent.

The train moved past the final outpost tenements into a verdant landscape with the river on one side—the Hudson, in which tides soon would rise to sweep high and far over the Palisades. Tony glanced back, once, toward the teeming city. The first flood would not top those tallest towers etched there; the pinnacles of man's triumphs would, for a while, rise above the tides; but all the rest? Tony turned away and looked out at the river, trying not to think of it.

CHAPTER 9—HOW THE WORLD TOOK IT

SETTLED in a chair, Tony glanced around the comfortable furnishings of the student's room and then gazed at the student himself. A lanky youth with red hair, good-humored blue eyes and a sprinkling of freckles that carried into his attained maturity more than a memory of the childhood he had so recently left.

"Yes," Tony repeated, "I'm from Cole Hendron. The dean told me about your academic work. Professor Gates showed me the thesis on Light which you turned in for your Ph.D. He said it was the finest thing he had had from the Graduate School since he'd held the chair of Physics."

Dull red came in the young man's face. "Nothing much. I just happened to have an idea. Probably never get another in my life."

Tony smiled. "I understand you were stroke in the varsity crew two years ago."

"That's right."

"That's the year you were rowing everybody out of the water, isn't it?"

"There weren't any good crews that year. We just happened to have the least bad ones."

Tony looked at the youth's hands, nervously clenching and unclenching. They were powerful hands, which nevertheless seemed to possess the capacity for minute adjustments. Tony smiled. "No need of being so modest, old fellow. It's just as I said. Cole Hendron in New York is getting together a bunch of people for some work he wants done during the next few months. It's work of a very private nature. I can't tell you what. I can't even assure you that he will accept you, but I'm touring around in the attempt to send him some likely people. You understand that I'm not offering you a job in the sense that jobs have been offered in the past. I don't know that any salary is attached to it at all. You will be supplied with a place to live, and provided with food, if you accept."

The tall youth grinned. "I suppose you know that offering a chance to associate with Cole Hendron, to a man like me, is just like offering the job of secretary to St. Peter, to a bishop."

"M-m-m. By the way, why did you stay here at the university when most of the graduate students have left?"

"No particular reason. I didn't have anything better to do. The university is on high ground, so it didn't seem sensible to move for that reason, and I thought I might as well go on with my work."

"I see," Tony replied.

His companion hesitated to say what was obviously on his mind, but finally broke the short silence. "Look here, Mr.— Mr.—"

"Drake. Tony Drake."

"Mr. Drake. I can't understand why on earth Hendron would want me. If he's planning to take a group of people to some safe spot in order to preserve scientific knowledge during the next year, he can find hundreds of people, thousands of people, that have more knowledge to save, and a better memory to save it in, than I have."

Tony looked at the good-humored blue eyes and liked the young man. He felt instinctively that here was one person whom Cole Hendron and the committee would surely accept. The name of the man before him, he recalled, was Jack Taylor—his record for a man of twenty-five was startling. He grinned at the youth's speculation. "You're a physicist, Taylor. If you were in Cole Hendron's shoes, and were trying to take a group of people to a place of safety, just where, under the circumstances we anticipate, would you take them?"

The other man was thoughtful for an instant. "That's just what worried me. I can't think of any place on earth that would offer a refuge essentially satisfactory."

"Exactly. No place *on earth*." Tony emphasized the last two words.

Jack Taylor frowned quickly, and suddenly the freckles on his face stood out because his color had departed.

"God Almighty! You don't mean to suggest—"

Tony lifted his hand and dropped it. "I'm offering you a letter than will give you an interview with Cole Hendron. Do you want to go and see him?"

For a minute Taylor did not answer. Then he said disjointedly: "Marvelous! My God—Hendron's just the man— the only man! To think that anybody would come around to give me a shot at such a thing!" Tears suddenly filled his eyes, and he stood up and walked in two mighty strides to the window.

Tony slapped his back. "See you in New York. Better get going right away. So long, old man."

Deeply moved, proud that any race, any civilization should produce human beings of the temper and fineness of young Taylor, Tony walked out onto the university campus and hurried to keep an appointment with an obscure but talented assistant professor of chemistry whose investigations of colloids had placed his name on the long list furnished to Tony by Hendron and his associates.

Tony, having applied himself for months to acquisition of the primitive proficiencies in growing things and in the manual arts, had found himself appointed by Cole Hendron as his personnel officer. Tony possessed, decidedly, a knack with people; and so Hendron was sending him about to recruit young men for the extraordinary duties of the crew of the Space Ship.

Her father had asked Eve to suggest, provisionally, the women who must go along; and Tony had met some whom Eve had selected.

Strange to think of them standing with you—and with a few other men out of all our world's creation—on the soil of an empty planet! What would they be to each other there?

Stranger still, to gaze at night into the sky, and see a spot of light beside a brighter orb and realize that you might—you *might* become a visitor to that spot in the sky!

Tony returned, three weeks later, to New York City, where Hendron now spent most of his time. He had workshops and laboratories started in several places, but the advantage of conveniences in New York was so great that he had decided not to abandon his work there until later.

Upon his arrival in the city, late on a July afternoon, Tony went at once to see Hendron and Eve. He had business with Hendron—none with Eve; he merely longed to see her and be with her, more than he dared display. Not much change was observable in the city. The station was a sea of people, as it had been on the day of his departure. The streets were more than normally crowded, and his taxicab made slow progress.

There were three policemen in the front offices of the laboratories, and he was admitted only after a wait. Eve came into the reception-room first, and shook hands with him coolly. That is, outwardly it was coolly; but inwardly, Tony felt sure, she was trembling, even as was he.

"Oh, Tony," she said, her voice almost giving way, "I'm so glad to have you back! I've read all your reports."

"I've read all your acknowledgments of them," said Tony

hoarsely. It was all that had passed between them. Reports and acknowledgments, in lieu of love-letters!

"Father will be right out. We've been working steadily ever since you left. You and Dad and I are going to have dinner together to-night."

"Any one else?" asked Tony jealously.

"No; who would there be?"

"Your South African, I thought probably."

"Not mine, Tony!"

"Your father's, then. He keeps him in the laboratory—for you."

Hendron, wearing his laboratory apron, walked briskly into the front office. "Hello, there, Drake! Delighted to see you back. Your candidates have been arriving daily, and we've put them all to work. Dodson and Smith and Greve are enthusiastic about them." He looked at his watch. "Five-fifty. I've got a little work to do here. Then we want you to come up to the house for dinner."

As Tony unlocked his apartment door, Kyto sprang to his feet.

"I take your presence," Kyto said, "with extravagant gratitude."

Tony laughed. "A bath, Kyto, a dinner jacket, something in the way of a highball—I haven't had a drink since I left. Good Lord! It's refreshing to see this digging again. You've missed me, eh?"

The little Jap ducked his head. "I have indulged my person in continual melancholy, which is now raised in the manner of a siege-gun."

"Swell," said Tony. "The drink, the bath, the clothes! Eat, drink and be merry, for to-morrow we die. There's something in it, Kyto."

"I have become apprised of the Bronson circumstances *in toto*, and about your statement am agreement itself."

Tony's eyebrows raised. "Know all about it, hey?"

"I have a nice storehouse of information on same."

"Good. How's my mother?"

"Excellent as to health. Telephoning daily."

"Maybe you'd better ring her up first. On second thought, that's the thing to do. I telegraphed her occasionally, but heaven only knows when I'll see her. She is a darn' good sport."

"A person of profound esteemableness."

Tony looked with surprise at the back of the Jap as he started toward the telephone. The approach of the Bronson bodies had made his servant more loquacious than he had ever before been. Aside from that, no change in Kyto was discernible—nor did Tony anticipate any change. He began to remove his travel-worn clothes, and was in a bath-

53

robe when Kyto succeeded in completing a telephone-connection with his mother's house in Connecticut.

Tony moved with a feeling of incredulity. The Hendron apartment was exactly as it had been. Leighton approached stiffly with a cocktail on a small silver tray. There was even jazz emerging softly from the radio. He smiled faintly. Funny that a girl of Eve's extraordinary education and taste should enjoy the monotonous rhythm of jazz coming over the radio, and yet she had always liked it.

Eve appeared—a new Eve who was a little different from the old Eve. She wore a green evening dress that he remembered from an hour spent long ago on the balcony.

"Hello, Tony." In her eyes was the same wonderment, the same surprise and unbelief that he felt. She took the cocktail which Leighton had brought, and held it up to the light. A pink hemisphere, a few drops of something that belonged to a life in a world already as good as dead. "Happy days!"

Hendron appeared immediately after his daughter. "Drake! Evening, old man. No cocktail, thanks, Leighton. Well, this is odd. Here we stand, just as we did in the old days, eh?"

"Don't say the old days, Father. We'll be doing it all the rest of our lives."

Hendron's extravagantly blue eyes twinkled. "If you expect me to furnish you with cocktail glasses and smuggled Bacardi in the years that lie ahead on Bronson Beta, Eve, you vastly overrate my paternal generosity and thoughtfulness. Let's have dinner. I want to get back to the laboratory for a conference at midnight."

The dining-room doors were opened. White, silver and red glittered under the indirect lights. "I point with pride," Eve said, "to the roses. It's something of an achievement these days."

They sat down. Leighton served consommé, and Tony picked up his silver spoon with a dreamy feeling of unreality which psychologists have noted and only badly explained.

Hendron brought him to his senses. "Tell us the news, Tony. We've been living down there at the laboratory ever since you left. This is Eve's and my first night off. Eating there, sleeping there. We have dormitories now on the floor above. What's going on in the world? You know, we even bar newspapers now. They're too much of a distraction, and Dodson has instructions to keep track of the news but not to give us any, unless it will have an effect on our work."

Tony sipped the consommé. "You mean to say you haven't kept tabs on the effect of your own society's bitter pill?"

Hendron shook his head. "Not anything to speak of. A

54

word here and there in reference to something else, that's all."

Eve said eagerly: "Go ahead, Tony! Tell us everything. What do you know about the world? What's it like in Boston? What do people think and say? What's the news from abroad? All we know is that the Government has at last done a little governing, and taken over the public utilities in order to keep them running."

Tony began to talk. He took what opportunity their questions gave, to eat.

"It hasn't made as much difference as you'd think. The Government at Washington is now less concerned with the fact that the populace should be moved away from the Coast, than it is with immediate problems. If you really have not read about them, I can give you some idea. There was a general strike in Chicago two weeks ago that tied up everything. No electric light and no water; nothing for a day. There was a terrific riot in Birmingham. The police forces in half a dozen cities walked out. The State governments weren't able to cope with the situation. In some cases it was just that the people decided not to work any more, and in others it was pure mob uproar. The Federal Government stepped in everywhere. They took over blanket control of the utilities, saw to it that trains were kept running, power-houses kept going, and so on. Nominally workers are jailed for dereliction, but actually I think they have found it necessary to execute them. Trouble began when I was in Boston, but in three days all the major functions of housing, food and transportation were working fairly well.

"I think the people looked first to the President, anyway; and the President had the good sense to kick politics in the face and take full authority upon himself to do anything and everything which he thought would keep the country in operation. There was some trouble in the Army and Navy, still more in the National Guard, especially with soldiers who were fathers and wanted to remain with their families. I suppose there are nearly half a million men doing police duty right now."

"It's strange," Eve said, "but I realized things were functioning, without even having the time to investigate precisely why they were going."

Her father looked keenly at Tony. "That's all according to the plan that the League worked out before the news broke. A man named Carey is largely responsible for it. He's an economist. I believe he's a guest at the White House right now, and has been for ten days."

"I've seen his name," Tony said, and continued: "As I was saying, it hasn't made as much difference as you would imagine. I saw one nasty riot in Baltimore between soldiers on one side and cops on the other, but in half an hour it was all over. I think that the work of keeping the public informed has been marvelous. The radio goes twenty-four hours a day, and the newspapers appear as often as they have anything fresh to print. People are kept encouraged and reassured and directed. Of course, part of the general calmness is due simply to mass inertia. For every person that will get hysterical or do something foolish, there are about ten who will not only fail to get hysterical, but who will not even recognize that their lives are presently going to be changed entirely. The whole city of Philadelphia, with the exception of the university, is almost unaltered. Anyway, that's the impression you get of it.

"And the unemployed have been corraled *en masse*. There is a project to turn the entire basin of the Mississippi north and west of Kansas City into an abode for the Coast populations, and the unemployed are building there, I understand, quarters of sorts for ten million people. Most of them are temporary. They are also planting vast areas of land in crops. I imagine that they are going to compel the migration when the interior of the country is prepared as well as possible to receive it, and when the danger of tidal waves draws near. As a matter of fact, every industrial center is working at top speed, and Chicago is headquarters for their produce. I don't just remember the figures, but an appalling quantity of canned goods, clothing, medical supplies and things like that are being prepared and distributed to bases in the Mississippi valley. Granted that the valley remains inhabitable, I really believe that a majority of our population will be successfully moved there and installed for an indefinite time."

"It's wonderful, isn't it?" Eve said.

Tony nodded. "The machinery which organized millions of men during the war was still more or less available for this much bigger undertaking, from the standpoint of plans and human cogs. The hardest thing is to convince the people that it must be done; but the leaders have recognized the fact, and are going ahead. A sort of prosperity has returned. Of course, all prices and wages are rigidly fixed now, but there is more than enough work to go around, and keeping busy is the secret of holding the masses in emotional balance."

Hendron nodded. "Exactly, Drake. I'm really astonished to hear that they've done so well. It's unthinkable, isn't it? Absolutely unthinkable! Just a few months ago we were a nation floundering in the depths of what we thought were great difficulties and tribulations, and to-day, facing an infinitely greater difficulty, the people are more intelligent, more united—and more successful."

"I think it's thrilling," Eve said.

Tony shook his head in affirmation. "I can't give you a really good picture of it. I really know very little of it. It all came in dashes—things read in newspapers, things heard over the radio, things told me; but this country at least has grasped the basic idea that there is going to be trouble, and great trouble, in a short time."

"Quite so," Hendron said. "Now how about the rest of the world?"

Tony's hand jerked as he buttered his roll. He looked up. "The rest of the world?" he repeated. "I don't know much about the rest of the world. What I do know I'll tell you, but you mustn't take my word as final. The information is garbled, contradictory and unreliable. For one thing, many of the European nations are still foolishly trying to keep their plans secret in order to protect their borders, and so on. In fact, I wouldn't be at all surprised if they fell to fighting. There seems to be small thought of coöperation, and they stick fiercely to national lines.

"England's labor troubles festered the minute she tried to institute compulsory work for those who tended her utilities. I believe London was without power or light for five or six days. There was a vast amount of sabotage. The police fought battles through Piccadilly and Trafalgar Square with armed mobs. A curious thing happened in India. One would think that the Hindus would be the last people in the world to recognize what was about to happen. One would believe that their reaction would be fatalistic acceptance. However, according to one report at least, there is something in the Veda which anticipated the Bronson bodies, or some similar cosmic manifestation; and with the spread of the news that disaster threatened the world, the Hindus and Brahmins rose together. Now no word comes from India at all. Every line of communication has been cut or silenced."

Tony paused, ate a little. "This is all very sententious. Most of what I'm saying is taken from the *clichés* of the newspapers. You'll have to forgive me, but you asked me to tell you."

"Don't stop, Drake, old man."

"Yes, go ahead, Tony."

"Australia and Canada, on the other hand, acted very much as the United States has acted. Their political leaders, or at least the ones who came immediately into prominence and power, accepted the fact that trouble was on the scene. They got down to brass tacks, and are doing what they can for and with their people. So is South Africa.

"The French are very gay about it, and very mad. They think it is very funny, and they think it is an insult to France at the same time. The whole country is filled with sputtering ineffective people. They're playing politics for all it's worth, and new cabinets come and go, sometimes at the rate of three a day, without ever getting anything accomplished at all. But at least they have kept functioning as a nation. Germany went fascist; a few communists were killed; and so were a few Jews.

"Communists are struggling to get control—not, with success. As for Russia, little is known. Of course it is a terrible blow to the Soviet. The heavy industries which they developed so painstakingly and at such awful cost are scattered over a wide area. I believe the Soviet Government is carrying on rather bitterly, but as best it can. China is still just China. So you can tell very little about it. In South America the news has served merely to augment the regular crop of revolutions."

Tony put down his fork. "That's all I know." He reached for a cigarette, and lighted it. "What to expect to-morrow or a week from to-morrow, no one can say. Since it's impossible to tell how high tides will be, how far inland they will rush, and what areas will be devastated, and since not even the best guess will be any indication whatsoever of where the land may rise, where it may fall, and what portions of it will witness eruptions and quakes, it may be that even the gigantic steps being taken by some governments will be futile. Am I not right?"

"My dear boy," Hendron replied after a pause, "you are eminently right. That is an amazingly clear picture you've given us. I'm surprised that any nation has had the intelligence to take steps, although I suppose, being patriotic in my heart, I rather hoped and expected that our own United States would leap from the backwash of villainous politics into a little good clear sailing before the crisis arrives. . . . Let's have our coffee in the other room."

After dinner Leighton, whose customary mournfulness had, by some perversity, bloomed into the very flower of good nature, ushered Ransdell into the apartment.

Tony was furious at Ransdell's arrival. He had hoped to have Eve to himself.

How he had hoped to have her, and with what further satisfaction, he did not define; but at least he knew that he wanted Ransdell away; and the South African would not go away.

"He has flown five or six times to Washington for Father," Eve explained. "And he's wonderful in the laboratory. He has a genius for mechanics."

The South African listened to this account of himself with embarrassment; and Tony, observing him, realized that under any other circumstances he would have liked him.

In fact, originally Tony had liked David Ransdell immensely—until he had realized that he also was to go with him—and with Eve—on the Space Ship!

BRIGHTER and brighter, and higher and higher, each night the strange stars stood in the southern skies.

Indeed, one ceased to resemble a star at all and appeared, instead, as a small full moon which grew balefully each night; and now the other also showed a disc even to the naked eye.

Each night, also, they altered position slightly relatively to each other. For the gravitational control of the larger—Bronson Alpha—swung the smaller, Bronson Beta, about it in an orbit like that of the moon about the earth.

Their plain approach paralyzed enterprise on the earth, while the physical effects of their rush toward the world was measurable only in the instruments of the laboratories.

Throughout the civilized world two professions above all others adhered most universally to their calling: day and night, in the face of famine, blood, fire, disaster and every conceivable form of human anguish, doctors and surgeons clung steadfast to their high calling; and day and night amid the weltering change of conditions and in the glut of fabulous alarms and reports, the men who gathered news and printed it, labored to fulfill their purposes.

Tony saw more of the world's activities than most of its citizens at this time. He had scarcely returned from his first tour of the Eastern cities when he was sent out again, this time to the Middle and Far West. That journey was arduous because of the increasing difficulties of travel. The railroads were moving the Pacific and the Atlantic civilizations inland, and passenger trains ran on uneasy schedules. He saw the vast accumulation of freight in the Mid-western depots. He saw the horizon-filling settlements being prepared. He saw the breath-taking reaches of prairie which had been put under cultivation to feed the new horde in the high flat country north and west of Kansas.

Along the Pacific Coast he observed the preparations being made for the withdrawal from the western ocean. Seattle, Tacoma, Portland, San Francisco, Los Angeles, San Diego, the cities inevitably doomed, were digging up their roots. Millionaires drove eastward in great limousines with their most priceless treasures heaped around them; and small urchins cast an anxious eye at the Pacific and turned to look with uncomprehending hope toward the mountains that ranged beside it.

Every citizen in the United States had some part in the migration. Relief maps of the United States were supplied by the Government, so that any man by looking at one could tell whether he had put a thousand feet or five thousand of altitude between himself and the menacing waters.

Tony's work was varied. He continued to send back by ones and twos those scientists whose counsel Hendron desired, and the flower of the young men and women who might be useful in the event of a great cataclysm.

Hendron's own ideas were still uncrystallized: he felt with increasing intensity the need for gathering together the best brains, the healthiest bodies and the stanchest hearts that could be found. He had a variety of plans. He had founded two stations in the United States, and was in the process of equipping them for all emergencies. Under the best conditions, the personality of his group might divide into two parts and move to those stations, there to remain until the first crisis passed so that afterward they could emerge as leaders in the final effort against doom.

Under the pressure of the impending destruction, his scientists had pushed their experiments in obtaining power from atomic disintegration to a point where the power of the atom could be utilized, within limits, as a propulsive force.

Hendron had thereupon succeeded in bombarding the surface of the moon with a projectile that was, in its essentials, a small rocket. He had settled the problems of hull composition, insulation and aëration, which would arise in such a vessel if made in a size to be occupied by men. He had devised rockets which could be directed. He had constructed a rocket with vents at both ends so that a discharge in the opposite direction would break its fall. Several such rockets he actually dispatched under remote control, hurtling many miles into the air, turning, descending part way under full force of their stern "engines," and checking their fall by forward discharges at the end of their flight, so that their actual landing had not destroyed even the delicate instruments they contained.

The chief problem that remained unsolved was a metal sufficiently resistant to the awful force Hendron employed. Even the experimental rockets often failed in their flight because the heat generated by the atomic combustion within them melted and blew away the walls intended to retain it. So, at the Hendron laboratories, the world's metallurgists concentrated their efforts upon finding an alloy capable of withstanding the temperatures and pressures involved in employing atomic energy as a driving force.

Tony visited both of Hendron's stations. One was in Michigan and one in New Mexico. He brought back reports on the progress being made there in the construction of laboratories, machine-shops and dormitories. He returned on the day on which the President made his impassioned and soul-searching speech on courage. More than forty million persons heard the President's voice as it came over the radio. Tony, standing in the crowded aisle of a train between Philadelphia and New York, caught some of the President's words:

"The world is facing an august manifestation of the handiwork of Almighty God. Whether this handiwork is provided as punishment for our failure to pursue His ways, or whether Nature in her inscrutable processes is testing the courage of her most tender product—man—we shall never know. But we stand on the brink of a situation from which we cannot hide, and which we cannot escape. We must meet this situation with fortitude, with generosity, with patience and endurance. We have provided punishments in our emergency decrees for the selfish. But so impoverished have our human resources become, that we can provide no reward for the noble, save that which they find in their own hearts.

"Many nations have already faltered and fallen in the outpouring of their own blood. Some nations, with obtuse stubbornness, have failed to accept the truth, and in stupid carelessness are endeavoring to ignore that which will presently devour them. America, recognizing the magnitude of the coming upheavals, has taken every step, bent every effort, and enlisted every man and woman and child to do his and her utmost, not only, as a great predecessor in my office has said, 'that the Nation shall not perish from the earth,' but that humanity itself shall not perish from the earth. To you, my fellow-countrymen, I can offer but one word of advice, one single lamp to penetrate the onrushing gloom"—and his voice sank to a whisper more penetrating than any shout—"*Courage.*"

As Tony listened, his heart swelled with pride, and he saw in the abstracted eyes of his fellow-passengers a new light appear.

Courage! Courage was needed.

When Tony reached New York, he found Hendron sleepless and icily calm in the midst of his multitudinous enterprises.

But Eve showed the strain more than her father, and during the first evening, which they spent together, she expressed her fear: "Father's greatest hope was that his ship would be successful. There is more information than has been given out about the Bronson bodies. We admit that they will come very close. Terribly close. We do not admit yet precisely how close."

They were standing together on the balcony overlooking the brightly lighted and still noisy city. Their arms were locked together in defiance of their oath to the league.

"He'll succeed," Tony said.

"He has succeeded, except that every rocket he builds is

61

limited in the distance it can fly and the power it can use by the fact that its propulsive tubes melt. There isn't a metal nor an alloy in the world that will withstand that heat."

Tony did not answer. After a long silence she spoke again. "It's an awful thing, Tony. Look down there. Look down on the city. Think of the people. Look at the lights, and then imagine water, mountains of it. Water that would reach to here!"

Tony held her arm more tightly. "Don't torture yourself, Eve."

"I can't help it. Oh, Tony, just think of it!"

"Well, that's the way things have to be, Eve." He could not say any more.

When Tony went down, the street was still filled with people. All the people were talking. They walked, but it did not seem to matter to them what direction they took or what chance company they shared.

The strange small moon, growing larger each night, shone palely in the sky.

Tony hailed a cab. His eyes settled on his shoes when he sat down. He thought grayly and without rhythm. Into every thought darted the face of Eve as he had last seen it—a face growing hourly more haggard. He remembered the downcasting of her eyes.

When he arrived at his apartment, Kyto was waiting. There was an expression of distinct anxiety on his usually inscrutable face. The emotion made him ludicrous—but Tony was more surprised than amused and Kyto commenced to talk immediately.

"All people frightful, now."

Tony tossed his hat aside. "Yes."

"Serious consequences close, you will inform me?"

"Of course. Do you want to leave now?"

"Contrarily. Safety surrounds you. Also charming good luck. I therefore prefer to stick."

"Right. And thanks."

Kyto padded softly away, and Tony stood thoughtfully in the center of his living-room for fully two minutes.

Next he called a number in Greenwich, Connecticut, waited an abnormally long time, then asked a maid for Mrs. Drake. His voice was warm and calm. "Hello, Mother. How are you?"

His mother's reply was controlled, but nerves stabbed through every word she said. "Tony, darling! I've tried and tried to reach you. Oh! I'm just an inch short of fainting. I thought something had happened to you."

"Sorry, Mother. I've been busy."

"I know. Come right out and tell me all about it."

"I can't."

There was a pause. "You can't put it in words?"

"No."

There was another long pause. Mrs. Drake's voice was lower, more tremulous—and yet it was not the voice of an hysterical or an unreasoning woman. "Tell me, Tony, how bad is it now to be?"

"The same as it was to be yesterday, Mother."

"Not hiding new developments, are you, Tony?"

"No, Mother; those we've announced that we expect, haven't really begun to happen yet."

"Yet you know more; I can feel you know more than you have ever told me."

"Mother, I swear you're being morbid—" How could he tell her that for her there was annihilation, but for himself some chance of escape? She would wish it for him, whatever happened to herself; but he could not accept it. A berth in the Space Ship, leaving her here! Leaving here millions of mothers—and children too!

Hendron did not permit himself such reflections; Hendron hardened himself and forbade it. He had to. If he began to let himself even consider the saving of individuals, and allowed himself personal judgment as to who should go,—as individuals,—he'd go mad. Stark, raving, crazy! He simply had to confine himself to selection on the sole point of saving the species—the race.

But probably no one at all would be saved, Tony recollected almost with relief. Work on the Space Ship, in recent days, was not really advancing. They were held up from lack of a material to withstand the power that science now could loose from the atom. The idea of escape was probably only a fantasy, utterly vain. So thinking, Tony ended his talk, and put up the receiver.

Taxicabs had been sent for Tony and his party. They made their way immediately downtown to the big building which housed the Hendron laboratories. The cab had covered a few blocks when Tony realized that not only on the waterfront, but throughout its length and breadth, Manhattan had been depopulated. Here and there a lone figure was visible—usually a figure in the uniform of a policeman or a soldier. Once he thought he caught sight of a man skulking in the shadows of a doorway. But he was not sure. And there were no women, no children.

After the sun had set, it was easy to appreciate why the last recalcitrant thousands of New York's populace had departed. The Bronson bodies, on this night, rose in frightful majesty: a sphere of lustrous white larger than the moon, and a second sphere much smaller, but equally brilliant. Their awesome illumination flooded the city, rendered superfluous the street-lights which, however, remained stubbornly burning. News of this augmented size had undoubtedly reached New York during the day—and the last unbeliever must surely have been convinced if he remained to witness the phenomenon.

There were few lights in the skyscrapers. As the taxies bowled through the murk and dark, unchecked by traffic signals, Tony and Jack Taylor shuddered involuntarily to see the black buildings which man had deserted. Had they but known, a second shudder might have seized them—for already the tide was lapping the sea-wall at the Battery.

At the elevator they were met by Eve. She kissed Tony, in an ecstasy of defiance, and then hurried to assist his group in the removal of their baggage, and in directing its disposal. Every one left the street reluctantly. The Bronson bodies were hypnotic.

In the laboratories there was the utmost confusion. No longer was the inner door closed. Only a skeleton crew had remained in New York, under Hendron. The scientist himself was introduced by Tony to each of the new arrivals, and to each he said a few words of welcome. Several were already known to him.

Then Hendron made an announcement to all of them—a statement which was repeated afterward in French and German. "Ladies and gentlemen—you will sleep in the dormitories above here to-night. To-morrow we will remove by airplane to my field station in Michigan. The others are already there. In bidding you good-night, I must also request no one to leave the building. A splendid view of the firmament may be had from the roof. But the streets are entirely unsafe. The last wave of emigration left New York at sundown this evening. The people who remain are either law officers or marauders. I regret that I will be unable to entertain you myself, but I leave you in the hands of my assistants."

Jack Taylor was beside Tony when they reached the roof. "As God lives, that's a marvelous thing!" He stared at the two yellow discs in the sky. "Think of it! The heavens are falling upon us—and a few hundred men, here and there, are sitting on this stymied golf-ball figuring how to get away!"

CHAPTER 11—THE LAST NIGHT IN NEW YORK

"LOOK down, now," said a different voice, "at the street." It was a young man's voice, carefully controlled, but in spite of its constraint, ringing with an unusually vibrant and vital quality.

Tony looked about at the speaker before he gazed down, and he recognized a recruit whom he had not himself selected. It was Eliot James, an Englishman from Oxford, and a poet. By profession and by nature, he was the most impractical of all the company; and one of the most attractive, in spite of his affectation—if it was that—of a small beard. The beard became him. He was tall, broad-shouldered, aquiline in feature, brown.

The baleful moonlight of the Bronson Bodies glinted up from the street.

"Water," some one said.

"Yes; that's the tide. It's flowing in from the cross-streets from the Hudson, and from the East River too."

"There's some coming up from the Battery along the avenues—see the flow down there!"

"How high will it rise to-night? Oh, how high?"

"Not above the bridges to-night. They're not in danger—to-night. But of course the power-houses will go."

"And the tunnels will be filled?"

"Of course."

"There are people down there, wading in the street! . . . Why did they stay? They've been warned enough."

"Why did we stay? We gave the warning."

"We've business here."

"So had they—they supposed, and as important to them as we imagined ours to be to us. Besides, they're safe enough to-night. Just that few of them. They can climb three stories in almost any building and be safe. The tide ebbs, of course, in six hours."

"Then comes again higher!"

"Yes—much higher. For the Bronson Bodies are rushing at us now."

"Exactly how," asked Eliot James, "do they look through the telescope?"

"The big one—Bronson Alpha," replied Jack Taylor, as they all looked up from the street, "not very different from before. It seems to be gaseous, chiefly—it always was chiefly gaseous, unlike the earth and Mars, but like Jupiter and Saturn and Neptune. Its approach to the sun has increased the temperature of its envelope, but has brought out no details of its geography, if you could call it that. Bronson Alpha offers us no real surface, as such. It seems to be a great globe with a massive nucleus surrounded by an immense atmosphere. What we see is only the outer surface of the atmosphere."

"Could it ever have been inhabited?" the poet asked.

"In no such sense as we understand the word. For one thing, if we found ourselves on Bronson Alpha, we would never find any surface to live on. There is probably no sudden alteration of material such as exists on the earth when air stops and land and water begin."

"But the other world—Bronson Beta—is different."

"Very different from its companion up there, but not so different from our world, it seems. It has a surface we can see, with air and clouds in its atmosphere. The clouds shift or disappear and form again; but there are fixed details which do not change, and which prove a surface crust exists. The atmosphere was frozen solid in the long journey through space, but the sun has thawed out the air and has started, at least, on thawing out the seas."

"You're sure there are seas too?"

"There are great spaces that seem to be seas, that satisfy every visual and spectroscopic test of seas."

"Have you seen," asked the poet, "anything like—cities?"

"Cities?"

"The ruins of cities, I mean. That globe seems to be so much like the earth; and sometimes it has had its sun. It lived in the sunshine of a star that was an octillion, octillion miles away. I thought just now, looking at it, that perhaps on it were cities like this, where people once watched the coming of whatever pulled them loose from their sun, and dropped them into the black mouth of space."

Some of the company about him were looking up and listening; others paid no attention to him. He did not care; a few had shared his feeling; and among them was Eve, who stood near him.

"Would you rather we went that way?" she said to him.

"Slipping into space, falling away, all of us in the world together retreating farther and farther away from our sun, gradually freezing as we went into darkness?" Eliot James shook his handsome head. "No; if I had my choice, I think I'd elect our way. Yet I wonder how they faced it—what they did?"

"I wonder," said Eve, her eyes upon the yellow orb, "if we'll ever know."

"Look," proclaimed some one else who was gazing down, "the lights are beginning to go."

He meant the street-lamps of New York, which had been switched on as usual and maintained to this minute.

Thousands of them still prevailed, indeed; but a huge oblong, which had been lighted before, was darkened now.

"The flood has caught the conduits!" And with the word, the little gleaming rows which etched the streets throughout another district died; but the rest burned on in beautiful defiance.

The city officially was abandoned; but men remained. Some men, whatever the warning, whatever the danger, refused to surrender; they stuck to their duties and to their services to the last. Some men and some boys; and some women and girls too. And so, on this night, New York had lights; it kept communication—telephone and telegraph too.

But now another pattern of blocks disappeared; Brooklyn went black. Beacons burned—airplane-guides and lighthouses. Ships, having their own electric installations, could be seen seeking the sea.

That too, thought Tony, was only a splendid gesture; yet the sight of the ships, like the stubborn persistence of the lights, threw a tingle in his blood and made him more proud of his people. They couldn't give up—some of them! To leave the ships at the dock to take the tide that now was flooding in, was certain destruction. What use to steer them out to sea? For what would they be saved? Yet captains and crews could be found to steer and stoke them.

More blocks were black; the lights from the awful orbs of the Bronson Bodies slanted sharp across the streets, their shadows unbroken by the last lamps of the city's defiance.

Now the street gave up sounds—the rush of water as the loud edge of the flood advanced filling the last floor of the cañons between the buildings. All over the world at the sea-board it must be the same, except that some cities already were overswept and this tide was now retiring. To rise higher yet twelve hours later; and then still higher!

Eliot James moved closer to Eve.

"What does it do to you?" he said.

She answered: "Too much."

"Yes," he said. "And it's only begun?"

"It's not begun," whispered Eve. "This—this is really nothing. To-night, the waters will merely rise over the lower buildings of the city, and then subside. We will all leave in the ebb tide."

"Which, I suppose, will drain the rivers dry? There was clearly no practical purpose for staying this twelve hours longer; but I am glad we did. I would not have escaped this sensation. I wonder where the people have gone who also stayed for it—whom we saw in the streets awhile ago?"

Eve attempted no answer; nor did Tony.

"I imagine," persisted the poet, "they are also glad they remained. It is a new intoxication—annihilation. It multiplies every emotion."

Tony so fully agreed with him that he drew Eve away. He made the excuse that, her father having retired, she also should sleep; but having taken her away from the others, he kept her to himself.

"Eve, we've got to marry!"

"My dear, what would marriage mean now?"

"But you feel it—don't you?"

"Need for you—"

"As never before, Eve?"

"Yes, Tony. It's as he said—oh, my dear! The waters overwhelm you—the flood rising and rising, with scarcely a

67

sound, and those two yellow discs doing it! And no one can
stop them! They're coming on, Tony! They're coming on, to
lift the waters higher and higher; they're coming on to crack
open the shell of the earth! Tony—oh, hold me!"

"I have you, Eve. You have me! Here we are, two of us
together. . . . They're in pairs wherever they are in New York
to-night, Eve. Didn't you see them? Wherever they waited, a
woman waited with a man. There's only one answer to—
annihilation. That's it."

"Tony!"

"My dear—"

"What's that. . . . Your name? Some one's searching for
you. A message seems to have come."

"How could a message come?"

Yet in the yellow light on the roof, they could see a uniformed boy; and Tony stepped out to meet him.

He had arrived at the building an hour ago, the boy was
saying; with the elevators stopped, he had climbed the roof
by the stairs.

Tony took his telegram, tore it open and, in the light of
the two baleful Bodies, he read:

MRS. MADELINE DRAKE MURDERED BY LOOTERS WHO RAIDED
SEVERAL CONNECTICUT FARMS AND ESTATES LATE TO-DAY.

The paper dropped from Tony's fingers. He slumped to a
bench and covered his face with his hands.

He felt Eve's hand and looked up, utter despair on his face.

"Read that." He saw that she held his telegram.

"I have read it. Tony—"

"I should have gone to her; or I should have taken her away
—but I believed it best to leave her in her home as long as
possible. I was going to her to-morrow. Now—now—"

She checked his flow of recrimination, sitting down on the
bench beside him and reaching up to smooth his hair as if
he were only a child. "You couldn't have done a thing, Tony.
This might have happened wherever you had taken her. All
over the country, bands of men have been running like
wolves; and to-day they became more merciless."

Tony leaped to his feet. "I'll go to her, and find them, and
kill them!"

"You'll never find them, Tony. They'll have moved on; and
no one will have stayed to tell you who they were. . . .
Besides, Tony, they'll be punished without any one raising
a hand. Perhaps already they are dead."

"But I must go to her!"

"Of course; and I'll go with you; but we must wait for the
tide to fall."

"Tide?" He stalked to the edge of the roof and stared

down; for, strangely, he had forgotten it. Now he saw the streets running full, not with the foul water of the harbor, but with a clean green flood. The Bronson Bodies lit it almost to dim daylight.

Tony gazed up at them, aghast. "My mind, my mind can understand it, Eve; but, good God, she was my mother! *Murdered!* Cornered somewhere in her house—my home where I was a little boy, and where I ran to her with my triumphs and my troubles, Eve. I wonder where she was, in what room they struck her down, the damned cowards—" He did not finish. He was racked by a succession of great sobs.

Eve caught his hand and brought him again to the bench. Still they were alone, and she sat close beside him, holding him in her arms.

"We'll go to her, Tony, as soon as we can. . . . This is happening to everybody. It's horrible, fiendish, unbelievable —and inevitable. It was frightful that they killed her; and yet probably, Tony, they did it instantly, and surely without agony for her; so perhaps it is much better that she went now, than that she should live through the next months as we know they will be—months of starvation and savagery and horror; leading only to the final catastrophe."

Tony looked bleakly at the girl. "Yes, I know that! but I can feel only that they killed her."

For a long time they said nothing more; then they arose, returned to the parapet and gazed down at the water.

Strange sounds rose with the flow of the flood; the collapse of windows under the weight of water; the outrush of air, the inrush of the tide. Away on other streets not citadeled by the massive towers whose steel skeletons reached down to the living rock, the walls were beginning to fall. Smoke drifted like a mist between the buildings as the water, the final enemy of fire, began to cause conflagrations.

Somewhere it "shorted" an electric current, perhaps; somewhere else it had sent a family fleeing before a fire which ought first to have been extinguished; or the water itself entered into chemical combinations which caused heat. Doubtless many a hand deliberately set the flames. But there was no wind to-night; so the flood isolated each fire; here and there a building burned; but the huge terraced towers of Manhattan stood dark and silent, intact.

"You must try to sleep, Tony."

"And you!"

"Till the tide goes out; yes, Tony. I'll try, if you will." She kissed him, and they went in together, to separate at the door of the room where she was to sleep. Tony went on to the bed allotted him, and he lay down without undressing. In the next room Cole Hendron was actually asleep.

Tony, trying not to think, occupied himself with separating the sounds which reached him through the opened window —a woman's shriek, a bass voice booming a strange song, a flute.

Some one, seated above the flood, was piping in the unnatural light of the Bronson Bodies as the sea swept over the city; but for the most part the people who had remained were silent—paired off, here and there, sharing in each other's arms the terrible excitement of dawning doomsday.

Tony twisted on his bed and remembered his mother. When this tide turned—and enormous as it was, it must flow six hours, ebb for six before it flowed again, just like the moon tides—he must set off home for his last service to her.

"Lord, let me know mine end, and the number of my days, that I may be certified how long I have to live." The lines for the burial of the dead began echoing in his brain. *"Behold, thou hast made my days as it were a span long; and mine age is even as nothing in respect of thee; and verily every man living is altogether vanity."*

Tony had shut his eyes, and now he opened them to the light of the Bronson Bodies slanting into the room. . . . *"For when thou art angry, all our days are gone; we bring our years to an end, as it were a tale that is told."*

The woman had ceased to shriek; but the Negro's bass boomed on. Tony was sure it was a black man singing the weird chant which rode on the waters. The piper, too, played on. . . .

Tony was aware that some one was shaking him.

"Morning?" he complained.

"Not morning," Kyto's voice admitted. "But the tide now—"

"Oh, yes," said Tony, sitting up as he remembered. "Thank you, Kyto."

"Coffee," said Kyto modestly, "will be much as usual, I venture to hope."

Tony arose and stalked to the window to look down at water, now rushing seaward. The roll of the world, while he had slept, had turned the city and the coast away from the Bronson Bodies so that now they sucked the sea outward; and the wash made whirlpools at the cross-streets.

It was the gray light of dawn which showed him the whirlpools. In the west, the awful Bronson Bodies had set; but Tony knew that, though now for twelve hours they would be invisible, the force of their baleful violence, even upon the side of the world which had spun away from them, was in no sense diminished. The tide which had risen under them would flow out for six hours, to be sure; but then—though they were on the opposite side of the world—they would raise the frightful flow again just six hours later. . . .

70

"Coffee," reminded Kyto patiently, "you will need."

"Yes," admitted Tony, turning, "I'll need coffee."

"Miss Eve insists to pour it."

"Oh, she's up?"

"Very ready to see you."

An airplane hummed overhead; at some small distance, several others. Ransdell undoubtedly was in one of them. Inspection from the air of effects upon the earth was one of his duties—a sort of reconnaissance of the lines of destruction. Tony thought of Ransdell looking down and wondering about Eve. The flyer's admiration of her amounted to openly desirous adoration. There was the poet Eliot James, too.

They were bound with him—and with Eve—in the close company of the League of the Last Days whose function lay no longer in the vague future. The peculiar rules and regulations of the League already were operative in part; others would clamp their control upon him immediately.

Tony to-day resented it. He made no attempt to shake off his overpossessive jealousy of Ransdell or Eliot James over Eve. She would go home with him to-day—to his home, where his mother had been murdered. Eve and he would leave his home together—for what next destination? To return her to her father, who forbade Tony attempting to exercise any exclusive claim upon her? No; Tony would not return her to her father.

Hendron had arisen; and as if through the wall he had read Tony's defiance, he opened the door and entered.

He offered his hand. "I have heard, Tony, the news which reached you after I retired. I am sorry."

"You're not," returned Tony. It was no morning for perfunctory politeness.

"You're right," acceded Hendron. "I'm not. I know it is altogether better that your mother died now. I am sorry only for the shock to you which you cannot argue away. Eve tells me that she goes home with you. I am glad of that. . . . Last night, Tony, the Bronson Bodies were studied in every observatory on the side of the world turned to them. Of course they were closer than ever before, and conditions were highly favorable for observation. I would have liked to be at a telescope; but that is the prerogative of others. My duty was here. However, a few reports have reached me. Tony, cities have been seen."

"Cities?" said Tony.

"On Bronson Beta. Bronson Alpha continues to turn like a great gaseous globe; but Bronson Beta, which already had displayed air and land and water, last night exhibited— cities. . . . We can see the geography of Bronson Beta quite plainly. It rotates probably at the same rate it turned, making day and night, when it was spinning about its sun. It makes a rotation in slightly over thirty hours, you may remember; and it happens to rotate at such an angle relative to us that we have studied its entire surface. Something more than two-thirds of the surface is sea; the land lies chiefly in four continents with two well-marked archipelagoes. We have seen not merely the seas and the lines of the shores, but the mountain ranges and the river valleys.

"At points upon the seacoasts and at points in the river valleys where intelligent beings—if they once lived on the globe—would have built cities, there are areas plainly marked which have distinct characteristics of their own. There is no doubt in the minds of the men who have studied them; there is no important disagreement. The telescopes of the world were trained last night, Tony, upon the sites of cities on that world. Tony, for millions of years there was life on Bronson Beta as there has been life here. For more than a thousand million years, we believe, the slow, cautious but cruel process of evolution had been going on there as it has here.

"Recall the calendar of geological time, Tony. Azoic time —perhaps a billion years while the earth was spinning around our sun with no life upon it at all—azoic time, showing no vestige of organic life. Then archeozoic time—the earliest, most minute forms of life—five hundred million years. Then proterozoic time—five hundred million more—the age of primitive marine life; then paleozoic time, three hundred million years more while life developed in the sea; then mesozoic time—more than a hundred million years when reptiles ruled the earth.

"A hundred million years merely for the Age of Reptiles, Tony, when in the seas, on the lands and in the very air itself, the world was dominated by a diverse and monstrous horde of reptiles!

"They passed; and we came to the age of mammals—and of man.

"Something of the sort must have transpired on Bronson Beta while it was spinning about its sun. That is the significance of the cities that we have seen. For cities, of course, cannot 'occur.' They must have thousands and tens of thousands of years of human strife and development behind them; and behind that, the millions of years of the mammals, the reptiles, the life in the seas.

"It is a developed world—a fully developed world which approaches us, Tony, with its cities that we now can see."

"Not inhabited cities," objected Tony.

"Of course not inhabited now; but once. There can be no possible doubt that every one on that world is dead. The point is, they lived; so very likely we also can live on their world —if we merely reach it."

"Merely," repeated Tony mockingly.

72

"Yes," said Hendron, ignoring his tone. "It is most likely that where they lived, we can. And think of stepping upon that soil up there, finding a road leading to one of their cities—and entering it!"

He recollected himself suddenly and extended his hand. "You have an errand, Tony, to complete between the tides. I gladly lend you Eve to accompany you. She will tell you later what we all have to do."

He led Tony to Eve's door but did not linger, thereafter. Tony went in alone.

She was at a tiny table where a blue flame burned below a coffee percolator, and where an oil lamp, following the failure of electricity, augmented the faint gray of approaching dawn.

Was it the light, he wondered, or was Eve this morning really so pale?

He came to her, and whatever the rules for this day, he claimed her with his arms and kissed her.

"Now," he said with some satisfaction, "you're not so pale."

She did not disengage herself at once; and before she did, she clung tightly to him for a moment. Then she said:

"You've got to have your coffee now, Tony."

"I suppose so. . . . But there's no stimulant in the world like you, Eve."

"I'll be with you all day."

"Then let's not think of anything beyond."

She turned the tiny tap of the silver coffeepot, filled a cup for him, one for herself. A few minutes later they went down together.

The rushing ebb of the tremendous tide was swirling less than a foot deep over the pavement, and was falling so rapidly that the curb emerged even while they were watching. From upper floors, where many automobiles had been stored against the tide, cars were reaching the street. One drove in the splash before Tony and Eve and stopped. The driver turned it over to them; and Tony took the wheel with Eve beside him.

They went with all possible speed, no longer encountering the tide itself, but lurching through vast puddles left by the retreating water. Débris from offices, shops and tenements swept by the tides bestrewed the street.

A few people appeared; a couple of motorcycle police, not in the least concerned with cars, were making some last inspection of the city.

Bodies lay in the street; and now on the right a haze of smoke drifted from an area that had burned down during the night.

The morning, though the sun had not yet risen, felt sticky.

73

The passage of water over Manhattan had laden the air with moisture so that driving between the forsaken skyscrapers was like journeying in a strange, gaunt jungle.

Tony noticed many things mechanically, with Eve at his side, traversing the reëchoing streets; the rows of smashed windows along Fifth Avenue—tipped-over dummies, wrecked displays; piles of useless goods on the sidewalks, the result of looting; the Empire State Building standing proudly against the blue sky, ignorant of its destiny, still lord of man's creation.

The East River, when they reached it, was a torrent low in its channel being sucked dry toward the sea. Wreckage strewed the strangely exposed bottom. The bridge; a few miles more of flood débris in steaming streets. Then towns and villages which also had been overswept.

Now the country with its higher hills whereon Tony and Eve marked in the first sunlight, the line left by the water at its height. They dipped through empty villages and rose to hamlets whose inhabitants still lingered, staring in a dulled wonderment at the speeding car. The effect of the vast desolation beat into the soul; derelict, helpless people, occasional burning houses, a loose horse or a wandering sheep—emptiness, silence.

They dipped into a hollow which was a pool not drained but which could be traversed; they climbed a slope with a sharp turn which was blocked; and there two men sprang at them.

Tony jerked out his pistol; but to-day—and though he was on his way to his mother who was murdered—he could not pull the trigger on these men. He beat down one with the butt, instead, and with the barrel cowed the other.

He got the car clear and with Eve drove on, realizing they would have killed him and taken Eve with them. Why had he left them alive?

Ah—here was the road home! Home! His home, where he had been born and where he was a little boy. Home, the home that had been his father's and his grandfather's and before that for four generations. Down this road from his home, some man named Drake had gone to fight in the Great War, the War of the Rebellion, in 1812, and to join the army of Washington.

Tony recalled how his earliest remembrances were of strangers coming to peer about the house which they called "historic," and how they raved about the things they called "old." The house was high on a hillside, and as he drove along the winding road, he rode over the mark where the water had risen the night before, and thought what a mere moment in geologic time the things "old" and "historic" here represented.

He tried not to think about his mother yet.

Eve, beside him, placed her hand over his which held the steering-wheel.

"You'll let me stay close beside you, Tony," she appealed.

"Yes. We're almost there."

Familiar landmarks bobbed up on both sides, everywhere: a log cabin he had built as a boy; here was the way to the old well—the "revolutionary well."

A thousand million years, at least, life had been developing upon this earth; a thousand million years like them had been required for the process which must have preceded the first molding of the bricks which built the cities on Bronson Beta —which, some countless æons ago, had come to an end. For a thousand million years, since their inhabitants died, they might have been drifting in the dark until to-day, at last, they found our sun, and the telescopes of the world were turned upon them.

It was useful to think of something like this when driving to your home where your mother lay. . . .

There was the tree where he had fashioned his tree dwelling; the platform still stood in the boughs. It was hidden from the house, but within hailing distance. Playing there, he could hear his mother's voice calling; sometimes he'd pretended that he did not hear.

How long ago was that? How old was he? Oh, that was fifteen years ago. Fifteen, in a thousand million years.

Time was beginning to tick on a different scale in Tony's brain. Not the worldly clock but the awful chronometer of the cosmos was beginning to space, for him, in enormous seconds. And Tony realized that Hendron, speaking to him as he had done, had not been heartless; he had attempted to extend to him a merciful morphia from his own mind. What happened here this morning could not matter, in the stupendous perspective of time. . . .

"Here we are."

The house was before them, white, calm, confident. A stout, secure dwelling with its own traditions. Tony's heart leaped. How he loved it—and her who had been its spirit! How often she had stood in that doorway awaiting him!

Some one was standing there now—an old woman, slight, white-haired. Tony recognized her—Mrs. Haskins, the minister's wife. She advanced toward Tony, and old Hezekiah Haskins took her place in the doorway.

"What happened?"

Not what happened to the world last night; not what happened to millions and hundreds of millions overswept or sent fleeing by the sea. But what happened here?

Old Haskins told Tony, as kindly as he could:

"She was alone; she did not feel afraid, though all the

village and even her servants had fled. The band of men came by. She did not try to keep them out. Knowing her—and judging by what I found—she asked them in and offered them food. Some of them had been drinking; or they were mad with the intoxication of destruction. Some one shot her cleanly—once, Tony. It might have been one more thoughtful than the rest, more merciful. It is certain, Tony, she did not suffer."

Tony could not speak. Eve clung to his hand. "Thank God for that, Tony!" she whispered.

Briefly Tony unclasped his hand from Eve's and met the old minister's quivering grasp. He bent and kissed Mrs. Haskin's gray cheek.

"Thank you. Thank you both," he whispered. "You shouldn't have stayed here; you shouldn't have waited for me. But you did."

"Orson also remained," Hezekiah Haskins said. Old Orson was the sexton. "He's inside. He's—made what arrangements he could."

"I'll go in now," Tony said to Eve. "I'll go in alone for a few minutes. Will you come in, then, to—us?"

"Lord, thou hast been our refuge in all generations. Before the mountains were brought forth, or ever the earth and the world were made: thou are God from everlasting, and world without end."

Old Hezekiah Haskins and his wife, and Orson the sexton, and Tony Drake and Eve Hendron stood on the hilltop where the men of the Drake blood and the women who reproduced them in all generations of memory lay buried. A closed box lay waiting its lowering into the ground.

"Hear my prayer, O Lord; and with thine ears consider my calling. . . . For I am a stranger with thee, and a sojourner as all my fathers were.

"Oh, spare me a little, that I may recover my strength before I go hence, and be no more seen."

Old Hezekiah Haskins held the book before him, but he did not read. A thousand times in his fifty years of the ministry he had repeated the words of that poignant, pathetic appeal voiced for all the dying by the great poet of the psalms: *"For I am a stranger with thee, and a sojourner as all my fathers were."*

Tony's eyes turned to the graves of his fathers; their headstones stood in a line, with their birth-dates and their ages.

"The days of our age are three score years and ten."

What were three score and ten in a thousand million years? To-day, in a few hours, the tide would wash this hilltop.

Connecticut had become an archipelago; the highest hills were islands. Their slopes were shoals over which the tide swirled white. The sun stood in the sky blazing down upon this strange sea.

"*Thou turnest man to destruction; again thou sayest, Come again, ye children of men.*"

Men and children of men on Bronson Beta too. Men millions and thousands of millions of years in the making. Azoic time—proterozoic time—hundreds of millions of years, while life slowly developed in the seas. Hundreds of millions more, while it emerged from the seas; a hundred million more, while reptiles ruled the land, the sky and water. Then they were swept away; mammals came; and man—a thousand millions years of birth and death and birth again before even the first brick could be laid in the oldest city on Bronson Beta, which men on earth had seen last night with their telescopes.

"*For a thousand years in thy sight are but as yesterday; seeing that is past as a watch in the night.*

"*For when thou art angry, all our days are gone; we bring our years to an end as it were a tale that is told.*"

The sexton and old Hezekiah alone could not lift the box to lower it. Tony had to help them with it. He did; and his mother lay beside her husband.

To-night, when the huge Bronson Alpha and Bronson Beta with its visible cities of its own dead were on this side of the world again, the tide might rise over this hill. What matter? His mother lay where she would have chosen. A short time now, and all this world would end.

"I'll take you away," Tony was saying to the old minister and his wife and the older sexton. "We're flying west to-night to the central plateau. We'll manage somehow to take you with us."

"Not me," said the old sexton. "Do not take me from the will of the Lord!"

Nor would the minister and his wife be moved. They would journey to-day, when the water receded, into the higher hills; but that was all they would do.

CHAPTER 12—HENDRON'S ENCAMPMENT

THE airplane settled to earth on the high ground between Lake Michigan and Lake Superior, just as the Bronson Bodies, appallingly large, rose over the eastern horizon. Nearly a thousand people came from the great cantonment to greet Tony and Hendron's daughter. The scientist had given up his New Mexico venture entirely, and brought his congregation of human beings all to his Michigan retreat.

Greetings, however, were not fully made until the Bronson Bodies had been observed. Beta now exceeded the moon, and it shone with a pearly luster and a brilliance which the moon had never possessed. Around it was an aureole of soft radiance where its atmosphere, thawed by the warmth of the sun it so rapidly approached, had completely resumed its gaseous state.

But Bronson Beta did not compare with the spectacle of Alpha. Alpha was gigantic—bigger than the sun, and seemingly almost as bright, for the clouds which streamed up from every part of its surface threw back the sun's light, dazzling, white and hard. There was no night. Neither Eve nor Tony had seen the camp in its completion; and when wonderment over the ascending bodies gave way to uneasy familiarity, Eliot James took them on a tour of inspection.

Hendron had prepared admirably for the days which he had known would lie ahead of his hand-picked community. There were two prodigious dining-halls, two buildings not unlike apartment houses in which the men and women were domiciled. In addition there was a building resembling a hangar set on end, which towered above the surrounding forests more than a hundred feet. At its side was the landing-field, space for the sheltering of the planes, and opposite the landing-field, a long row of shops which terminated in an iron works.

It was to the machine-shops and foundry that Eliot James last took his companions.

"The crew here," he said to Eve, "has already finished part of the construction of the Ark which your father is planning. If we wanted to, we could build a battleship here; in the laboratories anything that has been done could be repeated; and a great many things have been accomplished that have never been done before. By to-morrow night I presume that the entire New York equipment will have been reinstalled here."

Tony whistled. "It's amazing. Genius, sheer genius! How about food?"

Eliot James smiled. "There is enough food for the entire congregation as long as we will need it."

"Now show us the 'Ark.'"

Eve's father came out from the hangar to act as their guide.

From the hysterical white glare of the Bronson Bodies they were taken into a mighty chamber which rose seemingly to the sky itself, where the brilliance was even greater. A hundred things inside that chamber might have attracted their attention—its flood-lighting system, or the tremendous bracing of its metal walls; but their eyes were only for the object in its center. The Ark on that late July evening—the focal-point, the dream and hope of all those whom Hendron had gathered together—stood upright on a gigantic concrete block in a cradle of steel beams. Its length was one hundred and thirty-five feet. It was sixty-two feet in diameter, and its shape was cylindrical. Stream-lining was unnecessary for travel in the outer reaches of space, where there was no air to set up resistance. The metal which composed it was a special alloy eighteen inches in thickness, electro-plated on the outside with an alloy which shone like chromium.

After Tony had looked at it for a long time, he said: "It is by far the most spectacular object which mankind has ever achieved."

Hendron glanced at him and continued his exposition. "A second shell, much smaller, goes inside; and between the inner shell and its outer guard are several layers of insulation material. Inside the shell will be engines which generate the current, which in turn releases the blast of atomic energy, store-chambers for everything to be carried, the mechanisms of control, the aëration plant, the heating units and the quarters for passengers."

Tony tore his eyes from the sight. "How many will she carry?" he asked quietly.

Hendron hesitated; then he said: "For a trip of the duration I contemplate, she would be able to take about one hundred people."

Tony's voice was still quieter. "Then you have nine hundred idealists in your camp here."

The older man smiled. "Unless I am greatly mistaken, I have a thousand."

"They all know about the ship?"

"Something about it. Nearly half of them have been working on it, or on apparatus connected with it."

"You pay no wages?"

"I've offered wages. In most cases they've been refused. I have more than three million dollars in gold available here for expenses encountered in dealing with people who still wish money for their time or materials."

"I see. How long a trip do you contemplate?"

Hendron took the young man's breath. "Ninety hours. That is, provided,"—and his voice began to shake,—"provided we can find proper materials with which to line our blast-tubes. Otherwise we wouldn't be able to propel this thing for more than a few minutes. I—"

Eve looked at her father. "Dad, you've got to go to bed. You'd better take some veronal or something, and don't worry so. We'll find the alloy all right. We've done everything else, and the things we've done were even more difficult."

Hendron nodded; and Tony, looking at him, realized for the first time how much the scientist had aged recently. They went through the door of the hangar in single file, and high up among the beams and buttresses that supported it, a shower of sparks fell from an acetylene welding-torch.

Outside, the wind was blowing. It sighed hotly in the

near-by trees—wind that presaged a storm. The lights in the foundry and laboratories, the power-house and the dormitories made a ring around them, a ring of yellow fireflies faint beneath the glare of the Bronson Bodies. Tony looked up at them, and it seemed to him that he could almost feel and hear them in their awful rush through space: Beta, a dazzling white world, and Alpha, an insensible luminous disc of destruction. Both bodies seemed to stand away from the vault of the heavens.

Hendron left them. Soon afterward James withdrew with the apology that he wished to write to bring up to date his diary. Tony escorted Eve to the women's dormitory. A phonograph was playing in the general room on the ground floor. One of the girls was singing, and another was sitting at a table writing what was apparently a letter. They could all be seen through the open windows, and Tony wondered what postman that girl expected would carry her missive. Eve bade him good night, then went inside.

Tony, left alone, walked over the gleaming ground to the top of a neighboring hill. Hendron's village looked on the northern side like a university campus, and on the southern side like the heart of a manufacturing district. All around it stretched the Michigan wilderness. The ground had been chosen partly because of the age and grimness of its geological base, and partly because of its isolation.

He sat down on a large stone. The hot night wind blew with increasing violence, and the double shadows, one sharp and one faint, which were cast by all things in the light of the Bronson Bodies, were abruptly obliterated by the passage of a dark cloud.

Tony's mind ran unevenly and irresolutely. "Probably," he thought, "this little community is the most self-sufficient of any place on earth. All these people, these brilliant temperamental men and women, have subsided and made themselves like soldiers in Hendron's service—amazing man. . . . Only a hundred people. . . . I wonder how many of those I brought to New York they'll take."

Fears assailed him: "Suppose they don't complete the Ark successfully, and she never leaves the ground? Then all these people would have given their lives for nothing. . . . Suppose it leaves the earth and fails—falls back for hundreds of miles, gaining speed all the way, so that when it hit the atmosphere it would turn red-hot and burn itself up just like a meteor? What hideous chances have to be taken! If only I were a scientist and could help them! If only I could sit up day and night with the others, trying to find the metal that would make the ship fly. . . ."

A larger cloud obscured the Bronson Bodies. The wind came in violent gusts. The great globes in the sky which disturbed sea and land, also enormously distorted the atmospheric envelope.

The steady sound of machinery reached Tony's ears, and the ring of iron against iron. The wind wailed upon the æolian harp of the trees. Tony thought of the tides that would rise that night and on following nights; and faintly, like the palpitation of a steamer's deck, the earth shook beneath his feet as if in answer to his meditation. And Tony realized that the heart of the earth was straining toward its celestial companions.

Chapter 13—The Approach of the Planets

ON the night of the twenty-fifth, tides unprecedented in the world's history swept every seacoast. There were earthquakes of varying magnitude all over the world. In the day that followed, volcanoes opened up, and islands sank beneath the sea; and on the night of the twenty-sixth the greater of the Bronson Bodies came within its minimum distance from the earth on this their first approach.

No complete record was ever made of the devastation.

Eliot James, who made some tabulation of it in the succeeding months, could never believe all that he saw and heard, but it must have been true.

The eastern coast of the United States sustained a tidal wave seven hundred and fifty feet in height, which came in from the sea in relentless terraces and inundated the land to the very foot of the Appalachians. Its westward rush destroyed every building, every hovel, every skyscraper, every city, from Bangor in Maine to Key West in Florida. The tide looped into the Gulf of Mexico, rolled up the Mississippi Valley, becoming in some places so congested with material along its foaming face that the terrified human beings upon whom it descended saw a wall of trees and houses, of stones and machinery, of all the conglomerate handiwork of men and Nature—rather than the remorseless or uplifted water behind it. When the tide gushed back to the ocean's bed, it strewed the gullied landscape with the things it had uprooted.

It roared around South America, turning the Amazon Basin into a vast inland sea which stretched from what had been the east coast to the Andes Mountains on the west coast. The speed of this tide was beyond calculation.

Every river became a channel for it. It spilled over Asia. It inundated the great plain of China. It descended from the arctic regions and removed much of France, England and Germany, all of Holland and the great Soviet Empire, from the list of nations. Arctic water hundreds of feet deep flowed into the Caspian Sea and hurled the last of its august inertia upon the Caucasus.

Western Asia and Arabia, southern India, Africa and much of Australia remained dry land. Those who saw that tide from mountain-tops were never afterward able to depict it for their fellows. The mind of man is not adjusted for a close observation of phenomena that belong to the cosmos. To see that dark obsidian sky-clutching torrent of water moving inward upon the land at a velocity of many hundreds of miles an hour was to behold something foreign to the realm of Nature, as Nature even at its most furious has hitherto appeared to man.

More than half the population of the world died in the tides that rose and subsided during the proximity of the Bronson Bodies. But those who by design or through accident found themselves on land that remained dry were not necessarily spared.

The earthquake which Tony felt in Michigan was the first of a series of shocks which increased steadily in violence for the next forty-eight hours, and which never afterward wholly ceased. Hendron had chosen his spot well, for it was one of the relatively few portions of the undeluged world which was not reduced to an untenable wasteland of smoking rock and creeping lava.

Nothing in the category of earthquakes or eruption occurring within the memory of the race could even furnish criteria for the manifestations everywhere on the earth's crust on that July twenty-sixth. Man had witnessed the explosion of whole mountains. He had seen the disappearance and the formation of islands. Yards of sea-coast had subsided before his very eyes. Fissures wide enough to contain an army had opened at his feet; but such occurrences were not even minutiæ in the hours of the closest approach of the Bronson Bodies.

As hour by hour the earth presented new surfaces to the awful gravitational pull of those spheres, a series of stupendous cataclysms took place. Underneath the brittle slag which man considers both solid and enduring lie thousands of miles of dense compressed molten material. The earth's crust does not hold back that material. It is kept in place only by a delicate adjustment of gravity; and the interference of the Bronson Bodies distorted that balance. The earth burst open like a ripe grape! From a geological standpoint the tides which swept over were a phenomenon of but trifling magnitude.

The center of the continent of Africa split in two as if a mighty cleaver had come down on it, and out of the grisly incision poured an unquenchable tumult of the hell that dwells within the earth. Chasms yawned in the ocean floor, swallowing levels of the sea and returning it instantaneously in continents of steam. The great plateau of inner Thibet dropped like an express elevator nine hundred feet. South America was riven into two islands one extending north and south in the shape of a sickle, and the other, roughly circular, composed of all that remained of the high lands of Brazil. North America reeled and shuddered, split, snapped, boomed and leaped. The Rocky Mountains lost their immobility and danced like waves of water. From the place that had been Yellowstone Park a mantle of lava was spread over thousands of square miles. The coastal plain along the Pacific disappeared, and the water moved up to dash itself in fury against a range of active volcanoes that extended from Nome to Panama.

Gases, steam and ashes welled from ten thousand vents into the earth's atmosphere. The sun went out, the stars were made visible. Blistering heat blew to the ends of the earth. The polar ice melted and a new raw land emerged, fiery and shattered, mobile and catastrophic.

Those human beings who survived the world's white-hot throes were survivors for the most part through good fortune. Few escaped through design—on the entire planet only a dozen places which had been picked by the geologists as refuges remained habitable.

Upon millions poured oceans of seething magma carrying death more terrible than the death which rolled on the tongue of the great tides. The air which was breathed by other millions was suddenly choked with sulphurous fumes and they fell like gassed soldiers, strangling in the streets of their destroyed cities. Live steam, blown with the violence of a hurricane, scalded populous centers and barren steppes impartially. From a sky that had hitherto deluged mankind only with rain, snow and hail, fell now burning torrents and red-hot sleet. The very earth itself slowed in its rotation, sped up again, sucked and dragged through space at the caprice of the bodies in the sky above. It became girdled in smoke and steam, and blasts of hot gas; and upon it as Bronson Alpha and Beta drew away, there fell torrential rains which hewed down rich land to the bare rock, which cooled the issue from the earth to vast metallic oceans, and which were accompanied by lightnings that furnished the infernal scenery with incessant illumination, and by thunder which blended undetectably with the terrestrial din.

At Hendron's camp forty-eight hours in the Pit were experienced; and yet Hendron's camp was on one of the safest and least disturbed corners of the world.

The first black clouds which Tony had observed marked the beginning of an electrical storm. The tremor he felt presaged a steady crescendo of earth-shakings. He left his hill-top soon and found that the population of the colony which, an hour before, had retired for the night, was again awake. He met Hendron and several scientists making a last tour of inspection; and he joined them.

"The dormitories," Hendron said, "are presumably quake-proof. I don't think any force could knock over the buttresses we have put around the projectile."

Even as he spoke, the wind increased, lightning stabbed the sky, the radiance of the Bronson Bodies was permanently extinguished, and the gusty wind was transformed to a steady tempest. Lights were on in every building; and as shock followed shock, people began to pour into the outdoors.

Tony tried to locate Eve, but was unable to do so in the gathering throng. The darkness outside the range of lights was absolute. The temperature of the wind dropped many degrees, so that it seemed cold in comparison to the heat of early evening. It was difficult to walk on the wide cleared area between the various buildings, for the ground underfoot frequently forced itself up like the floor of a rapidly decelerated elevator. The lightning came nearer. The thunder was continual. It was hard to hear the voice of one's nearest neighbor. Word passed from person to person in staccato shouts that all buildings were to be evacuated. Tony himself, with half a dozen others, rushed into the brightly illuminated women's dormitory and hurriedly brought from it into the tumult and rain those who had remained there.

By ten o'clock the violence of the quakes was great enough so that it was difficult to stand. The people huddled like sheep in a storm in the lee of the buildings. Lightning hammered incessantly on the tall steel tower which surrounded the space-flyer. Tony moved through the assembled people shouting words of encouragement he did not feel.

Shortly after eleven an extraordinarily violent shock lifted one end of the men's building so that bricks and cement cascaded from its wall. Immediately Tony located Hendron, who was sitting wrapped in a tarpaulin on a stone in the center of the crowd, and made a suggestion which was forthwith carried out. The flood-lights were thrown on the landing-field, and every one migrated thither. They congregated again in the center of smooth open space, a weird collection in their hastily assumed wraps, with their white faces looking upward picked out through the rain by the flood-lights and the blue flashes from the heavens.

Before midnight some caprice of the seismic disturbance snapped off the power. At one o'clock in the morning a truck from the kitchens of the dining-halls floundered through the mud with sandwiches and coffee. At two o'clock the temperature of the wind dropped again, and the wet multitude shivered and chattered with cold. Hail fell in place of rain.

Half an hour later the wind stopped abruptly, and in that sudden silence, between bursts of thunder, human voices rose in a loud clamor of a hundred individual conversations. The wind puffed, veered, and came back from the southwest. It blew fifty miles an hour, a hundred, and then rose from that velocity to an immeasurable degree. Leaves and whole branches shot through the air. Every man and woman was compelled to lie face down on the muddy earth, the undulations of which increased.

They lay for an hour or more, shivering, gasping for breath, hiding their faces. Then a particularly violent shock suddenly separated the landing-field into two parts, one of which rose eight or nine feet above the other, leaving a sharp diminutive precipice across the middle of the field. A dozen people had been actually straddling the point of fracture; and some fell on the lower side, while others, crawling away from the new and terrifying menace, were lifted up. Fortunately no crevice opened, although the split edges of the underlying rocks ground against each other with a noise that transcended the tumult. Toward morning the temperature of the wind began to rise.

There was no dawn, no daylight, only a diffused inadequate grayness through which the tumbling streaming clouds could be dimly apprehended. The people lay on the ground, each man wrapped in the terrors of his own soul, with fingers clutching the grass or buried in the earth. And so the day began. The air grew perpetually more warm. An augmented fury of the gale brought a faint odor of sulphur.

Midday held no respite. It was impossible to bring up food against the gale, impossible even to stand. The sulphurous odors and the heat increased. The driven rain seemed hot. Toward what would have been afternoon, and in the absolute darkness, there was a sudden abatement; and the wind, while it still blew strong, allowed the shaken populace to rise and to stare through the impenetrable murk. Fifty or more of the men made a rush for the dining-halls. They found them, and were surprised that they had not collapsed. The low hills around had furnished them with protection. There was no time to prepare food. Snatching what they could, and loading themselves with containers of drinking-water, they fought their way back to the field. There, like animals, the people drank and ate, finishing in time only to throw themselves once again on the bare ground under the renewed fury of the storm.

Night came again. The sulphur in the air, the fumes and gases, the heat and smoke and dust, the hot rain, almost extinguished their frantically defended lives. They lay now in the lee of the fault, but even there the down-swirl of the tempest and lash of the elements were almost unendurable.

The dust and rain combined with the wind to make a diagonal downfall of fœtid mud which blistered them and covered the earth. Through that second night no one was able to talk, to think, to move, to do more than lie prone amid the chaos, gasping for breath.

CHAPTER 14—THE FIRST PASSING

THE respite brought by morning was comparative rather than real. The wind abated; the torrential rain became intermittent; and the visibility returned, though no one could have told whether it was early morning or twilight.

Tony rose to his feet the instant the wind slacked. Through all the long and terrible hours he had been absent from Eve. It would have been utterly unthinkable to attempt to locate her in the midst of that sound and fury. He found, however, that there was no use in looking for her immediately. So heavy had been the downpour of rain and ashes from the sky, that it not only reduced the field to a quagmire, but it covered the human beings who had lain there with a thick chocolate-colored coating, so that as one by one the people arose to sitting and standing postures, he found it difficult even to distinguish man from woman.

He was compelled to put Eve from his mind. It was necessary to think of all and not one. Succor was needed sorely. Many of those who had been in the field were unable to rise. Several had been injured. Of the older men a number were suffering perhaps fatally from exposure.

Tony found that his limbs would scarcely support him when he did regain them; but after he had staggered for some distance through the murk, his numbed circulation was restored, and his muscles responded. He held brief conversations with those who were standing:

"Are you all right?" If the answer was in the negative, he replied: "Sit down. We'll take care of you. But when it was in the affirmative, he said: "Come with me. We'll start things going again. I think the worst is over."

Out of the subsiding maelstrom he collected some thirty or forty persons, most of them men. They walked off the field together; and as they walked, slowly and painfully, their feet sucking in the quagmire and stumbling on débris, Tony proceeded with his organization.

"Any of you men working on the power plant?" he shouted. . . . "Right. You two come over here. Now who else here was in the machine-shop? . . . Good. You fellows get to work on starting up the lights. They'll be the first thing. Now I want half of you to get beds in shape in the women's hall." He counted the number he required, slapping them on the shoulders and dispatching them toward the halls, which loomed in the distance. "If they don't look safe," he shouted after the disappearing men, "find a place that is safe, and put the beds there. We'll have to have a hospital."

With the remnant of his men he went to the dining-halls. One of these buildings was a complete wreck, but the other still stood. They entered the kitchen. Its floor was knee-deep in mud. He recognized among those still with him Taylor, the student of light, whom he had sent to Hendron from Cornell. "Take charge in here, will you, Taylor? I'll leave you half these men. The rest of us are going out to round up the doctors and get medical supplies ready. They'll want coffee out there, and any kind of food that they can eat immediately." He saw Taylor's mouth smile in assent, and heard Taylor begin to issue instructions for the lighting of a fire in one of the big stoves.

Once again he went outdoors. It was a little lighter. His anxious gaze traveled to the tower that housed the Ark, and from its silhouette he deduced that it was at least superficially intact. The shouting he had done had already rendered him hoarse, for the air was still sulphurous. It irritated the nose and throat, and produced in every one a dry frequent cough. Tony was apprehensive for fear the gases in the air might increase in volume and suffocate them, but he banished the thought from his mind: it was but one of innumerable apprehensions, many of them greater, which numbed his consciousness and the consciousness of all his fellows during that terrifying forty-eight hours. Besides the irritating vapors in the air, there was heat, not the heat expected any day in July, but such heat as surrounds a blast furnace—a sullen withering heat which blanched the skin, parched the lips and was unrelieved by the rivulets of perspiration that covered the body.

Tony went back alone to the flying-field. It was a little lighter. Mist motions were visible in the sky, and threads of vapor were flung over the Stygian landscape by the wind. People were returning from what had been the flying-field to the partial wreck at the camp in twos and threes, many of them limping, some of them being carried. They made a stream of humanity like walking wounded—a procession of hunger, thirst, pain and exhaustion struggling across a landscape that would have credited Dante's Inferno itself, struggling through a nether gloom, slobbered with mire, breathing the hot metallic atmosphere. He found Eve at last, just as he reached the edge of the flying-field. She was helping two other girls, who were trying to carry a third. She recognized him and called to him.

"Are you all right, Eve?" His soul was in his rasping voice. He came close to her. He looked into her eyes. She nodded, first to him and then toward the unconscious girl. She put her lips close to his ear, for she could speak only in a whisper: "Give us a hand, Tony. This girl needs water. She fainted."

He picked up the girl, and they followed him through the slough to the main hall of the women's dormitory. Beds were being carried there, and many of the beds were already filled. Some one had found candles and stuck them in window-sills so that the room was lighted. Already two men who were doctors were examining the arrivals. Tony recognized one of the men as Dodson when he heard the boom of his voice: "Get hot water here, lots of it, boiling water. Don't anybody touch those bandages. Everything has to be sterilized. See if you can find anybody who knows anything about nursing. Get the rest of the doctors."

Somehow Dodson had already managed to wash, and his heavy-jowled face radiated power and confidence. In the candle-light Tony recognized other muddy faces on the beds. A German actress seemed to have a broken leg, and a dignified gray-haired Austrian pathologist was himself a victim of the barrage that had fallen from the heavens.

Tony went outdoors again. It seemed to him that the air had freshened somewhat, and that the temperature had dropped. A gong boomed in the kitchen, and he remembered his thirst and hunger. For almost forty-eight hours he had had little to eat and little to drink. He knew he could not deny the needs of his body any longer. He hastened in the direction of the gong. Around a caldron of coffee and a heap of sandwiches, which were replenished as fast as they disappeared, were grouped at least two hundred people. Tony stood in the line which passed the caldron, and was handed a cup of coffee and a sandwich. The coffee tasted muddy. The sandwich had a flavor not unlike the noxious odor in the air. Tony's craving was for water, but he realized that for the time being all liquids would have to be boiled to eliminate their pollution. With his first sip of coffee he realized that brandy had been added to it. He wet his burning throat and swallowed his sandwich in three mouthfuls, and joined the line again.

His senses reasserted themselves. He realized that the wind was dying, the oppressiveness was departing and the temperature had lowered perceptibly. He was able for the first time to hear the conversation of people around him, and even in his shocked and shocking state, he was moved by mingled feelings of compassion and amusement. The heavy hand of the gods had scarcely been lifted. Its return might be expected imminently, and yet the marvelous resilience of humankind already was asserting itself.

". . . Ruined my dress, absolutely ruined!" he heard one woman say.

And some one else laughed. That sentence spread. "Her dress was ruined. Too bad!"

From the men there came a different sort of comment: "When I say I never saw anything like it before in my life, I mean I've never seen anything like it before in my life. . . ."

The excited voice of one of the scientists: "Amazing, the way things survived. Almost nothing has been damaged in the machine-shops and the power-houses. Those places were built like bank vaults. Great genius for organization, that man Hendron."

Another man spoke: "I inspected the seismograph first. The needle had shot clear off the roll the night before last and put it out of business. Then I looked at the barometric record. Air-pressure changed around here inches in minutes. The barometer went out of business too. You could almost feel what was happening to the earth. I had sensations of being lifted and lowered, and of pressure coming and going on my ears.

"I wonder how many people survived. The volcanic manifestations must have been awful. They must still be going on—although I can't tell whether it's earthquake now, or just my legs shaking. And smell the sulphur in the air."

Tony saw Peter Vanderbilt sitting pacifically on a log, a cup of coffee in one hand, a sandwich in the other, and his bedraggled handkerchief spread over his knees for a napkin. The elegant Vanderbilt's mustache was clogged with mud. His hair was a cake of mud. His shoes were gobs of mud. One of his pant-legs had been torn off at the knee. His shirt-tails had escaped his belt and festooned his midriff in stained tatters, and yet as Tony approached him, he still maintained his attitude of cosmic indifference, of urbanity so complete that nothing could succeed in ruffling it spiritually.

Vanderbilt rose. "Tony, my friend," he exclaimed. "What a masquerade! What a disguise! I recognized you only by the gauge in which heaven made your shoulders. Sit down. Join me in a spot of lunch."

Tony sat on the log, which apparently the wind had moved into position especially for Mr. Vanderbilt. "I'll have a snack with you," he replied. "Then I must get back to work."

The quondam Beau Brummell of Fifth Avenue nodded understandingly. "Work, my dear fellow! I never saw so many people who were so avid for work, and yet there's something exalting about it. And the storm was certainly impressive. I admit that I was impressed. In fact, I proclaim that I was impressed. Yet its whole moral was futility."

"Futility?"

"Oh, don't think that for a minute I was being philosophical. I wasn't referring to the obvious futility of all man's efforts and achievements. They were quite apparent before this—this—ah—disturbance. I was thinking of myself entirely. I was thinking of the many years I had spent as a lad in learning geography, and how useless all that knowledge was to me now. I should imagine that the geography I learned at twelve was now completely out of date."

Tony nodded to the man on the log. "So I should imagine. You'll excuse me, but I'm needed."

Peter Vanderbilt smiled and put his cup beside Tony's on the ground. Then without a word he rose and followed the younger man. They found Hendron emerging from the great hangar. His condition was neither worse nor better than that of the others. He seized Tony's shoulder the minute his eyes lighted upon him. "Tony, son, have you seen Eve?"

"Yes."

"She's all right?"

"She's entirely all right. She's working over at the emergency hospital."

Behind Hendron stood a number of men. He turned to them. "You go ahead and inspect the machine-shop. I'll join you in a minute."

He then noticed that Tony had a companion. "Hello, Vanderbilt. Glad to see you're safe." And again he spoke to Tony. "What was the extent of the injury to personnel?"

Tony shook his head. "I don't know yet."

Vanderbilt spoke. "I just came from the field hospital before I had my coffee. I was making a private check-up. So far as is known, no one here was killed. There are three cases of collapse that may develop into pneumonia, several minor cases of shock, two broken legs, one broken arm, a sprained ankle; one of the men who made coffee during the storm got burned, and there are forty or fifty people with more or less minor scratches and abrasions. In all less than seventy-five cases were reported so far."

Hendron's head bobbed again. He sighed with relief. "Good God, I'm thankful! It was more terrifying out there, apparently, than it was dangerous."

"It was not unlike taking a Turkish bath on a roller coaster in the dark," Vanderbilt replied.

Hendron rubbed his hand across his face. "Did you men say something about coffee?"

"With brandy in it," Tony said.

Vanderbilt took Hendron's arm. "May I escort you? You're a bit rocky, I guess."

"Just a bit. Brandy, eh? Good." Before he walked away, he spoke to Tony. "Listen, son—" The use of that word rocked Tony's heart. "This was much more than I had anticipated, much worse. But by the mercy of Providence the major dangers have passed, and we seem to be bloody but unbowed. The ship is safe, although one side was dented against its cradle. That's about all. If I had foreseen anything like this, I could have been better prepared for it, although perhaps not. An open field was about the only habitable sort of place. I've got to get some rest now. I'm just a few minutes away from unconsciousness. I want you to take over things, if you think you can stand up for another twelve hours."

"I'm in the pink," Tony answered.

"Good. You're in charge, then. Have me waked in twelve hours."

Tony began the rounds again. In the hall of the women's dormitory, Dodson and Smith were hard at work. Their patients sat or lay in bed. There was a smell of anæsthetics and antiseptics in the air. Eve, together with a dozen other women, was acting as nurse. She had changed her clothes, and washed. She smiled at him across the room, and Dodson spoke to him. "Tell Hendron we're managing things beautifully in here now. I don't think there's anybody here that won't recover."

"He's asleep," Tony replied. "I'll tell him when he wakes."

He looked at Eve again before he went out, and saw her eyes flooded with tears. Immediately he realized his thoughtlessness in not telling her at once that her father was safe, but there was no reproof in her starry-eyed glance. She understood that the situation had passed the point at which rational and normal thoughtfulness could be expected.

Tony went next to the machine-shop. A shift of men was at work clearing away the infiltrated dust on the engines and the mud that had poured over the floors. Another group of men lay in deep sleep wherever there was room enough to recline. One of the workers explained: "Nobody around here can work for long without a little sleep, so we're going in one-hour shifts. Sleep an hour, clean an hour. Is that all right, Mr. Drake?"

"That's fine," Tony said.

At the power-house a voice hailed him.

"You're just in time, Mr. Drake."

"What for?"

"Come in." Tony entered the power-house. The man conducted him to a walled panel and pointed to a switch. "Pull her down."

Tony pulled. At once all over the cantonment obscurity was annihilated by the radiance of countless electric lights. The electrician who had summoned Tony grinned. "We're using a little emergency engine, and only about a quarter of the lights of the lines are operating. That's all we've had time to put in order. It's jerry-made, but it's better than this damn' gloom."

Tony's hand came down firmly on the man's shoulder. "It's marvelous. You boys work in shifts now. All of you need sleep."

The electrician nodded. "We will. Some of the big shots are inside. Shall I tell them to come out to see you?"

An idea suddenly struck Tony. "Look here. Why shouldn't I go see them if I want to? Why is it you expect them to come out and see me?"

"You're the boss, aren't you?"

"What makes you think I'm the boss?"

The man looked at him quizzically. "Why, it said so in the instruction-book we got when we were all sent out here. Everybody got a copy. It said you were second in command in any emergency to Mr. Hendron; and this is an emergency, isn't it?"

Tony was staggered by this new information. "It said that in a book?"

"Right. In the book of rules that everybody that lives here got the day they came. I had one in my pocket, but I lost pocket, book and all, out there on the landing-field."

Tony conquered his surprise. It flashed through his mind that Hendron was training him to be in command of those who stayed behind and launched the Space Ship. He was conscious of a naïve pride at this indication of the great scientist's confidence in him. "I won't bother the men here," he said. "Just so long as we get as many lights as possible in operation, as fast as possible."

He found a group of men standing speculatively in front of the men's hall. One of the side walls had been shattered, and bricks had cascaded from the front walls to the ground. Tony looked at the building critically, and then said: "I don't think anybody should occupy it."

"There are a good many men in there asleep right now. Probably they entered in the dark without noticing the condition of the building."

Tony addressed the crowd. "If two or three of you care to volunteer to go in with me, we'll get them all out. The men will sleep for the time being on the floor in the south dining-hall."

He went into the insecure building, and practically all of the men who had been regarding it from the outside accompanied him. They roused the sleepers.

The floor of the dining-hall was dry: men in dozens, and then in scores, without speech, among themselves, pushed aside the tables and stretched out on the bare boards, falling instantly to sleep.

Next Tony went to the kitchen. Fires were going in two

stoves; more coffee was ready, the supply of sandwiches had overtaken the demand, and kettles of soup augmented it. Taylor was still in charge, and he made his report as soon as he saw Tony.

"The big storehouses are half underground, as you probably know, and I don't think the food in them has been hurt much, although it has been shaken up. I didn't know anything about the feeding arrangements, but I've located a bunch of men who did. There's apparently a large herd of livestock and a lot of poultry about a quarter of a mile in the woods. I've sent men there to take charge. They already reported that the sheep and goats and steers didn't budge, although their pens and corrals were destroyed. They're putting up barbed-wire for the time being. Everything got shaken up pretty badly, and the water and mud spoiled whatever it got into, but most of the stuff was in big containers. The main that carried the water from the reservoir is all smashed to hell, and I guess the water in the reservoir isn't any good anyway. I'm boiling all that I use, but somebody has just got the bright idea of using the fire apparatus and hoses from some of these young lakes."

"You've done damned well, Taylor," Tony said. "Do you think you can carry on for a few hours more?"

"Sure. I'm good for a week of this."

Tony watched the innumerable chores which were being done by men under Taylor's instruction. He noticed for the first time that the work of reclaiming the human habitations was not being done altogether by the young men, the mechanics and the helpers whom Hendron had enlisted. Among Taylor's group were a dozen middle-aged scientists whose names had been august in the world three months before that day. Unable for the time to carry on their own tasks, they were laboring for the common weal with mops and brooms and pails and shovels.

When Tony went outdoors again, it was four o'clock, though he had no means of knowing the time. Once again he noticed that the air was cooler. He made his way down the almost impassable trail to the stockyards, and found another group of men working feverishly with the frightened animals and the clamorous poultry. Then he walked back to the "village green." So far as he could determine, every effort was being bent toward reorganizing the important affairs of the community. He had at last the leisure in which to consider himself and the world around him.

Perspiration had carried away the dirt on his face and hands, but his clothes were still mucky. The dampness of the air had prevented that mud from drying. His hair was still caked. He walked in the direction of the flying-field, and presently found what he sought—a depression in the ground which had been filled with water to a depth of three or four feet, and in which water the mud had settled. He waded into the pool carefully so as not to disturb the silt on the bottom. The water was warm. He ducked his head below the surface and laved his face with his hands.

When he stepped out, he was relatively clean, though his feet became immediately encased in mud again.

Slowly he walked to the top of the small hill from which he had watched the Bronson Bodies on the evening before. He felt a diminution of the sulphur and other vapors in the air, His throat was raw, but each breath did not sting his lungs as it had during the last hours when they had been lying in the open field. He noticed again a quality of thinness in the air which persisted in spite of the heat and moisture. He wondered if the entire chemistry of the earth's atmosphere had been changed—if, for example a definite percentage of its normal oxygen had been consumed. That problem, however, was unsolvable, at least for the time.

By straining his eyes into the distance, and aiding their perceptions with imagination, he could deduce the general changes in the local landscape. The hurricane had uprooted, disheveled and destroyed the surrounding portions except where hill-crests protected small patches of standing trees. One-half of the flying-field had been lifted eight or ten feet above the other, so that its surface looked like two books of unequal thickness lying edge to edge. The open space inside the "U" of buildings which Hendron had constructed was littered with rubbish, most of it tree-branches. One dining-hall had collapsed. The men's dormitory was unsafe until it could be repaired. Everywhere was an even coat of soft brown mud which on the level must have attained a depth of ten inches—and the rain which still fell in occasional interludes continued to bring down detritus from the skies.

What had happened to the rest of the world, to what had been Michigan, to the United States, to the continents and the oceans would have to be determined at some future time.

For the moment, calm had come. The Bronson Bodies not only had passed and withdrawn toward the sun, but they shone no longer in the night sky. If atmospheric conditions permitted, they would be visible dimly by day; but only by day. As a matter of fact, from the camp they were completely invisible; not even the sun could be clearly seen.

But the night came on clear—clear and almost calm. The mists had settled, and the clouds moved away. Dust and gases hung in the air; still the stars showed.

The moon, too, should be shining, Tony thought. To-night there should be a full moon; but only stars were in the sky. Had he reckoned wrong?

He was standing alone, looking up and checking his mental calculations, when some one stopped beside him.

"What is it, Tony?" Hendron said.

"Where's the moon to-night?"

"Where—that's it: where? That's what we'd like to know —exactly what happened. We had to miss it, you see; probably nowhere in the world were conditions that permitted observation when the collision occurred; and what a thing to see!"

"The collision!" said Tony.

"When Bronson Alpha took out the moon! I thought you knew it was going to happen, Tony. I thought I told you."

"Bronson Alpha took out the moon! . . . You told me that it would take out the world when we meet it next on the other side of the sun; but you didn't mention the moon!"

"Didn't I? I meant to. It was minor, of course; but I'd have given much to have been able to see it. Bronson Alpha, if our calculations proved correct, collided with the moon in a glancing blow. That is, it was not a center collision; but it surely broke up the moon into fragments. Most of them may have merged with the far greater body; but others we may see later. There are conditions under which they would form a band of dust and fragments about the earth like the rings about Saturn. In any case, there is no use looking for the moon, Tony. The moon has met its end; it is forever gone. I wish we could have seen it."

Tony was silent. Strange to stare into a sky into which never again the moon would rise! Strange to think that now that the terrible tides raised by the Bronson Bodies had fallen, there would not be any tide at all. Even the moon tides were gone. The seas, so enormously upsucked and swept back and forth, were left to lap at their shores in this unnatural, moonless calm.

"However," said Hendron, "when the world encounters Bronson Alpha, we'll see that, I hope."

"See it—from the world?" said Tony.

"From space, I hope, if we succeed with our ship—from space on our way to Bronson Beta. What a show that will be, Tony, from space with no clouds to cut if off! And then landing on that other world, whose cities we have seen!"

"Yes," said Tony.

Chapter 15—Reconnaissance

SO through the darkness of that moon-lost night, Tony continued to work. He mustered new gangs for the dreary tasks of salvage, and of rehabilitating and reconstructing the shelters.

He organized, directed, exhorted and cheered men on, wondering at them as they responded and redoubled their efforts. He wondered no less at himself. What use, in the end, was all this labor? A few months, and they would meet the Bronson Bodies again; and this time, Bronson Alpha would not pass the world. As it had extinguished the moon, it would annihilate the earth too! This solid ground!

Tony stamped upon it.

No wonder, really, that these men responded and that he exhorted and urged them on. They, and he, could not realize that the world was doomed, any more than a man could realize that he himself must die. Death is what happens to others! So other worlds may perish; but not ours, on which we stand!

Tony clapped his hands together loudly. "All right, fellows! Come on! Come on!" Clouds gathered again, and rain was pouring down.

When light began again to filter through the darkly streaming heavens, Hendron re-awoke. He found Tony drunk with fatigue, carrying on by sheer effort of will, and refusing to rest.

Hendron called some of the men who had been taking Tony's commands, and had him carried bodily to bed. . . .

Tony opened his eyes. One by one he collected all the disjointed memories of the past days. He perceived that he was lying on a couch in Hendron's offices in the west end of the machine-shop and laboratory building. He sat up and looked out the window. It was notably lighter, although the clouds were still dense; and as he looked, a stained mist commenced to descend. A slight noise in one corner of the room attracted his attention. A man sat there at a desk quietly scribbling. He raised his eyes when Tony looked at him. He was a tall, very thin man, with dark curly hair and long-lashed blue eyes. His age might have been thirty-five—or fifty. He had a remarkably high forehead and slim, tactile hands. He smiled at Tony, and spoke with a trace of accent.

"Good morning, Mr. Drake. It is not necessary to ask if you slept well. Your sleep was patently of the most profound order."

Tony swung his feet onto the floor. "Yes, I think I did sleep well. We haven't met, have we?"

The other man shook his head. "No, we haven't; but I've heard about you, and I should imagine that you have heard my name once or twice in the last few weeks." A smile flickered on his face. "I am Sven Bronson."

"Good Lord!" Tony walked across the room and held out his hand. "I'm surely delighted to meet the man who—" He hesitated.

The Scandinavian's smile returned. "You were going to say, 'the man who was responsible for all this.' "

Tony chuckled, shook Bronson's hand, and then looked down at the bedraggled garments which only partially covered him. "I've got to find some clothes and get shaved."

"It's all been prepared," Bronson said. "In the private office, there's a bath of sorts ready for you, and some clean clothes and a razor."

"Somebody has taken terribly good care of me," Tony said. He yawned and stretched. "I feel fine." At the door he hesitated. "What's the news, by the way? How are things? How is everybody?"

Bronson tapped his desk with his pencil. "Everybody is doing nicely. There are only a dozen people left in the hospital now. Your friend Taylor has the commissary completely rehabilitated, and everybody here is saying pleasant things about him. I don't know all the news, but it is picturesque, to say the least. Appalling, too! For instance the spot on which we now reside was very considerably raised last week. It has apparently been lifted again, together with no one knows how much surrounding territory, so the elevator sensations we felt in the field were decidedly accurate. We presume that many thousands of square miles may have been raised simultaneously; otherwise there would have been more local fracture. The radio station has been functioning again."

"Good Lord!" Tony exclaimed. "I forgot all about the radio station last night—that is to say, to-day is to-morrow, isn't it? What day is this?"

"This is the twenty-ninth." Tony realized that he has been asleep for twenty-four hours. "The man in the wireless division went to work on the station immediately. Anyway, not much has come in, though we picked up a station in New Mexico, and a very feeble station somewhere in Ohio. The New Mexico station reports some sort of extraordinary phenomena, together with a violent eruption of a volcanic nature in their district; the one in Ohio merely appealed steadily for help."

At once Tony inferred the import of Bronson's words. "You mean to say that you've only heard two stations in all this country?"

"You deduce things quickly, Mr. Drake. Of course the static is so tremendous still that it would be impossible to hear anything from any foreign country; and doubtless other stations are working which we will pick up later, as well as many which will be reconditioned in the future; but so far, we have received only two calls."

Tony opened the door to the adjacent office. "That means, then, that nearly everybody has been—"

The Scandinavian's long white hands locked, and his eyes affirmed Tony's speculation. . . .

"I'll get myself cleaned up," said Tony.

And he stepped into a big galvanized tub of water that had been kept warm by a small electric heater. He bathed, shaved and dressed in his own clothes, which had been brought from his quarters in the partly demolished men's dormitory. Afterward he went to the laboratories and found Hendron.

"By George, you look fit, Tony!" were Hendron's first words. "Eve is impatiently waiting for you. She's at the dining-hall."

Tony found Eve cheerful and bright-eyed. With a dozen or more women, she was rearranging and redecorating the dining-hall, which had been immaculately cleaned. She went out on the long veranda with him.

"Notice how much clearer the air is?" Eve asked. "Most of the fumes have disappeared. . . . It's hard to shake the superstition that natural disasters are directed at you, isn't it, Tony?"

"Are we sure it's a superstition, Eve?"

"After all, what has happened to us is only the sort of thing that has happened before, thousands of times, on this earth of ours, Tony, on a smaller scale—at Pompeii, at Mt. Pelée and Krakatao and at other places. What can be the differences in the scale of the God of the cosmos, whether He shakes down San Francisco and Tokio twenty years apart, buries Pompeii when Titus was ruling Rome, and blows up Krakatao eighteen hundred years later—or whether he decides to smash it all at once? It's all the same sort of thing."

"Yes," agreed Tony. "It's only the scale of the performance that's different. Anyway, we've survived so far. I heard you were safe, Eve; and then when I could hear no more, I supposed you were safe. You *had* to be safe."

"Why, Tony?"

"If anything was to keep any meaning for me." He stared at her, himself amazed at what he said. "The moon's gone, I suppose you know!"

"Yes. It was known that it would go."

"And we—the world goes like the moon, with the return of Bronson Alpha!"

"That's still true, Tony," she said, standing before him, and quivering as he did.

He gestured about. "They all know that now."

"Yes," she said. "They've been told it."

"But they don't *know* it. They can't *know* a thing like that just from being told—or even from what they've just been through."

"Neither can we, Tony."

98

"No; we think we—you and I, at least—are going to be safe somehow. We are sure, down in our hearts—aren't we, Eve?—that you and I will pull through. There'll be some error in the calculations that will save *us;* or the Space Ship will take us away; or—something."

She nodded. "There's no error in the calculations, Tony. Too many good men have made them, independently of each other."

"Did they all count in the collision with the moon, Eve?"

"All the good ones did, dear. There's no chance of escape because of the encounter with the moon. It deflected the Bronson Bodies a little, of course; but not enough to save the world. I know that with my head, Tony; but—you're right—I don't know it with my heart. I don't know it with —*me.*"

Tony seized and held her with a fierceness and with a tenderness in his ferocity, neither of which he had ever known before. He looked down at her in his arms, and it was difficult to believe that any one so exquisite, so splendidly fragile, could have survived the orgy of elemental passion through which they all had passed. Yet that—he knew— was nothing to what would be.

He kissed her, long and deeply; and when he drew his lips away, he continued to stare down at her whispering words which she, with her lips almost at his, yet could not hear.

"What is it, Tony?"

"Only—an incantation, dear."

"What?" she asked; so he repeated it audibly:

" '*A thousand shall fall beside thee, and ten thousand at thy right hand; but it shall not come nigh thee!*' Remember it, Eve?"

"The psalmist!" whispered Eve.

"He must have seen some one he loved, threatened," said Tony. " '*For he shall give his angels charge over thee,*' " he continued, " '*to keep thee in all thy ways.*

" '*They shall bear thee in their hands; that thou hurt not thy foot against a stone.*'

"It stayed in my head, hearing it at the church where Mother used to take me. I'd read it in the responses, too. I remember that, I suppose, because it's beautiful—if no more."

"If no more," said Eve; and very gently, she freed herself from him; for, far more faithfully than he, she heeded her father.

He sighed. She looked up at him. "They tell me, Tony, that you kept the whole camp going single-handed," she returned him to practical affairs.

"I just rallied around and looked at people who were doing something and said: 'Great! Go ahead.' That's all I did."

She laughed, proud of him. "You put heart in them all again. That's you, Tony. . . . Did you know Professor Bronson is here?"

"Yes; I saw him—spoke to him. Funny feeling I had, when I heard his name. Bronson—of the Bronson Bodies. It made him almost to blame for them. How did he happen to come?"

"He'd arrived in the country and was almost here when the storm struck. He's known about what was to happen, and he's been figuring it out for a longer time than any one else. He's had the highest respect for Father. Of course you know it was to Father that he sent his results. They had to get together, Father and he. They agreed it was better to work here than in South Africa; so he did the traveling. He'll be invaluable—if we do get away."

"You mean, if we get away from the world."

"Yes. You see, Father's chief work has been—and will be—on the Space Ship; how to get away from the world and reach Bronson Beta, when it returns."

"And before Bronson Alpha smashes us as it did the moon," said Tony grimly.

Eve nodded. "That's all Father can possibly arrange—if not more. He can't take any time to figuring how we'll live, if we reach that other world. But Professor Bronson has been doing that for months. For more than a year he practically lived—in his mind—on Bronson Beta. So he's here to make the right preparation for the party that goes on the ship: who they should be, what they should carry, and what they must do to live—if they land there."

In three days the static in the air vanished to such an extent that messages from various parts of the world became audible. Out of those messages a large map was constructed in the executive offices. It was a speculative map, and its accuracy was by no means guaranteed. It showed islands where Australia had been, two huge islands in the place of South America, and only the central and southern part of Europe and Asia. There was a blank in place of Africa, for no one knew what had happened to the Dark Continent. A few points of land were all that was left of the British Isles, and over the air came the terrible story of the last-minute flight from London across the Channel, in which the populace was overwhelmed on the Great Lowland Plain. Among the minor phenomena reported was the disappearance of the Great Lakes, which had been inclined from west to east and tipped like trays of water into the valley of the St. Lawrence. On the fifth day they learned that an airplane flight had been made over what was the site of New York. The Hudson

River Valley was a deep estuary; the sea rolled up to New-burgh; and the entire coast along its new line was scoured with east-to-west-running valleys which were piled high with the wreckage of a mighty civilization. Everywhere were still foetid plains of cooling lava; and in many areas, apparently, the flow from the earth had been not molten rock but metal, which lay in fantastic and solidified seas already red with rust.

It was impossible to make any estimate whatsoever of the number of people who had survived the catastrophe. Doubtless the figure ran into scores of millions; but except in a few fortunate and prearranged places, they were desti-tute, disorganized and doomed to perish of hunger and ex-posure.

On the tenth day the sun shone for the first time. It pierced the clouds for a few minutes only, and even at its strongest it was hazy, penetrating the belts of fog with scarcely enough strength to cast shadows. . . .

At the end of two weeks it would have been difficult to tell that the settlement in Michigan had undergone any great cataclysm, save that the miniature precipice remained on the flying-field, and that great mounds of chocolate-colored earth were piled within view of the inhabitants.

On the evening of the fifteenth day a considerable patch of blue sky appeared at twilight, and for three hours afforded a view of the stars. The astronomers took advantage of that extended opportunity to make observation of the Bronson Bodies, which had become morning stars, showing rims like the planet Venus as they moved between the earth and the sun.

Carefully, meticulously, both by direct observation and by photographic methods, they measured and plotted the course of the two terrible strangers from space; and with infinitesimal differences, the results of all the observers were the same. Bronson Beta—the habitable world—on its return would pass by closer than before; but it would pass.

There would be no escape from Bronson Alpha.

In all the fifteen days the earth had not ceased trembling. Sometimes the shocks were violent enough to jar objects from shelves, but ordinarily they were so light as to be barely detectable.

In all those fifteen days, furthermore, there had been no visitor to the camp from the outside world, and the radio station had contented itself for the most part with the mes-sages it received, for fear that by giving its position and broadcasting its comparative security, it might be over-whelmed by a rush of desperate and starving survivors.

At the end of three weeks one of the airplanes which had

escaped the storm was put in condition, and Eliot James and Ransdell made a five-hundred-mile reconnaissance. At Hendron's request the young author addressed the entire gathering in the dining-hall after his return. He held spellbound the thousand men and women who were thirsty for any syllable of information about the world over the horizon.

"Mr. Ransdell and myself," James began, "took our ship off the ground this morning at eight o'clock. We flew due north for about seventy-five miles. Then we made a circle of which that distance was the radius, covering the territory that formerly constituted parts of Michigan and Wisconsin.

"I say 'formerly,' ladies and gentlemen, because the land which we observed has nothing to do with the United States as it once was, and our flight was like a journey of discovery. You have already been told that the Great Lakes have disappeared. They are, however, not entirely gone, and I should say that about one-third of Lake Superior, possibly now landlocked, remains in its bed.

"The country we covered, as you doubtless know, was formerly heavily wooded and hilly. It contained many lakes, and was a mining center. I will make no attempt to describe the astonishing aspect of the empty lake-bed, the chasms and flat beaches which were revealed when the water uncovered them, or the broad cracks and crevices which stretch across the bed. I am unable to convey to you the utter desolation of the scene. It is easier, somewhat, to give an idea of the land over which we flew. Most of the forests have been burned away. Seams have opened underneath them, which are in reality mighty cañons, abysses in the naked earth. Steam pours from them and hovers in them. All about the landscape are fumaroles, hot springs, geysers and boiling wells.

"In the course of our flight we observed the ruins of a moderate-sized town and of several villages. We also saw the charred remains of what we assumed were farms, and possibly lumber- and mining-camps. Not only have great clefts been made, but hills have been created, and in innumerable places the earth shows raw and multicolored—the purplish red of iron veins, the glaring white of quartz, the dark monotony of basalt intermingled in a giant's conglomerate. I can only suggest the majesty and the unearthliness of the scene by saying it closely resembled my conception of what the lunar landscape must have been.

"We observed a few areas which, like our own, were relatively undisturbed. There were a number of oases in this destruction where forests still stood, apparently sheltered from the hurricanes and in no danger of conflagration. This district, as you know, is sparsely settled. I will complete my wholly inadequate report to you by satisfying what must be your major curiosity: we saw in the course of our flying a number of human beings. Some of them wandered over this nude, tumultuous country alone and obviously without resources for their sustenance. Others were gathered together in small communities in the glades and sheltered places. They had fires going, and they were apparently secure at least for the time being. All of them attempted to attract our attention to themselves, and it is with regret that I must say that not only is their rescue inadvisable from the sheer necessity of our own self-preservation, but that in most cases it would be difficult if not impossible, as we found no place in which we might have landed a plane, if the surface of the water that remains in Lake Superior be excepted, and a few other ponds and lakes. And it would be difficult indeed to go on foot to the succor of those unfortunates."

After the speech, people crowded around James. Peter Vanderbilt, moving through the crowd, glimpsed Ransdell as he was walking through the front doors of the hall. The New Yorker stepped out on the porch beside the pilot; the sophisticated Manhattan *dilettante* with his smooth, graying hair, his worldly-wise and -weary eyes, his svelte accent, beside the rugged, tan-faced, blue-eyed, powerful adventurer. One, the product of millions, of Eastern universities and of society at its most sumptuous, the other a man whose entire resources always had been held in his own hands, and who had lived in a world of frontiers.

"I wanted to ask you something," Vanderbilt said. Ransdell turned, and as usual he did not speak but simply waited.

"Has Hendron commissioned you to do any more flying?"

"No."

"Do you think it would be possible to hop around the country during the next few months?"

"With a good ship—an amphibian."

Vanderbilt tapped his cigarette-holder delicately against one of the posts on the porch. "You and I are both supernumeraries around here, in a sense. I was wondering if it might not be a good idea to make an expedition around the country and see for ourselves just what has happened. If this old planet is really going to be smashed,—and from the evidence furnished two weeks ago I'll believe it,—yet there's something to see on its surface still. Let's look at it."

Ransdell thought inarticulately of Eve. He was drawn to her as never to any girl before; but, he reckoned, she must remain here. Not only that, but under the discipline which was clamped upon the settlement, no rival could claim her while he would be gone. And the adventure that Vanderbilt offered tremendously allured him.

"I'd like to try it," Ransdell replied simply.

"Then I'll see Hendron; we must have his consent, of course, to take a ship."

Ransdell was struck by a thought. "Shall we take James too? He'd join, I think."

"Excellent," Vanderbilt accepted. "He could write up the trip. It would be ignominious, if any of us got to Bronson Beta, with no record of the real history of this old earth's last days."

Together they broached the subject to Hendron. He considered them for several minutes without replying, and then said: "You realize, of course, that such an expedition will be extremely hazardous? You could carry fuel and provisions for a long flight, but nothing like what you'd need. You'd have to take pot-luck everywhere you went; gasoline would be almost impossible to find—what hasn't leaked away must have been burned, for the most part; and whenever you set the ship down, you would be a target for any and every person lurking in the vicinity. The conditions prevailing, physically, socially and morally, must be wholly without precedent."

"That," replied Vanderbilt calmly, "is precisely why we cannot be men and fear to study them."

"Exactly," jerked Hendron; and he gazed at Ransdell.

The gray-blue eyes fixed steadily on Hendron's, and the scientist abruptly decided: "Very well, I'll sanction it."

Ransdell and Vanderbilt knocked on the door of Eliot James' room, from which issued the sound of typewriting. The poet swung wide the door and greeted them with an expression of pleasure. "What's up?"

They told him.

"Go?" James repeated, his face alight with excitement. "Of course I'll go. What a record to write—whether or not any one lives to read it!"

Tony received the news with mingled feelings. He could not help an impulse of jealousy at not being chosen for the adventure; but he understood that Ransdell hardly would have selected him. Also, he realized that his position as vice to Hendron in command of the cantonment did not leave him free for adventure.

Yet it was almost with shame that Tony assisted in the take-off of the big plane two days later. Eve emerged from the crowd at the edge of the landing-field and walked to Ransdell; and Tony saw the light in her eyes which comes to a woman watching a man embark on high adventure. The very needlessness, the impracticalness of it, increased her feeling for him—a feeling not to be roused by a man performing a merely useful service, no matter how hazardous. Tony walked around to the other side of the plane and stayed there until Eve had said good-by to the pilot.

The motor was turning over slowly. The mechanics had made their last inspection. The maximum amount of fuel had been taken aboard, and all provisions, supplies, ammunition, instruments and paraphernalia which were deemed needful. Many of the more prominent members of the colony were grouped near the plane shaking hands with Vanderbilt and Eliot James. Bronson was there, Dodson, Smith and a dozen more, besides Hendron. Vanderbilt's farewells were debonair and light. "We'll send you postcards picturing latest developments." Eliot James was receiving last-minute advice from the scientists, who had burdened him with questions, the answers of which they wished him to discover by observation. Ransdell came around the fuselage of the plane, Eve behind him.

He cast one look at the sky, where the heavy and still numerous clouds moved on a regular wind, and one at the available half of the landing-field, on which the sun shone tentatively.

"Let's go," he said.

There were a few last handshakes; there was a shout as the chocks were removed from the wheels of the plane. It made a long bumpy run across the field, rose slowly, circled once over the heads of the waving throng, and gradually disappeared toward the south.

Eve signaled Tony. "Aren't they fine, those three men? Going off into nowhere like that."

Tony made his answer enthusiastic. "I never thought I'd meet three such people in my life—one, perhaps, but not three. And there are literally hundreds of people here who are capable of the same sort of thing."

Eve was still watching the plane. "I like Dave Ransdell."

"No one could help liking him," Tony agreed.

"He's so interested in everything, and yet so aloof," went on Eve, still watching. "In spite of all he's been through with us, he's still absolutely terrified of me."

"I can understand that," said Tony grimly.

"But you've never been that way around me."

"I didn't show it that way; no. But I know—and you know —what it means."

"Yes, I know," Eve replied simply.

The sun, which had been shielded by a cloud, suddenly shone on them, and both glanced toward it.

Off there to the side of the sun, hidden by its glare, moved the Bronson Bodies on their paths which would cause them to circle the sun and return—one to pass close to the earth and the other to shatter the world—in little more than seven months more.

105

"If they are away only thirty days, we're not to count them missing," Eve was saying—of the crew of the airplane, of course. "If they're not back in thirty—we're to forget them. Especially we're not to send any one to search for them."

"Who said so?"

"David. It's the last thing he asked."

Chapter 16—The Saga

THE thirty days raced by. Under the circumstances, time could not drag. Nine-tenths of the people at Hendron's encampment spent their waking and sleeping hours under a death-sentence. No one could be sure of a place on the Space Ship. No one, in fact, was positive that the colossal rocket would be able to leave the earth. Every man, every woman, knew that in six months the two Bronson Bodies would return from their rush into the space beyond the sun; even the most sanguine knew that a contact was inevitable.

Consequently every day, every hour, was precious to them. They were intelligent, courageous people. They collaborated in keeping up the general morale. The various department heads in the miniature city made every effort to occupy their colleagues and workers—and Hendron's own foresight had assisted in the procedure. . . .

The First Passage was followed by relative calm. As soon as order had been restored, a routine was set up. Every one had his or her duty. Those duties were divided into five parts: First, the preparation of the rocket itself; second, the preparation of the rocket's equipment and load; third, observation of the receding and returning Bodies to determine their nature and exact course; fourth, maintenance of the life of the colony; fifth, miscellaneous occupations.

Hendron, in charge of the first division, spent most of his time in the rocket's vast hangar, the laboratories and the machine-shop. Bronson headed the second division. The third duty was shared by several astronomers; and in this division Eve, with her phenomenal skill in making precise measurements, was an important worker. The maintenance division was under the direction of Dodson, and under Dodson, a subcommittee headed by Jack Taylor took charge of sports and amusements. Tony was assigned to the miscellaneous category, as were the three absent adventurers.

The days did not suffice for the work to be done, particularly in preparation of the Space Ship.

Hendron had the power. Under the pressure of impending doom, the group laboring under him had "liberated" the amazing energy in the atom—under laboratory conditions. They had possessed, therefore, a potential driving power enormously in excess of that ever made available before. They could "break up" the atom at will, and set its almost endless energies to work; but what material could harness that energy and direct it into a driving force for the Space Ship?

Hendron and his group experimented for hour after desperate hour through their days, with one metal, another alloy and another after another.

At night, in the reaction of relaxation, there were games, motion pictures which had been preserved, and a variety of private enterprises which included organization and rehearsal of a very fine orchestra. There were dances, too; and while the thin crescents of the Bronson Bodies hung in the sky like cosmic swords of Damocles, there were plays satirizing human hopes and fates in the shed next to that wherein the Space Ship, still lacking its engine, was being prepared.

The excellent temper of the colony was flawed rarely. However, there were occasional lapses. One night during a dance a girl from California suddenly became hysterical and was carried from the hall shouting: *I won't die!* On another occasion a Berlin astronomer was found dead in his bed—beside him an empty bottle of sleeping-powders holding down a note which read: *"Esteemed friends: The vitality of youth is required to meet the tension of these terrible days with calmness. I salute you."* The astronomer was buried with honors.

Tony perceived an evidence of the increasing tension in Eve when they walked, late one afternoon, through the nearby woods.

She saw on the pine-needle carpet of the forest a white flower. She plucked it, looked at it, smelled it and carried it away. After they had proceeded silently for some distance, she said: "It's strange to think about matters like this flower. To think that there will never be any more flowers like this again in the universe—unless we take seeds with us!"

"That impresses you, perhaps," said Tony, "because we can come closer to realizing the verdict—no more flowers—than we can the verdict 'no more us.'"

"I suppose so, Tony. Did David ever tell you that, in his first conference at Capetown with Lord Rhondin and Professor Bronson, they were excited over realizing there would be no more lions?"

"No," said Tony, very quietly. "He never mentioned it to me."

"Tell me, Tony," she asked quickly, "you aren't jealous?"

"How, under the conditions laid down by your father," retorted Tony, "could anybody be 'jealous'? You're not going to be free to pick or choose your own husband—or mate—or whatever he'll be called, on Bronson Beta. And if we never get there, certainly I'll have nothing to be jealous about."

The strain was telling, too, on Tony.

"He may not even return to us here," Eve reminded. "And we would never know what happened to the three of them."

"It would have to be a good deal, to stop them. Each one's damn' resourceful in his own way; and Ransdell is sure a flyer," Tony granted ungrudgingly. "Yet if the plane cracked, they'd never get back. There's not a road ten miles long that isn't broken by some sort of landslip or a chasm. Land travel has simply ceased. It isn't possible that there's a railroad of any length anywhere in operation; and a car would have to be an amphibian as well as a tank to get anywhere.

"Sometimes, when day follows day and nobody arrives or passes, I think it must mean that every one else in the world is dead; then I remember the look of the land—especially of the roads, and I understand it. This certainly has become a mess of a world; and I suppose the best we can expect is some such state awaiting us," Tony smiled grimly, "if we get across to Bronson Beta.

"No; that's one of the funny things about our possible future situation. If we get across to Bronson Beta, we'll find far less damage there."

"Why?" Tony had not happened to be with the scientists when this had been discussed.

"Because Bronson Beta seems certain to be a world a lot like this; and it has never been as close as we have been to Bronson Alpha. It wasn't the passing of Bronson Beta that tore us up so badly; it was the passing of the big one, Bronson Alpha. Now, Bronson Beta has never been nearly so close to Bronson Alpha, as we have been. Beta circles Alpha, but never gets within half a million miles of it. So if we ever step upon that world, we'll find it about as it has been."

"As it has been—for how many years?" Tony asked.

"The ages and epochs of travel through space. . . . You ought to talk more with Professor Bronson, Tony. He just *lives* there. He's so sure we'll get there! Exactly how, he doesn't bother about; he's passed that on to Father. His work assumes we can get across space in the Ship, and land. He starts with the landing; what may we reasonably expect to find there, beyond water and air—and soil? Which of us, who may make up the possible crew of the ship, will have most chances to survive under the probable conditions? What immediate supplies and implements—food and so on—must we have with us? What ultimate supplies—seeds and seedlings to furnish us with food later? What animals, what birds and insects and crustacea, should we take along?

"You see, that world must be dead, Tony. It must have been dead, preserved in the frightful, complete cold of absolute zero for millions of years. . . . You'd be surprised at some of the assumptions Professor Bronson makes.

"He assumes, among other things, that we can find some

108

edible food—some sort of grain, probably, which absolute zero would have preserved. He assumes that some vegetable life—the vegetation that springs from spores, which mere cold cannot destroy—will spring to life automatically.

"Tony, you must see his lists of the most essential things to take with us. His work is the most fascinating here. What animals, do you supose, he's figured we must take with us to help us to survive?"

On the tenth of September, the inhabitants of the strangely isolated station which existed for the perfection of the Space Ship, began to look—although prematurely—for the return of the explorers into the world which had been theirs.

The three had agreed on the fourteenth as the first possible day for their return; but so great was the longing to learn the state of the outside world, that on the twelfth even those who felt no particular concern for the men who ventured in the airplane, began to watch the sky, casting upward glances as their duties took them out of doors.

It was difficult for anyone to work on the appointed day. The fourteenth was bright. The wind was gentle and visibility good—although the weather had never returned to what would have been considered normal for northern Michigan in the summer. There was always a moderate amount of haze. Sometimes the sky was obscured by new and interminable clouds of volcanic dust. The thermometer ranged between eighty and ninety-five, seldom falling below the first figure. From the laboratory, the dining-halls, the shops, power-house, kitchens and the hangar, men and women constantly emerged into the outdoors to stand silently, inspecting the sky.

No one went to bed that night until long after the usual hour. Then, reluctantly, those overwearied, those who had arduous tasks and heavy responsibilities on the morrow, regretfully withdrew. Fears now had voices.

"They're so damn' resourceful, I can't believe they could miss out."

"But—after all—what do we know about outside conditions?"

"Think of the risks! God only knows what they might have faced. Anything, from the violence of a mob to a volcanic blast blowing them out of the sky."

Tony was in charge of the landing arrangements. At three A.M. he was sitting on the edge of the field with Eve. Hendron had left, after giving instructions that he was to be wakened if they arrived. They had little to say to each other. They sat with straining eyes and ears. Coffee and soup simmered on a camp-stove near the plane-shed against which they leaned their chairs. Dr. Dodson lay on a cot, ready in case the landing should result in accident.

At four, nothing had changed. It began to grow light. Since the passing of the Bronson Bodies, dawn had been minutes earlier than formerly.

Eve stood up stiffly and stretched. "Maybe I'd better leave. I have some work laid out for morning."

But she had not walked more than ten steps when she halted.

"I thought I heard motors," she said.

Tony nodded, unwilling to break the stillness. A dog barked in the camp. Far away toward the stockyards a rooster crowed. The first sun rays tipped the lowest clouds with gold.

Then the sound came unmistakably. For a full minute they heard the rise and fall of a churning motor—remote, soft, yet unmistakable.

"It's coming!" Eve said. She rushed to Tony and held his shoulder.

He lifted his hand. The sound vanished, came back again —a waspish drone somewhere in the sky. Their eyes swept the heavens. Then they saw it simultaneously—a speck in the dawning atmosphere. The speck enlarged. It took the shape of a cross.

"Tony!" Eve breathed.

The ship was not flying well. It lurched and staggered in its course.

Tony rushed to the cot where Dodson slept. "They're coming," he said, shaking the Doctor. "And they may need you."

The ship was nearer. Those who beheld it now appreciated not only the irregularity of its course, but the fact that it was flying slowly.

"They've only got two motors," somebody said. The words were not shouted.

Scarcely breathing, they stood at the edge of the field. The pilot did not wiggle his wings or circle. In a shambling slip he dropped toward the ground, changing his course a little in order not to strike the ten-foot precipice which had bisected the field. The plane was a thousand yards from the ground. Five hundred.

"She's going to crash!" some one yelled.

Tony, Dodson and Jack Taylor were already in a light truck. Fire-apparatus and stretchers were in the space behind them. The truck's engine raced.

The plane touched the ground heavily, bounced, touched again, ran forward and slewed. It nosed over. The propeller on the forward engine bent.

Tony threw in the clutch of the car and shot toward it. As he approached, he realized that fire had not started. He leaped from the truck, and with the Doctor and Jack at his heels, he flung open the cabin door and looked into the canted chamber.

Everything that the comfortable cabin had once contained was gone. Two men lay on the floor at the forward end—Vanderbilt and James. Ransdell was unconscious over the instrument panel. Vanderbilt looked up at Tony. His face was paper-white; his shirt was blood-soaked. And yet there showed momentarily in the fading light in his eyes a spark of unquenchable, deathless, reckless and almost diabolical glee. His voice was quite distinct. He said: "In the words of the immortal Lindbergh, *'Here we are.'*" Then he fainted.

James was unconscious.

The truck came back toward the throng very slowly and carefully. In its bed, Dodson looked up from his three charges. He announced briefly as way was made for them: "They've been through hell. They're shot, bruised, half-starved. But so far, I've found nothing surely fatal." Then to Tony, who was still driving: "You can put on a little speed, Tony. I want to get these boys where I can treat them."

Two or three hundred people waited outside the surgery door for an hour. Then a man appeared and said: "Announcements will be made about the condition of the flyers in the dining-hall at breakfast time."

The waiting crowd moved away.

An hour later, with every member of the community who could leave his post assembled, Hendron stepped to the rostrum in the dining-hall.

"All three will live," he said simply.

Cheering made it impossible for him to continue. He waited for silence. "James has a broken arm and concussion. Vanderbilt has been shot through the shoulder. Ransdell brought in the ship with a compound fracture of the left arm, and five machine-gun bullets in his right thigh. They undoubtedly have traveled for some time in that state. Ransdell's feat is one of distinguished heroism."

Again cheering broke tumultuously through the hall. Again Hendron stood quietly until it subsided. "This evening we will meet again. At that time I shall read to you from the diary which James kept during the past thirty days. I have skimmed some of its pages. It is a remarkable document. I must prepare you by saying, my friends, that those of our fellow human beings who have not perished, have reverted to savagery, almost without notable exception."

A hush followed those words. Then Hendron stepped from the platform, and a din of excited conversation filled the room. The scientist stopped to speak to three or four people, then came over to his daughter. He seemed excited.

"Eve," he said, "I want you and Drake to come to the office right away."

111

Bronson and Dodson were already there when they arrived.

A dozen other men joined them; and last to appear was Hendron himself. Every one was standing, and Hendron invited them to sit down. It was easy to perceive his excitement now. His surpassingly calm blue eyes were fiery. His cheeks concentrated their color in two red spots. He commenced to speak immediately.

"My friends, the word I have to add to my announcement in the hall is of stupendous importance!

"When we took off Ransdell's clothes, we found belted to his body, and heavily wrapped, a note, a map, and a chunk of metal. You will remember, doubtless, that Ransdell was once a miner and a prospector. His main interest had always been diamonds. And his knowledge of geology and metallurgy is self-taught and of the practical sort."

Bronson, unable to control himself, burst into speech. "Good God, Hendron! He found it!"

The scientist continued impassively: "The eruptions caused by the passage of the Bodies were of so intense a nature that they brought to earth not only modern rock, but vast quantities of the internal substance of the earth—which, as you know, is presumably of metal, as the earth's total density is slightly greater than that of iron. Ransdell noticed on the edge of such a flow a quantity of solid unmelted material. Realizing that the heat surrounding it had been enormous, he secured specimens. He found the substance to be a metal or natural alloy, hard but machineable. Remembering our dilemma here in the matter of lining for the power tubes for the Space Ship, he carefully carried back a sample—protecting it, in fact, with his life.

"My friends,"—Hendron's voice began to tremble—"for the past seventy-five minutes this metal has withstood not only the heat of an atomic blast, but the immeasurably greater heat of Professor Kane's recently developed atomic furnace. We are at the end of the quest!"

Suddenly, to the astonishment of his hearer, Hendron bowed his head in his arms and cried like a woman.

No one moved. They waited in respect, or in a gratitude that was almost hysterical. In a few moments Hendron lifted his face.

"I apologize. These are days when nerves are worn thin. But all of you must realize the strain under which I have labored. Perhaps you will forgive me. I am moved to meditate on the almost supernatural element of this discovery. At a time when nature has doomed the world, she seems to have offered the means of escape to those who, let us hope and trust, are best fitted to save her most imaginative gesture of creation—mankind."

112

Hendron bowed his head once more, and Eve came wordlessly to his side.

Hendron stood before an audience of nearly a thousand persons. It was a feverish audience. It had a gayety mingled with solemnity such as, on a smaller scale, overwhelmed the thoughtful on a night in November in 1918 when the Armistice had been signed.

Hendron bowed to the applause.

"I speak to you to-night, my friends, in the first full flush of the knowledge that your sacrifices and sufferings have not been in vain. Ransdell has solved our last technical problem. We have assured ourselves by observation that life on the planet-to-be will be possible. My heart is surging with pride and wonderment when I find myself able to say: man shall live; we are the forefathers of his new history."

The wild applause proclaimed the hopes no one had dared declare before.

"But to-night I wish to talk not of the future. There is time enough for that. I wish to talk—or rather to read—of the present." He picked up from a small table the topmost of a number of ordinary notebooks. "I have here James' record of the journey that brought us salvation. I cannot read you all of it. But I shall have it printed in the course of the next few days. I anticipate that printing merely because I understand your collective interest in the document.

"This is the first of the seven notebooks James filled. I shall read with the minimum of comment."

He opened the book. He read:

"'August 16th. To-night Ransdell, Vanderbilt and I descended at six o'clock precisely on a small body of water which is a residue in a bed of Lake Michigan. We are lying at anchor about a mile from Chicago.

"'Our journey has been bizarre in the extreme. Following south along what was once the coast of Lake Michigan, we flew over scenes of desolation and destruction identical with those described after our first reconnaissance. In making this direct-line flight, it was forced upon our reluctant intelligence that the world has indeed been wrecked.

"'The resultant feeling of eeriness reached its quintessence when we anchored here. Sharply outlined against the later afternoon sun stood the memorable skyline of the metropolis—relatively undamaged! With an emotion of indescribable joy, after the hours of depressive desolation, I recognized the Wrigley Building, the Tribune Tower, the 333 North Michigan Avenue Building, and others. My companions shouted, evidently sharing my emotions.

"'We had landed on the water from the north. We anchored near shore and quickly made our way to land. We exercised certain precautions, however. All of us were armed. Lots were drawn to determine whether Ransdell or Vanderbilt would remain on guard beside the ship. I was useless in that capacity, as I would be unable to fly it in case of emergency. It was agreed that the lone guard was to take off instantly upon the approach of any persons whatever. Our ship was our only refuge, our salvation, our life-insurance.

" 'Vanderbilt was elected to remain. Ransdell and I started off at once toward the city. The pool on which we lay was approximately a mile in diameter and some two hundred feet below the level of the city. We started across the weird water-bottom. Mud, weeds, wrecks, débris, puddles, cracks, cliffs and steep ascents impeded our progress. But we reached the edge of what had been a lake, without mishap. The angle of our ascent had concealed the city during the latter part of our climb.

" 'Our first close view was had as we scrambled to the top of a sea-wall. The streets of the metropolis stretched before us—empty. The silence of the grave, of the tomb. Chicago was a dead city.

" 'We stood on the top of the wall for a few minutes. We strained our ears and eyes. There was nothing. No light in the staring windows. No plume of steam on the lofty buildings. We started forward together. Unconsciously, we had both drawn our revolvers.

" 'Behind us and to the right was the Navy Pier, which I remember as the Municipal Pier. Directly ahead of us were the skyscrapers of the northern business district. We observed them from this closer point only after we had been reassured by the silence of the city, and had slipped our revolvers back into our pockets. Large sections of brick and stonework had been shaken from the sides of the buildings, leaving yawning holes which looked as if caused by shell-fire. The great windows had been shaken into the street, and wherever we went, we found the sidewalks literally buried in broken glass. A still more amazing phenomenon was noticeable from our position on the lake shore: the skyscrapers were visibly out of plumb. We made no measurements of this angulation, but I imagine some of the towers were off center by several feet, perhaps by as much as fifteen or twenty feet. No doubt the earthquakes in the vicinity had been relatively light, but the wavelike rise and fall of the land had been sufficient to tilt these great edifices, much as if they had been sticks standing perpendicularly in soft mud.

" 'Ransdell and I commented on the strangeness of the spectacle, and then together we moved forward into the business district. We had crossed the railroad tracks before we found any bodies; but on the other side they appeared here and there—most of them lying underneath the cascades of glass, horribly mangled and now in a state of decomposition.

" 'It was Ransdell who turned to me and in his mono-syllabic, taciturn way said: "No rats. Noticed it?"

" 'I was stricken by a double feeling of horror, first in the realization that upon such a ghastly scene the armies of rats should be marching, and second by the meaning of Ransdell's words—that if there were no rats, there must be some dreadful mystery to explain their absence.

" 'We walked over the rubble and glass in the streets. Here and there it was necessary to circumvent an enormous pile of débris which had cascaded from the side of one of the buildings. It was immediately manifest that the people who had left Chicago had taken with them every object upon which they could lay their hands, every possession which they coveted, every article for which they thought they might find use. The stores were like open bazaars; their glass windows had been broken in by marauders or burst out by the quakes, and their contents had been ravaged.

" 'We continued to notice that the dead on the street did not represent even a tithe of the metropolitan population, and I expressed the opinion that the passing of the Bronson Bodies must have caused a mighty exodus.

" 'Ransdell's reply was a shrug, and abruptly my mind was discharged upon a new course. "You think they're all up-stairs?" I asked.

" 'He nodded. A block farther along, we came to an open fissure. It was not a large fissure in comparison with the gigantic openings in the earth which we had seen hitherto, but it appeared to go deep into the earth, and a thin veil of steam escaped from it. As we approached it, the wind blew toward us a wisp of this exuding gas, and instantly we were thrown into fits of coughing. Our lungs burned, our eyes stung and our senses were partially confounded, so that with one accord we snatched each other's arms and ran uncertainly from the place.

" ' "Gas," Ransdell said, gasping.

" 'No other words were necessary to interpret the frightful fate of Chicago; nothing could better demonstrate how profound was the disturbance under the earth's crust. For in this region noted for its freedom from seismic shocks and remote from the recognized volcanic region, it was evident that deadly, suffocating gases such as previously had found the surface only through volcanoes, here had seeped up and blotted out the population. When the Bronson Bodies were nearest the earth and the stresses began to break the crust—when, doubtless, part of the population in that great interior metropolis were madly fleeing and another part was grimly holding on—there were discharged somewhere in the vicinity deadly gases of the sort which suffocated the people about Mt.

Pelée and La Soufrière. Only this emission of gas—whether through cracks in the crust or through some true new crater yet to be discovered—was incomparably greater. Like those gases, largely hydrochloric, it was heavier than air; and apparently it lay like a choking cloud on the ground. When those who escaped the first suffocating currents—and apparently they were in the majority—climbed to upper floors to escape, they were followed by the rising vapors. That frightful theory explained why there were so few dead on the street, why no one had returned to the silent city, and above all, why there were no rats.

" 'We would have liked to climb up the staircases of some of the buildings to test the accuracy of our concepts so far as it might concern the numbers who had remained in the city, to be smothered by gas, but darkness was approaching.

" 'We were sure of Vanderbilt's safety, for we had heard no shot. It was odd to think that we could expect to hear such a shot at a distance of more than a mile when we were standing in a place where recently the machine-gun fire of gangsters had been almost inaudible in the roaring daylight. Moreover, our single experience with the potency of the gas even in dilution warned us that a deeper penetration of the metropolitan area was more than dangerous.

" 'We found Vanderbilt sitting upon a stone on the shore beside the plane. We pushed out to it in the collapsible boat; and while we ate supper, we told him what we had seen.

" 'His comment perhaps is suitable for closing this record of the great city of Chicago: "Sitting alone, I realized what you were investigating; and for the first time, gentlemen, I understand what the end of the world would mean. I have never come so close to losing my nerve. It was awful." ' "

Hendron looked up from the book. "I think, my friends, we will all find ourselves in agreement with Mr. James and Mr. Vanderbilt." He turned a few pages, and their whisper was audible in the silence of his audience. "I am now skipping a portion of Mr. James' record. It covers their investigation of the Great Lakes and describes with care the geological uplifting of that basin. From Chicago they flew to Detroit. In Detroit they found a different form of desolation. The waters of Lake Huron had poured through the city and the surrounding district, completely depopulating it and largely destroying it. They were able to land their plane on a large boulevard, a section of which was unbroken, and they refueled in the vicinity. They were disturbed by no one, and they saw no one. Cleveland had suffered a similar fate. Then they continued their flight to Pittsburgh. I read from Mr. James' record:

" 'Like God leading the children of Israel, Pittsburgh remains in my memory as a pillar of cloud by day and of fire by night. My astonishment may be imagined when I say that, as we approached the city after our visit to the ravaged metropolises of Ohio, we saw smoke arising against the sky. Presently the lichen-like area of buildings began to clarify in the morning haze. Vanderbilt dampered the motors and we dropped toward the Monongahela River, which was full to the brim of the levees and threatened to inundate the city. Earthquakes had half wrecked its structures. They lay broken and battered on "The Point" which lies between the two rivers. Smoke and steam emerged from a rent in Mt. Washington. The bridges were all down. I noticed that one of them had fallen directly upon a river steamer in which human beings had evidently sought to escape.

"'Our ship came to rest, and we taxied cautiously toward one of the submerged bridges—every landing on water was dangerous, because of the likelihood of unsuspected snags, and we always exercised the maximum of care. From the top of the pontoon I threw a rope over one of the girders, and we made fast, the perceptible current keeping us clear. We went ashore by way of the taut rope.

"'It was easy to perceive the cause of the smoke. A large area of Pittsburgh, or what remained of Pittsburgh, was in flames, and to our ears came clearly a not distant din. We had already guessed its identity in our descent. It was the din of battle. Rifles cracked incessantly; machine-guns clattered; and occasionally we heard the cough of a hand-grenade.

"'It was not wise to proceed farther. Nevertheless, bent upon discovering the nature of the combat, I insisted on going forward while my companions returned to guard our precious ship. I had not invaded the city deeply before I saw evidence of the fighting. Bullets buzzed overhead. I took cover. Not far away, in a street that was a shambles, I saw men moving. They carried rifles which they fired frequently; and they wore, I perceived, the tattered remnants of the uniform of the National Guard.

"'A squad of these men retreated toward me, and as they did so, I perceived their enemy. Far down the street a mass of people surged over the barricade-like ruins of a building. They were terrible to see, even at that distance. Half naked, savage, screaming, armed with every tool that might be used as a weapon—a mob of the most desperate sort. The retreating squad stopped, took aim and several of the approaching savages fell. In their united voices I detected the tones of women.

"As the guardsmen reached my vicinity, one of them clapped his hand to his arm, dropped his rifle and staggered away from his fellows to shelter. The squad was at that instant reënforced by a number of soldiers who carried a machine-gun. The mob was temporarily checked by its clatter.

" 'I made my way to the wounded man, and he gratefully accepted the ministrations I could offer from the small kit I carried in my pocket. His right arm had been pierced. It was from him that I was able to learn the story of Pittsburgh. Some day I hope I may expand his tale into a complete document, but since my time at the moment is short, and since we are now flying southward and writing is difficult, I will compress it.

" 'The man's name was George Schultz. He had been a bank-clerk, married, the father of two children, and had joined the National Guard because it offered an opportunity for recreation. He told me rather pitifully that he had doubted the menace of the Bronson Bodies, and that he had compelled his wife to keep the children in their flat, against her better judgment. His wife had wished to take them to their aunt's home in Kansas. On the night of the twenty-sixth, although frightened by the size of the Bronson Bodies, he had nonchalantly gone out to a drug-store for cigarettes, and the first tremor which struck Pittsburgh had shaken down his home on the heads of his family. He was not very clear about the next forty-eight hours.

" 'The mills at Pittsburgh had been working to the last moment. The Government deemed that the great steel city was in no danger from the tides, and had used it for manufacturing during the last days. Schultz described to me the horrible effect of the earthquakes in the steel-mills, as blast furnaces were upset and as ladles tipped their molten contents onto the mill floors. Hundreds perished in the artificial hell that existed in the steel mills; but tens of thousands died in the city proper. In many parts of the city area the effect of the earthquakes was rendered doubly more frightful by the collapse of the honeycomb of mine galleries underlying the surface. Blocks of buildings literally dropped out of sight in some places.

" 'After the quake, what was left of the administrative powers immediately organized the remnant of the police and National Guard. Food, water and medical attention were their first objectives, and policing only a secondary consideration. However, food ran low; medical supplies gave out; the populace rebelled.

" 'Three days before our arrival, a mob had armed itself, stormed one of the warehouses in which a commissary functioned, and captured it. Encouraged by that success, the mob had attempted to take over the distribution of the remaining food and supplies.

" 'I had appeared on the scene apparently after the mob and the forces of law and order had been fighting for three days; and it was not necessary for Schultz to explain to me that in a very short time the National Guardmen and police would be routed: their numbers were vastly inferior; their ammunition was being exhausted, and organized warfare was out of the question in that madman's terrain.

"'I abandoned Schultz to his comrades and made my way back to the river.

"'We lost no time in taking off; and as we flew over Pittsburgh, we could see below us, moving antlike through the ruins, the savage mob, with scattered bands of guardsmen and police opposing it.'"

Again Hendron looked up from the notebook.

"That, my friends, ends the account of the fate of Pittsburgh.

"Mr. James' diary next describes a hazardous flight across the Appalachians and their arrival at Washington, or rather the site of Washington: 'It is not possible to describe our feelings when we actually flew over the site of Washington. We had passed the state in which emotions may be expressed by commonplace thought. We had reached a condition, in fact, where our senses rejected all feeling, and our brains made a record that might be useful in the future while it was insensible in the present. When I say that the ocean covered what had been the Capital of our nation, I mean it precisely. No spire, no pinnacle, no monument, no tower appeared above the blue water that rippled to the feet of the Appalachian chain. There was no trace of Chesapeake Bay, no sign of the Potomac River, no memory of the great works of architecture which had existed at the Capital. It was gone— gone into the grave of Atlantis; and over it was the inscrutable salt sea, stretching to the utmost reaches of the eye. The Eastern seaboard has dropped. We turned back after assuring ourselves that this condition obtained along the entire East Coast.'

"Mr. James," Hendron said, "now describes their return across the mountains. He adds to our geographical knowledge by revealing that the whole Mississippi Basin, as well as the East Coast and Gulf States, has been submerged. Cincinnati is under water. The sea swells not only over Memphis but over St. Louis, where it becomes a wide estuary stretching in two great arms almost to Chicago and to Davenport.

"They next investigated the refuge area in the Middle West. Here they found indescribable chaos, and although order was being made out of it, although they were hospitably received by the President himself in Hutchinson, Kansas, which had become the temporary Capital of the United States, they found the migrated population in a sorry plight. Mr. James uses the President's own words to describe that predicament. Again I refer to the diary.

"'Following the directions we had been given, we flew to Hutchinson. For a number of reasons, Hutchinson had been chosen as the temporary Capital of the States refuge area. It is normally fifteen hundred feet above sea level. It is in the center of a rich grain, farm, poultry, dairy, live-stock and lumber region. It has large packing plants, grain elevators, creameries, flour-mills. It is served by three railroads, and hence is an excellent site for the accumulation of produce. Thither, in the weeks preceding the passage of the Bronson Bodies, the multitudes of the United States flocked.

" 'The speed of that migration accelerated greatly after the Bronson Bodies had appeared above the southern horizon, and the most obtuse person could appreciate in their visible diameter the approach of something definite and fearful. It is estimated that more than eleven million people from the East Coast and three million from the West Coast actually reached the Mississippi Valley before the arrival of the Bodies. More than half of them were exterminated by the tide which rushed up the valley and which remained in the form of a gigantic bay in the new sunken area that now almost bisects the United States. We found Hutchinson a scene of prodigious military and civil activity—it resembled more than anything else an area behind the front lines in some titanic war.

" 'After presentation of our credentials and a considerable wait, we left our plane, which was put under a heavy guard, and drove in an automobile to the new "White House"—a ramshackle rehabilitation of a huge metal garage. Here we found the President and his Cabinet; and here sitting around a table, we listened to his words. The President was worn and thin. His hand trembled visibly as he smoked. We learned later that he had been living on a diet of beans and bacon. He looked at us with considerable interest and said: "I sent for you, because I wished to hear about Cole Hendron's project. I know what he is planning to do, and I'm eager to learn if he thinks he will be successful."

" 'We explained the situation to the President, and he was delighted to know that we had survived the crises of the Passing. He then continued gravely: "I believe that Hendron will be successful. You alone, perhaps, may carry away the hope of humanity and the records of this life on earth; and I will return to the tasks confronting me here with the solace offered by the knowledge that the enterprise could be in no—" ' "

Here Hendron stopped, realizing that he was reading praise of himself to his colleagues. A subdued murmur of sympathetic amusement ran through the crowd of listeners, and the scientist read again from James' journal.

" ' "The theory of migration to the Western Plains," the President told us, "was correct in so far as it concerned escape from the tides. It was mistaken only in that it underestimated the fury of the quakes, and particularly the force and

120

velocity of the hurricane which accompanied them. I removed from Washington on the night of the twenty-fourth. At that time the migration was proceeding in an orderly fashion. Transcontinental highways, and particularly the Lincoln Highway, were choked with traffic, and railroads were overburdened; but the cantonments were ready, the food was here, the spring crops were thriving and I felt reasonably certain that with millions of my countrymen the onslaught might be survived. I doubted, and I still profoundly doubt, that the earth itself will be destroyed by a collision. Accurate as the predictions of the scientists may be, I still trust that God Himself will intervene if necessary with some unforeseen derangement and save the planet from total destruction.'

" 'The President then described the passing of the Bronson Bodies and their effect on the prodigious Plains Settlement on the night of the twenty-fifth.

" ' "We were as nearly ready as could be expected. People arrived in the area at the rate of three hundred thousand per hour that night. Tent colonies if nothing better, bulging granaries and a hastily made but strong supply organization were ready for them.

" ' "Then the blow fell. Throughout the district the earth opened up. Lava poured from it. On the western boundary of our territory, which extended into Eastern Colorado, a veritable sea of lava and molten metal poured into the country drained by the Solomon, Saline, Smoky Hill and Arkansas rivers. A huge volcanic range was thrown up along the North Platte. Many if not most of our flimsily constructed buildings were toppled to the ground in utter confusion. However, for the first few hours of this awful disaster most of our people escaped. It was the hurricane which went through our ranks like a scythe. In this flat country the wind blew unobstructed. Those who could, hastened into cyclone-cellars, of which there are many. These cellars, however, often collapsed from the force of the earthquakes, and many died in them. No one knows what velocity the wind attained, but an idea of it may be had by the fact that it swept the landscape almost bare, that it moved our stone buildings.

" ' "This wind-driven scourge, which continued for thirty-six hours, abated on a scene of ruin. When I emerged from the cellar in which I had remained, I did not believe that a single one of my countrymen had survived it until I saw them reappear slowly, painfully, more often wounded than not, like soldiers coming out of shell-holes after an extensive bombardment. Our titanic effort had been for nothing. With the remnant of our ranks, we collected what we could find of our provisions and stores. In that hurricane my hopes of a united and re-formed United States were dashed to the ground. I now am struggling to preserve, not so much the nation, but

121

that fraction of the race which has been left under my command; and I struggle against tremendous odds.'

" 'Those were the words of the President of the United States. After the interview he wished us God-speed and good fortune in our projected journey; and we left him, a solitary figure whose individual greatness had been like a rock to his people.' "

Hendron put down the fifth of the notebooks from which he had been reading. "We now come," he said, "to the last stages of this remarkable flight. James' sixth diary describes the grant of fuel to them by the President, and their departure from the ruins of the great mushroom area that had grown up in Kansas and Nebraska, only to be destroyed. They made an attempt at flight over the Rockies, but found there conditions both terrestrial and atmospheric which turned them back. Hot lava still belched from the age-old hills; the sky was sulphurous and air-currents and temperature wholly uncertain. They had been flying for three weeks, sleeping little, living on bad food, and it was time for them to return if they were to keep their pledged date. They decided to go back by way of St. Paul and Milwaukee.

"On the way to St. Paul, they were forced down on a small lake and it was there that Ransdell noticed the unmelted metal in a flow of magma. The country was apparently deserted, and they investigated a tongue of molten metal after an arduous and perilous journey to reach it. When they were sure of its nature, they collected samples and brought them back to the plane. Repairs to the oil-feeding system were required, and they were made. They took off on the day before their return, and reached the vicinity of St. Paul safely. It was in St. Paul—which as you will realize, is less than two hundred miles from here—that they received the injuries with which they returned. St. Paul was in much the same condition as Pittsburgh, except that it had undergone the further decay occasioned by two additional weeks of famine and pestilence. They landed on the Mississippi River near the shore, late that night. Almost immediately they were attacked, doubtless because it was believed they possessed food. The last words in James' diary are these, 'Boats have put out toward us. One of them has a machine gun mounted in the bow. Ransdell has succeeded in starting the motors, but the plane is listing. I believe that bullets have perforated one of the pontoons, and that it is filling. We may never leave the water. Vanderbilt is throwing out every object that can be removed, in order to lighten the ship. Our forward progress is slow. It may be that it will be necessary to repulse the first boat-load before we can take off. . . . It is.' "

Hendron dropped the seventh notebook on the table. "You

may reconstruct what followed, my friends. The hand-to-hand fight on the plane with a boatload of hunger-driven maniacs—a fight in which all three heroic members of the airplane company were hurt. We may imagine them at last beating back their assailants, and with their floundering ship taking off before a second boatload was upon them. We may imagine Ransdell guiding his ship through the night with gritted teeth while his occasional backward glances offered him little reassurance of the safety of his comrades. The rest we know. And this, my friends, completes their saga."

CHAPTER 17—THE ATTACK

AUTUMN had set in, but it was like no autumn the world had ever known before. The weather remained unnaturally hot. The skies were still hazy. An enormous amount of fine volcanic dust, discharged mostly from the chain of great craters that rimmed the Pacific Ocean, remained suspended in the upper air-currents; and when some it settled, it was constantly renewed.

Vulcanists had enumerated, before the disturbance of the First Passage, some four hundred and thirty active volcanic vents. Counting the cones which, because of their slightly eroded condition, had been considered dormant, there had been several thousand. All of these, it now was calculated, had become active. Along the Andes, through Central America, through the Pacific States into Canada, then along the Aleutian chain of craters to Asia, and turning southward through Kamchatka, Japan and the Philippines into the East Indies stood the cones which continued to erupt into the atmosphere. The sun rose red and huge, and set in astounding haloes. Tropical rains, tawny with volcanic dust, fell in torrents. Steam and vapors, as well as lavas and dust, were pouring from innumerable vents out from under the cracked and fissured crust of the world.

The neighboring vent, opened in the vicinity of St. Paul, supplied Hendron with more than the necessary amount of the new metal, which could be machined but which withstood even the heat of the atomic blast. Hendron had not waited for his explorers to recover. On the day after the reading of the diaries, he had flown with another pilot, found a source of the strange material from the center of the earth; and he had loaded the plane. Repeated trips had thereafter provided more than enough metal for the tubes of the atomic engines.

The engine-makers could not melt the metal by any heat they applied; they could not fuse it; but they could cut it, and by patient machining, shape it into lining of tubes which, at last, endured the frightful temperatures of the atom releasing its power.

The problem of the engine for the Space Ship was solved. There existed no doubt that it could, when required, lift the ship from the earth, successfully oppose the pull of gravity and propel it into interplanetary regions.

This transformed the psychology of the camp. It was not merely that hope appeared to be realized at last. The effect of Ransdell's discovery was far more profound than that.

The finding of the essential metal became, in the over-emotionalized mind of the camp, no mere accident, or bit of good luck, or result of intelligence. It became an event "ordained," and therefore endowed with more than physical meaning. It was a portent and omen of promise—indeed, of more than promise.

And now there ensued a period of frantic impatience for the return of the Bronson Bodies! For the camp, in its new hysteria, had become perfectly confident that the Space Ship must succeed in making its desperate journey. The camp was resolved—that part of it which should be chosen—to go.

"When a resolution is once taken," observed Polybius nearly two millennia before, "nothing tortures men like the wait before it can be executed."

Tony kept on at his work, tormented by a torture of his own. Together with Eliot James and Vanderbilt, who had been less hurt than he, Ransdell had now recovered from his wounds.

For his part in the great adventure which James had reported in detail, the pilot would have become popular, even if he had not also proved the discoverer of the metal that would not melt. That by itself would have lifted him above every other man in the camp.

Not above Hendron in authority; for the flyer never in the slightest attempted to assert authority. Ransdell became, indeed, even more retiring and reserved than before; and so the women of the camp, and especially the younger ones, worshiped him.

When Eve walked with Ransdell, as she often did, Tony became a potential killer. In reaction, he could laugh at himself; he knew it was the hysteria working in him—his fear and terrors at facing almost inevitable and terrible death, and at knowing that Eve also must be annihilated. It was these emotions that at moments almost broke out in a demonstration against Ransdell.

Almost but never did—quite.

When Tony was with Eve, she seemed to him less the civilized creature of cultured and sophisticated society, and more an impulsive and primitive woman.

Her very features seemed altered, bolder, her eyes darker

and larger, her lips softer, her hair filled with a bright fire. She was stronger, also, and more taut.

"We're going to get over," she said to him one day. "To get over" meant to make the passage successfully to Bronson Beta, when it returned. The camp had phrases and euphemisms of its own for the hopes and fears it discussed.

"Yes," agreed Tony. No one, now, openly doubted it, whatever he hid in his heart. "How do you—" he began, and then made his challenge less directly personal by adding: "How do you girls now like the idea of ceasing to be individuals and becoming 'biological representatives of the human race'—after we get across?"

He saw Eve flush, and the warmth in her stirred him. "We talk about it, of course," she replied. "And—I suppose we'll do it."

"Breed the race, you mean," Tony continued mercilessly. "Reproduce the type—mating with whoever is best to insure the strongest and best children for the place, and to establish a new generation of the greatest possible variety from the few individuals which we can hope to land safely. That's the program."

"Yes," said Eve, "that's the purpose."

For a minute he did not speak, thinking how—though he temporarily might possess her—so Ransdell might, too. And others. His hands clenched; and Eve, looking at him, said:

"If you get across, Tony, there probably must be other wives—other mates—for you too."

"Would you care?"

"Care, Tony?" she began, her face flooded with color. She checked herself. "No one must care; we have sworn not to care—to conquer caring. And we must train ourselves to it now, you know. We can't suddenly stop caring about such things, when we find ourselves on Bronson Beta, unless we've at least made a start at downing selfishness here."

"You call it selfishness?"

"I know it's not the word, Tony; but I've no word for it. *Morals* isn't the word, either. What are morals, fundamentally, Tony? Morals are nothing but the code of conduct required of an individual in the best interests of the group of which he's a member. So what's 'moral' here wouldn't be moral at all on Bronson Beta."

"Damn Bronson Beta! Have you no feeling for me?"

"Tony, is there any sense in making more difficult for ourselves what we may have to do?"

"Yes; damn it," Tony burst out again, "I want it difficult. I want it impossible for you!"

Wanderers from other places began to discover the camp. While they were few in number, it was possible to feed and clothe and even shelter them, at least temporarily. Then there was no choice but to give them a meal and send them away. But daily the dealings with the desperate, reckless groups became more and more ugly and hazardous.

Tony found that Hendron long ago had forseen the certainty of such emergencies, and had provided against it. Tony himself directed the extension of the protection of the camp by a barrier of barbed-wire half a mile beyond the buildings. There were four gates which he sentineled and where he turned back all vagrant visitors. If this was cruelty, he had no alternative but chaos. Let the barriers be broken, and the settlement would be overwhelmed.

But bigger and uglier bands continued to come. It became a commonplace to turn them back at the bayonet-point and under the threat of machine-guns. Tony had to forbid, except in special cases, the handing out of rations to the vagrants. The issuance of food not only permitted the gangs to lurk in the neighborhood, but it brought in others. It became unsafe for any one—man or woman—to leave the enclosure except by airplane.

Rifles cracked from concealments, and bullets sang by; some found their marks.

Ransdell scouted the surroundings from the air; and Tony and three others, unshaven and disheveled, crept forth at night and mingled with the men besieging the camp. They discovered that Hendron's group was hopelessly outnumbered.

"What saves us for the time," Tony reported to Hendron on his return, "is that they're not yet united. They are gangs and groups which fight savagely enough among themselves, but in general tolerate each other. They join on only one thing. They want to get in here. They want to get us—and our women.

"There are women among them, but not like ours; and they are too few for so many men. Our women also would be too few—but they want them.

"They talk about smashing in here and getting our food, our shelters—and our women. They'd soon be killing each other in here, after they wiped us out. That desire—and hate of us—is their sole force of cohesion."

Hendron considered silently. "There was no way for us to avoid that hate. And there is no hate like that of men who have lost their morale, against those who have retained it."

Tony looked away. "If they get in, we'll see something new in savagery."

The attack began on the following night. It began with gunfire, raking the barriers. A siren on top of the power-house sounded a wholly unnecessary warning. "Women to cover! Men to arms!"

126

Low on the horizon that night, which was speckled here by gunfire, shone two new evening stars. They were the Bronson Bodies which now had turned about the sun and were rushing toward their next meeting-place with the earth: one of them to offer itself for refuge, the other to end the world forever.

CHAPTER 18—THE FINAL DEFENSE

TONY, directing the disposal of his men, longed for the moon—the shattered moon that survived to-night only in fragments too scattered and distant to lend any light. The stars had to suffice. The stars and the three searchlights fixed on the roofs of the laboratories nearest to the three fronts of the encampment.

One blazed out—and instantly became a target for a machine-gun in the woods before it. For a full minute, the glaring white beam swung steadily, coolly back and forth, picking out of the night men's figures, that flattened themselves on the ground between the trees as the searchlight struck them.

Then the beam tipped up and ceased to move. The next moment, the great glaring pencil was snuffed out. The machine-gun in the woods had got the light-crew first, and then the light itself.

Other machine-guns and rifles, firing at random but ceaselessly, raked the entire camp. Tony stumbled over friends that had fallen. Some told him their names; some would never speak again. He recognized them by flashing, for an instant, his pocket-light on their still faces. Scientists, great men, murdered in mass! For this was not war. This was mere murder; and it would be massacre, if the frail defenses of the camp failed, and the horde broke in.

A defending machine-gun showed its spatter of flashes off to the right; Tony ran to it, and dropped down beside the gun-crew.

"Give me the gun!" he begged. He had to have a shot at them himself; yet when he had his finger on the trigger, he withheld his fire. The enemy—that merciless, murderous enemy—was invisible. They showed not even the flash of gunfire; and outside the wire barriers, there was silence.

The only firing, the only spatters of red, the only rattle, was within the defenses. It was impossible that, so suddenly, the attack had ceased or had been beaten off. No; this pause must have been prearranged; it was part of the strategy of the assault.

It alarmed Tony far more than a continuance of the surrounding fire. There was more plan, more intelligence, in the attack than he had guessed.

"Lights!" he yelled. "Lights!"

They could not have heard him on the roofs where the two remaining searchlights stood; but they blazed out, one sweeping the woods before Tony. The glare caught a hundred men before they could drop; and Tony savagely held the trigger back, praying to catch them with his bullets. He blazed with fury such as he never had known; but he knew, as he fired, that his bullets were too few and too scattered. His targets were gone; but had he killed them? The searchlight swept by and back again, then was gone.

Machine-guns were spitting from the woods once more, and both lights were blinded.

A rocket rasped its yellow streak into the air and burst above in shower of stars. A Fourth of July rocket, unquestionably a signal!

Tony fired at random into the woods; all through the camp, rifles and machine-guns were going. But no attack came.

A second rocket rasped up and broke its spatter of stars. Now the camp held its fire and listened. It heard—Tony heard, only a whistle, like a traffic whistle, or the whistle that summoned squads to attacking order.

A third rocket went up.

"Here they come!" some one said; and Tony wondered how he knew it. Soaked in perspiration, Tony glared into the blackness of the woods. He longed for the lights; he longed for military rockets. But there never had been any of these. Hendron, in making his preparation, had not foreseen this sort of attack. He had imagined vagrants in groups, or even mobs of desperate men, but nothing that the wire would not stop or a few machine-guns scatter. That is, he had imagined nothing worse until it was too late to prepare, adequately, for—this.

Now machine-guns in the woods were sweeping the camp enclosure. The fire radiated from a few points; and as it was certain the attackers were not in the path of their own fire, but were in the dark spaces between, Tony swept these with his bullets.

The gun bucked under his tense fingers. Yells rewarded him. He was wounding, killing the attackers—units of that horde that had sent that murderous fire to mow down the men, the splendid men, the great men who had whispered their names quietly to Tony as he had bent over them before they died.

Shouts drowned the yells of the wounded—savage, taunting shouts. There must be a thousand men on this bit of the front alone, more than all the men in the camp. Tony heard his voice bawling over the tumult: *"Get 'em! Get 'em! Don't let 'em by!"*

His machine-gun was overheating. A little light came from somewhere; Tony could not see what it was, except that it flickered. Something was burning. Tony could see figures at the wire, now. He could not reckon their numbers, did not try to. He tried only to shoot them down. Once through that wire,—that wire so weak that he could not see it,—and that thousand with the thousand behind them would be over him and the men beside him, they would be over the line of older men behind; then they would reach the women.

Tony's lips receded from his teeth. He aimed the gun with diabolic care, and watched it take effect as wind affects standing wheat. The attackers broke, and ran back to the woods.

In the central part of the cantonment the growth afforded better cover and gave the assault shorter range. Men went in pairs to the tops of the buildings, and through loopholes which had been provided for such a contingency began sniping at those who moved in the territory around the buildings.

Every one was overmastered by the same sort of rage which had possessed Tony. The reason for their existence had been to them a high and holy purpose. They defended it with the fanaticism of zealots. They could not know that the flight of their planes to and from the Ransdell metal-supply had indicated to the frantic hordes that somewhere human beings lived in discipline and decency. They could not know how for weeks they had been spied upon by ravenous eyes. They could not know how the countryside around, and the distant cities, had been recruited to form an army to attack them. They could not know that nearly ten thousand men, hungry, desperate, most of them already murderers many times over, armed, supplied with crafty plans which had been formulated by disordered heads once devoted to important, intelligent pursuits—how these besieged them now, partly for spoils, but to a greater degree in a fury of lust and envy. They had traveled on broken roads, growing as they marched. It was a heathen horde, a barbaric and ruthless horde, which attacked the colony.

The siege relaxed to an intermittent exchange of volleys. At this machine-gun station, Tony, suffering acutely from thirst, with six of his comrades lying dead near by, fought intermittently.

Reënforcements came from the center of the camp—Jack Taylor and two more of the younger men.

"Hurt, Tony?" Tyalor challenged him.

"No," replied Tony; and he did not mention his dead; for Taylor, creeping up, had encountered them. "Who's killed in the buildings?"

"Not Hendron," said Taylor, "or Eve—though she might have been. She was one of the girls that went out to attend to the wounded. Two of the girls were hit, but not Eve. . . . Hendron wants to see you, Tony."

"Now?"

"Right now."

"Where is he?"

"At the ship. I'll take over here for you. Good luck!"

Tony stumbled through the dark to the buildings, black except for faint cracks of light at the doors behind which the wounded were collected. He found Hendron inside the Space Ship, and there, since its metal made an armor for it, a light was burning. Hendron sat at a table; it was now his headquarters.

"Who's hurt?" said Tony.

"Too many." Hendron dimissed this. "What do they think *they* are doing?" he challenged Tony abruptly.

"Getting ready to come again," Tony returned.

"To-night, probably?"

Tony glanced at his wrist-watch; it was eleven o'clock. "Midnight, would be my guess, sir," he said.

"Will they get in next time?" Hendron demanded.

"They can."

"What do you mean by that?"

"I mean, if they come on more resolutely. They can do more than they have done."

"Whereas we," Hendron took up for him, "can scarcely do more."

"Yes, sir," said Tony. "We used all the defenses we had; and they could have carried us an hour ago, if they'd come on."

"Exactly," nodded Hendron. "And now we are fewer. We will be fewer still, of course, after the next attack; and fewer yet, after they get in."

"Yes, sir."

"However," observed Hendron thoughtfully, "that will be, in one way, an advantage."

Tony was used, by now, to be astonished by Hendron; yet he said: "I don't follow you, sir."

"We will defend the enclosure as long as we can, Tony," Hendron said. "But when they are in,—if they get in,—no one is to throw himself away fighting them uselessly. They must be delayed as long as they can be; but when they *are* in, we gather—all of us that are left, Tony—here."

"Here?"

"Inside this ship. Hadn't that occurred to you, Tony? Don't you *see?* Don't you *see?*"

Tony stared at his chief, and straightened, the blood of hope racing again hot within.

130

"Of course I see!" he almost shouted. "Of course I see!"

"Very well. Then issue cloths—white cloths, Tony; distribute them."

"Cloths?" repeated Tony, but before Hendron answered, he realized the reason.

"For arm-bands, Tony; so, in the dark, we will know our own."

"Yes, sir."

"No time to lose, Tony."

"No, sir. But—Eve is safe?"

"She is not hurt, I hear. You might see her for an instant. The women are tearing up bandages."

Tony found her, but not alone; she was in a room with twenty others, tearing white cloth into strips. At least, he saw for himself that she was not yet hurt; at least he had one word with her.

"Tony! Take care of yourself!"

"How about you, Eve?"

She disregarded this; said only:

"Get back to the ship, Tony, after the fight. Oh, get back to the ship!" He went out again. A bullet pinged on the wall beside him; bullets were flying again. Behind Tony, on the other edge of the camp, sporadic firing flashed along the road and in the woods. The bursts of machine-gun fire sounded uglier; there were groans again, and screams. Tony could sense rather than see the gathering of attackers on this edge; then firing broke out on the other side too.

He wondered how many of his runners with the arm-bands and with the orders would fall before they reached the first line of the defense. With his own burden of machine-gun cartridges, he returned to the post he had fought.

"That you, Tony?" Jack Taylor hailed. "Cartridges? Great! We'll scrap those bimboes. Hell! Just in time, I'd say. . . . Here they come!"

"Listen!" yelled Tony, giving his orders with realization that, if he did not speak now, he might never: "If they get in, delay them but don't mix with them; each man tie a white cloth on his sleeve—and retreat to the ship!" And he issued the strips he had brought with him.

From the buildings, reënforcements arrived—six men with guns slung over their shoulders, and bayonets that caught a glint from the firing. They were burdened with more cartridge-cases, and they carried another machine-gun. Tony placed them almost without comment.

One of the new men produced a Very pistol. His private property, he explained, which he had brought along "for emergencies."

"It's one now," Tony said simply, and took the pistol from him. He fired it; and the Very light, hanging in the air, re-

131

vealed men at the wire everywhere. A thousand men—two thousand; no sense even in estimating them.

In the green glare which showed them, Jack Taylor looked at Tony. "My God, I forgot," he said, and shoved Tony his canteen.

Tony tasted the whisky and passed it on, then again he claimed the machine-gun. He made a flat fan of the flashes before him as he swung the gun back and forth. He was killing men by scores, he knew; but he knew, also, that if the hundreds had the nerve to stick, they were "in."

Chapter 19—Escape

THEY were in! And Tony did not need the green flare of the last light from the Very pistol to tell him so.

"Fall back! Fall back to the ship—fighting!" Tony yelled again and again.

He did not need to tell his men to fight. They were doing that. The trouble was, they still wanted to fight, holding on here.

What saved them was the fact that the machine-gun ammunition was gone. The machine-guns were useless; nothing to do but abandon them.

"Fall back!" Tony yelled. "Oh, fall back!"

A few obeyed him. The rest could not, he suddenly realized; and he had to leave them, dying. Jack Taylor was beside him, firing a rifle. They were five altogether who were falling back; firing, from the machine-gun post.

Figures from the black leaped at them, and it was hand to hand. Tony fought with a bayonet, then with a clubbed rifle, madly and wildly swinging. He was struck, and reeled. Some one caught him, and he clutched the other's throat to strangle him before his eyes got the patch of gray which was a white arm-band.

"Come on!" cried Jack Taylor's voice; and with Taylor, he ran in the dark. Clear of the attack for an instant, they rallied—the two of them—found a pistol on a body over which they stumbled, emptied it at the attackers, and fell back again.

They reached the buildings. Gunfire was flashing from the laboratories which otherwise were black. The dormitories sprang into light; windows shone, and spread illumination which showed that they were deserted and were being used, now, by the defenders of the camp to light the space already abandoned. The final concentration was in the center, dominated by the looming black bulk of the Space Ship standing in its stocks.

The lights from the dormitories were holding up the advance of the attackers. They could not shoot out hundreds of globes so simply as they had smashed the searchlights. And they could not advance into that illuminated area, under the machine-guns and rifles of the laboratories. They had first to take the deserted dormitories and darken them.

They were doing this; but it delayed them. It held them up a few minutes. Here and there a few, drunker or more reckless than the rest, charged in between the buildings, but they dropped to the ground dead or wounded—or waiting for the support that was soon to come.

Room by room, dormitory windows went black. The lights were not being turned out; they were being smashed and the window-panes were crashing. Yells celebrated the smashing, and shots.

The yells ceased; and the defenders knew that some sort of assault was being reorganized.

Tony moved in the dark, recognized by his voice, and knowing others in the same way.

"Keep down—down—down," he was crying. "Below the window-line. Down!" For bullets from machine-guns, evidently aimed from the dormitory windows, were striking in.

Many did not obey him; he did not expect them to. They had to fight back, firing from the windows. Yells at the farther end of the main laboratory told that it was hand-to-hand there, in the dark. A charge—a rush had been pushed home.

Tony found Taylor beside him; they had stuck together in the dark; and a dozen others rose and ran with them into the mêlée.

Men of science, Tony was realizing even as he stumbled in the dark, the best brains of the modern world, fighting hand to hand with savages! Shoot and stab and club, wildly, desperately in the dark!

Your comrade went down; you stepped back over him, and shot and stabbed again; yelling, groaning, slipping, struggling up again. But many did not get up. More and more lay where they fell. Tony, stumbling and slipping on the stickily wet floor, realized that this rush was stopped. There was nobody left in the room to fight—nobody but two or three distinguished as friends by the spots of the arm bands.

"Jack?" gasped Tony; and Taylor's voice answered him. They were staggering and bleeding, both of them; but they had survived the fight together.

"Who was here!" Tony asked. Who of their comrades and friends were dead and dying at their feet, he meant. Tony found the flash-light which, all through the fight, he had in his pocket, and he bent to the floor and held it close to the faces.

He caught breath, bitterly. Bronson was there. Bronson,

the discoverer of the two stranger planets whose passing had loosed this savagery; Dr. Sven Bronson, the first scientist of the Southern Hemisphere, lay there in his blood, a bayonet through his throat! Beside him Dodson was dying, his right arm hacked almost off. He recognized Tony, spoke two words which Tony could not hear, and lost consciousness.

A few of those less hurt were rising.

"To the ship! *Into the ship!*" Tony cried to them. "Everybody into the ship! Spread the word! Jack! . . . Everybody, everybody into the ship!" There was no alternative.

Three-fourths of the camp was in the hands of the horde; and the laboratories could not possibly beat off another rush. They could not have beaten back this, if it had been more organized.

Bullets flew through the dark.

"To the ship! *To the ship!*"

Creeping on hands and knees, from wounds or from caution, and dragging the wounded with them, the men started the retreat to the ship. Women were helping them.

Yells and whistles warned that another rush was gathering; and this would be from all sides; the laboratories and the ship were completely surrounded.

Tony caught up in his arms a young man who was barely breathing. He had a bullet through him; but he lived. Tony staggered with him into the ship.

Hendron was there at the portal of the great metal rocket. He was cooler than any one else. "Inside, inside," he was saying confidently.

"Where's Eve?" Tony gasped at him.

"I saw her—a moment ago."

"Safe?"

Her father nodded.

Tony bore in his burden, laid it down. Ransdell confronted him. From head to foot, the South African was dabbled and clotted with blood. He was three-quarters naked; a bullet had creased his forehead; a bayonet had slashed his shoulder. His lips were set back from his teeth. His eyes, the only portion of him not crimson, gazed from the pit of his face, and a voice that croaked out of his wheezing lungs said: "Seen Eve?"

"Her father has, Dave. She's all right," replied Tony.

Ransdell pitched head foremost toward the floor as Tony caught him.

The second rush was coming. No doubt of it, and it would be utterly overwhelming. There would be no survivors—but the women. None. For the horde would take no prisoners. They were killing the wounded already—their own badly wounded and the camp's wounded that they had captured.

Eliot James, a bullet through his thigh, but saved by the

134

dark, crawled in with this information. Tony carried him into the ship.

They were all in the ship—all the survivors. The horde did not suspect it. The horde, as it charged in the dark, yelling and firing, closed in on the laboratories, clambered in the windows, smashing, shooting, screaming. Meeting no resistance, they shot and bayoneted the bodies of their own men and of the camp's which had been left there.

Then they came on toward the ship. They suddenly seemed to realize that the ship was the last refuge. They surrounded it, firing at it. Their bullets glanced from its metal. Somebody who had grenades bombed it.

A frightful flame shattered them. Probably they imagined, at first, that the grenade had exploded some sort of a powder magazine within the huge metal tube, and that it was exploding. Few of those near to the ship, and outside it, lived to see what was happening.

The great metal rocket rose from the earth, the awful blast from its power tubes lifting it. The frightful heat seared and incinerated, killing at its touch. A hundred of the horde were dead before the ship was above the buildings.

Hendron lifted it five hundred feet farther, and the blast spread in a funnel below it. A thousand died in that instant. Hendron ceased to elevate the ship. Indeed, he lowered it a little, and the power of the atomic blast which was keeping two thousand tons of metal and of human flesh suspended over the earth, played upon the ground—and upon the flesh on the ground—as no force ever released by man before.

Tony lay on his face on the floor of the ship, gazing down through the protective quartz-glass at the ground lighted by the garish glare of the awful heat.

In the midst of the blaring, blinding, screaming crisis, a man on horseback appeared. His coming seemed spectral. He rode in full uniform; he had a sword which he brandished to rally his doomed horde. Probably he was drunk; certainly he had no conception of what was occurring; but his courage was splendid. He spurred into the center of the lurid light, into the center of the circle of death and tumult, stiff-legged in stirrups of leather, like one of the horrible horsemen of the Apocalypse.

He was, for a flaming instant, the apotheosis of valor. He was the crazed commander of the horde.

But he was more. He was the futility of all the armies on earth. He was man, the soldier.

Probably he appeared to live after he had died, he and his horse together. For the horse stood there motionless like a statue, and he sat his horse, sword in hand. Then, like all about them, they also crumpled to the ground.

Half an hour later, Hendron brought the ship down.

A PALE delicate light carried away the depths of night. From the numbness and exhaustion which had seized it, the colony roused itself. It gazed with empty eyes upon that which surrounded it. The last battle of brains against brutality had been fought on the bosom of the earth. And the intelligence of man had conquered his primeval ruthlessness. But at what cost! Around a table in the office of the laboratories a few men and women stared at each other; Hendron pale and shaken, Tony in shoes and trousers, white bandages over his wounds, Eve staring from him to the short broad-shouldered silent form of Ransdell, whose hands, blackened, ugly, hung limply at his sides, whose gorilla-like strength seemed to have deserted him; the German actress, her dress disheveled, her hands covering her eyes; Smith the surgeon, stupefied in the face of this hopeless summons to his calling.

At last Hendron sucked a breath into his lungs. He spoke above the nerve-shattering clamor which penetrated the room continually. "My friends, what must be done is obvious. We must first bury the dead. There are no survivors of the enemy. If others are gathering, I believe we need fear no further attack. Doctor Smith, you will kindly take charge of all hospital and medical arrangements for our people. I will request that those who are able to do so appear immediately on the airplane field, which I believe is—unobstructed. I shall dispatch the majority of them to your assistance, and with those who remain, I shall take such steps as are necessary. Let's go."

Only three hundred and eighty persons were counted by Tony as they struggled shuddering to the landing-field. Almost half of them were women, for the women, except in the case of individuals who joined the fighting voluntarily, had been secluded.

As in the the other emergency, Taylor was assigned to the kitchen. He walked to the kitchen with his men. Tony with ten other men, a pitiful number for the appalling task that confronted them, went down to the field and began to gather up in trucks the bodies there. Not far from the cantonment, on what had been a lumber road, an enormous fissure yawned in the earth. . . .

All that day they tended their own wounded. Many of them perished.

In those nightmare days no one spoke unless it was necessary. Lifelong friendships and strong new friendships had been obliterated. Loves that in two months had flowered into vehement reality were ended. And only the slowest progress was made against the increasing charnel horror surrounding the cantonment. For two weeks abysmal sadness and funereal silence held them. Only the necessary ardors of their toil prevented many of them from going mad. But at the end of two weeks Tony, returning from an errand to the fissure where the last bodies had been entombed by a blast of dynamite, stood on the hill where he had so often regarded the encampment, and saw that once again the grass grew greenly, once again the buildings were clean and trim. The odor of fresh paint was carried to his nostrils, and from far away the droning voices of the cattle in the stockyards reached his ears. He was weary, although for the last few nights he had been allowed adequate sleep, and his heart ached.

While he stood there, his attention was attracted by a strange sound—the sound of an airplane motor; and the plane itself became visible. It was not one of their own planes, and he looked at it with hostile curiosity. It landed presently on their field, and Tony was one of several men who approached it. The cabin door opened, and out stepped a man. There was something familiar about him to Tony, but he could not decide what it was. The man had a high crackling voice. His hair was snow-white. His features were drawn, and his skin was yellow. His pilot remained at the controls of the plane, and the old man hobbled toward Tony, saying as he approached:

"Please take me to Mr. Hendron."

Tony stepped forward. "I'm Mr. Hendron's assistant. We don't allow visitors here. Perhaps you will tell me your errand."

"I'll see Hendron," the other snapped.

Tony realized that the man constituted no menace. "Perhaps," he said coldly, "if you will tell me your reason for wanting to see Hendron, I can arrange for the interview."

The old man almost shrieked. "*You* can arrange an interview; I tell you, young fellow, I said I would see Hendron, and that's all there is to it." He came abruptly closer, snatched Tony's lapel, cocked his head and peered into his face. "You're Drake, aren't you, young Tony Drake?"

Suddenly Tony recognized the man. He was staggered. Before him stood Nathaniel Borgan, fourth richest man in America, friend of all tycoons of the land, friend indeed of Hendron himself. Tony had last seen Borgan in Hendron's house in New York, when Borgan had been immaculate, powerful, self-assured and barely approaching middle age. He now looked senile, degenerate and slovenly.

"Aren't you Drake?" the crackling voice repeated. Tony nodded mechanically. "Yes," he said, "come with me."

Hendron did not recognize Borgan until Tony had pronounced his name. Then upon his face there appeared briefly a look of consternation, and Borgan in his shrill grating voice began to talk excitedly. "Of course I knew what you were doing, Hendron, knew all about it. Meant to offer you financial assistance, but got tangled up taking care of my affairs in the last few weeks. I haven't been able to come here before, for a variety of reasons. But now I'm here. You'll take me with you when you go, of course." He banged his fist on the table in a bizarre burlesque of his former gestures. "You'll take me, all right, all right, and I'll tell you why you'll take me—for my money. When all else fails, I'll have my money. I ask only that you spare my life, that you'll take me from this awful place, and in turn go out to my plane, go out to the plane that is waiting there for you. Look inside." Suddenly his voice sank to a whisper, and his head was shot forward. "It's full of bills, full of bills, Hendron, hundred-dollar bills, thousand-dollar bills, ten-thousand-dollar bills—stacked with them, bales of them, bundles of them—millions, Hendron, millions! That's the price I'm offering you for my life."

Hendron and Tony looked at this man in whose hands the destiny of colossal American industries had once been so firmly held; and they knew that he was mad.

Oddly enough, the arrival of Nathaniel Borgan and his effort to purchase passage on the Space Ship with millions in bills as worthles as Civil War shin-plasters, acted as a sort of catalyst on the survivors of the attack. The deep melancholy which had settled upon them, and which in many cases had been so powerful an emotion that all interest in the future was swept away, evaporated as the story of Borgan ran through the colony. To people living in a normal world, the millionaire's behavior might have seemed shocking. But Hendron's colonists were beyond the point where they could be shocked. Instead they were reawakened to an intense consciousness of their unique position and their vast responsibilities.

They sent Borgan away with his pilot and his plane full of money; and the last words of the financier were pronounced in a voice intended to be threatening as he leaned out of the cabin door: I'll get an injunction against you from the President himself. I'll have the Supreme Court behind me within twenty-four hours."

Somebody laughed, and then somebody else. It was not gay laughter, but Homeric laughter, the sort of laughter that contains too many emotions to be otherwise expressed.

After the plane disappeared in the sky, people found themselves talking to each other about their lives once more. On the following morning a small quota of bathers appeared and plunged into the pool. Their voices were still restrained; but Hendron, watching from the roof of the laboratory, sighed with infinite relief. He had almost reached the point when he would have given way to utter despair over the morale of his people. That evening the strains of phonograph music floated over the place that had been a battlefield. They played old favorites for a while; but when some one put on a dance record, there was no objection.

The energy of interest returned to their work, replacing the energy of dogged and bleak determination. . . .

At that time, nearly three weeks after the attack, a census was retaken. There were two hundred and nine uninjured women, one hundred and eighty-two uninjured men. There were about eighty men and women who were expected wholly to recover. There were more than a hundred who would suffer some disability. Four hundred and ninety-three people had been killed or had died after the conflict.

Work of course was redistributed. More than five months lay ahead of them. The Space Ship could be completed, even with this reduced group, in three weeks. The greatest loss was in the death of men, specialists in various fields of human knowledge. That their branches of learning might not be unrepresented, schools were immediately opened, and more than two hundred men and women began an intensive training in a vast variety of the branches of science. . . .

On one of the unseasonably warm afternoons in December Tony received what he considered afterward the greatest compliment ever paid to him in his life. He was making one of his regular tours of the stockyards when Ransdell, walking alone on the road, overtook him. In all their recent encounters, Ransdell had not spoken a hundred words to Tony; but now finding him alone, he stopped him and said almost gruffly: "I'd like to speak to you."

Tony turned and smiled with his usual geniality.

The South African hesitated, and almost blushed. "I'm not talkative," he said bluntly, "but I've been trying to find you alone for weeks." Again he hesitated.

"Yes?"

"That fight you put up—" Ransdell took a huge pocket-knife from his flannel shirt and commenced to open and shut its blade nervously. "That was a damn' fine piece of work, fellow."

"What was yours?" Tony replied, heartily. Ransdell held out his hand. They gripped, and in that grip the hands of lesser men would have been broken.

From that time on, those rivals in love were as blood brothers. They were seen together more often than Ransdell was seen with his two companions of the long flight; they made an odd pair, the tall garrulous good-humored Tony striding here and there on his numerous duties, accompanied by the short, equally broad and herculean British-American.

Another general meeting was held in the dining-hall. It began a little quietly, for those who gathered there were reminded intensely of the diminution of their numbers by the number of empty seats. Hendron again took charge, and his words from the beginning to end were a complete surprise to the community.

In his office and at his business a relatively silent man, Hendron none the less enjoyed making speeches. He stood on the platform that night, his hair a little grayer than formerly, the lines around his eyes a little deeper, the square set of his shoulders slightly bowed, and his mouth fixed in a more implacable line than before. The five-hundred-odd people who listened to him appreciated from the first moment that Hendron had something of importance to impart, and something which he knew would please them.

"I have called you together," he began, "for two distinct purposes: I shall dispatch the first of these with what I know will be your approval; and the second I am sure will meet with equal approval.

"I want each one of you to-night to forget for the moment the tragedies that have overtaken us. I want each of you to-night to think of yourself as a member of the human race who, buffeted by fortune, overwhelmed by Nature, threatened by your fellow-men, is nevertheless steadfastly continuing upon the greatest enterprise mankind has ever undertaken.

"And while you are thinking that, I will draw your attention to the fact that certain of our number have made, at the risk of their own lives and with the exhibition of incredible heroism, contributions to our lives here, the value of which cannot be expressed.

"I am thinking of Peter Vanderbilt, Eliot James and David Ransdell, who brought to us a record of the fate of our nation, and especially of Ransdell, who not only carried home his companions when he was severely wounded, but who discovered and brought back the substance which will make our escape from here possible."

Applause and cheering checked Hendron for a while. Then he continued:

"I am thinking also of Jack Taylor and Anthony Drake, whose courageous defense is largely responsible for our presence here to-day." The cheers were redoubled.

"'Because we are all human, and because we wish to recognize by some token services so extraordinary and distinguished as these, I have had struck off five gold medals." Hendron held up his hand to check the tumult. "These medals bear on one side the motto of the United States of America, which I think we might still adopt as our own. Out of the many nationalities represented before, we intend to create a

140

single race. Therefore the medals bear the inscription, 'E pluribus unum,' the names of their recipients, and beneath the names the words 'For valor.' On the opposite face of these medals is the head of Sven Bronson, who first discovered the Bronson Bodies, who gave warning to the world, and who was one of those who surrendered his life, that the rest of us might not perish."

There was now silence in the room. One by one Hendron called the names of the five men to whom he wished to do honor. As each rose and stepped forward, he spoke a few words descriptive of the reasons for awarding the medal, and the occasion which had won the award. Vanderbilt and James were gracefully embarrassed. Jack Taylor was dumb-stricken and crimson. Tony shuffled to and from the platform with a bent head, and Ransdell accepted his medal with a white face and a military precision which showed clearly the emotional price he was paying for every step and gesture he made.

When the applause had at last died, Hendron began again in a different tone: "The second matter which I have to discuss with you is one which will come, I am sure, as a distinct surprise. It is the result of my earnest thought and of careful calculations. I arrived at it no sooner, because I anticipated neither the temper nor the quality of the people who would be gathered before me at this time, and because I was uncertain of the mechanical facilities that would be available to us. From the standpoint of realism,—and I have learned that all of you are courageous enough to face truths, —I am forced to add that my decision has been made possible by the diminution of our numbers.

"All of you know that I founded this village of ours for the purpose of transferring to the planet that willl take the place of Earth a company of about one hundred people, with the hope that they might perpetuate our doomed race. The number I considered was in a measure arbitrary, but it seemed to me that a ship large enough to accommodate such a number might be fabricated and launched by the one thousand persons who were originally assembled here. It is obvious, of course, that the more intelligent and healthy the units of humanity we are able to transfer to the planet, the better the chance for founding a new race will be."

He paused and his eyes roved over the throng. Not a breath was drawn, and not a word was spoken. Many guessed in a blinding flash of ecstasy what Hendron was going to say.

"My friends, we are five hundred in number. There is not one man or woman left among us who bears such disability as will prevent him from surviving, if any one may, the trip through space; there is not one but who, if we effect our landing upon Bronson Beta and find it habitable, will be fit to propagate there the human race.

"On the night of the attack, we all of us—and some who since have died—crammed into the Space Ship. We all realize that no such crowding will be possible on the voyage through space; we all realize that much cargo, other than humanity, must be stowed on the ship if there is to be any point and purpose in our safe landing upon another planet. One hundred persons remains my estimate of the probable crew and passenger-list of the ship which saved us all on that night.

"But I have come to the conclusion that, by dint of tremendous effort and coöperation, and largely because of the success of the experiments which we have made with Ransdell's metal, it will be possible within the remaining months of time to construct a second and larger vessel which will be capable of removing the entire residual personnel of this camp."

Hendron sat down. No cheer was lifted. As if they had seen the Gorgon's Head, the audience was turned to stone. The sentence imposed by the death-lottery had been lifted. Every man and woman who sat there was free. Every one of them had a chance to live, to fight and to make a new career elsewhere in the starlit firmament.

They sat silently, many with bowed heads, as if they were engaged in prayer. Then sound came: A man's racking sob, the low hysterical laughter of a woman; after that, like the rising of a great wind, the cheers.

CHAPTER 21—DIARY

IN Eliot James' diaries the days appeared to be crammed with events. A glance at its pages would have made the observer believe that life was filled with excitement for the dwellers in Hendron's colony, although to the dwellers themselves, the weeks passed in what seemed like a steady routine, and James had been so busy that he was unable to write voluminously:

"Dec. 4th: To-day what we call the keel of the second Space Ship was laid. The first has been popularly named 'Noah's Ark,' and we have offered a prize of five thousand dollars in absolutely worthless bank-notes for anybody who will contrive a name for the second. It was a spectacular affair—all of us dressed in what we call our best clothes, Hendron making another of his usual speeches, full of stirring words and periodic sentences, and the molten metal pouring into its forms.

"Dec. 7th: To-day was a gala day for Tony Drake. Kyto, the Japanese servant whom he had had for some years in New York, and of whom he was inordinately fond, walked peacefully into camp, after he had been supposedly lost on the trip here from New York. The inscrutable little Jap walked up to Tony, whose back was turned. Kyto's face was like a smiling Buddha's; and fully appreciating the drama of the situation, he said in his odd voice: 'With exceedingly humbleness request possibilities of return to former employment.' Peter Vanderbilt and I had brought him up to Tony, and when Tony spun around, I thought he was going to faint. Immediately afterward he began thumping Kyto's back so hard that I personally feared for the Jap's life. But he seems to be wiry; in fact, he must have the constitution of a steel spring, for he has traveled overland more than eight hundred miles in the past two months, and his story, which I am getting out of him piecemeal, is one of fabulous adventure. Eve seemed almost as much pleased to see Kyto as was Tony himself. She took his hand and held it and cried over him, while he stood there blinking and saying that he was humbly and honorably this and that.

"*Dec. 8th:* Four deer wandered into the camp to-day, and were corralled for our menagerie after a very exciting chase.

"*Dec. 19th:* Hendron is a curiously ingenious devil. I discovered only to-day that he has used for insulation, between the double walls of the now completed Ark, two thick layers of asbestos, and between them, books. The books make reasonably good insulating material, and when we arrive at our future home, if we do not arrive with too hard a blow, we will be provided with an enormous and complete library. I even saw a first edition of Shelley which was designated for the lining of the second ship. Amazing fellow, Hendron.

"*Dec. 31st:* We had our Christmas dinner last Thursday, and except for the absence of turkey, it was complete, even to plum pudding. The weather continues to be warm, and the gardens which we replanted have flourished under this new sub-tropical climate, so that already we are reaping huge harvests which are being stored in the Space Ships.

"*Jan. 18th:* A flight was made to the 'mines' from which Ransdell's metals have been taken, and in the course of it the plane passed over St. Paul and Minneapolis. Apparently the mobs in those two cities have for the most part either perished or migrated, as there was very little sign of life— smoke columns rising here and there amid the ruins betokening small cooking-fires, and an occasional figure on the streets, nothing more. However, we have not drawn in the outposts stationed around the cantonment after the last attack, and if we should be again attacked in force, we shall be warned in time and shall not temporize but use the final weapon at once. However, no one expects another attack. Even in this dying world, the word of our weapon has spread.

"*Jan. 20th:* There was dancing in the hall of the women's

dormitory and Ransdell so far overcame his almost animal shyness that he danced twice with Eve. The rivalry between Ransdell and Tony is the most popular subject of discussion among the girls and women. I myself have been much interested in the triangle, and for a while I was disturbed about it, but such a bond has grown between the two men that I know whoever is defeated in the contest, if there is victory or defeat, will take his medicine honorably and generously. I am wondering, however, about that business of victory and defeat. The women here slightly outnumber the men. It will be necessary for them to bear children on the new planet. Variation of our new race will be desirable. To care for the same, fifty girls and twenty-five men are already deeply immersed in the study of obstetrics, nursing, pediatry, child psychology, etc. Perhaps we will resort in the main to polyandry and abolish, because of biological necessity, all marriage. There are a good many very real love-affairs existent already. That is to be expected, when the very flower of young womanhood and the best men of all ages are segregated in the wilderness. I myself doubtless reflect the mental attitude of most of the men here. There are a hundred women, I shall say two hundred, any one of whom I would be proud to have as my wife. But so great have been the trials of our life, so enormous is the need for our concentrated efforts, that little energy or time has been left to them to think about love or marriage.

Jan. 31st: It is too bad that the change in the earth's orbit and the inclination of its axis did not occur long ago. Generations of people who have been snowbound at this time in Michigan would rub their eyes in wonderment if they could see the trees still in leaf, the flowers still in bloom, the fields still green, sunshine alternating with occasional warm rains, and the thermometer standing between 65 and 85 every day.

"*Feb. 17th:* In a little more than a month it will be time for our departure. As that solemn hour approaches, all of us tend to think back into our lives, rather than forward toward our new lives. Hendron has not hesitated to make it clear that our relatively short jump through space will be dangerous indeed. The ships may not have been contrived properly to withstand what are at best merely theoretical conditions. The cold of outer space may overwhelm us. The sun may beat through the sides of the ship and consume us. The rays which travel through the empty reaches when we thrust ourselves among them clad in the thin cylinders of our Ark may assert a different potency from that experienced under the layer of Earth's atmosphere. Either or both of our two projectiles may collide with a wandering asteroid, in which case the consequences will be similar to those anticipated for the collision of Earth with Bronson Alpha. Hendron assures us

144

only that the ships will fly, and that if they reach the atmosphere of Bronson Beta, it will be possible to land them.

"*Feb. 22nd:* The Bronson Bodies have reappeared in the sky with visible discs. Alpha once more looks like a coin, and Beta not unlike the head of a large pin. Observations through our modest telescope show clearly that Bronson Beta, warmed by the sun, has a surface now completely thawed. Its once solid atmosphere is drifting about it filled with clouds, and through those clouds we are able to glimpse patches of dark and patches of brilliance, which indicate continents and oceans. At the first approach, an excellent spectroscopic analysis was made of the planet's composition. The analysis denoted its fitness to support human life, but we stand in such awe of it that we say to ourselves only: 'Perhaps we shall be able to live if we ever disembark there'; but we cannot know. There may be things upon its mysterious surface, elemental conditions undreamed of by man. However, there is some mysterious comfort, a sort of superstitious courage, afforded to many of our numbers by the fact that as our doom approaches, a future home is also waxing brightly in the dark sky. We spend many evenings staring toward the heavens.

"*Feb. 28th:* Tremendous effort is being expended upon the second Ark. The task of accumulating metal for its construction was tremendous, inasmuch as the vast stores accumulated by Hendron for the building of the first ship in the cantonment itself were insufficient. There was no time to smelt iron from the deposits in this district, and it had to be collected from every possible source. The hangar which had protected the first ship was confiscated. Two steel bridges across what used to be a river near by have furnished us with much of the extra material required, but we are now engaged in smelting every object for which we shall have no future use. Copper is at a premium, and our lighting system is now being conducted over iron wires, to the great detriment of its efficacy. Women are doing tasks that women have never done before, and we are all working on a sixteen-hour-a-day schedule. Hendronville looks like a little Pittsburgh—its furnaces going all night, its roads rutted by heavy trucking, and its foundries shaking with a continual roar of machinery. The construction of the second Ark in such a record time would have been impossible had it not been for the adaptability of Hendron's solution of atomic disintegration. Power and heat we have in unlimited quantities, but we are making progress, and we shall finish in time.

"*March 6th:* The day and hour of departure have been announced. In order to intercept the Bronson Body at its most advantageous point, we shall leave the Earth on the 27th of this month at 1:45 A.M. precisely. It is estimated that the journey will require about ninety hours, although it could be made much more quickly.

"*March 18th:* In running over my notes, I find I have not mentioned one source of constant interest and speculation here at the camp. From time to time, when our own receiving apparatus has been functioning, we have overheard radio broadcasts from the world outside. The static is still tremendous, and these broadcasts, whether on spark sets or over regular stations, have been most unsatisfactory. Once in November and again in January we heard the President of the United States. He recited in a very strained and weary voice a few fragmentary details of life in his small kingdom. Not in any hope of aid, but as if he wished to inform any one else who might be listening, what the situation was. He did not address his own constituents, so we may assume they have no receiving sets and are still struggling against appalling handicaps which Ransdell and myself observed. On three or four occasions through the rattle in the earphones we have caught snatches of broadcasts from foreign stations. But, except for a lull immediately after the storms, we have never been able to overhear enough so that we know anything definite about the situation in Europe or elsewhere, except that on the night of, I think, December 8th, we heard a short segment of a Frenchman's oration which evidently was intended to move his hearers toward peace. We assumed that in spite of the appalling conditions that must prevail abroad as they do here, Europe, still sticking stubbornly to her nationalism, is again engaged in some form of warfare.

"*March 20th:* A week from to-night we shall leave the Earth. The approach of this zero hour has cast a spell on the colonists. They move as if in a dream. When they talk, they use only trivialities and commonplaces as a medium for their expression. Nervous tension is enormous. I saw two of the girls sitting on the steps of their dormitory discussing dressmaking for half an hour with the utmost seriousness; and yet neither replied to anything the other had said, and neither said anything that might be remotely considered sensible.

"Everything is in readiness; a few perishables will be moved into the ships in the last hours; the stock and poultry have already been domiciled in their quarters, although they have not been lashed fast. I have been given by Hendron, to include with my papers, a complete list of the contents of both ships. In spite of their enormous size,—the second ship looks like three gas-storage tanks piled on top of each other, and also has the same shining exterior as the first,—it is impossible to believe that they could contain all the items in these lists.

"It is the most incredible assortment of the gear that belongs to mankind ever assembled in any one place. What our ships contain might well be samples of our civilization collected wholesale by some curious visitors from another world and taken home in order that their weird fellows might look upon the wisdom, the genius, the entertainment and the interests of men. We are ready."

CHAPTER 22—AVE ATQUE VALE

"WHEN I think," Tony said to Eve as they sat side by side on a small hilltop watching the descent of twilight into the busy valley, "of the foresight and ingenuity of your father, I am appalled. He was ahead of most of the people in the world in his idea for leaving the earth, and he was ahead of all of us when he saw the possibility and the practicability of taking everybody who was left after the struggle, to the new planet. It's odd. I used to imagine scenes that would exist when the Ark was ready to leave, and of the thousand of us here only a hundred would be chosen. It would have been a terrible period for every one. Then I used to think what would have happened if the world knew about the Ark. Hundreds of men like Borgan would have offered their millions in return for a ticket. Husbands would have deserted their wives and their children. People would have fought until they were killed, trying to get aboard. Prospective stowaways would have offered fabulous prices. No wonder he insisted on isolation and secrecy. And now we can all go—"

Eve hugged herself with her arms and looked at him sidewise. "I knew all about Dad's plans for the departure, and I knew something else. You were not to go, were you?"

"Me? Of course not. What good would I have been?"

Eve smiled. On this evening, an evening so close to the great adventure, she seemed radiant and unusually tender. "You're modest, Tony. That's one of your greatest charms. Let me tell you: Once I saw the list Dad had made up. He had given Bronson first place. I came second. Dodson was third. Ransdell was fourth. And you were fifth, Tony. When he could pick almost as he wished from the whole world, he made you fifth. That's pretty high up."

"Your father must be sentimental to consider me at all. But I am glad he gave Ransdell that fourth position. I can't imagine any situation in the world which Dave couldn't handle."

Eve ignored the compliment. "Father took the list away from me, and he was very angry that I had seen it. Peter Vanderbilt was on it. There are a good many high-minding and high-binding communists—that is, there used to be a good many—who would be mighty sore to think that into the blood of the future race would go that of the American aristocracy which they so passionately hate. Funny! I got into the habit of thinking, just as Dodson and the other men were thinking, about whom to preserve, and when you consider it, Vanderbilt has as much to offer as almost any one. The delicacy that comes from overbreeding, a wiry nervous constitution, an artist's temperament, taste, a learned mind, a gorgeous sense of humor and courage. Probably he's wasteful, spendthrift, decadent and jaded—or at least he used to be; but how greatly his positive virtues outweigh his vices!"

"He's a good egg," Tony replied. "I knew him for years. His sister went to school with my mother."

"Another thing: Dad's name wasn't on that list. I think when Dad thought he could save only a hundred people, he figured that he was too old, and that his work had been done; and I'll bet if the first ship had been ready to leave and there had been none other, Dad would have been missing at the crucial time, so that they would have been compelled to go without him."

"Yes," Tony said thoughtfully. "That's exactly what your father would have done. And how calmly we are able to consider that! It's strange the way people change. I remember once when I was in college, seeing a man in Boston struck by an automobile. I don't suppose he was really badly injured, and yet for days afterward I was actually sick. And I used to brood about the awfulness of people being locked up in prisons, about electrocution and operations.

"I couldn't stand the thought of people being hurt. I used to lie in my bed at night in a cold sweat thinking about the, to me, impossible courage of men who volunteered during the wars to go on missions that meant sure death. And now"—he shrugged his shoulders—"death has lost all its meaning. Suffering has become something we accept as the logical accompaniment of life. I am not even shocked when I think that your father would deliberately commit suicide on this planet if he decided his biological usefulness was at an end—although, of course, such a decision would have been mistaken."

Eve nodded in agreement. "He intended to do it, I think, as a lesson—a sort of instruction—to the others."

A silence fell between them. In the cantonment a mechanical siren tooted, and the night-shift exchanged places with the day-shift to the noisy undertone of moving trucks and banging doors. Lights sparkled in all the windows of the dining-hall, and as the doors opened and closed, a streak of vivid purplish light darted across the open campus. Tony began to talk again. "I have changed my ideas about everything, Eve—not only about life and death! I think that even my ideas about you are changing. When Ransdell came to New York under such dramatic circumstances, and when I saw your interest in him, I was jealous. I pretended I wasn't,

148

even to myself; but I was. And in some small way—some small-minded way—I felt superior to him. I was better educated, better bred, better trained socially. Since I've come to know that man, I've learned that from the standpoint of everything that counts, he's a man, and I'm still in short pants.

"It would have been hard to talk to you about such things at one time; in fact it would have been impossible, because I would have considered it bad form. Now it's all different. The day after to-morrow we are going to sail. I may not have a chance to see you alone again between now and then. I don't want to burden you with a feeling of unnecessary responsibility. There isn't any responsibility on your part. But I must tell you that I love you. I've told you that before, long ago, and what I said then has nothing to do with what I feel now. In saying it I am asking you for nothing. I mean that you shall know only that whatever happens, whatever you decide, whatever either of us does in the future, cannot alter the fact that I now do and always shall hold for you intact the most fundamental part of all that any man can feel toward any woman."

He had finished his words with his face turned toward her, and his eyes looking into her eyes.

Eve spread her palms on the ground behind her and leaned back. "I love you too, Tony. I shall always love you."

A long second passed, and then he said in a startled and absent-minded tone: "What?"

"I said I shall always love you. What did you expect me to say?"

"I don't know," Tony replied.

"Can a girl say anything more?"

"I guess not."

"Well, what's the matter with you then?"

Tony thrust his hand against his forehead. "I don't know. I can't believe it. I don't think either of us can guess what we will 'always' do—if we reach Bronson Beta."

Eve was still leaning on her straightened arms. "Whether we'll have marriage on the other planet or not, I can't tell. Maybe I'll be expected to share you with some of the other girls. I think the old system of living will never quite return. You're thinking of Ransdell: I admire him; I'm fascinated by him. Sometimes I have brief periods in which I get a tremendous yen for him. So much manhood in one person is irresistible. Probably I'm the first girl in the world who thrust into one of these intimate *tête-à-têtes* a statement of the truth. I am assuring you I love you. I'm telling you something that every human being knows and that every human being tries to pretend is not true—that love on a night like this can always be pledged as enduring; but that love through the years invariably proves to be something that is capricious,

149

something that waxes and wanes. I'm not saying that I love you with reservations, Tony. I'm saying only that I'm human."

Tony took her in his arms then and kissed her.

"I'll try to understand what you've told me," he said a long time afterward. "I don't deserve this."

Eve laughed softly. Her copper hair was disheveled, and her black eyes were luminous in the dark. Tony, looking down into them, was frightened even when he heard her laughter, and the words that followed it. "I'll be the person who decides in the future about your merits and demerits. Perhaps in giving up the power to choose the men she loves, the fathers for her children, by accepting our false single standards, woman has thrown away the key to freedom for both sexes. Anyway, let's not worry about that right this minute."

"You whistle so persistently and so cheerfully," Jack Taylor said to Tony on the following morning, "that it makes me irritable."

"Good!" Tony replied, and kept on whistling.

"I came here to bring you news, various kinds of news. The first item is interesting and historical: Ransdell is just in from a flight, and says he found how all those people got up here from the cities to attack us. There's a road reasonably undamaged that leads nearly three-quarters of the way from St. Paul here. The places wrecked by the earthquakes have been hastily repaired, and the whole road is littered with broken-down automobiles. Most of that mob must have driven a good part of the way. They must have spent weeks getting ready to strike."

Tony looked up from the suitcase which he was strapping in his room. He had stopped whistling. "That a fact? Well, that's one mystery cleared up, anyway."

"The second item is that the list of who goes in which ship has just been posted."

"Huh."

"I thought that word would get a rise out of you. Don't worry, don't worry. You're in the first ship, with Eve, all right. Hendron's in command. You're a lieutenant. James is with you. But guess who's in command of the second ship."

"Jessup?"

"Guess again."

"Kane?"

"Nope; you're all wet. Those two noble scientists are second in command. The big ship is going out under the instructions of your good friend David Ransdell."

"That's grand," Tony said; "but will he have sufficient technical knowledge to run the thing?"

"Oh, Jessup and Kane will do that all right. Ransdell's only going to be a figurehead until they get to Bronson Beta. But isn't that sweet?"

"That's swell."

"I mean for you and Eve. Think of it. Alone together in the reaches of utter space for ninety whole hours, cooped up with only about a hundred other people."

Tony groaned, kicked the lock on his suitcase shut, and said: "Jack, how'd you like to be lying on this floor unconscious?"

"Sure you could make the grade?"

"What do you think?"

Jack scratched his head in mock calculation.

"Well, remember back in Cornell when you were sounding me out to see if I'd be a likely candidate for this jaunt? Remember your asking me if I hadn't rowed on a crew, and my telling you that I had, but it wasn't much of a crew, and we were champions that year because the others were still worse?"

Tony nodded with mock menace. "I remember. What about it?"

"Well, on thinking it over, I've decided that that was a pretty good crew, after all. Now on this matter of whether I'm going to be lying on the floor unconscious, or you, I have another item to point out beside my quondam skill at the oars. I was a little bit rattled the day you came into my room, and I forgot to mention that I was also captain of the boxing team."

Tony stepped back. "Professionalism rearing its ugly head, eh? All right. We'll find something else to decide our positions. How about baseball-bats?"

"My idea exactly. Celluloid baseball-bats."

"Fine. I'll meet you and your seconds out behind the power-house in half an hour. In the meantime I've got to get packed up here. You know we're going places to-morrow."

Jack sat down on the bed. "That reminds me: I'm going on the second ship too."

Tony's face fell. They were serious again.

Jack said: "When you are all set, they want you down at the Ark. Everybody's going through it, and getting assigned to their quarters."

Tony walked up a long flight of steps to the airlock. As he went, he cast an upward glance at the elaborate structure of beams which supported the Ark, and which workmen were now removing. The interior of the Ark was brilliantly lighted by electricity. Through its center ran a spiral staircase, and a long taut cable inside the stairs. At eight-foot intervals steel floors cut the cylinder into sections. The two forward sections were crammed with machinery and instruments, and across them ran the great thrust-beams against which the atomic tubes would exert their force. A ring of smaller tubes pointing outward around the upper and lower sections like spokes were provided to give free dimensional control of the ship, and to make the adjustments necessary for grounding. It had been planned to travel head-on for the greater part of the distance. When the reaction forces were started, the whole ship would be upside down for some time, and eventually the landing would be made after turning it end for end; and although the probabilities of depositing the ship precisely upon her stern, and of keeping her in that position, were small, it was felt that after she had landed she might tip over, —a motion that would be broken by the use of the horizontal jets,—or that she might even roll, which could also be stopped by the jets, as had been done on the short and simple hop from the ground on the night of the attack.

Tony walked up the spiral staircase from the stern's engine-room. Above it were stockrooms with their arrangements for lashing fast the livestock which the Ark carried. Above the stockrooms were storerooms reaching to the center of the ship, and tightly packed. In the center of the ship were the human quarters, their walls carefully padded, and lashings, similar to but more comfortable than those provided for the animals, arranged along the floor.

These accommodations were not alluring. They suggested that the journey would be cramped and unpleasant, but inasmuch as it would take only ninety hours if it was successful, everything had been sacrificed to utility. On the side walls were water-taps, and in steel closets food for a considerably longer time than four days had been stored; but in their journey through space the travelers would enjoy no comfortable beds, eat no hot meals and divert themselves with no entertainments. The exact conditions of flight through space were unknown; and underneath the springs and paddings which lined the passengers' quarters was apparatus both for refrigeration and for heating. Tony passed through the double layer of passenger quarters, through the layers of storerooms and the engine-room at the front end of the great cylinder, climbing all the way on the spiral stairs. There he found Hendron, who was testing some of the apparatus.

"You sent for me?" Tony asked.

"No. Oh, I see what it was. They were giving out the numbers of your slings down below. I've asked every one to get in slings before we start and when we land, as I'm not sure, from the single test, exactly what the general effect will be. I think King was in charge of the list, but if you see him any time within the next few hours, he will tell you your number and position."

As Tony was about to go, Hendron recalled him. "I never showed you my engines, did I?"

"No," Tony said.

Hendron waved his arm around the chamber. It looked

very much like the interior of a submarine. "This is the forward power-cabin," he began. "The breeches of the main tubes are concealed behind a wall which is reënforced by the thrust-beams. Those are the ones which are to break the force of our fall; but you can see here the breeches of the smaller surrounding tubes. They are not unlike cannon, and they work on the same principle. Acting at right angles to our line of flight, they can turn the ship and revolve it end for end, in fact, like a thrown fire-cracker, if we should turn on jets on opposite sides and opposite ends. The breech of each of these little tubes,"—at that point Hendron turned a wheel with a handle on it, and the rear of one of the tubes slowly opened,—"is provided with the tubes which generate the rays that split atoms of beryllium into their protons and nuclei. The forces engendered in the process, which is like a molecular explosion, but vastly greater, together with the disrupted matter, is then discharged through the gun, the barrel of which is lined with Ransdell's metal. The consumption of fuel, so to speak, both in quantity and rate, is regulated by a mechanism on the breech itself. The rate and volume of the discharge will be, of course, immensely greater for leaving the earth, than it was on the mere hop from the ground on the night of the assault. The ship proved itself then to be a gun, or rather a number of guns, which we will fire steadily on the trip through space. By Newton's Law, which Einstein has modified only in microscopic effects, for every action there is an equal and positive reaction, so that through space the speed and energy of the discharge from the tubes—which we also call the engines and motors, rather inaccurately—are what will determine the speed and motion of the ship."

Tony looked at the breech of the tube and nodded.

"Journeying through space we will be a rocket that can be fired from both ends and from all around the sides of both ends?"

"Exactly, although the side firing is of lesser intensity. We have twenty stern vents and twenty forward, you see, and twelve around the circumference at each end." Hendron smiled. "It is very beautiful, our ship; and according to the laws of physics, by the release of more power, it will navigate space as surely as it hopped from the ground, when we required it to. We'll leave this world, Tony; and, I believe, we'll land upon Bronson Beta."

Tony stared at him: "And we'll live?"

"Why not, Tony? I can control the landing as I can control the leaving."

"I meant," said Tony, "granting that—granting we travel through space and reach that other planet and land upon it safely, will we live afterward?"

"Why not?" Hendron returned again. "We can count upon

vegetation on Bronson Beta almost surely. No, surely, I should say. Higher forms of life must have been annihilated by the cold; but the spores of vegetation could survive.

"Arrhenius, the great Swedish physicist, demonstrated years ago that the germinating of spores may be preserved rather than killed by intense cold. He cited, indeed, micro-örganisms that had been kept in liquid air, at a temperature of some two hundred degrees below zero, Centigrade, for many months without being deprived of their germinating power.

"We know too little about the lower temperatures; but what we have discovered indicates that the germinating power of microörganisms and spores should be preserved at lower temperatures for much longer periods than at our ordinary temperatures.

"Arrhenius made calculations on a cold of only minus 220 Centigrade, which is much warmer than the almost 'absolute cold' in which all organisms on Bronson Beta have been preserved."

Hendron referred to a notebook: " 'The loss of germinating power,' Arrhenius observed, 'is no doubt due to some chemical process, and all chemical processes proceed at slower rates at lower temperatures than they do at higher. The vital functions are intensified in the ratio of 1:2.5 when the temperature is raised by ten degrees Centigrade.'

"So in the case of spores at a distance from the sun of the orbit of Neptune, after their temperature had been lowered to minus 220, their vital energy would, according to this ratio, react with one thousand millions less intensity than at ten plus. Arrhenius figured that the germinating power of spores would not deteriorate in three million years at minus 220 more than it would in *one day* at an ordinary earthly temperature. It is not unreasonable, therefore, to believe that at the much lower temperatures which must have prevailed on Bronson Beta, spores and microörganisms could have been preserved indefinitely.

"These, now, have been thawed, and are being revived by the sun; so I feel we can count at least upon vegetation upon Bronson Beta."

"At least!" Tony caught up his words. "You will not deny, then, that there may be a possibility of higher life surviving or capable of being revived—too?"

Hendron shook his head. "I have seen too many incredible things occur, Tony," he replied, "to deny any possibility—particularly under conditions of which no one on this world has had any experience. But I do not expect it. I do expect vegetation, especially vegetation that grows from spores.

"In the early days on this world, the great majority of plants did not reproduce by seeds, but by the far more resistant spores, which have survived as the method of reproduction of many varieties. So we will count upon a native flora which, undoubtedly, will appear very strange to us. Of course, as you know, we are taking across with us our own seeds and our own spores."

"I know," said Tony, "and even our own insects too."

"An amazing list—isn't it, Tony?—our necessities for existence. We take so much for granted, don't we? You do not realize what has been supplied you by nature on this world of ours—until you come to count up what you must take along with you, if you hope to survive."

"Yes," said Tony, "ants and angleworms—and mayflies."

"Exactly. You've been talking with Keppler, I see. I put that problem entirely up to Keppler.

"Our first and most necessary unit for self-preservation proved to be the common honey bee, to secure pollination of flowering plants, trees and so on. Keppler says that of some twenty thousand nectar insects, this one species pollinates more than all the rest put together. The honey bee would take care of practically of this work, as his range is tremendous. There are a few plants—Keppler tells me—such as red clover, which he cannot work on; but his cousin the bumblebee, with his longer proboscis, could attend to them. So, first and foremost among living things, we bring bees.

"We also take ants, especially the common little brown variety, to ventilate, drain and work the soil; and, as you have observed, angleworms also.

"Since we are going to take with us fish eggs to hatch into fish over there, we have to take mayflies. Their larvæ, in addition to providing food for the fish, are necessary to keep the inland waters from becoming choked with algæ and the lower water plants.

"In the whole of the Lepidoptera there is not, Keppler says, one necessary or even useful species; but for sheer beauty's sake—and because they take small space—we will take six butterflies and at least the Luna moth.

"And we must take one of the reputed scourges of the earth."

"What?" said Tony.

"The grasshopper—the locust. Such an insect will be vitally necessary to keep the greenery from choking our new earth; and the one best suited for this job is, paradoxically enough, one of mankind's oldest scourges, the grasshopper. He is an omnivorous feeder and would keep the greenery in check—after he got his start. Our first problem may be that he will not multiply fast enough; and then that he multiply too fast. So to keep him in check, and also the butterfly and the moth, we will take parasitic flies. We will have to have these—two or three of the dozen common Tachinidæ have been chosen.

155

"These will be the essential insects. Here on earth, with a balanced and bewilderingly intricate economy already established, a tremendously longer list would be vital to provide the proper checks and balances; but starting anew, on Bronson Beta, we can begin, at least, with the few insects we have chosen. Unquestionably, differentiation and evolution will swiftly set in, and they will find new forms.

"We are bringing along vials of mushroom and other fungi spores. Otherwise vegetation would fall down, never disintegrate, and pile up till everything was choked. A vial the size of your thumb holds several billion spores of assorted fungi—in case the spores of the fungi of Bronson Beta have not survived. They are absolutely essential.

"Also, besides our own water supply for the voyage, we are taking bottles of stagnant pond-water and another of seawater containing our microörganisms such as diatoms, plankton, unicellular plants and animals which form the basis for our biotic economy and would supplement, or replace, such life on the other globe.

"About animals—" He halted.

"Yes, about animals," Tony urged.

"There is, naturally, still discussion. Our space is so limited, and there is most tremendous competition. Birds offer a somewhat simpler problem; but possibly you have heard some of the arguments over them."

"I have," said Tony, "and joined in them. I confess I argued for warblers—yellow warblers. I like them; I have always liked them; and meadow larks."

"The matter of dogs and cats is the most difficult," Hendron said, closing the subject. Air pumps murmured somewhere within the ship, which seemed half-alive. Electric generators hummed, and from somewhere came the high note of one of the electronic engines. Tony left Hendron and went from the ship.

That night, the emigrants from the Earth gathered again in the dining-hall. Hendron addressed them, outlining the general final preparations which were augmented by specific, printed instructions to meet such contingencies as could be foreseen.

The large ship, an exact duplicate of the original Ark with the exception of its greater proportions, stood on a concrete platform three hundred yards from its smaller companion.

After the meeting, the crowd moved outdoors and stood awhile, looking at the Bronson Bodies. As in their former approach their size had increased in diametric proportion during the last few days and nights, and they now dominated the heavens, Alpha eclipsed by Beta, which rushed toward the earth ahead of it, in the same position as that held by a planet in transit across the face of the sun. The spectacle was one of weird beauty, and one calculated to strike terror in the bravest. Bronson Alpha looked like the rising moon, except that it was much larger than any moon had ever seemed to be; and its edges, instead of being sharp, were furred with a luminous aura which indicated its atmosphere. Riding as if on the bosom of Bronson Alpha was its smaller comrade, and it was sometimes difficult for the eye to delineate it exactly, for both planets gave off a brilliant white light. On Beta dark irregular "continental" splashes could be seen, and similar areas of maximum brightness doubtless indicated great oceans.

It seemed as they rose over the horizon on that last night that they increased visibly in size as the onlookers regarded them.

And such might have been the case, for now the earth was no longer rushing away from the stranger bodies, but toward them.

Already the desolate and wounded surface of man's world was stirring to their approach. Slight earthquake shocks were felt from time to time, and the very winds seemed to be moving in a consciousness of the awful cataclysm that was drawing near. All over the world, the tides—unnaturally absent since the shattering of the moon—rose again and licked up the sides of the fresh, raw shores; the people who huddled on mountains and prairie plateaus that night knew instinctively that this was indeed the end.

Chapter 23—The Last Night on Earth

TONY sought out Eve.

"Come walk with me," he said.

"I'd like to. It's so strange to wait, with everything done that matters. For it's all done, Tony; everything that we're to take with us has been prepared and put in place. Except the animals and ourselves."

"Dull lot of animals, mostly," complained Tony. He was excited and on edge, with nerves which he tried to quiet and could not.

He did not want to talk to Eve to-night about animals; but he might as well, for people were all about, alone or in pairs, likewise restless and excited.

"It would be madness to try to bring the interesting animals along, wouldn't it?" Eve said agreeably. "Like lions and tigers and leopards."

"I know," admitted Tony. "Meat-eaters. We can't cart along meat for them, of course; and we can't expect meat on Bronson Beta. All we can hope for is grass and moss; so we load up with a cow, and a young bull, of course; a pair of sheep of proved breeding ability, a couple of reindeer, and a colt and a young mare. Half humanity lived on horsemeat once and milked the mares. We'll be allowed goats, too. And deer, if our big ship gets over. Do you supose there'll be other ships starting from this side of the world tomorrow night and from the other side, the evening after?"

"Father doesn't know. When the radios were working well, months ago, he broadcast the knowledge of David's metal. It must have become obtainable from volcanic eruptions in other places. But we've no real news of any one else ready to start. One thing is certain. No party can count upon the arrival of any other. Each crew has to assume that it may be the only one that gets across to Bronson Beta."

"And damn' lucky if it lands, too," agreed Tony. "However, I hope the Australians are making a try, and will start with a kangaroo. And if the South Africans have a ship, they ought to show some originality in animals, even if they too feel confined to grass- and moss-eaters. Who has a chance of sending up a ship, anyway?"

"The English, Father thinks, surely have preserved enough organization to build and equip one ship, and the French, the Germans and Italians ought to do the same. Then there are the Russians and the Japanese at least with the potential ability to do it. There's a chance in Australia and another in South Africa—Lord Rhondin would head any party there, Father thinks."

"Any one else?"

"A possibility in Argentina and also in China."

"That makes twelve, counting our two."

"Possibilities, that's all. Of course, we know nothing about them. Father guesses that if twelve are trying, perhaps five may get ships out into space."

"What five?" demanded Tony.

"He did not name them."

"Five into space beyond the attraction of the world."

"The world won't be left then, Tony," Eve reminded him.

"Right. Funny how one keeps forgetting that, isn't it? So there'll be no place for them to drop back to, if they miss Bronson Beta. They just stay—out there in space—in their rocket, with their air-purifiers and oxygen-machines and their compressed food and their seeds and insects and birds or birds' eggs, and carefully chosen grass-eating animals. . . . I imagine they'll eat the animals, at last, out there in space; and then—"

Eve stopped him.

"Why deny the possibilities?" he objected.

"Why dwell on those particular ones, Tony, when they may be the ones we ourselves will meet? We—or our friends in our other ship. . . . It's funny how you men complain about

158

missing the wild animals. Do you know, Tony, that Dave told me that Dr. Bronson thought about the impossibility of taking over lions when he first began planning with Father the idea of the space ships? That night Lord Rhondin and Professor Bronson walked about the room and spoke about how there would be no more lions."

"Funny to think of meeting Rhondin for the first time on Bronson Beta," said Tony, "if we and the South African ship get over. Good egg, Lord Rhondin, from all I hear from Dave."

They were off by themselves now, and Tony drew her nearer to him. She neither encouraged nor resisted him. He tightened his arm about her, and felt her softness and warmth against him. For a moment she remained motionless, neutral; then suddenly her hands were on his arms, clasping him, clinging to him. Her body became tense, thrilling, and as he bent, her lips burned on his.

She drew back a little, and at last he let her. In silence he kissed her again; then her lips, close to his, said: "Farewell to earth, Tony!"

"Yes," he said, quivering. "Yes; I suppose this is our last sure night."

"No; we leave to-night, Tony."

"To-night? I thought it was to-morrow."

"No; Father feared the last night—if any one knew it in advance. So he said to-morrow; but all his calculations make it to-night."

"How soon, Eve?"

"In an hour, dear. You'll hear the bugles. He deceived even you."

"And Dave?" asked Tony jealously. Dave Ransdell now was his great friend. Dave was to be in command, except as to scientific matters, of the party in the second ship; Tony was himself second only to Hendron on the first ship; and Tony had no jealousy of Dave for that. Moreover, Eve was to travel in the ship with her father and Tony; if he was saved, so would be she! And Dave might, without them, be lost. Tony had told himself that he had conquered his jealousy of Dave; but here it still held him.

"No," said Eve. "Father told Dave to-morrow, too. But we leave the earth to-night."

"So to-morrow," said Tony, "to-morrow we may be 'ourselves, with yesterday's seven thousand years.' I had plans— or dreams at least, Eve—of the last night on earth. It changes them to find it barely an hour."

"I should not have told you, Tony."

"Why? Would you have me go ahead with what I dreamed?"

"Why not?" she said. "An hour before the bugles; an hour

159

before we leave the world, to fall back upon it from some frightful height, dear, and be shattered on this globe's shell; or to gain space and float on endlessly, starving and freezing in our little ship; or to fall on Bronson Beta and die there. Or perhaps, Tony—perhaps, to live!"

"Perhaps," repeated Tony; but he had not, this time, gone from the world with her in his mind. He held her again and thought of his hour—the last hour of which he could be sure.

"Come away," he said. "Come farther away from—"

"From what, Tony?"

"From everybody else." And he drew her on. He led her, indeed, toward the edge of the encampment where the wires that protected it knitted a barrier. And there, holding her, he heard and she heard a child crying.

There were no children in the encampment. There never had been. No one with little children had been chosen. But here was a child.

Eve called to it, and the child ceased crying; so Eve had to call again for a response that would guide her to it in the dark. . . .

There were two children, together and alone. They were three and four years old, it appeared. They knew their names —Dan and Dorothy. They called for "Papa." Papa, it appeared, had brought them there in the dark and gone away. Papa had told them to stay there, and somebody would come.

Eve had her arms between the wires, and the children clung to her hands while they talked. Now Tony lifted them over the wires; and Eve took them in her arms.

In the awful "moonlight" of Bronson Beta, the children clung to her; and the little girl asked if she was "Mamma." Mamma, it appeared, had gone away a long time ago.

"Months ago only," Eve interpreted for Tony, "or they wouldn't remember her."

"Yes. Probably in the destruction of the First Passage," Tony said; and they both understood that the mother must be dead.

"He brought them here to us," Eve said; and Tony understood that too. It was plain enough: Some father, who had heard of the camp and the Space Ships, had brought his children here and left them—going away, asking nothing for himself. . . .

Clear and loud in the night, a bugle blew; and Tony and Eve both started.

"Gabriel's horn," muttered Tony. "The last trump!"

"Father advanced the time," returned Eve. "He decided to give a few minutes more of warning; or else he fooled me, too."

"You are carrying that child?" asked Tony. Eve had the little girl.

"Yes," said Eve. "You are carrying the boy?"

"Yes," said Tony. "Rules or no rules; necessities or no necessities, if we can take sheep and goats, I guess we can take these two."

"I guess so," said Eve; and she strode strongly beside him into the edge of illumination as the great floodlights blazed out.

The buildings were all alight; and everybody was bustling. The loading of the two Arks long ago had been completed, as Eve had said—except for the animals and the passengers and crew. The animals now were being driven aboard; and the passengers ran back and forth, calling, crying, shaking hands, embracing one another.

They were all to go; every one in sight was billeted on the Space Ships; but some would be in one ship, some on the other. Would they meet again—on Bronson Beta? Would either ship get there? Would they rise only to drop from a great height back upon this earth? What would happen?

Tony, hurrying to his station, appreciated how wisely Hendron had acted in deceiving them all—even himself—as to the night.

Here he was, second in command of the first Space Ship, carrying a strange child in contravention of all orders. The chief commander's daughter also carried a child.

No one stopped them. Not Hendron himself. It was the last hour on earth, and men's minds were rocking.

The bugles blew again; and Tony, depositing the boy with Eve, set about his business of checking the personnel of his ship.

Three hundred yards away, Dave Ransdell checked the personnel of his larger party. Jessup and Kane, there, were in the navigating-room as Hendron was in the chief control-room here.

Ransdell, for a moment, ran over. He asked for Hendron, but he sought, also, Eve.

Tony did not interfere; he allowed them their last minutes together.

A third time the bugles blew. This meant: "All persons at ship stations!" All those who were to leave the earth forever, aboard ship!

Chapter 24—Starward Ho!

TONY completed his check of crew and passengers. Thrice he blew his whistle.

From off to the right, where the second ship lay, Dave Ransdell's shrill signal answered.

"Close valves and locks!"

There was no one on the ground. No one! They were all aboard. All checked and tallied, thrice over. Yet as Tony left the last lock open to gaze out again and listen, he heard a faint cry. The father of the children?

Could he take him too? One man more? Of course they could make it. If it was only one man more, they must have him. Tony withheld the final signal.

With a quick command, he warned those who were closing the lock. It swung open again. The voice was faint and far away, and in its thin notes could be detected the vibrations of tense anxiety. Tony looked over the landscape and detected its direction. It came from the southwest, where the airplane-field lay. Presently he made out syllables, but not their meaning.

"Hello," he yelled mightily. "Who is it?"

Back came the thinly shouted reply: *"C'est moi, Duquesne! Attendez!"*

Tony's mind translated: *"It's I, Duquesne! Wait."*

On the opposite side of the flying-field a lone human figure struggled into the rays of the flood-lights. It was the figure of a short fat man running clumsily, waving his arms and pausing at intervals to shout. Duquesne! The name had a familiar sound. Then Tony remembered. Duquesne was the French scientist in charge of building the French space ship that had been reported to him by James long ago. Instinctively he was sure that this Duquesne who ran ludicrously across the flying-field was the same man.

He turned to the attendants at the airlock.

"Get Hendron," he said; "he'll be in the stern control-room now. Tell him Duquesne is here alone." He operated the winch which moved the stairway back to the hull of the ship.

The short fat man trotted across the field, stopping frequently to gesticulate and shout: *"Attendez! C'est moi, Duquesne!"*

At last he scrambled up the steps of the concrete foundations to the ship. He rushed across the platform and arrived at the airlock. He was completely out of breath, and could not speak. Tony had an opportunity to look at him. He wore the remnants of a khaki uniform which did not fit him. Protruding from the breast pocket of the tunic was the butt of a revolver. He was black-haired, black-eyed and big-nosed. He regarded Tony with an intensity which was almost comical, and when he began to speak brokenly, he first swore in French and then said in English: "I am Duquesne! The great Duquesne! The celebrated Duquesne! The famous Duquesne! The French physicist, me, Duquesne. This I take for the ship of Cole 'Endron—yes? Then, so I am here. Tell him I have come from France in three months, running a steamboat by myself, flying across this foul country with my plane, which is broken down near what was Milwaukee, and to here I have walked by myself alone these many days. You are going now, yes? I see you are going. Tell him to go. Tell him Duquesne is here. Tell him to come and see me. Tell him to come at once. Tell him I leave those pigs, those dogs, those cows. those onions, who would build such a foolish ship as they will break their necks in. I said it would not fly, I, Duquesne. I knew this 'Endron ship would fly, so I have come to it. Bah! They are stupid, my French colleagues. More suitable for the motormen of trams than for flyers in outer space!"

At that instant Hendron arrived at the top of the spiral staircase.

He rushed forward with his eyes alight. "Duquesne! By God, Duquesne! I'm delighted. You're in the nick of time. In forty minutes we would have been away from here."

Duquesne gripped Hendron's hand, and skipped around him as if he were playing a child's game. With his free fist he smote upon his breast. Whether he was ecstatic with joy or rage could not have been told, for he shouted so that the entire chamber reverberated: "Am I a fool that you should have to tell me what hour was set for your departure? Have I no brains? Do I know nothing about astronomy? Have I never studied physics? Have I run barefoot across this whole United States of America for no other reason than because I knew when you would have to leave? Do I not carry the day on the watch in my pocket? Idiots, charming friends, glorious Americans, fools! Have I no brain? Can I not anticipate? Here I am."

Suddenly after this broadside of violent speech he became calm. He let go of Hendron's hand and stopped dancing. He bowed very gravely, first to Hendron, then to Tony, then to the crew. "Gentlemen," he said, "let's be going. Let's be on our way."

Hendron turned to Tony, who in reaction burst into a paroxysm of laughter. For an instant the French scientist looked deeply wounded and as if he might burst into expletives of anger; then suddenly he began to laugh. "I am ridiculous, am I not?" he shouted. He roared with laughter. He rocked with it. He wrapped his arms around his ample frame, and the tears rolled down his cheeks. "It is magnificent," he said. "Yes. It is to laugh."

"What about the ships that were being built in other countries in Europe?" Hendron asked him.

"The English?" returned Duquesne. "They will get away. What then, who knows? Can you 'muddle through' space, Cole 'Endron? I ask it. But the English are sound; they have a good ship. But as to them, I have made my answer. I am here."

"The Germans?" demanded Hendron.

The Frenchman gestured. "Too advanced!"

"Too advanced?"

"They have tried to take every contingency into account—too many contingency! They will make the most beautiful voyage of all—or by far the worst. Again I reply, I am here. As to all the other, again I observe, I have preferred to be here."

And in that fashion Pierre Duquesne, France's greatest physicist, was at the eleventh hour and the fifty-ninth minute added to the company of the Ark. He went off with Hendron to the control-room, talking volubly. Tony superintended the closing of the lock. He went up the spiral staircase to the first passenger deck. Fifty people lay there on the padded surface with the broad belts strapped around their legs and torsos. Most of them had not yet attached the straps intended to hold their heads in place. Their eyes were directed toward the glass screen, where alternately views of the heavens overhead and of the radiant landscape outside the Space Ship were being shown.

Tony looked at his number and found his place. Eve was near by him, with the two children beside her. She had sat up to welcome him. "I've been terribly nervous. Of course I knew you'd come, but it has been hard waiting here."

"We're all set," Tony said. "And the funniest thing in the world has just happened." He began to tell about the arrival of Duquesne, and everybody in the circular room listened to his story. As he talked, he adjusted himself on the floor harness.

Below, in the control-room, the men took their posts. Hendron strapped himself under the glass screen. He fixed his eyes to an optical instrument, across which were two hair lines. Very close to the point of their intersection was a small star. The instrument had been set so that when the star reached the center of the cross, the discharge was to be started. About him was a battery of switches which were controlled by a master switch, and a lever that worked not unlike a rheostat over a series of resistances. His control-room crew were fastened in their places with their arms free to manipulate various levers. Duquesne had taken the place reserved for one of the crew, and the man who had been displaced had been sent up to the passenger-cabins.

The French scientist glanced at his watch and put it back into his pocket without speaking. Voluble though he was, he knew when it was time to be silent. His black, sparkling eyes darted appreciatively from one instrument to another in the chamber, and on his face was a rapt expression as his mind identified and explained what he saw. Hendron looked away from the optical instrument. "You religious, Duquesne?"

The Frenchman shook his head and then said: "Neverthe-less, I am praying."

Hendron turned to the crossed hairs and began to count. Every man in the room stiffened to attention.

"One, two, three, four, five—" His hand went to the switch. The room was filled with a vibrating hum. "—Six, seven, eight, nine, ten—" The sound of the hum rose now to a feline shriek. "—Eleven, twelve, thirteen, fourteen, fifteen—ready! Sixteen, seventeen, eighteen, nineteen, twenty—" His hand moved to the instrument that was like a rheostat. His other hand was clenched, white-knuckled, on his straps. "Twenty-one, twenty-two, twenty-three, twenty-four, twenty-five." Simultaneously the crew shoved levers, and the rheostat moved up an inch. As he counted, signals flashed to the other ship. They must leave at the same moment.

A roar redoubling that which had resounded below the ship on the night of the attack, deafened all other sound.

Tony thought: "We're leaving the earth!" But strangely, thought itself at such a moment supplied no sensation. The physical shocks were too overpowering.

A quivering of the ship that jarred the soul. An upthrust on the feet. Hendron's lips moving in counting that could no longer be heard. The eyes of the men of the crew watching those lips so that when they reached fifty, a second switch was touched, and the room was plunged into darkness re-lieved only by the dim rays of tiny bulbs over the instruments themselves. A slight change in the feeling of air-pressure against the eardrums. Another forward motion of the steady hand on the rheostat. An increase of the thrust against the feet, so that the whole body felt leaden. Augmentation of the hideous din outside.

An exchange of glances between Hendron and Duquesne—both men's eyes flashing with triumph.

In the passenger-cabin, Tony's recitation of the arrival of Duquesne was suddenly interrupted by the fiendish uproar. "We've started!" fifty voices shouted, and the words were soundless. The deck on which they lay pressed up against them. The glass screen overhead went dark. Tony reached toward Eve, and felt her hand stretching to meet his.

CHAPTER 25—THE JOURNEY THROUGH SPACE

ON the doomed earth, observers must have seen the Space Ship lying brass-bright in the light of the Bronson Bodies and the cantonment flood-lamps, as immobile as if part of the earth. They must have seen it surrounded abruptly in golden fire, fire that drove toward the earth and lifted in immense clouds which bellowed and eddied toward the other larger ship simultaneously rising above a similar cloud. They must have heard the hideous torrent of sound, and then they must have seen the ship rise rapidly into the air on its column of flame. They must have watched it gain altitude vertically. They would have realized that it gathered momentum as it rose, and they would have seen that long trail of fire beneath each ship stretch and stretch as the shimmering cylinder shot into the night until it detached itself from the earth. But— there were no known observers left immediately below. If any one from outside the camp had happened to approach too closely, he must certainly have been annihilated by the blast.

Tony, clinging to his straps, thought of the father who had brought the children; and Tony hoped, irrationally, that he had fled far away. But what difference whether he was annihilated alone now—or in the wreck of all the world a little later?

He could see the fiery trail of the second Ark rising skyward on its apex of scintillating vapor. Already it was miles away.

Below, on the earth, fires broke out—a blaze that denoted a forest burning. In the place where the ship had been, the two gigantic blocks of concrete must have crumbled and collapsed. The power-house, left untended, continued to hum, supplying lights for no living thing. Far away to the south and west, the President of the United States, surrounded by his Cabinet, looked up from the new toil engendered by the recommencing earthquakes, and saw, separated by an immeasurable distance, two comets moving away from the earth. The President looked reverently at the phenomenon; then he said: "My friends, the greatest living American has but now left his home-land."

In the passenger-chamber the unendurable noise rose in a steady crescendo until all those who lay there felt that their vital organs would be rent asunder by the fury of that sound. They were pressed with increasing force upon the deck. Nauseated, terrified, overwhelmed, their senses foundered, and many of them lapsed into unconsciousness.

Tony, who was still able to think, despite the awful acceleration of the ship, realized presently that the din was diminishing. From his rather scanty knowledge of physics he tried to deduce what was happening. Either the Ark had reached air so thin that it did not carry sound-waves, or else the Ark was traveling so fast that its sound could not catch up with it. The speed of that diminution seemed to increase. The chamber became quieter and quieter. Tony reflected, in spite of the fearful torment he was undergoing, that eventually the only sound which would afflict it would come from the breeches of the tubes in the control-rooms, and the rooms themselves would insulate that. Presently he realized that the ringing in his ears was louder than the noise made by the passage of the ship. Eve had relaxed the grip on his hand, but at that moment he felt a pressure.

It was impossible to turn his head. He said, "Hello," in an ordinary voice, and found he had been so deafened that it was inaudible. He tried to lift his hand, but the acceleration of the ship was so great that it required more effort than he was able yet to exert. Then he heard Eve's voice and he realized that she was talking very loudly: "Are you all right, Tony? Speak to me."

He shouted back: "I'm all right. How are the children?" He could see them lying stupefied, with eyes wide open.

"It's horrible, isn't it?" Eve cried.

"Yes, but the worst is over. We'll be accelerating for some time, though."

Energy returned to him. He struggled with the bonds that held his head, and presently spoke again to Eve. She was deathly pale. He looked at the other passengers. Many of them were still unconscious, most of them only partly aware of what was happening. He tried to lift his head from the floor, but the upward pressure still overpowered him. He lay supine. Then the lights in the cabin went out and the screen was illuminated. Across one side was a glimpse of the trail which they were leaving, a bright hurtling yellow stream, but it was not that which held his attention. In the center of the screen was part of a curved disk. Tony realized that he was staring up at half of the northern hemisphere of the Earth. The disk did not yet have the luminous quality that the moon used to possess. It was in a sort of hazy darkness which grew light on its eastern edge.

Tony thought he could make out the outline of Alaska on the west coast of the United States, and he saw pinpoints of light which at first he thought of as signs of human habitation, but which he presently realized must have represented vast brilliant areas. He identified them with the renewal of volcanic activity. The screen flashed. Another view appeared. Constellations of stars, such stars as he had never seen, blazing furiously in the velvet blackness of the outer sky. He realized that he was looking at the view to be had from the side of the ship. The light went out again, and a third of the four periscopes recorded its field. Again stars, but in their center and hanging away from them, as if in miraculous suspension, was a small round bright-red body which Tony recognized as Mars.

Once again Eve pressed his hand, and Tony returned the pressure.

In the control-room, Hendron still sat in the sling with his hand on the rheostat.

His eyes traveled to a meter which showed their distance from the Earth. Then they moved on to a chronometer; then

167

for an instant, as if in concession to his human curiosity, they darted to Duquesne. Duquesne had loosened himself from his sling and was lying on the floor, unable to rise. His expression in the dim light was extremely ludicrous. He struggled feebly, like a beetle that has been turned on its back, and Hendron smiled at him and pointed to the chronometer, but Duquesne did not seem to understand his meaning.

The control-room was filled with the throb that was contained in the breeches, but Hendron could do nothing to alleviate it. He had already determined the time necessary for acceleration—one hundred and twelve minutes—and he could not shorten it. In the end, Duquesne managed to pull himself to a sitting position underneath the glass screen where he was perfectly content to sit and contemplate the heavens as they appeared in reflection from outer space.

Tony felt that he had been lying on the floor for an eternity. His strength had come back, and he realized that it would be possible to sit up, even to move about, but they had been instructed to remain on the floor until the speed of their ascent was stabilized. Minutes dragged. It was becoming possible to converse in the chamber, but few people cared to say anything. Many of them were still violently ill. Others were glad to lie motionless, and watch the screen as Duquesne was doing several decks below.

At three minutes of five, Hendron slowly moved back the handle of the rheostat, and almost abruptly conditions in the ship changed. The volume of sound radiating from the engine-room decreased. Hendron unbuckled his bonds and stepped from them. Duquesne stood up. He walked unsteadily across the floor to take the hand of Hendron.

"Magnificent! Stunning! Beautiful! Perfect! How fast do we now travel?" He was compelled to shout to make himself heard.

Hendron pointed at a meter; its indicator hovered between the figures 3,000 and 3,500.

"Miles?" the Frenchman asked.

Hendron nodded.

"Per hour?"

Hendron nodded again.

The Frenchman made his mouth into the shape required for a whistle, although no note could be heard.

Hendron operated the switch controlling the choice of periscopes. In the midst of the glass screen, the Earth now appeared as a round globe, its diameter in both directions clearly apparent. More than half of it lay in shadow, but the illuminated half was like a great relief map. The whole of the United States, part of Europe and the north polar regions, were revealed to their gaze. In wonder they regarded the world that had been their home. They could see clearly the colossal changes which had been wrought upon it. The great inland sea that occupied the Mississippi Valley sparkled in the morning sun. The myriad volcanoes which had sprung into being along the Western cordillera were for the most part hidden under a pall of smoke and clouds.

Duquesne pointed solemnly to that part of Europe that was visible. Hendron, looking at the screen for the first time, was shocked to see the disappearance of the Lowland Plain.

The Frenchman moved closer to him and shouted in his ear. "We abandoned the ship outside of Paris when we realized it was not on high enough ground. We started a new one in the Alps. I told those pigs: 'Gentlemen, it will melt. It is but wax, I know it.' They replied: 'If it melts, we shall perish.' I responded: 'If you perish, it shall be without me.'" Suddenly the Frenchman popped out his watch. "*Sapristi!* The world has turned so that these fools are to leave now." He moved his lips while he made a rapid calculation. "We shall observe, is it not so? In an hour my idiot friends will burn themselves to death. I shall laugh. I shall roar. I shall shout. It will be one grand joke. Yes, you will give me a focus upon France in this remarkable instrument of yours an hour from now, will you not?"

Hendron nodded. He signaled a command to his crew, who had been standing unbuckled from their slings, at attention. They now seated themselves.

Hendron shouted at the Frenchman: "Come on up with me. I'll introduce you to the passengers. I'm anxious to know about them."

When Hendron reached the first deck of passengers' quarters, he found them standing together comparing notes on the sensations of space-flying. Many of them were rubbing stiff arms and legs. Two or three, including Eliot James, were still lying on the padded deck in obvious discomfort. They had turned on the lights, apparently more interested in their own condition than in the astounding vista of the Earth below. Tony had just opened the doors of the larder and was on the point of distributing sandwiches.

Hendron brought the shabby Duquesne into their midst.

"I'd like to present my friend Professor Pierre Duquesne of the French Academy, a last-minute arrival. I assure you that except for its monotony, the trip will offer you no further great discomfort until we reach Bronson Beta, when we shall be under the necessity of repeating approximately the same maneuver. I want to call your attention to the following phenomena: In something less than an hour we are going to turn the periscope on France in an effort to observe the departure of the French equivalent of our ships. We are at the moment engaged in trying to locate our second Ark, which took its course at a distance from us to avoid any chance of collision, and being between us and the sun, is now temporarily lost in the glare of the sun.

"I will have the sun thrown on the screen at intervals, as some of the phenomena are extremely spectacular. At about mid-point of our voyage we will concentrate our attention on the collision between the Earth and Bronson Alpha. I think at this point I may express my satisfaction in the behavior of the Ark. As you all are aware, we have escaped from the earth. We are still well within the field of its gravitational control, in the sense that if our propellent forces ceased, we undoubtedly would fall back upon the earth; but the pull of gravity is constantly weakening. It diminishes, as most of you know, not directly in relation to the distance, but in relation to the square of the distance. It is the great lessening of the pull of gravity which has ended our extreme distress.

"Except for the small chance of striking an astrolite, we are quite safe and will continue so for some time. When we approach Bronson Beta, our situation will, of course, become more difficult. You will please excuse me now, as I wish to convey the same information to the passengers on the deck above."

Hendron departed, and his feet disappeared through the opening in the ceiling which contained the spiral staircase.

Duquesne immediately made himself the center of attention, praising alternately Hendron's ship and his own prowess in completing the journey from France. The reaction from the initial strain of the voyage took, in him, the form of saluting, shouting, joking with the men and flirting with the women.

Tony saw to the distribution of food and water. The ship rushed through the void so steadily that cups of milk, which Eve held to the lips of the children, scarcely spilled over. The passengers, having eaten a little, found that they could move from floor to floor without great trouble, and several became garrulous. The ship was spinning very slowly, exposing one side after the other to the sun, and this served to equalize the temperature, which was fiery hot on the sun-side, deadly cold on the other.

Fans distributed the air inside the ship. Outside, there was vacuum against which the airlocks were sealed. The air of the ship, breathed and "restored," was not actually fresh, although chemically it was perfectly breathable. The soft roar of the rocket propulsion-tubes fuddled the senses. There was no sensation of external time, no appreciation of traveling from morn to night. The sun glared in a black sky studded with brilliant stars. . . . The sun showed its corona, its mighty, fiery prominences, its huge leaping tongues of flame.

To the right of the sun, the great glowing crescents of Bronson Alpha and Bronson Beta loomed larger and larger.

Eve sat with Tony as a periscope turned on them and dis-

170

played them on the screen. They could plainly see that Bronson Alpha was below and approaching the earth; Bronson Beta, slowly turning, was higher and much nearer the ship.

"Do you see their relation?" she asked.

"Between the Bronson Bodies?" said Tony. "Aren't they nearer together than they have ever been before?"

"Much nearer; and as Father—and Professor Bronson—calculated. Bronson Beta, being much the smaller and lighter, was revolving about Bronson Alpha. The orbit was not a circle; it was a very long ellipse. Sometimes, therefore, this brought Bronson Beta much closer to Alpha than at other times. When they went around the sun, the enormous force of the sun's attraction further distorted the orbit, and Bronson Beta probably is nearer Alpha now than it ever was before. Also, notice it is at the point in its orbit which is most favorable for us."

"You mean for our landing on it?" asked Tony.

"For that; and especially is it favorable to us, after we land —if we do," amended Eve; and she gathered the children to her. She sat between them, an arm about each, gazing at the screen.

"You see, the sun had not surely 'captured' Bronson Beta and Bronson Alpha. They had arrived from some incalculable distance and they have rounded the sun, but, without further interference than the sun's attraction, they would retreat again and perhaps never reappear; they would not join the family of familiar planets circling the sun.

"But on the course toward the sun, Alpha destroyed the moon, as we know, and this had an effect upon both Alpha and Bronson Beta, controlled by Alpha. And now something even more profound is going to happen. Alpha will have contact with the world. That will destroy the earth and will send Bronson Alpha off in another path—perhaps will will prove to be a very long ellipse, but more probably it will be a hyperbola. No one can quite calculate that; but one almost certain effect of the catastrophe is that it will break Bronson Beta away from the dominating control of Bronson Alpha and leave Beta subject to the sun. That will provide a much more satisfactory orbit for us about our sun."

"Us?" echoed Tony.

"Us—if we get there," said Eve; and she bent and kissed the children. "What purpose could there be in all that"—she nodded to the screen when she straightened—"if some of us aren't to get there? We see God not only sending us that world, Tony,"—she spoke a little impatiently—"but arranging for us an orbit for it about the sun which will let us live."

"Do you know the Wonder Clock?" Danny, the little boy, looked up and demanded. "Do you know Peterkin and the li'l Gray Hare?"

"Certainly," said Eve. "Once there was a giant—"

At the end of the hour all the lights in the passenger quarters were turned out, and the Earth was again flashed on the screen. Its diminution in size was already startling; and the remains of Europe, stranded in a new ocean, looked like a child's model flour-and-water map.

Duquesne lay on his back on deck and stared up at the scenery. He gave an informal lecture as he looked. "As we are flinging ourselves away from the Earth below, we are putting distance between ourselves and a number of prize fools. These fellows are my best friends. You will pick out faintly the map of Europe. Directly south of those shadows which were once the British Isles, you see the configuration of the Alps. In the center of the western range are the fools of whom I spoke. At any moment now, providing we are able to see anything at all, we shall witness their effort at departure. They built a ship not dissimilar to this, but unfortunately relying upon another construction than that valuable little metal discovered by Mr.—whatever his name is. I have told them they shall melt. I hope that we shall be able to see the joke of that fusion."

Duquesne glanced again at his watch, and looked up at the screen on which, like a stereopticon picture, hung the Earth. Suddenly he sat bolt upright. "Did I not tell you?"

A point of light showed suddenly in the spot he had designated. It was very bright, and as a second passed, it appeared to extend so that it stood away from the Earth like a white-hot needle. Tony and Eve and many others glanced at Duquesne.

But Duquesne was not laughing as he had promised. Instead he sat with his head bent back, his hands doubled into fists which pounded his knees, while in an outpouring of French he cajoled and pleaded frantically with that distant streak of fire.

The seconds passed slowly. Every one under the glass screen realized that here, perhaps, would be companions for them after they had reached Bronson Beta. Since they had just undergone the experience which they knew the Frenchmen were suffering in their catapulted departure from the Alps, they watched gravely and breathlessly. Only the rocket trail of the ship could be seen, as the ship itself was too small and too far away to be visible.

Duquesne was standing. He suddenly seemed conscious of those around him. "They go, they go, they go, they go! Maybe they have solved this problem. Maybe they will be with us."

Suddenly a groan escaped him. The upshooting light curved, became horizontal and shot parallel with Earth, moving apparently with such speed that it seemed to have traversed a measurable fraction of the Alps while they watched.

Abruptly, then, the trail zigzagged; it curved back toward the Earth, and the French ship commenced to descend, impelled by its own motors. In another second there was a faint glow and then—only a luminous trail, which disappeared rapidly, like the pathway of fire left by a meteor.

Duquesne did not laugh. He wept.

They tried to console him but he shrugged them away angrily. After a long time he began to talk, and they listened with sympathy. "Jean Delavoi was there, handsome Jean. And Captain Vivandi. Marcel Jamar, my own nephew, the greatest biologist of the new generation. And yet I told them, but it was their only hope, so they were stubborn." He looked at the people in the chamber. "Did you see? It melted. First the right tubes, throwing it on a horizontal course, then all of it. It was quickly over—*grâce à Dieu.*"

But other flashes rose and traveled on. The English, the Germans, perhaps the Italians had got away.

The implications of these sights transcended talk. Conversation soon ceased. Exhaustion, spiritual and physical, assailed the travelers. Eve's children fell into a sleep-like stupor. The motion of the ship seemed no more than a slight sway, and those who remained awake found it possible to talk in more ordinary tones.

Gravity diminished steadily, so that gestures were easier to make than they had been on Earth. Time lost all sequence. Twelve hours in the past seemed like an eternity spent in a prison; and only the waning Earth, which was frequently flashed on the screen by men in the control-room, marked progress to the passengers. They were spent by their months of effort and by the emotional strains through which they had passed. Stupefied like the children by the unusualness of this voyage, they were no longer worldly beings, but because all their vision of outer space came vicariously, their sensations were rather of being confined in a small place than of being lost and alone in the unfathomable void.

Their habit of relying upon the attractive force of the Earth resulted in an increasing number of mishaps, some of them amusing and some of them painful. After what seemed like eons of time some one asked Tony for more food. Tony himself could not remember whether he was going to serve the fifth meal or the sixth, but he sprang to his feet with earnest willingness—promptly shot clear to the ceiling, against which he bumped his head. He fell back to the floor with a jar and rose laughing. The ceiling was also padded, so that he had not hurt himself.

The sandwiches were wrapped in wax paper, and when some one on the edge of the crowd asked that his sandwich be tossed, Tony flipped it toward him, only to see it pass high over the man's head and entirely out of reach, and strike against the opposite wall. The man himself stretched to catch the wrapped sandwich, and sat down again rubbing his arm, saying that he had almost thrown his shoulder out of joint.

People walked in an absurd manner, stepping high into the air as if they were dancers. Gestures were uncontrollable, and it was unsafe to talk excitedly for fear one would hit one's self in the face.

Before this condition reached its crisis, however, Hendron himself appeared in the passenger-cabin for one of his frequent visits. He arrived, not by way of the staircase, but by way of the cable which was strung tautly inside the spiral, hauling himself up hand over hand with greater ease and rapidity than was ever exhibited by any sailor. He was greeted with pleasure—any slight incident had an exaggerated effect upon the passengers; but his demeanor was serious.

"I want you all to be witnesses of the reason for this journey," he said soberly.

He switched off the lights. The screen glowed, and on it they saw the Earth. At the hour of their departure the Earth had occupied much more than the area in the screen now reflected overhead, darkened on one side as if it were a moon in its third quarter, or not quite full. At the very edge of the screen was a bright curve which marked the perimeter of Bronson Alpha. Bronson Beta could not be seen.

CHAPTER 26—THE CRASH OF TWO WORLDS

NOW for an hour the passengers watched silently as Bronson Alpha swept upon the scene, a gigantic body, weird, luminous and unguessable, many times larger than Earth. It moved toward the Earth with the relentless perceptibility of the hands of a large clock, and those who looked upon its awe-inspiring approach held their breaths.

Once again Hendron spoke. "What will take place now cannot be definitely ascertained. In view of the retardation of Bronson Alpha's speed caused by its collision with the moon, I have reason to believe that its course will be completely disrupted."

Inch by inch, as it seemed, the two bodies came closer together. Looking at the screen was like watching the motion picture of a catastrophe and not like seeing it. Tony had to repeat to himself over and over that it was really so, in order to make himself believe it. Down there on the little earth were millions of scattered, demoralized human beings. They were watching this awful phenomenon in the skies. Around them the ground was rocking, the tides were rising, lava was bursting forth, winds were blowing, oceans were boiling, fires were catching, and human courage was facing complete frustration. Above them the sky was filled with this awful onrushing mass.

To those who through the smoke and steam and hurricane could still pierce the void, it would appear as something no longer stellar but as something real, something they could almost reach out and touch. A vast horizon of earth stretched toward them across the skies. They would be able, if their reeling senses still maintained powers of observation, to see the equally tumultuous surface of Bronson Alpha, to describe the geography of its downfalling side. They would perhaps, in the last staggering seconds, feel themselves withdrawn from the feeble gravity of their own Earth, to fall headlong toward Bronson Alpha. And in the magnitude of that inconceivable manifestation, they would at last, numb and senseless, be ground to the utmost atoms of their composition.

Tony shuddered as he watched. A distance, short on the screen—even as solar measurements are contemplated—separated the two planets. In the chamber of the hurtling Space Ship no one moved. Earth and Bronson Alpha were but a few moments apart. It seemed that even at their august distance they could perceive motion on the planet, as if the continents below them were swimming across the seas, as if the seas were hurling themselves upon the land; and presently they saw great cracks, in the abysses of which were fire, spread along the remote dry land. Into the air were lifted mighty whirls of steam. The nebulous atmosphere of Bronson Alpha touched the air of Earth, and then the very Earth bulged. Its shape altered before their eyes. It became plastic. It was drawn out egg-shaped. The cracks girdled the globe. A great section of the Earth itself lifted up and peeled away, leaping toward Bronson Alpha with an inconceivable force.

The two planets struck.

Decillions of tons of mass colliding in cosmic catastrophe.

"It's not direct," Duquesne shouted. "Oh, God! Perhaps—"

Every one knew what he was thinking. Perhaps they were not witnessing complete annihilation. Perhaps some miracle would preserve a portion of the world.

They panted and stared.

Steam, fire, smoke. Tongues of flame from the center of the earth. The planets ground together and then moved across each other. It was like watching an eclipse. The magnitude of the disaster was veiled by hot gases and stupendous flames, and was diminished in awfulness by the intervening distances and by the seeming slowness with which it took place.

Bronson Alpha rode between them and the Earth. Then—on its opposite side—fragments of the shattered world reappeared. Distance showed between them—widening, scattering distance. Bronson Alpha moved away on its terrible course, fiery, flaming, spread enormously in ghastly light.

The views on the visagraph changed quickly. The sun showed its furious flames. The telescopic periscopes concentrated on the fragment of the earth.

"They're calculating," Hendron said.

During a lull of humble voices Kyto could be heard praying to strange gods in Japanese. Eliot James drummed on the padded floor with monotonous fingertips. Tony clenched Eve's hand. Time passed—it seemed hours. A man hurried down the spiral staircase.

He went directly to Hendron. "First estimates ready," he said.

Hendron's voice was tense: "Tell us."

"I thought perhaps—"

"Go ahead, Von Beitz. These people aren't children; besides, they have given up all expectations of the earth."

"They have seen the first result," Von Beitz replied. "The earth is shattered. Unquestionably much of its material merged with Bronson Alpha; but most is scattered in fragments of various masses which will assume orbits of their own about the sun."

"And Bronson Alpha?"

"We have made only a preliminary estimate of its deceleration and its deviation from its original course; but it seems to have been deflected so that it will follow a hyperbola into space."

"Hyperbola, eh?"

"Probably."

"That means," Hendron explained loudly, "we will have seen the last of Bronson Alpha. It will not return to the sun. It will leave our solar system forever. —And Bronson Beta?" Hendron turned to the German.

"As we have hoped, the influence of Bronson Alpha over Bronson Beta is terminated. The collision occurred at a moment which found Bronson Beta at a favorable point in its orbit around Bronson Alpha. Favorable, I mean, for us. Bronson Beta will not follow Alpha into space. Its orbit becomes independent; Bronson Beta, almost surely, will circle the sun."

Some of the women burst out crying in a hysteria of relief. The world was gone; they had seen it shattered; but another would take its place. For the first time they succeeded in feeling this.

A short time later, a man arose to bring the women water; he remained suspended in the air!

Tony reached up and turned on the lights. The man who floated was sinking slowly toward the floor, his face blank with amazement.

"We have come," announced Tony loudly, "very close to the point between Bronson Beta and Bronson Alpha where the gravity of one neutralizes the gravity of the other. Bronson Alpha and the fragments of our world, pulling one way, strike an equilibrium here with the pull of Bronson Beta, which we are approaching."

He saw Eve lifting the children and leaving them suspended in the air. For an instant they enjoyed it; then it frightened them. A strange panic ensued. Tony's heart raced. It was difficult to breathe. When he swallowed, it choked him; and as he swam through the air with every step, he felt himself growing faint, dizzy and nauseated.

He saw Eve, as if through a mist, make a motion to reach for the children, and rise slowly into the air, where she stretched at full length groping wildly for the children. Tony swam over to her and pushed them into her arms. His brain roared; but he thought: "Is this psychological or physical? Was it a physical result of lack of all weight or was it the oppressiveness of sensation?" He shouted the question to Eve, who did not reply.

The air was becoming filled with people. Almost no one was on the deck. The slightest motion was sufficient to cause one to depart from whatever anchorage one had. Hands and feet were outthrust. On every face was a sick and pallid expression. Tony saw Hendron going hand over hand on the cable through the stair, ascending head foremost, his feet trailing out behind him.

That was all he remembered. He fell into coma.

When his senses returned, he found himself lying on the deck under half a dozen other people, but their weight was not oppressive. The pile above him would have crushed any one on Earth, but here it made no difference. His limbs felt cold and weak; his heart still beat furiously. He struggled to free himself, and succeeded with remarkable ease. A wave of nausea brought him to his knees, and he fainted again, striking the floor lightly and bouncing into the air several times before he came to rest. . . .

Again consciousness returned.

This time he rolled over carefully and did not attempt to rise. He was lying on something hard and cold. He explored it with his fingers, and realized dully that it was the glass screen which projected the periscope views. It was the ceiling, then, on which the passengers were lying in a tangled heap, and not the deck. Their positions had been reversed. He thought that he was stone deaf, and then perceived that the noise of the motors had stopped entirely. They were falling toward Bronson Beta, using gravity and their own inertia to sustain that downward flight. He understood why he had seen Hendron pulling himself along the staircase. Hendron had been transferring to the control-room at the opposite end of the ship.

177

Tony's eyes moved in a tired and sickly fashion to the tangle of people. He knew that since he was the first to regain consciousness, it was his duty to disentangle them and make them as comfortable as possible. He crawled toward them. Whole people could be moved as if they were toy balloons. With one arm he would grasp a fixed belt on the deck, and with the other he would send a body rolling across the floor to the edge of the room. The passengers were breathing, gasping, hiccoughing; their hearts were pounding; their faces were stark white; but they seemed to be alive. The children were dazed but unhurt. Tony was unable to do more than to give them separate places in which to lie. After that, his own addled and confused body succumbed, and he lay down again, panting. He knew that they would be all right as soon as the gravity from Bronson Beta became stronger. He knew that the voyage was more than half finished; but he was so sick, so weak, that he did not care. He fell into a state between sleep and coma.

Some one woke him. "We're eating. How about a sandwich?"

He sat up. The gravity was still very slight, but strong enough to restore his sensations to something approaching normal. He started around the circular room which had become so familiar in the past hours. An attempt at a grin overspread his features. He reached inaccurately for the sandwich, and murmured his thanks.

An hour later conditions were improved for moving about the chamber, by the starting of the motors which were to decelerate the ship. The floor was firm again. On the screen now at their feet they could see Bronson Beta. It was white like an immense moon, but veiled in clouds. Here and there bits of its superficial geography were visible. They gathered around the screen, kneeling over it, the lurid light which the planet cast glowing up on their faces. In four hours the deceleration had been greatly increased. In six, Bronson Beta was visibly spreading on the screen. Deceleration held them tightly on the floor, but they would crawl across each other laboriously, and in turn stare at the floating, cloudy sphere upon which they expected to arrive.

The screen changed views now. It halted to catch the flight of Bronson Alpha from the sun, but most of the time those who operated it were now busy searching for the other American ship, of which they had seen no trace.

The hours dragged more, even, than they had on the outward journey. The surface of the planet ahead of them was disappointingly shrouded, as inspected for the last time. A word of warning went through the ship. The passengers took another drink of water, ate another mouthful of food, and once again strapped themselves to the floor. Hendron tripped

178

the handle of a companion to the rheostat-like instrument in the far end of the ship. He fixed a separate telescope so that he could see into it. He looked critically at his gauges. He turned on more power.

A half-hour passed, and he did not budge. His face was taut. The dangers of space had been met. Now came the last great test. At his side again was Duquesne. Above him, in layers, were the terrified animals and the half-insensible passengers. So great was the pressure of retardation that it was almost impossible for him to move, and yet it was necessary to do so with great delicacy. A fractional miscalculation would mean that all his work had gone for nothing.

In the optical instrument to which he screwed his eyes, the edges of Bronson Alpha had long since passed out of view. He stared at a bright foaming mass of what looked like clouds. A vast abyss separated him from those clouds, and yet its distance shortened rapidly. He looked at the gauge that measured their altitude from the surface of the planet, and at the gauge which reckoned their speed.

Duquesne followed his movements with eyes eloquent of his emotions.

Suddenly the clouds seemed to rush up toward him.

Hendron pressed a stud. The retardation was perceptibly increased. Sound began to pour in awful volumes to their ears.

Duquesne's eyes jerked up to the altimeter, which showed eighty-six miles. It was falling rapidly. The clouds on the screen were thicker. They fell through atmosphere. The roar increased and became as insufferable as it had been when they left the Earth. Perspiration leaked down Hendron's face and showed darkly through the heavy shirt he wore. The altimeter ran with diminishing speed from fifty miles to twenty-five. From twenty-five it crawled to ten. From ten to five. It seemed scarcely to be moving now.

Suddenly Hendron's lips jerked spasmodically, and a quiver ran through the hand on the rheostat. He pointed toward the screen with his free hand, and Duquesne had his first view of the new world. The same view flashed through the remnants of cloud to all the passengers. Below them was a turbulent rolling ocean. Where the force of their blasts struck it, it flung back terrific clouds of steam. They descended to within a mile of its surface, and then Hendron, operating another lever, sent out horizontal jets, so that the ship began to move rapidly over the surface of this unknown sea.

To every one who looked, this desolate expanse of ocean was like a beneficent blessing from God Himself. Here was something familiar, something interesting, something terrestrial. Here was no longer the incomprehensible majesty of the void.

The Space Ship had reached the surface of Bronson Beta and was traveling now at a slow, lateral velocity above one of the oceans. Hendron worked frantically with the delicate controls to keep the ship poised and in regular motion; yet it rose and fell like an airplane bounding in rough winds, and it swayed on its horizontal axis so that its pilot ceaselessly played his fingertips on the releases of the quick blasts which maintained equilibrium.

The sullen, sunless ocean seemed endless. Was there no land?

Where were the continents, where the islands and plains and the sites of the "cities" which the great telescopes of earth—the telescopes of that shattered world which survived now only in fragments spinning around the sun—once had shown? Had the cities, had the mountains and plains, been mere optical illusions?

That was impossible; yet impatience never had maddened men as now. Still the views obtainable from the side periscope flashed upon the screen and showed nothing but empty sea and lowering cloud.

Then, on the far horizon, land appeared dimly.

A cry, a shout that drowned in the tumult of the motors, broke from trembling lips. Speedily they approached the land. It spread out under them. It towered into hills. Its extent was lost in the mists. They reached its coast, a bleak inhospitable stretch of brown earth and rock, of sandy beach and cliff upon which nothing grew or moved or was. Inland the country rose precipitously; and Hendron, as if he shared the impatience of his passengers and could bear no more, turned the ship back toward a plateau that rose high above the level of the sea.

Along the plateau he skimmed at a speed that might have been thirty terrestrial miles an hour. The Ark drew down toward the new Earth until it was but a few feet above the ground. The speed diminished, the motors were turned off and on again quickly, a maneuver which jolted those who lay strapped in their places. There was a very short, very rapid drop; bodies were thrown violently against the padded floor; the springs beneath them recoiled—and there was silence.

Regardless of the fate of the others, the fate of Earth itself, Hendron with his hundred colonists had reached a new world alive.

The ship settled at a slight angle in the earth and rock beneath it.

The Ark was filled with a new sound—the sound of human voices raised in hysterical bedlam.

Chapter 27—The Cosmic Conquerors

COLE HENDRON turned to Duquesne. The bedlam from the passenger-cabin came to their ears faintly. On the visa-screen above them was depicted the view from one of the sides of the ship—a broad stretch of rolling country, bare and brown, vanishing toward ascending hills and gray mist. Hendron had relaxed for the first time in the past eight months, and he stood with his hands at his sides, his shoulders stooped and his knees bent. He looked as Atlas might have looked when Hercules lifted the world from his shoulders. It was an expression more descriptive than any words might have been.

Duquesne's emotions found speech. "Miraculous! Marvelous! Superb! Ah, my friend, my good friend, my old friend, my esteemed friend! I congratulate you. I, Duquesne, I throw myself at your feet. I embrace your knees; I salute you. You have conquered Destiny itself. You have brought this astounding ship of yours to the Beta Bronson. To you, Christopher Columbus is a nincompoop. Magellan is a child drooling over his toys. Listen to them upstairs there, screaming. Their hearts are flooded. Their eyes are filled. Their souls expand. Through you, to-day, humanity opens a new epoch!"

The Frenchman could not confine his celebration to the control-cabin. He seized Hendron and hauled him to the spiral staircase which functioned as well inverted as it had right-side up. He thrust Hendron before him into the first chamber, where the passengers from both decks were crowding. Duquesne himself was ignored; and he did not mind it.

"Hendron!" rose the shout; and men and women, almost equally hysterical, rushed to him. They had to clap hands on him, touch him, cry out to him.

Tony found himself shouting an excited harangue to which no one was paying attention. He discovered Eve at his side, struggling toward her father, and weeping. Some one recognized her and thrust her through the throng.

Men and women were throwing their arms about each other, kissing, and screaming in each other's faces. Duquesne, ignored and indifferent to it, made his way through the throng thumping the backs of the men and embracing the women, and beating on his own chest. Eliot James, who had been deathly ill during the entire transit, abruptly forgot his sickness, was caught in the tumult of the first triumph, and then withdrew to the wall and watched his fellows rejoice.

At last some one opened the larder and brought out food. People who had eaten practically nothing for the four days began to devour everything they could get their hands upon.

181

Tony, meanwhile, had somewhat recovered himself. He made a quick census and shouted: "We all are here. Every one who started on this ship survived!"

It set off pandemonium again, but also it reminded them of doubt of the safety of the second ship. "Where is it? Can it be sighted? . . . How about the Germans? . . . The English? . . . The Japanese?"

Their own shouts quieted them, so that Hendron at last could speak.

"We have had, for three days, no sight of our friends or of any of the other parties from earth," he announced. "That does not mean that they all have failed; our path through space was not the only one. Some may have been ahead of us and arrived when the other side of this world was turned; others may still arrive; but you all understand that we can count upon no one but ourselves.

"We have arrived; that we know. And none of you will question my sincerity when I repeat to you that it is my conviction that fate—Destiny—far more than our own efforts has brought us through.

"I repeat here, in my first words upon this strange, new, marvelous world what I said upon that planet which for millions and hundreds of millions of years supported and nourished the long life of evolution which created us—I repeat, what I said upon that planet which now flies in shattered fragments about our sun; we have arrived, not as triumphant individuals spared for ourselves, but as humble representatives of the result of a billion years of evolution transported to a sphere where we may reproduce and recreate the life given us. . . .

"I will pass at once to practical considerations.

"At this spot, it is now late in the afternoon of Bronson Beta's new day, which lasts thirty hours instead of the twenty-four to which we are accustomed. For the present, we must all remain upon the ship. The ground immediately under is still baked hot by the heat of our blast at landing. Moreover we must test the atmosphere carefully before we breathe it.

"Of course, if it is utterly unbreathable, we will all perish soon; but if it proves merely to contain some unfavorable element against which we must be masked at first until we develop iimmunity to it, we must discover what it is.

"While waiting, we will discharge one of the forward rocket tubes at half-hour intervals in the hope that our sister ship will see this signal and reply. We will also immediately put into operation an external radio system and listen for her. I wish to thank those of you who acted as my crew during this flight, and who in spite of shuddering senses and stricken bodies stuck steadfast to your posts. But there is no praise adequate in human language for the innumerable feats of courage, of ingenuity and perseverance which have been performed by every one of you. I trust that by morning we shall be able to make a survey of our world on foot, and I presume that by then we shall have heard from our sister ship."

Eve and Tony walked back and forth through the throng of passengers, arm in arm. Greetings and discussions continued incessantly. Every one was talking. Presently some one began to sing, and all the passengers joined in.

Up in the control-room Hendron and his assistants began their analysis of a sample of atmosphere that had been obtained through a small airlock. They rigged up the ship's wireless, and sent into the clouds the first beacon from the Ark's sky-pointing tubes. Lights were on all over the ship. Above the passenger quarters, several men were releasing and tending stock. The sheep and a few of the birds had perished, but the rest of the animals revived rapidly.

One of Hendron's assistants put a slip of paper before his chief. He read it:

Nitrogen	43%
Oxygen	24%
Neon	13%
Krypton	6%
Argon	5%
Helium	4%
Other gases	5%

Hendron looked at the list thoughtfully and took a notebook from a rack over the table. He glanced at the assistant and smiled. "There's only about a three-per-cent error in our telescopic analysis. It will be fair enough to breathe."

The assistant, Borden, smiled. He had been, in what the colonists came to describe as "his former life," a professor of chemistry in Stanford University. His smile was naïve and pleasing. "It's very good to breathe. In fact, I drew in a large sample and breathed what was left over for about five minutes. It felt like air; it looked like air; and I think we might consider it a very superior form of air—remarkably fresh, too."

Hendron chuckled. "All right, Borden. What about the temperature?"

"Eighty-six degrees Fahrenheit, top side of the ship—but the ground all around has been pretty highly heated, and the blast from the beacon also helped warm up the air. I should conjecture that the temperature is really about seventy-eight degrees. I didn't pick up much of that heat, because our thermometer is on the windward side."

Hendron nodded slowly. "Of course I don't know our latitude and longitude yet, but that seems fair enough. Pressure?"

"Thirty point one hundred thirty-five ten thousandths."

"Wind-velocity?"

"Eighteen miles an hour."

"Humidity?"

"Seventy-four per cent. But if I'm any judge of weather, it's clearing up."

"That's fine. We'll go out in the morning."

Another man approached the desk. "The radio set is working, Mr. Hendron. There's terrific static in bursts, but in the intervals listening has been pretty good. Everything's silent. I don't think anybody else made it."

"Right. You take the receivers until midnight on the new time, put Tarleton on for four hours and let Grange have it until dawn, and then Von Beitz. No one will leave the ship to-night. I believe that the situation here is favorable; but we will need every advantage for our first experience upon this planet. So we will wait for the sun."

The night came on clear. The visa-screen, which had been growing darker, showed now a dim, steady light. It was the light of the earth-destroyer Bronson Alpha, shining again upon the survivors of men as it set off on its measureless journey into infinite space. Other specks of light reënforced it; and the stars—glints from the débris of the world settling themselves in their strange circles about the sun.

Exhaustion allied itself to obedience to Hendron's orders. The emigrants from Earth slumped down and slept. Hendron strode quietly through the dimly lighted chambers, looking at the sleeping people with an expression almost paternal on his face. Within him leaped an exultation so great that he could scarcely contain it. . . .

Tony lay down but did not sleep. Around him the members of the expedition lay in attitudes of rest. A thought had been stirring in his brain for a long time. Some one would have to take the risk of being the first to breathe the air of Bronson Beta. A small sample was not decisive. Tony did not know how accurately its composition might have been measured. He thought that it might have an evil smell. It might be sickening. It might be chemically possible to breathe, but practically, hopeless. It might contain a trace of some rare poison that, repeatedly breathed, would kill instantly or in time.

He should test it himself. They should send him out first. If he did not go into spasms of nausea and pain, the rest could follow. It was a small contribution, in Tony's mind; but it would help justify his presence on the Ark. He had considered offering himself for this service for so long that he had created in his subconscious mind a true and very real fear of the possibilities in the atmosphere of Bronson Beta.

"They might send some one useful," he thought. "Hendron might sacrifice himself in the test."

The more he thought, the more he worried. His mind began to plan. If he wished, he could open the airlock and drop down to the ground. Of course, he could not get back without making a fuss—stoning the periscope outlet—and he might not remain conscious long enough. But in that case —his body would be a warning when they looked out in the morning. . . .

At last he rose. He went down the spiral staircase quietly. He shut doors behind him. In the bottom chamber he stood for a long time beside the airlock. He was trembling.

It did not enter his mind that the honor of being the first to step on the soil of Bronson Beta rightfully belonged to Hendron. It was self-sacrifice and not ambition which prompted him.

He lifted the levers that closed the inner door, balancing them so that they would fall automatically. He stepped between it and the outer door. The lock slammed; the levers fell. He was in pitch darkness.

He opened the outside door. He leaned out—his heart in his mouth. He drew in a breath.

A hot, rasping, sulphurous vapor smote his nostrils. He shuddered. Was this the atmosphere of the new planet? He remembered that the blast of the Ark had cooked the ground around it.

Gasping, wih running eyes, he lay down on the floor and felt with his feet for the iron rungs of the workmen's ladder that ran from the now inverted bow of the Ark to the upper door and matched that on the opposite end. He began to descend. He coughed and shuddered. With every step the heat increased.

His foot touched the ground. It gave off heat like the earth around a geyser. He ran away from the looming bulk of the ship. His first fifty steps were taken in the stinging vapors.

Then—cooler air blew on his face. Sweet, fresh, cool air!

He inhaled lungfuls of it. It had no odor. It was like earth air washed by an April rain. It did not make him dizzy or sick. He did not feel weakness or numbness or pain. He felt exhilarated.

He flung out his arms in ecstasy. It was a dancer's gesture, a glorious, abandoned gesture. He could make it only because he was alone—alone on the new earth. Bronson Beta's atmosphere was magnificent.

He flung his arms again.

Beside him a voice said quietly: "It's splendid, isn't it, Tony?"

He could have been no more startled if stones had spoken or a mummy had sat up in its sarcophagus. He stiffened, not daring to look. Then into his icy veins blood flowed. He had recognized the voice. He turned in the lush, starlit dark.

"Mr. Hendron, I—I—I—"

"Never mind." The older man approached. "I think I know why you came. You wanted to be sure of the air before any of the rest of us left the ship."

Tony did not reply. Hendron took his arm. "So did I. I couldn't sleep. I had to inspect our future home. I came out on the ladder half an hour ago." Hendron chuckled. "Duquesne was on my heels. I hid. He's gone for a walk. I heard him fall down and swear. What do you think of it? Did you see the aurora?"

"No." Tony looked at the stars. He had a feeling that the sky overhead was not the sky to which he had been accustomed. The stars looked slightly mixed. As he stared upward, a crimson flame shot into the zenith from the horizon. It was followed by torches and sheets in all colors and shades. "Lord!" he whispered.

"Beautiful, isn't it?" Hendron said softly. "Nothing like it on earth. It was in rippling sheets when I came out. Then in shafts—a colored cathedral. It made faint shadows of the landscape. I venture to say it's a permanent fixture. The gases here are different from those on earth. Different ionization of solar electrical energy. That red may be the neon. The blue— I don't know. Anyway—it's gorgeous."

"You mean—this thing will play overhead all night every night?"

"I think so. Coming and going. It seemed to me that it touched the ground over there—once." He pointed. "I thought I could hear it—crackling faintly, swishing. It's going to make radio broadcasting bad; and it'll affect astronomic observation. But it is magnificent."

"Like the rainbow that came on Ararat," Tony said slowly.

"Lord! So it is! God's promise, eh? Tony—you're an odd fellow for a football-player. Football! What a thing to hover in the mind here! Come—let's see if we can find Duquesne. The wily devil wanted to be first on Bronson Beta. He came out of the Ark like a shot. No. Wait—look."

Tony glanced toward the Ark. The lock was opening again. The aurora shone luminously on the polished sides, revealing the black rectangle of the open door in sharp contrast.

"Who is it?" Hendron whispered.

"Don't know." Tony was smiling.

They watched the fourth man to touch the new soil make his painful descent and run across the still hot earth. They saw him stop, a few yards away, and breathe. They heard his voice ecstatically. Then—they heard him weep.

Hendron called: "Hello—James!"

Tony saw Eliot James undergo the unearthliness of hearing that voice come through the empty air. Then James approached them.

186

"How beautiful!" he whispered. "I'm sorry. I thought some one should try the air. And—I admit—I was keen to get out. Wanted to be first, I suppose. I'm humiliated—"

Again Hendron laughed. "It's all right, my boy. I understand. I understand all of us. It was an act of bravery. When I came out, I half expected you others would be along. It's in your blood. The reason you came here one by one, alone and courageously, is the reason I picked you to come here with me. You all think, feel, act independently. You also all act for the common welfare. It makes me rather happy. Come on; Duquesne went this way."

"Duquesne?" James repeated. Tony explained.

They hunted for a long time. Overhead the stars showed brightly; and underneath them in varying intensity, with ten thousand spangles, the aurora played symphonies of light. Behind them was the tall cylinder of the ship, and behind it the range of hills. Ahead of them as they walked they could hear the increasing murmur of the sea.

They found Duquesne sitting on a bluff-head overlooking the illimitable sea. He heard them coming and rose, holding out his hands.

"My friends! *Salut!*"

"I saw you pop out of the ship," Hendron said, "and I was sorry you fell down."

The Frenchman was crestfallen. "You were out here?"

"Oh, yes."

"Ahead of me?"

"By a few minutes," Hendron answered.

Duquesne stamped his foot several times, and then laughed. "Well—you should be! But I thought to fool you. Duquesne, I told myself—the great Duquesne—shall be first to set foot on the new earth. But it was not to be. It was a sin. I even brought a small flag of France—my beautiful France—and planted it upon the soil."

"I saw it," Hendron said. "I took it down. We aren't going to have nations here. Just—people."

Duquesne nodded in the gloom. "That too is right. I am foolish. I am like six years old. But to-night we will forget all this, *n'est-ce pas?* We will be friends. Four friends. The mighty Cole 'Endron. The brilliant Monsieur James. The brave Tony Drake. And myself—Duquesne the great. Sit."

On the outcrop of stone ledge they seated themselves. They looked and breathed and waited.

Occasionally one of them spoke. Usually it was Hendron —casting up from his thoughts between periods of silence memories of the past and plans for the future.

"We are here alone. I cannot help feeling that our other ship has in some way failed to follow us. If, in the ensuing days, we hear nothing, we may be sure it is lost. Your French confrères, Duquesne—failed. We must admit that it seems probable that others failed. Bronson Beta belongs to us. It is sad—tragic. Ransdell is gone. Peter Vanderbilt is gone. Smith. That Taylor youngster you brought from Cornell. All the others. Yet—with all the world gone, who are we to complain that we have lost a few more of our friends?"

"Precisely!" exclaimed Duquesne emphatically. "And what are we, after all? What was that mankind, of our earth, which we alone perhaps survive to represent and reproduce?"

He had recoiled from his moment of inborn, instinctive patriotism, and become the scientist again.

"Is the creation of man the final climax toward which the whole Creation has moved? We said so, in the infancy of our thought, when we imagined the world made by God in six days, before we had any comprehension even of the nature of our neighboring stars, when we could not even have dreamed of the millions and millions of the distant stars shown us by our telescopes, when our wildest fancy would have failed before the facts of to-day—endless space spotted to the edges of time with spiral nebulæ, each a separate 'universe' with its billions of suns like our own.

"Behind us lay, on our own earth, five hundred millions of years of evolution; and billions of years before that, while matter cooled and congealed, the world was being made—for us?

"Can we say so? Or is it that our existence is a mere accidental and possibly quite unimportant by-product of natural processes, which—as Jeans, the Englishman, once suggested—really had some other and more stupendous end in view?"

"You mean," said Hendron, "perhaps it concerns only ourselves in our vanity, and not the universe at all, that any of us escaped from the cataclysm of earth's end and came here?"

"Exactly," pronounced Duquesne. "It is nothing—if we merely continue the earth—here. When I recollect the filth of our cities, the greed of individuals and of nations, the savagery of wars, the horrors of pauperism permitted to exist side by side with luxury and wealth, our selfishness, hates, diseases, filth—all the hideousness we called civilization—I cannot regret that the world which was afflicted by us is flying in fragments, utterly incapable of rehabilitation, about the sun. On the other hand, now we are here; and how are we to justify the chance to begin again?"

Tony moved away from them. He was stirred with a great restlessness. He wandered toward the ship; and he saw, in that glowing, opalescent night, a woman's form; and he knew before he spoke to her, that it was Eve.

"I was sure you'd be out," he said.

"Tony!"

"Yes?"

"Here are you and I. Here!" She stooped to the ground and touched it; the dry fiber of a lichenlike grass was between her fingers. She pulled it, and stood with it in her hand. They had seen it, they both remembered; it was what had made the ground brown in the light of the dying day.

"This was green and fresh, Tony, perhaps ten million years ago; perhaps a hundred million. Then the dark and cold came; the very air froze and preserved it. Do you suppose our cattle could eat it?"

"Why not?" said Tony.

"What else may be here, Tony? How can we wait for the day?"

"We aren't waiting!"

"No; we're not." For they were walking, hand in hand like children, over the bare, rough ground. The amazing aurora of this strange world lighted them, and the soil smoothed, suddenly, under their feet. The change was so abrupt that it made them stare down, and they saw what they had stumbled upon; and they cried out together: "A road!"

The ribbon of it ran to right and left—not clear and straight, for it had been washed over and blown over, but it was, beyond any doubt, a road! Made by what hands, and for what feet? Whence and whither did it run?

A hundred million years ago!

The clock of eternity ticked with the click of their heels on this hard ribbon of road, as they turned, hand in hand, and followed it toward the aurora.

"Where were they, said Tony, almost as if the souls of those a hundred million years dead might hear, "when they were whirled away from their sun? What stage had they reached? Is this one of their Roman roads on which one of their Varros was marching his men to meet a Hannibal at Bronson Beta's Cannæ? What was at one end—and what still awaits us there? A Nineveh of Sargon saved for us by the dark and cold? Or was this a motor road to a city like our Paris of a year ago? Or was it a track for some vehicle we would have invented in a thousand more years? And is the city which we'll find, a city we'd never dreamed of? Whatever it was, their fate left it for us; whereas our fate—the fate of our world—" He stopped.

"I was thinking about it," said Eve. "Out there is space— in scattered stones circling in orbits of their own about the sun; the Pyramids and the Empire State Building, the Washington Monument and the Tomb of Napoleon, the Arch of Triumph! The seas and the mountains! Here the other thing happened—the other fate that could have been ours if the world had escaped the cataclysm. What sort were they who faced it here, Tony? Human, with bodies like our own? Or with souls like our own, but other shapes?"

"On this road," said Tony, "this road, perhaps, we'll see."

"And learn how they faced it, too, Tony; the coming dark and the cold. I think, if I had the choice, I'd prefer the cataclysm."

"Then you believe our world was better off?"

"Perhaps I wouldn't have—if we had stayed," amended Eve. "What happened here, at least left their world behind them."

"For us," said Tony.

"Yes; for us. What will we make of our chance here, Tony? Truly something very different?"

"How different do you feel, Eve?"

"Very different—completely strange even to myself, at some moments, Tony; and then at other times—not different at all."

"Come here."

"Why?"

"Come here," he repeated, and drawing her close, he clasped her, and himself quivering, he could feel her trembling terribly. He kissed her, and her lips were hot on his. A little aghast, they dropped away.

"We seem to have brought the world with us. I can never give you up, Eve; or share you with any one else."

"We're too fresh from the world, Tony, to know. We've a faith to keep with—"

"With whom? Your father?"

"With fate—and the future. Let's go on, Tony. See, the road turns."

"Yes."

"What's that?"

"Where?"

She moved off the road to the right, where stood something too square and straight-edged to be natural. Scarcely breathing, they touched it, and found metal with a cold, smooth surface indented under their finger-tips.

"A monument!" said Tony, and he burned a match. The little yellow flame lighted characters engraved into the metal —characters like none either of them had ever seen before, but which proclaimed themselves symbols of meaning.

Swiftly Tony searched the two faces of the metal; but nothing that could possibly be a portrait adorned it. There were decorations of strange beauty and symmetry. Amazing that no one, in all the generations and in all the nations of the world, had drawn a decoration like this! It was not like the Chinese or Mayan or Egyptian, Greek or Roman, or French or German; but different from each and all.

190

Tony caught his breath sharply as he traced it with his fingers.

"They had an artist, Eve," he said.

"With five hundred million years of evolution behind him."

"Yes. How beautifully this writing is engraved! Will we ever read it? . . . Come on. Come on!"

But the monument, if it was that, stood alone; and consideration of others, if not prudence, dictated that they return.

But they did not reënter the ship. Duquesne was determined to spend the first night on the ground; and Hendron and James agreed with him. James had dragged out blankets from the Ark, and the five lay down on the ground of the new planet. And some of them slept.

Tony opened his eyes. The sun was rising into a sky not blue but jade green. A deep, bewildering color—the color of Bronson Beta's celestial canopy.

There would be no more human beings who wrote poetry about the blue sky. They would shape their romantic stanzas —as the stanzas in those strange, beautifully engraved characters must be shaped, if they mentioned the sky—to the verdancy of the heavens.

Tony lifted himself on his elbow. Below him, the sea also was green. It had been gray on the steamy yesterday. But an emerald ocean was more familiar than an emerald sky. He watched the white water roll on the summits of swells until it was dispersed by the brown cliff. He looked back at the Ark. It stood mysteriously on the landscape—a perpendicular cylinder, shining and marvelous, enormously foreign to the bare, brilliant landscape. Behind it the chocolate colored mountains stretched into opalescent nowhere—the mountain into which the road ran, the road beside which stood the stele adorned by a decoration like nothing else that had been seen in the world.

Tony regarded his companions. Hendron slept on a curled arm. His flashing eyes were closed. His hair, now almost white, was disheveled on his white forehead. Beside him Duquesne slept, half-sitting, his arms folded on his ample abdomen, and an expression of deep study on his swarthy face. Eliot James sprawled on a ledge which the sun now was warming, his countenance relaxed, his lips parted, his straggling red beard metal-bright in the morning rays.

Eve slept, or she had slept, near to Tony; and now she roused. She was lovely in the yellow light, and looked far fresher than the men.

Their clothes were stained and worn; and none of them had shaved, so that they looked more like philosophical vagrants than like three of the greatest men produced in the Twentieth Century on the Earth.

Tony watched Eve as she gazed at them, anxiously ma-

191

ternal. To be a mother in actuality, to become a mother of men, was to be her rôle on this reawakened world.

As she arose quietly, so as to disturb none of the others, Tony caught her hand with a new tenderness. They set off toward their road together.

Suddenly Tony saw something that took the breath from his lungs. It was a tiny thing—on the ground. A mere splotch of color. He hurried toward it, not believing his eyes. He lay down and stared at it. In a slight damp depression was a patch of moss the size of his hand.

He lay prone to examine it as Eve stooped beside him in excitement like his own. He did not know mosses—the vegetation resembled any other moss, on Earth. He recollected the hope that spores, which could exist in temperatures close to absolute zero for long periods, had preserved on Bronson Beta the power to germinate.

Mosses came—on Earth—from spores; and here, reawakened by the sun, was a remnant of life that had existed eons ago, light-years away.

Tony jumped up and ran about on the terrain; a few feet away, Eve stooped again. Other plants were burgeoning. Mosses, ferns, fungi—vegetation of species he could not classify, but some surely represented growths larger than mere mosses.

He heaped Eve's hands and his own, and together they ran back to the three who were staring, as they earlier had gazed, at the green sky.

Then Duquesne saw what Eve and Tony held. "Sacré nom de Dieu!" He leaped to his feet. Hendron and James were beside him.

With one accord, they rushed toward the Space Ship.

"Get Higgins!" Hendron shouted. "He'll go mad! Think of it! A whole new world to classify! . . . And it means that we will live!"

Before they reached the sides of the ship, the lock opened. The gangplank dropped to earth. Von Beitz appeared in the aperture, and Hendron shouted to him the news.

People poured from the Ark; they stepped upon the new soil. They waved their arms. They stared at the hills, the sky, the sea. They breathed deep of the air. They handled the mosses, and ran about finding more of their own. They shouted, sang. They laughed and danced.

The first day on the new earth had begun.

THE END

AFTER WORLDS COLLIDE

FOREWORD

EARLY in the middle third of the twentieth century a brilliant astronomer named Sven Bronson observed through a telescope in South Africa that two bodies were moving through space toward the solar system.

Bronson's calculations revealed to him that these wandering spheres would pass very close to the earth, make a circuit of our sun, and turn back toward space and infinity. The larger of the two wandering worlds would strike and annihilate the earth. Finer and more delicate calculations tended to show that the smaller body, which was of the same magnitude as the earth, would be "caught" by the sun and held in an orbit between the courses of Mars and Venus.

In other words, Bronson's discovery was an announcement of the end of the world.

It would be an end of the world preceded by the close passage of two mighty planets from some sun lost in the void—two planets which had been pulled from their pathways ages ago by a passing star. The world would be replaced by a new earth whose pathway would take it alternately out to the cold orbit of Mars and back again to the vicinity of Venus.

The bodies were named for their discoverer: the larger one, Bronson Alpha, and the smaller, Bronson Beta.

Sven Bronson knew the horrors that would attend the announcement of his awful findings.

He and Lord Rhondin, the Governor of the South African Dominion, summoned David Ransdell, a war veteran and flier, to carry the tangible demonstration to an American scientist, Cole Hendron. Ransdell started out with photographic plates which proved the discovery.

Cole Hendron, the greatest astrophysicist and engineer of the century, had already been notified of the approaching doom. He and his daughter Eve, who acted as his assistant, checked Bronson's calculations.

There was no doubt. The earth was doomed.

Hendron, Bronson and others united the foremost scientists of the world in a secret organization known as "The League of the Last Days" and these men kept the information from the public for some time. Among the first laymen to know, or guess the truth were Ransdell, the flier, and Anthony Drake, a young New York man-about-town who was in love with Eve Hendron.

Most of the informed scientists were ready to resign themselves to universal destruction. Cole Hendron, however, perceived a possibility of escape: if the planet which was to occupy the earth's position were habitable, and if a vessel capable of transporting human beings and their possessions through a few hundred thousand miles of space could be made, a small and select group of people might "jump" from the doomed earth to the new arrival in the solar system. This group could then set about reëstablishing mankind on a new earth.

Hendron and his assistants set to work at once. Atomic energy adequate to drive such a vessel exactly as a rocket is propelled was released in his laboratories. At first it could not be harnessed, as it fused everything with which it came in contact. Nevertheless Hendron persisted in his plans for the space ship. The "Ark" was the name given to the ship eventually built.

For its construction, Hendron established a vast manufacturing city in Michigan, and to it he took a thousand selected human beings—men and women with scientific training, healthy physiques, and great courage.

While Hendron labored frantically, the world found out what was in store for it.

Society disintegrated. The first, and relatively harmless "passage" of the Bronson bodies would be sufficiently close to cause vast terrestrial disturbances—tides, cyclones, terrific volcanic disturbances, and earthquakes. All the seacoast cities of the world were evacuated. New York, Boston, Philadelphia were cleared of their population, which was moved inland at the order of the President.

One bit of fortune came in the discovery of a new metal in the material forced from the depths of the earth during the great eruptions. Ransdell found it and brought it to camp where Hendron tested it. This metal proved able to withstand the heat of the atomic blast. The problem of propulsion of the "Ark" was solved.

In the fantastic days that followed, Hendron and his band manufactured the Ark, and found time and materials to make a second ship so that the balance of their heroic group could be transported to Bronson Beta and not sacrificed. The Michigan cantonment was attacked by bloodthirsty and hungry mobs. The first passage killed more than half of the people of the earth. Continents split apart. Seas rose. The internal fires of the earth burst to the surface. The moon was smashed to atoms.

Months afterward the celestial wanderers rounded the sun and returned. Hendron's two ships "took off" for Bronson Beta. Other ships, frantically constructed by other nations, also leaped into space as doom fell upon our world.

Bronson Alpha annihilated the earth and moved into the void.

Bronson Beta swung into a course about our sun.

Upon it, Hendron brought down the "Ark." With him was a company of a hundred and three human beings. Tony Drake was one of them, and his Japanese servant, Kyto. Eliot James, the diarist and historian of the party was in the "Ark." So was Dodson, the surgeon, and Duquesne, the French physicist who had been saved at the eleventh hour as the Ark stood ready to rise from Holocaust.

A safe landing was made. The air of Bronson Beta was found to be breathable.

But there was no word of the second ship—the vessel under Ransdell's command which had left with them. It was given up for lost. Ransdell, who also loved Eve, was presumed to have died somewhere in space with his brave companions—Jack Taylor, the college boy who had become one of Tony's best friends, and Peter Vanderbilt, the cynical and fearless New Yorker, and Greve and Smith, and four hundred others.

The arrivals on Bronson Beta could rouse no answer to their radio signals. They were forced into the awful realization that of all humanity they alone survived. They were alone on an unknown world where a nameless and dead race had once built cities—on a world which had been drifting through the absolute zero of space for nameless millenia. They faced the probem of survival. Responsibility for the future of the species was theirs.

Resolutely, they turned to their prodigious task.

CHAPTER I

ELIOT JAMES sat at a metal desk inside the space ship which had conveyed a few score human beings from the doomed earth to safety on the sun's new planet Bronson Beta. In front of Eliot James was his already immemorial diary, and over it he poised a fountain pen.

He had written several paragraphs:

"*April*—what shall I call it? Is it the 2nd day of April, or is it the first? Have we, the last survivors of the earth, landed upon our new planet on All Fools Day? That would be ironic, and yet trivial in the face of all that has happened. But as I meditate on the date, I am in doubt about how to express time in my diary.

"The earth is gone—smashed to fragments; and the companion of its destroying angel, upon which our band of one hundred and three Argonauts holds so brief and hazardous a residence, is still without names, seasons and months. But April has vanished with the earth; and for all I know, spring, winter, summer and fall may also be absent in the new world.

"I have pledged myself to write in this diary every day, as Hendron assures me there will be no other record of our adventures here until we have become well enough established to permit the compilation of a formal history. And yet it is with the most profound difficulty that I compel myself to set down words on this, man's first morning in his new home.

"What shall I say?

"That question in truth must be read by the future generations as a cry at once of ecstasy and despair. Ecstasy because even while the heavens fell upon them, my companions remained firm and courageous—because in the face of earthquakes, tornadoes, bloody battles and the unimaginable holocaust of Destruction Day itself, they not only preserved whatever claims the race of man may have to majesty, but by their ingenuity they escaped from the earth to this new planet, which has invaded and attached itself to our solar system.

"And I am in despair not only because, so far as we can tell, all but one hundred and three members of the human race have perished, not only because my friends, my home, the cities that were familiar to me, the trees and flowers I knew, the rivers and the oceans, the scent of the wind and the accustomed aspects of the sky have forevermore disappeared from the universe, and not only because I am incapable of setting down the emotions to which those cosmic calamities give rise, but for another reason: as vast, as stirring, as overwhelming to the mind as those foregoing, the responsibility for half a billion years of evolution which terminated in man rests upon myself and one hundred and two others.

"They stand there in the sunshine under the strange sky on our brown earth—forty-three men, fifty-seven women, two children. They have been singing—a medley of songs which under other circumstances might seem irrelevant. Many of them are foreigners and do not know the words, but they also sing—with tears streaming down their faces and a catch in their voices. They sang 'The Processional' and they sang 'Nearer, My God, to Thee.' After that they sang 'Hail, Hail, the Gang's All Here.' Then they sang 'The Marseillaise' with Duquesne leading—leading and bellowing the words, and weeping.

"What a spectacle! Beside it, the picture of Leif Ericsson or Columbus reaching green shores at last is dimmed to insignificance. For those ancient explorers found the path to a mere continent, while this band has blazed a trail of fire through space to a new planet.

"Cole Hendron is there, his magnificent head thrown back, and his face grave under its thatch of newly whitened hair. No doubt replicas of Hendron's head will be handed down through the ages, if ages are to follow us. His daughter Eve has been near him, and near to Tony Drake. In young Drake one sees the essence of the change which has taken place in all the members of our company. The fashionable, gay-hearted New Yorker is greatly changed. So many times in the past two years has he resigned himself to death, and so many times has he escaped from it only through courage, audacity and good fortune, that he seems superior to death. His face is no longer precisely young, and it contains, side by side, elements of the stoniest inflexibility and the most willing unselfishness. I have no doubt that if this colony survives, when the time comes to bury our leader and our hero,—the incomparable Cole Hendron,—it will be Drake who supersedes him in command. For by that day I am sure the great person in that young man will have availed itself of all our technical knowledge as a mere corollary of his remarkable character.

"And now,"—the pen wavered,—"to what I imagine whimsically as the new future readers of my notes, I make an apology. This is our first day on Bronson Beta. My impatience has exhausted my conscience. I must lay down my pen, leave the remarkable ship wherein I write, and go out upon the face of this earth untrod by man. I can restrain myself no longer."

Eliot James stepped to the gangplank that had been laid down from the Ark. The earth around the huge metal cylinder had been melted by the blasts of its atomic propulsion-jets. But now it was cool again. A space of two or three hundred yards lay between the Ark and the cliff which beetled over the unknown sea. In that space were the planetary pilgrims. They had stopped singing. Half of them stood on the top of the precipice regarding the waters that rolled in from a nameless horizon. The others were distributed over the landscape. With a smile James noted the botanist, Higgins, leaping from rock to rock, his pockets and his hands full of specimens of ferns and mosses which he had collected. Every few seconds his eye lighted upon a new species of vegetation, and he knelt to gather it. But his greediness resulted invariably in the spilling of specimens already collected, and the result was that he continued hopping about, dropping things and picking them up, with all the energy and disorganization of a distracted bird.

James walked down the gangplank and joined Tony, Eve and Cole Hendron.

The leader of the expedition nodded to the writer. "You certainly are a persistant fellow, James. Some day I hope to find a situation so violent and unique that it keeps you from working on your diary."

"We have been through a number of such situations," James answered.

"Nevertheless—" Hendron said. He checked himself. Several of the people on the edge of the cliff had turned toward the Ark and were marching toward him.

"Hendron!" they hailed him again. "Hendron! Cole Hendron!"

Their hysteria had not yet cleared away; they remained in the emotional excitement of the earth-cataclysm they had escaped but witnessed, and of the incomparable adventure of their flight.

"Hendron! Hendron! What do you want us now to do?" they demanded; for their discipline, too, yet clung to them— the stern, uncompromising discipline demanded of them during the preparation of the Ship of Escape, the discipline of the League of the Last Days.

Too, the amazements of this new place paralyzed them; and for that they were not to be blamed. The wonder was that they had survived, as well, the emotional shocks; so they surrounded again their leader, who throughout had seen farther ahead and more clearly than them all; and who, through Doomsday itself, had never failed them.

Hendron stepped upon an outcrop of stone, and smiled down at them. "I have made too many speeches," he said. "And this morning is scarcely a suitable hour for further thanksgiving. It may be proper and pleasant, later, to devote such a day as the Pilgrims, from one side of our earth to another, did;

11

but like them, it is better to wait until we feel ourselves more securely installed. When such a time arrives, I will appoint an official day, and we shall hope to observe it each year."

He cast his eyes over the throng and continued: "I don't know at the moment how to express my thoughts. While I am not myself a believer in a personal God, it seems evident to me in this hour that there was a purpose in the invention of man. Otherwise it is difficult to understand why we were permitted to survive. Whether you as individuals consider that survival the work of a God, or merely an indication that we had reached a plane of sufficient fitness to preserve ourselves, is of small moment to me now. And since I know all of you so well, I feel it unnecessary to say that in the days ahead lies a necessity for a prodigious amount of work.

"Your tempers and intelligences will be tried sorely by the new order which must exist. Our first duty will be to provide ourselves with suitable homes, and with a source of food and clothing. Our next duty will be to arrange for the gathering of the basic materials of the technical side of our civilization-to-be. In all your minds, I know, lies the problem of perpetuating our kind. We have, partly through accident, a larger number of women than men. I wish to discontinue the use of the word *morality;* but what I must insist on calling our biological continuum will be the subject of a very present discussion.

"In all your minds, too, is a burning interest in the nature and features of this new planet. We have already observed through our telescopes that it once contained cities. To study those cities will be an early undertaking. While there is little hope that others who attempted the flight to this planet have escaped disaster, radio listening must be maintained. Moreover, the existence of living material on this planet gives rise to a variety of possibilities. Some of the flora which has sprung up may be poisonous, even dangerous, to human life. What forms it will take and what novelties it will produce, we must ascertain as soon as possible. I think we are safe in believing that no form of animal life can have existed here, whether benign or perilous; but we cannot ignore the possibility that the plant life may be dangerous. I will set no tasks for this day,— it shall be one of rest and rejoicing,—except that I will delegate listeners for radio messages, and cooks to prepare food for us. To-morrow, and I use an Americanism which will become our watchword, we will all 'get busy.'"

There was a pause, then cheering. Cole Hendron stepped down from the stone. Eve turned to Tony and took his arm. "I am glad we don't have to work today."

"No," said Tony. "Your father knows better. He realizes that, in our reaction, we could accomplish nothing. It is the time for us to attempt to relax."

12

"Can you relax, Tony?"

"No," he confessed, "and I don't want even to attempt to; but neither do I want to apply myself to anything. Do you?"

Eve shook her head. "I can't. My mind flies in a thousand different directions simultaneously, it seems. Where are those cities which, from the world—our ended world, Tony—our telescopes showed us here? What remains may we find of their people? Of their goods and their gods and their machines? . . . What, when they found themselves being torn away from their sun, did they do? . . . That monument beside the road that we found, Tony—what was it? What did it mean? . . . Then I think of myself. Am I, Tony, to have children—here?"

Tony tightened his clasp upon her arm. Through all the terrors and triumphs, through all their consternations and amazements, instincts, he found, survived. "We will not speak of such things now," he said. "We will satisfy the more immediate needs, such as food—deviled eggs and sandwiches; and coffee! As if we were on earth, Eve. For once more we are on earth—this strange, strange earth. But we have brought our identical bodies with us."

"Sardines!" Duquesne said. He patted his vast expanse of abdomen—an abdomen which in his native land he had often maintained, and was frequently to assert with pride on Bronson Beta, consisted not of fat but of superior muscle. Indeed, although Duquesne was short of stature and some fifty years of age, he often demonstrated that he was possessed not only of unquenchable nervous energy, but of great physical strength and endurance. "Sardines!" He rolled his eyes at half a dozen women and several of the men who were standing near him. He took another bite of the sandwich in his hand.

Eve giggled and said privately to Tony: "All this expedition needed to make it complete was a comedian."

Tony grinned as he too bit a crescent in a sandwich. "A comedian is a great asset, and a comedian who was able even years ago to help Einstein solve equations, is quite a considerable asset."

"So many things like Duquesne's arrival have happened to us," Eve said. "Purely fortuitous accidents."

"Not all of them good."

"Who's in charge of lunch?" Eve asked a moment later.

Tony chuckled. "Who but Kyto? He, and an astronomer, and a mechanical engineer, and a woman who is a plant biologist like Higgins, are all working in happy harmony. Kyto seems to understand exactly what has taken place. In fact, there are moments when I think he is a high-born person. I had a friend once who had a Japanese servant like Kyto, who after seven years of service resigned. When my friend asked him what he was going to do, the Japanese informed him that he had been offered the chair of Behavioristic Psychology at a Middle Western university. He had been going to Columbia at night for years. Sometimes I think Kyto may be like that."

Eve did not make any response at the moment, because Duquesne was again talking in his loud bombastic voice. He had attracted the attention of Cole Hendron and of several others, including Dr. Dodson.

Dodson's presence on the Ark was due to the courage of a girl named Shirley Cotton. On the night of the gory raid on Hendron's encampment, Dodson had been given up for dead by Tony. The great surgeon's last gesture, in fact, had been to wave to Tony to carry his still living human burden to safety. However, before the Ark rose to sear and slay the savage hordes of marauders, Shirley Cotton had found the dying man.

In the space of a few moments she had put a turniquet around his arm, partly stanched a deep abdominal wound, and dragged him to a cellar in the machine-shop, intending to hide him there. It saved both their lives, for soon afterward the whole region was deluged by the atomic blast of the Ark as it rose and methodically obliterated the attackers of the camp.

Dodson had recovered, but he had lost one arm. As Tony was Hendron's chief in the direction of physical activities, Dodson became his creator of policies. He listened now to Duquesne.

"A picnic in the summer-time on Bronson Beta, children," Duquesne boomed. "And it is summer-time, you know. Fortunately, but inevitably from the nature of events, still summer. My observations of the collision check quite accurately with my calculations of what would happen; and if the deductions I made from those calculations are correct, quite extraordinary things will happen." He glanced at Hendron.

The leader of the expedition frowned faintly, as if Duquesne were going to say something he did not wish to have expressed. Then he shrugged.

"You might as well say it. You might as well tell them, I suppose. I wasn't going to describe our calculations until they had been thoroughly checked."

Duquesne shook his head backward and forward pontifically. "I might as well tell them, because already they are asking." He addressed those within earshot. "We will have a little class in astronomy." He put to use two resources—the smooth vertical surface of a large stone, and a smaller stone which he had picked up to scratch upon the bowlder.

As Duquesne began to talk, all the members of the group gathered around the flat bowlder to watch and listen.

"First," he began, "I will draw the solar system as it was." He made a small circle and shaded it in. "Here, my friends, is the sun." He circumscribed it with another circle and said: "Mercury." Outside the orbit of Mercury he drew the orbits respectively of Venus, Earth and Mars. He looked at the drawing with beaming satisfaction, and then at his listeners. "So this is what we had had. This is where we have been. Now. I draw the same thing without the Earth."

He repeated the diagram—this time with three concentric circles instead of four. A broad gap was left where the earth's orbit had been. Again he stepped away from the diagram and looked at it proudly. "So—Mercury we have; Venus we have; and Mars we have. The Earth we do not have. Bear in mind, my children, that these circles I have drawn are not exactly circles. They are ellipses. But they vary only slightly from circles. Mr. Cole Hendron's associates will give you, I do not doubt, very fine maps. This rock-scratching of mine is but a child's crude diagram. I proceed. I set down next the present position of this world on which we stand—Bronson Beta."

Every one watched intently while he drew an ellipse which, on one side, came close to the orbit of Venus, and on the other approached the circle made by the planet Mars on its journey around the sun.

"Here is our path, closer to the sun than the Earth has been; and also farther away. The hottest portion of this new path of this new planet about the sun already had been passed when we fled here. This world had made its closest approach in rounding the sun, and it had reached the point in its orbit which our earth had reached in April. Now we are going away from the sun, but on such a path that—and under such conditions that—only slowly will the days grow colder."

"They will become, when we get out on that portion of our path near Mars," a man among his hearers questioned, "how cold?"

Duquesne called upon his comic knack to turn this question. He shivered so grotesquely that the audience laughed. "This most immediately interesting feature of our strange situation will be, my friends, the amazing character of our days. Many of you have been told of that; so I ask you. Who will answer? Hands, please!" He pretended to be teaching a class of children. "How long will be our days?"

They nearly all laughed; and several raised their hands. "You, Mr. Tony Drake. You, I know, have become like so many others a splendid student of astronomy. How long will be our days?"

"Fifty hours, approximately," replied Tony.

"Excellent! For what determines the length of the day? Of course it is the time which the planet takes to turn upon its own axis. It has nothing whatever to do with the sun, or the path about the sun; it is a peculiarity of the planet itself, and inherent in it from the forces which created it at its birth. Bronson Beta happens to be rotating on its axis in approximately fifty hours, so our days—and our nights—will be a trifle more than twice as long as those to which we have become accustomed. Now—hands again—how long will our year be? Let one of the ladies speak this time!"

"Four hundred and twenty-eight days!" a girl's voice said. Her name was Mildred Pope.

"Correct," applauded Duquesne, "if you speak in terms of the days of our perished planet. It will take four hundred and twenty-eight of our old days for Bronson Beta"—Duquesne, not without some satisfaction, stamped upon it—"to circle the sun; but of the longer days with which we are now endowed, the circuit will consume only two hundred and five and a fraction. It tears up our old calendars, doesn't it? We start out, among many other adventures, with new calculations of time. So we will rotate in some fifty hours, and swing in toward Venus and our toward Mars, in our great elliptical orbit, making a circuit of the sun in four hundred and twenty-eight of our old days—which will live now only in our memories—or two hundred and five of our new days. Around and about, in and out, we will go—let us hope, forever."

His audience was silent. Duquesne let them study his sketches on his natural blackboard before he observed: "A few obvious consequences will at once occur to you."

Higgins, who had dropped his plants while he listened, gave his impromptu answer like a grade boy in a classroom: "Of course; our summers will be very hot, and our winters will be very cold and very long."

Duquesne nodded. "Quite so. But there is one fortunately favorable feature. What chiefly determined the seasons on the old earth," he reminded, "was the inclination of the earth upon its axis. If Bronson Beta had a similar or a greater inclination in reference to the plane of its orbit around the sun, all effects would be exaggerated. But we find actually less inclination here. Whether that may be a favorable feature 'provided' for us by some Power watching over this singularly fortunate party, or whether it is one of innumerable accidents of creation which have no real causative connection with our destinies, the fact remains: The equinoxes on Bronson Beta will not march back and forth on the northern and southern hemispheres with such great changes in temperatures. Instead, as we round the sun at its focus,"—he pointed with his chubby finger,—"there will be many, many long hot days. Perhaps our equator at that time will not be habitable. And later, as we round the imaginary focus out here in space so near to the orbit of Mars, it may be very cold indeed, and perhaps then only the equator will be comfortable. So we may migrate four times a year.

From the Paris of our new world to its Nice—I mean to say, from the New York City to its Miami. Does one think of anything else?"

Hendron was looking tentatively from one face to the next of his Argonauts. He had been reasonably sure that Bronson Beta would travel in the ellipse Duquesne had described; and from the behavior of the celestial bodies at the time of the collision, he had formed his calculations; but he had not wanted to worry them with thoughts of excessive heat and extreme cold in their new home, and he had enjoined the other mathematicians, astronomers and astrophysicists to say nothing. He was pleased with the reaction of the people. There was no fear in their faces, no dismay. Only a great interest.

The silence was broken by a question from Dodson: "How close will we come to Venus and Mars?"

Duquesne shrugged. Eve turned to Dodson and said: "If my figures are right, it will be three million miles at periods many, many years apart. Three million miles from Mars, and at the most favorable occasion about four from Venus."

Dodson's eyebrows lifted. "Is that dangerous?"

Eve shook her head. "The perturbations of all three planets will, of course, be great. But as far as danger of collision is concerned, there is none."

The group was thoughtful.

"There will be a great opportunity," Dodson said slowly, "to study those two planets at close range. We must build a good telescope."

"Telescope!" The word burst from Duquesne. His eyes traveled over the members of the group standing in front of him to the tall, shining cylinder of the Space Ship. There they remained; and slowly, one by one, the people turned to look at the Ark which had carried them from Earth to Bronson Beta. They realized the meaning of Duquesne's steady gaze. There would be an opportunity in the future not only to study Venus and Mars at close range—but to voyage to them.

Duquesne dropped the stone with which he had been drawing, and stepped away from his diagram.

Eliot James walked over to Tony and Eve. "That is something I didn't think of," he murmured. "Something I didn't think of. Stupendous! Colossal!"

Eve smiled. "Father and I thought of it independently a long time ago. It will make your journey around the United States after the first passing seem pretty trifling."

James shook his head in agreement. "I'd want Vanderbilt with me again if I went on such a trip. And Ransdell." Abruptly he stopped. Vanderbilt and Ransdell had been lost on the other Space Ship. James flushed, as he looked at Eve. "I'm sorry, Eve. For an instant I forgot."

17

"It's all right." She took Tony's arm. "I want to go over and look at the ocean. It's a funny thing—looking at the ocean. Every time I stared out to sea on earth, I always expected to see a shark's fin, or a big turtle, or a jellyfish, or a sail, or the smoke of a steamship; and I keep looking for such things on this one. And yet there can be nothing. Nothing at all." Her eyes traveled the expanse of ocean, and then she sighed. "Let's take a walk."

"Let's go back and look at that road in daylight."

Eve started. "We've left it all this time! Did you tell Father about it?"

"Not yet."

They went over to Cole Hendron. "Last night," Tony said, "Eve and I were out walking, and we found a road."

Ten minutes later every one was gathered around the highway. It was made of a metal-like substance. It ran to the bluff along the sea and then turned south. Except for that single curve—a graded curve, which suggested that the vehicles that once traveled the road moved very swiftly, there was no other turn. In the opposite direction it drove straight toward the dim and distant hills. Its surface was very smooth. As the Argonauts had gathered around Duquesne's natural lecture-platform, so they now gathered around the metal monument Tony and Eve had seen in match-light on the previous evening. Way was made for Bagsley, the paleontologist. He bent over and looked up with a curious smile.

"That isn't a job for me." His eyes were fastened on the inscription the metal slab bore. "You see, this is such a thing as might be found in the future of our earth, but not in the past. No ancient civilization in our world could make a road such as this, or use metal so skillfully."

"How about the writing?" some one asked.

Bagsley replied: "It's beautiful, isn't it? I wonder if we won't find that the curves in all those letters are mathematically perfect? That is, if they are letters. But I couldn't give you the faintest notion of what it says. It is not remotely related to Sanskrit, or Chinese, or Mayan, or cuneiform, or hieroglyphics, or runes; and it is equally remote from any modern writing."

Duquesne was taking again. "Anyway," he said, "whoever lived here had a language to write, and eyes to read it. They had roads to travel and vehicles to go upon them. So they had places to go and to come from. The cities we saw, or thought we saw, must have been real. My friends, great as our adventures have been, there lie ahead adventures infinitely more astounding."

In the face of so many necessities and so many unknown possibilities, any normal person would have lacked adequate judgment to do the right things in the right order. The

18

colonists of Bronson Beta succeeded in a logical procedure because they had been chosen from a multitude of human beings better than normal.

On the first day of their sojourn they had rested.

On the evening of that day Bronson Beta had exhibited another phenomenon. Soon after dark, when more than half the members of the colony had gone to sleep from fatitgue, a colossal meteor blazed across the sky and disappeared over the edge of the sea. It passed so close to the place where the Ark rested, that they had been able to hear a soft roar from it. It left a blaze upon the sky—a livid pathway of greenish-white fire which faded slowly. It was followed by another smaller meteor, and then half a dozen.

During the ensuing two hours countless thousands of meteors hurtled across the atmosphere of Bronson Beta in the vicinity of the Ark, and many of them fell to earth within the visual range of that spot.

Tony and Eve were outside when the aërolites commenced to fall. At first they were spellbound by the majesty of the spectacle, but when a great hurtling mass of molten material splashed into the sea less than a mile offshore and set the ocean boiling all around, so that clouds of hot steam drifted over it, they became alarmed. Hendron and Duquesne were alseep, but there were twenty-five or thirty people outdoors.

In the afternoon of that day Tony had made his way some distance down the coast, and he had found a precipice carved by an ancient ocean from living rock. At its base were shallow cave-like openings, and above it three or four hundred feet of solid stone.

When several of the great masses of material had hit the earth so hard that it trembled beneath their feet, Tony quickly commanded the little knot of people who were standing together, watching the spurts of fire across the sky, to go to these holes in the rock wall. They started, with Eve leading the way. Tony then entered the Ark and woke Hendron, whom he found lying on the padded floor in sound, exhausted slumber.

Hendron sat up. "What is it?"

So effective was the insulation of the ship that the fall of meteors was not perceptible on its interior.

"Meteors," Tony answered. "Three of them have landed within a mile of here in the last few minutes. Big ones. Any one of them would annihilate this ship if it hit it. There were about thirty people outdoors. I sent them up the coast to some shallow caves at the foot of a basalt cliff. I thought it was safer there."

As he said the last words, he was following Hendron down the spiral staircase. They debouched on the gangplank; and as they did so, a dazzling, dancing illumination and a crescendo roar announced the fall of another meteor. It hit on the brink of the cliff overlooking the sea some distance down the coast. A million bright, hot particles splashed over the barren landscape, and an avalanche of melted metal crashed into the ocean. Hendron looked up at the sky, and saw a dozen more of these spectacular missiles pursuing each other. He turned instantly to Tony. "If one of those things hit the cliff where you sent the people, would it knock the cliff down?"

"I don't know. It's safer than the Ark, anyway."

"Right." Hendron rushed up the stairs, followed by Tony. "How about the animals? Should we try to get them out?"

The living creatures—mammals, birds, insects—had been tended and fed but not yet moved. Where, outside, could they yet be established?

"The animals," said Tony, "will have to take their chances here."

But Hendron and he awakened all the pilgrims who had been asleep. They were commencing to leave the Ark in an orderly but fast-moving line. Hendron was at the door of the Ark, and as the people emerged, he divided them into groups of five, and sent each group running in a different direction, thus dispersing over a wide area those of the colonists who were not hiding under the rim of the cliff.

The number of the astrolites increased with every passing minute, until the sky seemed full of them. The terrain was as brightly illuminated as by daylight; and from the gangplank Tony could see the little bands scurrying in their appointed directions.

When they had all emerged, Hendron said to Tony shortly: "You go to the cliff and disperse the people there. I'll stay here with the last five."

The air was filled with parched, hot odors and clouds of steam. In the distance, around the craters made where the meteors had struck earth, there was a red glow. Half an hour passed. The pyrotechnics stopped. During that half-hour Cole Hendron had been busy in the upper control-room of the Ark with two electrical engineers; and when after five or ten minutes of normal darkness, interrupted only by spurts of the soft multi-colored aurora which frequently flickered on Bronson Beta, a few of the groups of five began to return to the Ark, they were halted by Cole Hendron's voice—a voice broadcast from the Ark by a mighty loud-speaker. It carried distinctly for a distance of two or three miles—a distance much greater than that which separated any of the bands.

"You will stay where you are," Hendron's voice commanded, "in groups of five for the remainder of the night. Try to sleep, if possible, but keep a long distance from the party nearest to you. I will summon you when the time comes."

Tony had rejoined Eve in a group of five along the base of the precipice. Eliot James was in that group, and two women— one of them Shirley Cotton, who was already a prominent person among the hundred and one odd people who had been prominent on earth. The two men and the three women slept fitfully on the hard earth that night; and in the morning with the first rays of dawn, Hendron's voice summoned every one together again.

No more meteors had fallen after the shower had ended. The human beings who trekked back over the bare landscape to the Ark were a little more grave than they had been on the previous day. Once again the frailness of their hold upon their new home had been made plain. Once again they had been reminded of the grim necessities by which they would have to live. For in order to insure that some of them, at least, would be safe, they had been compelled on a moment's notice to desert all that they had brought with them from the earth, and run like dislodged insects into the night, into hiding.

All of them, because of their weariness, and in spite of the hard ground, had slept. Most of the bands had kept one member awake in turn as a watchman. Since the night on Bronson Beta was longer than the night on earth, they had used the additional time for rest. Hendron first summoned them by calling on the loud-speaker; and then, for those who had marched out of sight of the Ark, he gave an auditory landmark by broadcasting over the powerful loud-speaker a series of phonograph musical records. The men and women in clothes now earth-stained, the former not shaven, and the latter not made up, straggled to the Ark to the music of "The Hymn to the Sun" and of Schubert's "Unfinished Symphony."

They answered a roll-call. No one had been harmed. The Ark was unscathed. They sat down to breakfast.

Hendron explained the unexpected dilemma of the previous night. "Unless I am greatly mistaken, our new planet passed through a cluster or path of fragments of the moon, destroyed, as you know, months ago. They would find orbits of their own about the sun; and we have approached again an area where we might encounter fragments of any size. I believe that the meteors which fell last night were débris from the moon— débris scattered and hurled into space by that cosmic collision.

"In the future we will probably be able to chart the position of such fragments, so that we will know when we are coming within range of them. It is my opinion that the phenomenon was more or less local here, that we attracted to our surface a unified group of fragments scattered along a curve coinciding with our orbit, so that they dropped virtually in one place.

"I regret that the night which I had planned should be so

peaceful for all was so profoundly disturbed. You are courageous. I would like to extend our period of rest to include this, our second day, on Bronson Beta. But so divergent and so pressing are the necessities of our work here, that I cannot do so. We will start immediately after breakfast to construct a cantonment which will be adequate at least temporarily."

CHAPTER II

CIVILIZATION RECOMMENCES

SUCH isolation, such solitude, such courage in the face of the unknown never before existed. One hundred and three people ate their breakfast—one hundred and three people laughing, talking, saluting each other, staring often at the ocean and the greenish sky, and still more often at the shining cylinder standing on end in their midst.

Cole Hendron walked over to Tony and Eliot James and his daughter, who were breakfasting together.

"Right after breakfast," he said, "I want you, together with Higgins, to start prospecting for farm lands."

Tony nodded. Two years before, the assignment would have appalled him. He would not have known whether beets were planted an inch under the surface of the soil or three feet, and whether one planted tubers or seeds; but he had been for a long time in charge of the farm in Michigan, and he was now well equipped for the undertaking.

"Bring back soil-samples. You understand the nature of the terrain which will be required—level and free from stones. It may be that you will find nothing in the vicinity that will be adequate; and if that is true we will consider moving the Ark. It is still good for a few hundred miles, I guess."

Eliot James grinned. "Or a few hundred million? Which?"

To the surprise of all three, Cole Hendron did not respond with a smile. Instead he said simply: "I'd risk taking it up if we had to move in order to find a suitable place to raise food."

Tony understood that the leader of the expedition was entirely serious, and said with sudden intensity: "What's the matter with the Ark?"

"In the laboratory tests," the gray-haired man answered, "and in the smaller furnaces and engines we designed, Dave Ransdell's metal did not fuse or melt. But under the atomic blast, as we came through space, it commenced to erode. About eighteen hours after we had started, we went off our course because, as I discovered, the lining of one of the outside stern jets was wearing out more rapidly than the others. I used one of the right-angle tubes to reëstablish our direction, and I made some effort to measure the rate of dissipation of Ransdell's metal. I couldn't be very accurate, since I could not turn off the jets, but I was not at all certain that the material would stand the strain until we had reached the point where we started falling on Bronson Beta."

"You mean to say," Eliot James exclaimed, "that we barely got here?"

Cole Hendron smiled, and yet his face was sober. "It turned out that we had a little margin. I examined the tubes yesterday, and I dare say we could use them for a trip of another five hundred miles. But at both ends of the ship our insulation is nearly gone. We could not, for example, circumnavigate this globe."

The writer looked depressed. "I had imagined," he said, "that we would be able to cruise at will on the surface of the planet from now on."

Hendron turned his face toward the ship, which represented the masterpiece of his life of engineering achievements. He regarded it almost sadly. "We won't be able to do that. In any case we would move her over the surface of the planet only to find good farm land, because we've got to take her to pieces."

"To pieces!"

Hendron assented. "We designed her for that very purpose. Those layer sections on the inside wall will be taken down, one by one, and set up again on the ground. The top section will be made into a radio station, so that we can make accurate measurements of our orbit and also study meteorological conditions. The next section below that will be a chemistry laboratory. The one below that will be a hospital, if we need it. The next three will be store-rooms, and we will turn the last section into a machine-shop. The steel on the outside hull will be our mineral source for the time being, and out of it we will make the things we need until it is exhausted."

His eyes twinkled. "I had anticipated we might have a great deal of trouble in finding a source of iron ore and in mining it, but I dare say that some of the meteorites which fell here last night will not have buried themselves very deeply, so that we may have many tons of first-rate metal at our disposal when we need it."

"An ill wind," Eliot James said. "Still, I hate to think of the Ark being torn down. I had imagined we would go hunting for the others in it."

Tony spoke. "I'd been thinking about that. It seems to me that if anybody had reached here, we would have heard some kind of signal from them by now."

"I agree with you," said Hendron.

"And when I thought about looking for them, it seemed darned difficult. After all, Bronson Beta has an area of more than five hundred million square kilometers, and any one of those five hundred million would be big enough to hide a ship like the Ark. Besides, we don't even know where the land is, except in a general way."

"I've got maps made for telescopic photographs," Eve said, "but they're not very good. Bronson Beta was mighty hard to observe—first with its atmosphere thawing, then its water. You could get a peek through the perpetual clouds at a little chunk of water or a small area of land now and again, but all the photographs I collected don't give a very good idea of its geography." She reached in her pocket and took out a piece of paper. "Here is a rough sketch I made of the East and West hemisphere; it isn't very good cartography, but it will give you some idea of what little we do know of the planet's surface."

They bent over the map for a few moments. Hendron said: "It would be like looking for a haystack on a continent, so that you could look for a needle in the haystack when you found it."

"And besides," Tony continued, "you might go over the place, where the people you were looking for were, at night, and in that case your jets would completely annihilate them."

Cole Hendron's face showed amazement. Then he said:

"By George, Tony, you're quite right! And do you know that although I spent a lot of time thinking about looking for other human beings here, and although I originally considered we would probably make long excursions in the Ark until I realized it would be more sensible to take it down at once, it never occurred to me for an instant that our jets would be dangerous to anybody underneath, even in spite of the fact that I used it to wipe out that army of hoodlums that attacked us. It just goes to show what you may omit when you think. Still, I am of the opinion that we arrived here alone out of all the expeditions. If our crops fail us entirely because of too much heat, or because it gets cold too soon, or for reasons we cannot anticipate now—" He paused.

"Twenty-five or thirty of us might get through the winter on the provisions I've brought. But all of us couldn't."

With the injection of that grim thought into their breakfast conversation, the meal was brought to an end.

"It therefore behooves me," Tony said, "to look for farm lands, and get some sort of crops in."

Half an hour later Tony started out with Higgins. Tony carried a knapsack in which there was food enough for two days for both of them. He also carried a pair of blankets and a revolver. He had objected to the revolver, as it had been his wish to appear in complete possession of himself. Reason argued that there would be no phenomenon on the new planet which might make firearms useful, but imagination made the possession of a gun a great comfort, and Hendron had insisted he take it.

As the two men started, the sound of hammering was already audible inside the Ark, and most of the members of the company were engaged in useful work.

A few watched their start. Tony reached into his pocket and took out a quarter. "I've carried this from Earth," he said to

Higgins, "for just such emergencies. Heads we go inland; tails we go along the coast."

The coin landed with the eagle up. Tony flipped it again, saying as it spun in the air: "Heads we go north, tails we go south." Again the eagle. Tony pointed toward the coastline and said: "Forward."

The people who were seeing them off waved and called: "Good luck!"

"You'll have to abandon your botanical pursuits, I'm afraid," Tony said to the elderly scientist. "I usually hit a pretty fast pace. If I go too fast, let me know."

"Very well," Higgins said, and he chuckled dryly. "But I'd like to tell you, young man, that I've spent three sabbatical years climbing mountains in Tibet and Switzerland and the Canadian Northwest, and I dare say I'll be able to keep up with you."

Tony glanced at the scrawny, pedagogical little man at his side, and once more he felt almost reverent toward Hendron. Who would have thought that this student of plants, this desiccated college professor, was also a mountain-climber? Yet, since a plant biologist of the highest capabilities was essential to the company of the Ark, how much better it was to take a man who not only knew his subject magnificently, but who also could scale rugged peaks!

For an hour they walked along the bluff that faced the sea— a continuation of the landscape upon which the Ark had landed. It was rocky and barren, except for such ferns and mosses as they had already observed. Of dead vegetation there seemed to be nothing which had grown as large as a tree or indeed even a bush. The whole area appeared to have been what on earth would have been called a moor—though Higgins could recall no earthly moor of this character or evident extent. The ground inland was a plateau ranged with low hills, and in the remote distance the tops of a mountain-range could be seen.

At the end of an hour they saw ahead of them an arm of hills that ran at right angles down to the ocean and extended out in a long rocky promontory. At the foot of the promontory was a cove, and in the cove were beaches. They climbed to the highest near-by elevation and surveyed the arid, rock-strewn plateau.

"I don't believe," said Tony, "that there is any farm land in this area."

Higgins shook his head. "I think if we can find a place to get down over the cliff to the edge, we can go around that point at water level."

They continued along a little way, and presently Higgins pointed to a "chimney" in the precipice. He looked at Tony with a twinkle in his eyes. "How about it?"

Tony stared into the narrow slit in the rock. It was almost perpendicular, and only the smallest cracks and outcroppings afforded footholds and handholds. He was on the point of suggesting that they find a more suitable place to descend, when he realized that the older man was laughing at him.

Tony set his jaw. "Fine!"

Higgins started down the chimney. He had not let himself over the edge before it was apparent that he was not only a skillful climber, but a man of considerable wiry strength.

Tony had always felt an instinctive alarm in high places, and he had no desire for the task ahead of him. Perspiration oozed from him, and his muscles quivered, as he lowered himself into position for the descent. It was ticklish, dangerous work. Two hundred feet below them lay a heap of jagged rocks, and around that the beach. Tony did not dare look down, and yet it was necessary to look for places to put his feet; and from the corner of his eye he was continually catching glimpses of the depth of the abyss below. His composure was by no means increased when the Professor below him called: "Maybe I should have gone last, because if you fall where you are now, you'll probably knock me off."

Tony said nothing. Twenty minutes later, however, he felt horizontal ground under his feet. He was standing on the beach. He was covered with perspiration; his clothes were soaked. His face was white. He looked up at the precipice which they had descended; and he said, with his best possible assumption of carelessness: "I thought that was going to be difficult. There was nothing to it."

The Professor gave him a resounding clap on the back. "My boy," he exclaimed, "you're all right! That was one of the nastiest little jobs I've ever undertaken."

There was sand under their feet now, and they slogged through it up to the end of the promontory, where the sea rolled in and broke in noisy gusts.

They walked around it. Before them was a vast valley. It stretched two miles or more to another series of hills. It disappeared inland toward the high mountains, and down its center meandered a wide, slow river.

Tony and Higgins stared at the scene and then at each other. The whole valley was covered with new, bright green, where fresh vegetation had carpeted the soil!

They ran, side by side, out upon the expanse of knee-deep verdure until they arrived, panting, at the river's edge. The water was cold and clouded. After they had regarded it, they turned their heads in unison toward the distant range; for they realized that this, the first river to be discovered on Bronson Beta, was the product of glaciers in the high mountains. Higgins stepped back from the bank a moment later, and pulled up a number of mosses and ferns, until he had cleared a little area of ground in which he began to dig with his hands. The soil was black and loamy, alluvial and rich. He beckoned Tony to look at it. They knew then that their mission had been fulfilled; for here, not more than half a dozen miles from the Ark, along the valley of this river, was as fine a farm land as could be found anywhere on the old Earth. Here too water would be available for irrigation, if no rains fell.

There were no tides on Bronson Beta to make the river brackish at its mouth. Some one in camp had already announced that the sea was salt, saltier even than the ocean on Earth. Now Tony went to the river's edge, scooped up a handful of water and tasted it. He was mindful as he did so that he might be exposing himself to an unknown spore or an unheard-of bacterium, but recklessness had so long been a part of necessary risk, that he did not heistate.

Higgins raised his eyebrows.

"Fresh," Tony said. "Fresh and cold." He unstrapped his canteen, poured out the drinking-water they had brought, and filled it with water from the river.

"We might as well go back," said Tony, "and tell them."

They collected samples of soil, then started back, side by side, avoiding the chimney by turning inland and following a gentle rise of ground over the promontory. They walked eagerly for a while, as they wished to hurry the news of their discovery to the camp; but they fell to talking, and their pace unconsciously slowed. It was not unusual that ardent conversation would occupy the colonists of Bronson Beta, for their problems were so grave, their hazards were so little understood, that they were constantly found in large or small groups, exchanging plans, suggestions, worries and ideas. Higgins was inclined, like many people of his type, to be pessimistic.

"My interest," he explained to Tony, "in finding various new forms of plant life on Bronson Beta was purely scientific. I regard their discovery as a very bad omen."

"Why?"

"Wherever ferns and mosses will grow, fungi will grow. Fungi are parasitical. The seeds we have brought from Earth have been chosen through countless generations to resist the fungi of earth. But many of them, if not all of them, will doubtless fall prey to smuts and rots and root-threads and webs, which they have never encountered before and against which they have no resistance. It would have been better if what I had always maintained to be true were a fact."

"Which was what?" Tony asked."

Higgins snorted. "I wouldn't have believed it! For years I have been teaching that the theory that spores could survive absolute zero was ridiculous. I have had some very bitter quarrels with my colleagues on the subject. In fact,"—he frowned uncomfortably,—"I fear I have abused them about it. I called Dinwiddie, who made experiments with spores kept in liquid hydrogen, a pinhead. It is unfortunate that Dinwiddie has not survived, although I can imagine nothing more detestable and odious than to have to apologize to such an egotist. Dinwiddie may have been right about one matter, but he was indubitably wrong about hundreds of other theories."

Tony grinned at this carry-over of this curious man's prejudices and attitudes. They surmounted the central ridge of the promontory and scanned the landscape. Tony's eyes lighted on a feature which was not natural, and he suddenly exclaimed: "By George, Higgins, we should have followed that road! It went south a little inland from the coast, and there it is."

Higgins grunted. "So it is! But we'd have missed that splendid little climb of ours."

They walked together to the road and stepped upon its smooth hard surface.

"It will give us a perfect highway from that valley to the Ark," Tony said jubilantly. "Let's go back a few hundred yards."

They returned along the highway to a point from which they could see its descent into the river valley, where it turned and ran west along the side of the watercourse. Having satisfied themselves that it served the valley, they turned again toward the Ark, following the road this time.

For several miles they came upon no other sign of the creatures that had lived upon the planet in the past ages—not even another of the slabs of metal neatly engraved with the unreadable writing. The road curved only when the natural topography made the problem of grading it very difficult. As a rule the Bronson Betans had preferred to cut through natural barriers or raise up a high roadbed over depressions rather than to curve their road around such obstacles.

"It looks," said Tony, "as if they built these roads for speed. They didn't like curves, and they didn't like bumps. They went through the hills and over the valleys, instead of up and down and around."

There were a few bends, however; and upon rounding one of these, they came abruptly upon an object which made both of the men scramble from the road and stand and stare silently. The object was a machine—or rather what was left of a machine. It was crushed against a pinnacle of rock at the end of one of the rare curves in the road. The very manner in which it stood against the rock wall suggested how it had arrived there: it had been one of the vehicles which the creatures of the planet drove or rode, and rounding the curve at too high a speed, it had shot off the highway and smashed head-on into the wall of stone.

The two men looked at it, then went closer and looked again.

They bent over it and touched it. They exchanged glances without speaking. The thing still glittered in the sunlight—the metal which composed it being evidently rust-proof. The predominating color of that metal was crimson, although many parts were steel blue, and some were evidently made of copper. An unidentifiable fragment lay on the ground beside it; and Tony, picking it up, found to his surprise that it was extremely light, lighter even than aluminum. The engine was twisted and mangled, as was the rest of the car. It was impossible to guess what the original shape of the vehicle had been, but it was conceivable that an expert, examining the débris, might decide what type engine had driven it.

Tony could not tell. He could see that it had not been a gasoline engine. It was not a reciprocating steam engine, or a turbine. Furthermore, it was not an atomic engine. There were wires and connections which suggested an electromotive force, but that was all. For a long time they looked at this mute record of age-old reckless driving. They could find no sign of the driver or of his clothing. Tony picked up the loose fragment of crimson, iridescent metal, and they went on down the road, for a while silent and thoughtful.

"An automobile," Higgins said at last.

"With an engine like none I have ever heard of."

"I know very little about such things. It looks like drunken driving, though."

"It must have been going frightfully fast."

"Did you see the wheels?"

"They were big."

"They didn't have pneumatic tires, just a ribbon of some yielding material around them."

"You wouldn't need rubber tires on a road as smooth as this."

"There were no people."

"Would they have been—people?"

Neither of them could answer that question. They walked quickly now and by and by in the distance they saw the summit of the Ark.

They ran to the encampment, bringing their news. . . .

Naturally the colonists were excited—even ecstatic—to know that apparently good farming land had been found within a few miles of the Ark. The value of the discovery was understood clearly by all of them. But they were human. It was the report of the strange machine wrecked by the roadside which set them ablaze with curiosity.

Even Hendron made no pretense of concealing it.

"The importance of finding the valley unquestionably outweighs your other discovery by a thousand to one. However, I share the feeling of every one else here. The minute you said you had found a vehicle, a score of questions burst into my mind. No matter how badly wrecked it is, we can certainly tell what its motive force was, and more than that, we can get some idea of the creature or creatures who operated it. We can tell from the position of its controls how big they were and how strong they were. In fact, although it had been my intention to postpone archæological research until we were more comfortably situated,"—Hendron smiled,—"I know that I, for one, cannot stay away from that machine, and I am going to let everybody who feels they would like to see it, accompany me with you to the spot at once."

An hour later nearly every one from the Ark was gathered around the machine. Bates and Maltby, who were perhaps the best engineers and mechanics among them, except Hendron, stepped out of the circle of fascinated onlookers. Behind them walked Jeremiah Post, the metallurgist of the company. These three men, together with Hendron, began painstakingly and slowly to examine the wreck. They worked without spoken comment, although occasionally one of them would point to a connection, or trace a cable with his finger; and even more frequently questioning looks and nods would be exchanged. They studied particularly the twisted and battered remnants of what had been the controls.

Finally Hendron, after a brief *sotto voce* colloquy with Post, Bates and Maltby, addressed the crowd of people. who had remained far enough away to leave room for those inspecting the discovery.

"Well, friends," he said simply, "until we have had time to take this apparatus back to camp and study it more thoroughly, we will be unable to make a complete report on it. But we four are agreed on a good many things that will interest you. In the first place, judging from the area of space for passengers and the division of that area, whoever occupied and operated this machine could not have been much larger or much smaller than ourselves. You will note,"—he walked over to the wreck and pointed,—"that although the force of the crash has collapsed this portion of the vehicle, we may assume that its operator sat here.

"I say sat, because this is manifestly a seat. The vehicle steered with a wheel which has been broken off. This is it. The braking mechanism was operated by either of two flat pedals on the floor; and on what corresponds to a dashboard there were manual controls. Whether the creatures on Bronson Beta had hands and feet like ours cannot be said. However, that they had four limbs that they were able to sit upright and that their upper pair of limbs terminated in members which could be used precisely as fingers are used, is very illuminating. In fact, I won't say that the builders of this very interesting and brilliant vehicle were human beings; but I *will* say that if the vehicle were intact, it could be operated by a human being."

31

He paused for a full minute, while a babble of conversation swept his audience.

The talking stopped, however, when he continued: "As for the machine itself, it was made very largely of beryllium. Beryllium was a very common element on earth. It is, roughly speaking, about half as heavy as aluminum, and about twice as strong as what we called duraluminum. It was rare and valuable in a pure state only because we had not as yet perfected a way of extracting beryllium cheaply. The brilliant coloring of the metal is due to the addition of chemicals during its refinement and smelting, and I think it is safe to assume that the color was added for decorative rather than for utilitarian purposes. It is interesting to remark in that connection that the metal, which was rust-proof and tarnish-proof, is very much superior to the enamel finishes which we used for similar purposes.

"The principle upon which this vehicle was propelled is obvious in the sense that we have all agreed upon what was accomplished by its engine, although further study will be necessary to reveal precisely how it was done.

"For the sake of those who are not physicists or engineers, I will explain that except for the atomic energy which we ourselves perfected, all terrestrial energy was thermal energy. In other words, it came from the sun. Oil represents the energy stored up in minute vegetation. Coal, the sunlight stored in larger plants. Water-power is derived from kinetic energy in water elevated by the sun to high places. Tidal energy may be also excepted, as it was caused by the attraction of the moon. Since we found electricity a more useful form of energy, we bent our efforts to the changing of thermal energy into electrical energy. Thus we burn coal and oil to run steam turbines, which in turn run dynamos, which generate electricity. We run other turbines by water-power, not to use their force directly, but in order again to generate electricity.

"All those systems were inefficient. The loss of energy between the water-fall and the power line, between the fire-box and the light bulb, was tremendous. It has been the dream of every physicist to develop a system whereby thermal energy could be converted directly into electrical energy. For most of you it will probably be difficult to understand more than that the engine of this vehicle of the ancient inhabitants of Bronson Beta was run by that precise method. Its machinery was capable of taking the energy of heat and turning it, in simple steps, into electricity."

Cole Hendron glanced at Duquesne and Von Beitz, who stood near the vehicle. He spoke as if to them: "A stream of superheated. ionized steam was discharged at a tremendous velocity upon a dielectric, and the induced current ran the driving motor." He turned to the others. "We must go back and go to work. As soon as we can spare the time, I will have this machine studied in complete detail." He smiled. "I'd like to do it myself, as you can all imagine, but just now planting beans is more important. One other thing before we go back to our labors: you will probably all be interested to know that the reason this car is in such a demolished condition is that it must have been able to attain a speed of at least three hundred and fifty miles an hour."

CHAPTER III

In Eliot James' diary appears the following anecdote. It is dated Day No. 14:

"Higgins has classified most of the local flora, and in that connection an amusing thing happened.

"For the first two weeks of our stay here he hopped around like a madman, gathering specimens; and except for his expedition with Tony, it was impossible to make him do anything else. The whole group was at lunch outdoors one day when he came running in with some miserable little fragments of vegetation, yelling: 'I've got the brother of one we had on earth! Identical! Identical in every way. One of the *Pteridophyte*. Light-pressure has probably carried these spores all through space. It is the *Lycopodium Clavatum*. Found a sample with a Prothallus bearing young sporophyte, with a single sporangium and adventitious roots!'

"Even among our learned company this burst of botanical terminology caused a ripple of laughter. Hendron took the plant gravely from Higgin's hand, stared at it and said: 'It's club moss, isn't it?'

"Higgins nodded so that he nearly shook off his little goatee. 'Exactly Hendron. Precisely. Club moss. We had it on earth.'

"Hendron then turned to his comrades and said: 'Dr. Higgins has brought up a principle which I have long intended discussing with you.' He held up the plant. 'Here is an insignificant bit of vegetation, which was known on earth as club moss, and also by the three jawbreakers the eminent Doctor has pronounced. To my mind, *club moss* is a fine name. To my mind, the use of Latin as a basis for terminology of the sciences is a little silly, especially since the last vestige of Rome is now reduced literally to atoms. So I was going to suggest that for the sake of the headaches of all future generations of students, as well as for the convenience of the human race which can memorize *club moss* more readily than *Lycopodium Clavatum*, we base the nomenclature of our new sciences, and reëstablish the terminology of the old, upon English.

" 'We will have plants which belong to the genus *Moss*, the cohort *Rock Moss*, the species *Club* or *Creeping Moss;* and instead of *cohort* and *genus* we will say *class* and *type*. The main artery in the arm will not be known as the axilliary, brachial and radial, hereafter, depending upon just what part

34

of the artery is meant, but it will be known as the main artery in the arm at the armpit, the elbow and the wrist. Of course, I speak carelessly now, and our simplification will have to be made so that no name-value is lost. But since we are going to be a strictly scientific civilization, I see no reason why science should remain esoteric; and I wish as much effort would be made to use familiar terms for our scientific facts and features as will be made to introduce scientific terms into common speech.'

"Higgins stood before Henderson, crestfallen, amazed. 'It couldn't be,' he said suddenly, almost tearfully. 'Why, I've spent years acquiring my technical vocabulary!'

"Hendron nodded. 'And you call a skunk—*Mephitis Mephitica?*'

"Higgins said: 'Quite so.'

" 'And what does *Mephitis Mephitica* mean?'

"Higgins flushed. 'It means something like—a—er—smelliest of the smelly.'

"Everybody giggled. Hendron, however, was serious. 'Quite so. Now, I think *skunk* is a better name than *the smelliest of the smelly,* so if we find any skunks on Bronson Beta—a discovery I seriously doubt,—we will call them not *Mephitis Mephitica,* but just plain skunks. And in our classrooms we will teach the fact that they are nocturnal, burrowing meat-eaters, but we will ignore the *Mephitis Mephitica.*'

"Higgins shook his head sadly. 'It will mean the reorganization of all science. It will mean beginning at the bottom. It will be tragic. I suppose, my dear Hendron, that you will forget the *Laminariæ* and the *Fuci,* and call their ash *kelp.*'

"Hendron nodded again. 'I shall certainly have different names from *Laminariæ* for them, but whether we shall call their ashes *kelp* or not, is for the simplifier to say. Maybe we could just call them *seaweed ashes* and let it go at that.'

"But perhaps my penchant for summarizing at anniversaries should be given a little chance to function. We have been here two weeks. We have been working furiously.

"Great cranes surmount the top of the Ark. Already the uppermost layer has been removed and reassembled on the ground. Our settlement looks like a shipbuilding yard, but I think all our hearts are heavy with the knowledge that we are not building, but wrecking our ship. We have cut off escape to anywhere else. We have committed ourselves to life here.

"The peril of the planets in the sky on Earth, and the last tribulations of civilization, were great nervous driving forces in the days before the destruction. Those stimuli exist no longer. We sweat. Our atomic winches purr, and chunks of metal clank to the earth. At night our forges glow, and rivet-hammers ring.

"The food we eat is monotonous. No dietitian could give us

a better balanced diet; but on the other hand, none of us is able to gratify those daily trifling appetites, which were unimportant on earth, but which up here assume great proportions. I saw Lila Parker become hysterical one day because she couldn't have olives with her lunch. It was not that she wanted olives so badly, but just that she was making an expression of the frustrations of all of us in such respects. Bread and beans and johnny-cake and oatmeal, and bacon and lentil soup and sweet chocolate and rice, together with yeast which we cultivate and eat to prevent pellagra, and other vitamins which we take in tablets, form a diet nourishing beyond doubt, but tiresome in the extreme.

"Some of us still sleep in the Ark. Some sleep in the observatory, and some in two different groups of tents. We remain scattered because of the possibility of a recurrence of the meteoric shower.

"One of the small atomic engines Hendron brought has been converted into the motor of a tractorlike machine which pulls a flat four-wheeled trailer back and forth to the river valley.

"Tony and twenty other men and women live in that river valley. They have used the tractor to plow, and already they have several hundred acres under cultivation. They work frantically—not knowing how long the growing season will be—knowing only that our survival depends upon their success. The sun has been very hot these days, and the heat increases through a strange, tremendous noon. Several of the people, particularly the women, have been severely sunburned, as the actinic rays appear to be much stronger on Bronson Beta than they were upon Earth.

"None of us has yet adjusted himself to the difference in the length of the day, so that the hours of light seem interminable, and we reach darkness exhausted. I have seen workers on the Ark, and men and women on the farm, fall asleep at their jobs in the later afternoon. On the other hand, since we are accustomed to sleeping at the most nine or ten hours, we are apt to wake up long before dawn. We have ameliorated this problem somewhat by dividing the labor into eight-hour shifts, with eight more hours for recreation. But this brings the free periods of all of us frequently in the dark hours, and there is little in the way of recreation available then, or any time; so we go on working, although nearly always a number of those who are enjoying a rest-period may be found in the circular observation-building, watching Von Beitz or one of the other electrical engineers as they continue their long and manifestly hopeless vigil at the radio-receivers. They occasionally vary that vigil by sending out into the empty universe a description of our position and an account of our situation.

"The soil at the farm was judged excellent by the chemists. Bacteria have been sowed in it. Ants have been loosed there. Our grasshoppers are fattening on the local flora; their buzzing is the only familiar living sound except our own, and the occasional noises of the animals we tend. Every day the tractor brings over the Other People's road an iron tank of drinking- and cooking-water from the river. We had at first utilized sea-water, which we distilled; but the water in the river was found to be pure and apparently without bacteria, so we have given up our distillation.

"We would like to restock the sea with fish, but we are doubtful about the possibility of establishing a biological econ-omy there. We have numerous fishes in an aquarium on the Ark, and perhaps at some later date we shall make the at-tempt.

"Shirley Cotton has fallen more or less in love with Tony. I would not enter this in a diary that is perhaps to be history, except for the fact that she announced it to every one the other day, and said that she was going to move for a system of marriage codes by which she could compel him to become her mate as well as Eve's. It must have saddened Eve, although she has said nothing about it, and appears not to mind. But Shirley has pointed out what every one has often thought privately—there are thirteen more women than men. All the women but five are under forty years of age. Nearly half the men are more than fifty. Our other party, which appears lost, contained more of the younger people.

"So at the end of two weeks we find ourselves disturbed by many questions, working hard, and realizing slowly the tre-mendous difficulties to be conquered.

"Yesterday and the day before it rained. The days were like any rainy ones on earth, with gray skies and an incessant heavy drizzle that crescendoed to occasional downpours. The river at the farm rose. The earth around us became a slough of mud, and we tramped in and out of the Ark dejected, de-spondent, soaked and uncomfortable. When the skies cleared, however, Tony was jubilant. His wide acres were covered with even rows of green, and indeed, the farm was a beautiful spectacle. Hendron ordered Kyto to serve a meal which was an anticipatory thanksgiving.

"We have moved our animals to the farm and put them in stockades where some—the most valuable, fortunately, the cows and sheep—thrive so far, on the ferns and mosses which we have mixed with the last of the fodder brought from earth. Other of the animals do not do so well; and if they die, it is the last we shall see of their species. But shall we our-selves survive?

"On reading the above, it seems that my tone is melan-choly; and I feel that it cannot be otherwise. Pressure of work and the reaction to our months of strain and danger, and contemplation of the awful though splendid perils of the flight from earth, have brought about this state of mind. We may be—are, for all we know—the only living, intelligent beings in all the cosmos; one hundred and three of us,—many past the prime of life,—stranded in this solitude with two cows and a bull, two sheep and rams, two deer, a few. ants, grasshoppers, fungi, bacteria and bees that we have brought with us. We are now feeling the grinding despair that castaways must know, except that we cannot have the hope of rescue, and still worse, we have abandoned the hope of any other fellowship than our own. Solitude—exile—loneliness!

"The children—the little boy and girl whom, thank God, we brought—are the bright lights in our emotional gloom. Their eagerness, their amusing behavior, their constant loyalty and affection, point us more powerfully than anything else to an untiring hope.

"If there were more children—if babes were born among us, new members of our race, this awful feeling of the *end* might be lifted. But who would dare to bear children here? Eve? Shirley?"

Eliot James, on this despairing note, interrupted his record.

Two matters recommend themselves for comment at this point. One concerns Kyto, the quick-witted, obedient Japanese, who had so honorably, as he would have said, followed his master's cause and was now one of the mysteries of Bronson Beta. Everybody talked to Kyto. Naturally, the little Jap was no longer Tony's servant. No one would have servants again. His handiness in the matter of the preparation of meals had made him gravitate to the commissariat in the first few days. But it began to appear at once that Kyto was more than a good cook.

On the third day, when Shirley Cotton had been instructed to inform Kyto on the matter of vitamins and balanced diets, she discovered that he knew fully as much about the subject as she. His budgeting of the food supply was a masterpiece. Unaided, he organized a storeroom system and made plans for its transference. Indeed the eventual discoveries about Kyto surpassed even the wildest guesses of the colonists.

The other matter concerned Hendron:

Others beside Eliot James had observed, and with concern, the change in the leader; and they began to discuss it.

Tony knew that he himself was talked of as a candidate for commander of the group—governor of the camp—if Hendron was to be replaced; so Tony was especially careful to refrain from criticism. In addition to his sincere loyalty and devotion to Hendron, there was the further fact that Eve became even more fanatically devoted to her father as his difficulties increased.

"Tony," she asked him, "what do they—the opposition—say about Father?"

"There's no real opposition," Tony denied. "We'd be crazy to oppose each other; we'd be stark insane! A hundred and three of us upon an empty planet. Surely we've more sense than that."

"Tony, tell me," insisted Eve, "what you hear them say! Father's through? They want another leader; isn't that it?"

"No," denied Tony. "They want him to *lead* again; that's all. He's not doing it now as he did, you know."

"But he will again!"

"Of course he will."

"They're so unfair to Father!" Eve cried. "How much more can they expect of a man? He brought them—those who criticize him—he brought us all through the greatest venture and journey of mankind; and they complain that now he rests a little, that he does not immediately explore. Does it occur to nobody that perhaps Father is too wise to explore or to permit others to wander off—exploring?"

"I've told them I agree with your father," Tony said. "I agree that our first procedure should be to establish ourselves where we are by hard work."

"But do you really agree, Tony?"

"Well," said Tony honestly, "it would certainly be more pleasant to explore."

"But it must not be done now; not yet. And you know why."

"Yes," said Tony; for he too was familiar with Hendron's fears—which were these: since the spores of certain plants had manifestly survived upon Bronson Beta, it was probable up to the practical point of certainty that spores of disease-inducing bacteria also had survived. These would be found where the previous "hosts" of the bacteria had dwelt and died—that is, in the villages and the cities of the Other People.

So Hendron, in this new mood of his, feared the finding of dwellings of the Other People; he forbade, absolutely, further exploration.

Hendron was tired; he had borne too much. He had brought his people over through space, having dealt with and conquered the most tremendous risks; and now he would risk no more. He became obsessed with a passion to preserve and keep safe these followers of his, whom he considered the last survivors of the human race.

Yet, against all his care and caution, death came to the camp. On the morning of the twentieth day, after the slow, dragging dawn when the sun so leisurely arose, two men were found lying in a strange stuper. They were Bates and Jeremiah Post. Before sunset of that long day, twenty more—both men and women—were afflicted, and the physicians had isolated all the sick and ailing.

The epidemic, while somewhat resembling the "sleeping sickness" of earthly days, differed from it in important aspects. It might be, Dodson announced, due to an infection carried from the world and which had developed on this new planet, and which, in the strange environment, exhibited different characteristics. It might be caused by some infective agent encountered on Bronson Beta.

Was it significant that Bates and Jeremiah Post, who had dug from the soil the wreck of the Other People's vehicle, were the first affected? And Maltby soon afterward was sick. Twenty-six persons altogether fell ill; and three died—Bates, and Wardlow, a chemist, and one of the girls who had served as a nurse to the sick—Lucy Grant. The rest made complete recoveries; no one else was later affected; the strange plague passed from the camp.

But of the hundred and three emigrants from earth—perhaps the sole survivors of humanity in all creation—three were dead. And Tony Drake ordered the breaking of the strange soil of Bronson Beta for the first burials of Earth People! Three new interments to add to the uncountable graves of the Other People who were yet to be discovered!

Hendron, who himself had not fallen sick, was by far the most disturbed by these deaths that had come to the camp; thereafter he doubled his restrictions.

It was Higgins the botanist, who at length openly defied the leader.

Higgins took four of the younger men—and under other circumstances Tony unquestionably would have joined them —and went off. At that time Hendron was endeavoring to make a new set of gears, and a chassis and a body, for a second atomic-engine vehicle, using metal from the wall of the Ark; and although he engaged more than twenty people in the operation, it was progressing very slowly. Moreover they had just passed through another three days of heavy rain, and while it was good for the gardens, nevertheless the people who lived in tents were extremely miserable. They were studying the possibility of having to live altogether in one or two of the round sections of the Ark during the coming winter, as it would be impossible to erect metal houses by that time; and every one was dejected over the idea of passing nearly two earth years sleeping on the padded floor of a chamber in the Ark in one great communal group.

Higgins and his party were gone for four days, and anxiety about him became so acute that music was played on the great broadcasting machine constantly during the day, and at night a searchlight shot into the air a vertical beam which was visible for many miles.

Late on the afternoon of the fourth day the exploring party returned.

The five came down the Other People's road from the west, walking with rapid, swinging strides, plainly in triumphant excitement.

Higgins reported for them all when they halted, surrounded by their friends:

"We covered about seventy-five miles. We saw a great desert. We went into a valley where a mighty tangle of fern trees is beginning to rise toward the heavens. We saw glaciers on the top of those distant mountains. I have seen excavations in an old pit where the fossils of animals that were extinct during the civilized period on this planet were being dug out. And we encountered, not ten miles from here, on the Other People's road, something that will very largely relieve one of our great difficulties."

With that he unstrapped his pack, opened it, and dumped out at Hendron's feet a dozen objects upon which Hendron dropped eagerly.

They were wood, chips of wood. Hard wood—soft wood. Finely grained wood, and wood with a coarse, straight grain.

"Is there much of it?" Hendron asked, as he examined the chips.

Higgins nodded. "It isn't related to any of the wood on earth, and there are many interesting features about this vegetation which I will outline in a monograph later, but it is vegetation. It is wood. It comes from the trunks of trees, and there is enough of it standing, seasoned, perfectly preserved, to supply us with all the lumber we can use for generations.

"You have assumed," he continued, speaking directly to Hendron, "that this planet upon which we stand was long ago drawn away from its orbit about some distant sun—some star. We had assumed that, for uncounted ages, this planet followed its prescribed course about its sun until, by the close passing of some other star, its orbit was disturbed, and this planet, with its companion world which destroyed our earth, was cast out into space and cold and darkness.

"The appearance of the forest that we found completely accords with your theory of this planet's past history. There stood a great forest of many varieties of trees, none exactly resembling those of our world, yet of their general order. They seemed to have been deciduous trees mostly; their leaves had fallen; they lay on the ground; the boughs were bare.

"There must have been a long, last autumn followed by a winter without parallel on our world and previously on this planet. All water froze; air froze, preserving the forest as it was at the end of that awful autumn when no thaw came

41

through the millions of years in outer space until this planet found our sun.

"I have said that the trees I examined were unlike the trees on earth; yet their trunks and boughs were wooden; their leaves encumbered the ground. Here are a few of the leaves. . . . I am taking the liberty of calling this one maple, and this one oak, and this one spruce, and this one elm."

The exiles from earth pushed close to finger the leaves and bits of wood, so strange and yet suggesting the familiar. These promised them homes, rooms of their own, chairs, tables, cupboards and book-shelves and writing desks, and a thousand other things dear to their emotional memories. And yet it was odd to see Duquesne, the great French physicist, weeping, and Dodson, the dignified dean of New York surgery, hurling an old felt hat into the air and yelling at the top of his lungs, simply because a wiry little man with a goatee had showed them a few chips of wood.

Tony drew close to Eve. "We'll be outcasts no longer—outcasts!" he emotionally murmured. "We'll have a house and a wood fire again!"

"We?" whispered Eve. "We? You and I? We'll be allowed to marry and live by ourselves?"

They were near to Hendron, but he seemed not to hear them.

"Did you go to the other edge of the forest?" he asked of Higgins.

"There was no sign of the edge as far as we went. The road we followed went through the forest, and before we came to the woods, there were two crossroads. We considered both of them; but we went on, as we have told you, deep into the forest; and returned, as you see."

They were all sitting around a fire on that night, after those first moments of gentleness and of affection when they had been brought electrically back to the happy past, when once again their hopes had risen.

It was night, and dark; and there was no moon. Nor would there ever be a moon. They had been singing softly; and one of their number—Dimitri Kalov—had slipped away from the fire and talked to Hendron, and gone to the Ark and come back with a piano-accordion strapped around his shoulders. No one had seen him return, but suddenly from out of the darkness came a ripple of music.

The singing stopped, and they listened while Dimitri played. He played old songs, and he played some of the music from Russia which his father had taught him. Then, between numbers, when the applause died and a hush fell over the group, as they waited for him to begin again, there was a sound.

It was soft and remote, and yet it transfixed every one instantly, because it was a sound that did not belong to any human being. It was a sound that did not belong to their colony. A sound foreign and yet familiar. A sound that rose for a few instants, and then died out to nothing, only to return more strongly than before.

One by one they turned their faces up, for the sound was in the sky. It approached rapidly, above them, in the dark. There was no mistaking it now. It was the motor of an airplane. An airplane on Bronson Beta! An airplane piloted by other human beings, or perhaps—they did not dare to think about the alternative.

Nearer and nearer it came, until some of them could discern the splotch of darkness against the stars. But then the ship in the heavens seemed to see their fire on the ground and be alarmed by it, for it switched its course and started back in the direction from which it had come.

Hendron rushed toward the observatory and shouted to Von Beitz, who was on duty at the radio, to turn on a searchlight. Von Beitz must have heard the airplane too, for even as Hendron shouted, a long finger of light stabbed across the sky and began combing it for the vanishing plane. It caught and held upon the ship for a fraction of a second before it plunged through a sleazy cloud, but that second was not long enough for any one to tell what manner of ship it was, or even whether it was a ship such as might have been made by the people of the earth. A speck—a flash of wing surface. And the clouds.

They sat, stricken and numb. Surely, if there had been human beings in that ship—surely if it had contained other refugees from the destruction of the earth—it would have circled over their fire time and again in exultation.

But it had fled. What could that mean? Who could be in it? What intelligence could be piloting it?

The pulsations of the motor died. The light was snapped off. The colonists shuddered.

They were not alone on Bronson Beta.

CHAPTER IV

WHAT WAS IT?

SOMEBODY threw a log onto the fire. It blazed up freshly, and illuminated the strained, immobile faces of the emigrants from earth. Nobody spoke. They only looked at each other.

Out of the night, out of the darkness, out of the remote, infinitely distant, impersonal Nowhere, had come that humming, throbbing reality. Somewhere on Bronson Beta there were other human beings. Another still more dreadful thought curdled the imaginations of the people who sat around the camp-fires: were those other beings human?

Hendron, the leader of these brave people, had never felt upon himself pressure for greater leadership—had never felt himself more incompetent to explain the mystery of that night.

He moved among his fellows almost uncertainly. He walked up to the camp-fire and addressed his comrades. "I think," he said slowly, "that the thought now engraving the imaginations of many of you may be discarded. I mean the thought that the plane which approached our camp was piloted by other than human beings."

Eliot James interrupted, speaking with a confidence he did not feel. "It looked like an ordinary airplane."

Cole Hendron shook his head. "From the glimpse we had, no one could say. What we saw was merely a glint upon some sort of material. However, we must use our reason to rescue us from impossible conclusions. We must infer from our glimpse of that machine in the sky, and from the sound of its flight, that some other party on earth was successful in completing a ship capable of taking the leap from Earth to Bronson Beta; and that, also, they were fortunate in the flight; and that they have succeeded, as well as we, in establishing themselves here."

"They must be established very well," somebody else said grimly. "We haven't got a plane."

Hendron nodded. "No; nor did we include an airplane in the equipment of our larger Ark. Therefore it could not have been our comrades from our own camp on Earth whom we heard in this sky. Were they the English, perhaps? Or the Russians? The Italians? Or the Japanese?"

"If they were any people from earth," Jeremiah Post countered, "why should they have approached so near, and yet not give any sign they had seen us?"

Cole Hendron faced this objector calmly. He was aware that

Post was one of the younger men who believed that he, the leader of the party on earth, and the captain on the voyage through space, had served his purpose. "Have you come to believe," he challenged the metallurgist, "that any of the people native to this planet could have survived?"

"I believe," retorted Post, "that we certainly are not safe in excluding that possibility from our calculations. As you all know," he continued, addressing the whole group now rather than Hendron, "I have given extended study to the vehicle of the Other People which we have found. Not only in its mechanical design and method of propulsion was it utterly beyond any vehicle developed on earth, but its metallurgy was in a class by itself—compared to ours. These People had far surpassed our achievement in the sole fields of science from which we yet have any sample. Is it not natural to suppose that, likewise, they were beyond us in other endeavors?"

"Particularly?" Hendron challenged him.

"Particularly, perhaps, in preservation of themselves. I will not be so absurd as to imagine that any large number of them could have survived the extreme ordeals of—space. But is it utterly inconceivable that a few could?"

"How?" said Hendron.

"You know," Jeremiah Post cast back at his leader, "that is not a fair question. I suggest a possibility that some people of this planet may have survived through application of principles or processes far beyond our knowledge; and then you ask me to describe the method. Of course I can't."

"Of course not," agreed Hendron apologetically. "I withdraw that question. However, in order that each of us may form his and her own opinion of the possibilities, I will ask Duquesne to acquaint you with the physical experience of this planet as we now perceive it."

The Frenchman readily arose and loomed larger than ever in the flickering flare of the fire:

"My friends, it is completely plain to all of us that once this world, which has given us refuge, was attached to some distant sun which we, on the world, saw as a star.

"That star might have been a sun of the same order as our sun, which this world has now found. If such were the case, it seems likely that Bronson Beta circled its original sun at some distance similar to our distance from our sun; for the climatic conditions here seem in the past to have been similar, at least, to the conditions on earth.

"There are two other alternatives, however. The original star, about which Bronson Beta revolved, might have been a much larger and hotter sun; in that case, this planet must have swung about that star in an enormous orbit with a year perhaps ten or fifty times as long as our old years. On the other hand, the original sun might have been smaller and feebler—a 'white dwarf,' perhaps, or one of the stars that are nearly spent. In that case, Bronson Beta must have circled it much more closely to have obtained the climate which once here prevailed, and which has been reëstablished now that this planet has found our sun.

"These are fascinating points which we hope to clear up later; we can only speculate upon them now. However, whether the original sun for this planet was a yellow star of moderate size, like our own sun, or whether it was one of the giant stars, or a 'white dwarf,' this world must have been satisfactorily situated with regard to it for millions and hundreds of millions of years.

"Orderly evolution must have proceeded for an immense period to produce, for instance, that log—the material which we burn before me to give us, to-night, light and heat; and to produce the People who made the vehicle which my colleague Jeremiah Post so admirably has analyzed.

"Beings of a high order of intelligence dwelt here. We have evidence that in science they had progressed beyond us— unfortunately for themselves. Poor fellows!"

Dramatically, Duquesne stopped.

Some one—it was a girl—did not permit him the full moment of his halt. "Why unfortunately?"

"Their science must have showed them their doom so plainly and for so frightfully long a period—a doom from which there scarcely could have been, even for the most favored few, any means of escape. Theirs was a fate far more terrible than was ours—a fate incomparably more frightful than mere complete catastrophe.

"Attend! There they were, in some other part of the heavens, circling, at some satisfactory distance, their sun! For millions and millions of years this world upon which now we stand went its orderly way. Then its astronomers noticed that a star was approaching. A star—a mere point of light on its starry nights—swelled and became brighter.

"We may be sure that telescopes upon this world turned upon it; and the beings—whose actual forms we have yet to discover—made their calculations. Their sun, with its retinue of planets, was approaching another star. There would be no collision; we do not believe that such a thing occurred. There was merely an approach of another sun close enough to counteract, by its own attraction, the attraction of the original sun upon this planet, and upon Bronson Alpha.

"The suns—the stars—battled between themselves from millions and perhaps hundreds of millions of miles away; and neither conquered completely. The new sun tore the planets away from the first sun, but it failed to capture them for itself. Between the stars, this planet and its companion, which we called Bronson Alpha, drifted together into the darkness and cold of space.

"The point is, that this must have been a torturingly prolonged process for the inhabitants here. The approach of a star is not like the approach of a planet. We discovered Bronson Alpha and Bronson Beta only a few months before they were upon us; the Beings here must have known for generations, for centuries, the approach of the stranger star!

"Knowing it, for hundreds of years, could any of the inhabitants here have schemed a way of saving themselves? That seems to be the question now before us.

"I cannot say that they could not. I can only say that we could not have devised anything adequate to meet their situation. Yet—*they* might have. They knew more than we: they had much more time, but their problem was terrific—the problem of surviving through nearly absolutely cold and darkness, a drift through space, of a million or millions of years. If any of you believe that problem could have been met by the Beings here, he has as much right to his opinion as I have to mine."

"Which is?" Jeremiah Post demanded.

"That the People here tried to solve that problem," replied Duquesne without evasion, "and failed; but that they made a magnificent attempt. When we find them, we will find—I hope and believe—the method of their tremendous attempt."

Shirley Cotton stood up. She always moved with an almost languid voluptuousness. Now, in these tense moments, her actions were seemingly doubly calculated to be slow and indolent.

"What, M. Duquesne," she inquired, "would be the attitude of the Beings if they survived and found us here?"

The Frenchman shook his head. "Before imagining their attitude, I must first imagine them surviving. I have confessed my failure at that task."

"But *if* some of them survived?" Shirley persisted.

"Their attitude, after awaking from a million years' sleep, would combine, among other elements, surprise and caution, I should suggest," the Frenchman concluded courteously. "But, engaging as such speculations may be, our position demands that we be practical. We must assume that aircraft we saw in these skies came from earth. If there are other people from our world upon Bronson Beta, we prefer to be friends with them. That attitude, besides being rational, is our natural inclination. However,"—he shrugged his huge shoulders eloquently,—"it does not therefore follow that another party of emigrants from earth would want to be friendly to us. We cannot assume that the same emotions sway them. It is possible that, finding themselves here, they prefer private possession of this planet."

Eve, sitting beside Tony, leaned toward him and whispered: "I can imagine that. Can't you?"

Tony nodded. "That's what I've been doing. I was in Russia during the days on earth," he said, and repeated, *"during the days on earth,"* feeling how it seemed an epoch long ago, though it was not yet a month since they fled before the final catastrophe; and as Duquesne had reminded them, it was less than two years since they all had been living on the world unwarned that its end was at hand. Only a little more than two years ago, Tony had traveled as he liked on the world, and had visited, among other countries, Russia.

"Suppose that a Russian party made the hop," Tony continued. "Since we did, why not? They worked along lines of their own, but they had some of the world's best scientists. If they made it, you may be sure they packed their ship with first-class communists—the most vigorous and the most fanatic. When they found themselves here, what would they feel most?"

"I know," Eve nodded. "They'd feel that they had a world to themselves, where they could work out the millennium according to their own ideals."

"And," Tony finished for her, "that they must beat down, at the very outset, possible interference."

They were whispering only to each other; but many heads bent near to listen; and Hendron, seeing that Tony caught this attention, called to him: "You have a suggestion?"

"Two," said Tony, rising to his feet. "I suggest, Cole, that we organize at once an adequate exploring expedition; and at the same time, prepare defenses."

Nobody in the encampment had ever before called Hendron by his first name. Tony's use of it was involuntary and instinctive. Having to oppose his leader in again urging exploration, he took from it any air of antagonism by addressing him as "Cole."

Hendron appreciated this.

"Will you lead the exploring party—and choose its members?" he asked Tony.

"Gladly."

"I," said Hendron, "will be responsible for the defenses here."

The people about Tony pressed closer. "Take me! . . . Me! . . . Tony, I want to go! Take me!"

From the gloom, where Eliot James sat rose his calm, twangy voice: "So we have come to the end of our honeymoon!"

Eve reached for Tony's arm and clung to him as he moved out of the group gathered about him.

"Take me too, Tony."

"Not you."

"Why not?"

"I wouldn't on earth; why would I here? Besides, I want to come back to you. I want to feel, when I'm away, I'm risking whatever we happen to risk, for you. You see, I love you. It's like on earth, when I'm with you away from the others. See the stars up there." The clouds were cleared from a patch in the sky. "There's Cepheus and the Dragon; and Vega and the Swan, as we've always seen them. And the earth hard and cold at our feet; so comfortably solid and substantial, this earth, which came to us torn from some distant star for a couch, sometime, for you and me!"

Night deepened. The company of emigrants from the earth heaped higher the fire with the wood from the forest which had leafed on this land of Bronson Beta a million years ago. Some of the company—men as well as women—shivered with a chill not instilled in their veins by the sharpness of night, as this side of the planet turned away from the sun it had found at the end of its incalculable wandering. Slowly, lazily, the stars swung in the sky; for this planet rotated much less swiftly than the earth upon its axis. The earth people had learned not to lie down too soon to sleep, but to wait out the first hours of the long night in talk; and doubts, terrors, phantasms, easier to dismiss by day, plagued them.

That night, as Eliot James had said, they felt "the honeymoon over." The triumph of their flight, the enormous excitement and relief at finding themselves safe on the new world, could suffice them no longer. Others besides themselves were on this world.

Survivors of the People of the Past! That idea would not down. Contrarily, it increased with the night.

Survivors of the People of the Past—or other emigrants from Earth who had made the journey safely, established themselves and already were exploring, and who, having found this encampment, had swung away again to report. Report what? And to whom?

Nothing happened.

Days passed—the long, slow days of Bronson Beta. The murmuring specter of the sky put in no further appearance; but the consequences of its evanescent presence continued. The camp was roused to a feverish activity which reminded the emigrants of the days of the Ark-building on earth. Indeed, this was Ark-building again, but on a far smaller scale; for the Ark was being taken down, and its materials—especially the last of the lining of the propulsion tubes—were being adapted to an exploration ship.

In the section of building which had been originally dedicated to research, rivet-hammers now rang, and metal in work glowed whitely. The crew that manned the farm was still at its post. Lumber was still being brought from the forest. But the most skillful and the most energetic members of the colony were working upon a small metal jet-propulsion ship hastily designed to travel in Bronson Beta's atmosphere—a ship with lifting surfaces—but a ship with an enclosed cockpit; a ship which could travel very rapidly through the atmosphere of the new planet, and which could rise above that atmosphere if it became necessary.

The throbbing of the motor of the strange plane had changed the entire tempo of the lives of the colonists; it had rearoused them to themselves. If they were to preserve the intelligent pattern of their plans, it was essential to learn at once what interference threatened them. They could look upon themselves no longer as law unto themselves. Some other beings—survivors of the People of this planet or others from the earth—shared this new world with them.

Hendron's people no longer could endure delay in learning, at whatever risks, what lay beyond these silent horizons.

On the morning of the fifty-sixth Bronson Beta day after their arrival, the airship was ready. Streamlined, egg-shaped, with quartz glass windows and duraluminum wings, with much of the available Ransdell-metal lining its diagonally down-thrust propulsion tubes, it stood glittering in the sunshine five hundred yards from the half-wrecked cylinder of the Ark. At about noon of that day Tony and Eliot James climbed into the hatch of the ship after Tony, under Hendron's tutelage, had been familiarizing himself with the controls.

They were to make the exploration alone; the ship had been built only for pilot and observer. Both carried pistols.

It was proof of Hendron's high practicality that, among the implements cargoed from earth, were pistols and ammunition. Policing might have to be done, if there were no other use for arms; and so there were pistols not only for Tony and Eliot James, but for others who remained in the camp.

As long as the explorers stayed in their ship, they possessed, of course, weapons far more deadly than pistols—the jet-propulsion tubes which had proved their terrible deadliness on the night of the raid on the camp in Michigan.

The camp here owned the same weapons; for all of the tubes from the Ark had not been broken up to supply the little exploration ship. Hendron, keeping his word to prepare defense for the camp, had had the extra tubes prepared and mounted almost like cannon—which he hoped never to use. But he had them.

Hendron watched Eliot James establish himself in the cockpit beside Tony; then he beckoned him out. Hendron would make one last trial flight with Tony at the controls. So James reluctantly stepped out; Hendron stepped in, and the ship rose.

It rose—shot, indeed, crazily forward, spun, jumped still higher and finally rushed southward along the coast till the camp was nearly out of sight. Then Tony brought it back, pushing away Hendron's hands that wanted to help him. He made a landing on the barren acres selected a mile from the camp; and after waiting a few minutes, Tony and then Hendron leaped over the hot earth which surrounded the ship, and went to meet the people hurrying from the camp.

Eve was with the first of them; and Tony saw her pale and shaken. "Oh, Tony!" she exclaimed. "You nearly—"

He looked at her and grinned. "I certainly nearly did whatever you were going to say."

Hendron said: "He did well enough."

"All right now?" asked Eliot James eagerly.

"All right," said Hendron; and yet he held them, reluctant to let them go. "I've had everything put in place—everything you are likely to need. In all our observations from the earth, we made out a great continent here nearly two thousand miles wide and seven thousand in length. We believe we landed about the middle of the east coast of that continent."

He had reviewed this time and time again with Tony and Eliot James, separately and together; yet he had to do it again at the last moment before he let them go:

"Your charts have spotted in them the sites of the cities that we thought we observed. Go to the nearest points first, and then as much farther as—as circumstances dictate.

"If you get into any kind of trouble, radio us. We may not be able to help; yet it is essential to us to learn what may be happening to you. Remember you have a deadly weapon of defense in your tubes.

"Remember, if you come upon survivors of the original People of this planet, their first impulse may be to protect themselves against you. I cannot myself imagine how any of the People of this planet could have survived; yet I must admit the possibility. If they live, they probably have weapons or materials of defense and offense utterly strange to us. . . . Far more probably, you may find other people from earth. If you possibly can, avoid conflict of any sort with them. Nothing could be more tragic than warfare between us here. Yet—if they attack, you must defend yourselves. Fight to kill—to annihilate, if need be! May the God of this world go with you!"

He stepped back and, for a moment, Tony merely stared at him. No moment since they had gained the ground of this strange planet had been as pregnant with the emotions of the Earth. Fight to kill—to annihilate, if need be!

It was the sensible thing; and for it, Tony was himself prepared. Yet it was shocking to hear it announced on this desolate world resuming life again after its long journey through dark and cold.

Eve broke the spell. She stepped forward. "Good-by, Tony."

She gave him her hand; and he longed to draw her to him, and though before them all, to clasp her close and kiss her again. Suddenly, defiantly, he did it. She clung to him. It was another very earthly moment.

His eyes caught Hendron's and found in her father's—in his leader's—no reproach. Hendron, indeed, nodded.

Shirley Cotton spoke to him; he grasped her hand, and she kissed his cheek. She kissed also Eliot James. Others crowded about.

Eliot himself saved the situation.

"It's awfully nice of all you girls to see me to the train," he half declaimed, half chanted, in his comedy twang, a refrain of years ago. "So long, Mary!"

Then Hendron signaled men and women alike away from the ship. Tony and Eliot climbed in; but they waited until their friends had retreated nearly half a mile before they set the jet-propulsion tubes in action.

There was a tremendous roar. The ship bounded forth and took the air. A few moments later it was out of sight; a spark in the sunshine—then nothing.

Eve sat down and wept. Hendron knelt beside her, encircling her with his arms, and remained there staring toward the west in silence.

Travel in the hastily contrived combination of rocket-ship and airplane was not pleasant. Its insulation and cooling systems were inadequate, so that its interior became hot.

Tony flew at a height of five thousand feet. At this height the blast of the Ark would have seared the earth underneath, but the less powerful jets of the airship were dissipated before they reached the ground and caused no damage.

They followed the Other People's road inland. When they had been flying for a few minutes, Eliot James pointed downward; and Tony, looking through a quartz window in the floor, had a fleeting glimpse of a magnificent metal bridge which carried the road across a deep valley. A little later they both concentrated their gaze upon a vast green thicket that reached to the horizon—a cover evidently composed of ferns. They soon left it behind them, and the mountains loomed directly ahead.

At their base was a desert valley some twenty miles in width. From the far side of the valley the mountains rose precipitously to the level at which Tony was flying. They were craglike raw mountains of red and bronze-colored stone, bleak and forbidding. The spore-generated vegetation did not seem to grow upon them, and as far as the fliers could tell, nothing had grown there even before disaster had wrenched Bronson Beta from its parent system.

Tony tilted the nose of the plane upward and gained sufficient altitude to clear their summits by a few thousand feet. He could see, as he looked downward, the direct course of the Other People's road through these mighty mountains—a road that leaped great chasms on spectacular bridges, a road that vanished occasionally in the bowels of some bronze or henna spur or shoulder.

Both men as they flew were particularly absorbed in their immediate uncomfortableness, but still more occupied by the same thought: what would lie upon the other side of this mighty range of mountains? Up to that moment they had seen nothing which gave any indication of the existence of living intelligence. The Other People's road was a monument in a dead world—and for the rest, all that lived and grew was vegetation.

They rose higher to surmount still loftier peaks, penetrating the upper altitudes of the thin greenish atmosphere of Bronson Beta. For almost half an hour they flew straight west across the mountains, and then, far away, they saw a break in the turmoil of upthrust peaks. The mountains turned into hills of lesser altitude which finally gave way to a broad flat plain. It was a plain that seemed endless and through its heart, like an arrow, ran the metal road.

Tony occupied himself with the business of losing altitude for a few moments and abruptly felt his arm gripped by James' hand. Once again he followed the outstretched finger of his companion and he drew in his breath in astonishment.

CHAPTER V

FAR away on the horizon, blazing in the pathway of the sun, was a mighty iridescent bubble. From the windows of the plane it appeared to be small, and yet its distance was so great that the senses immediately made the proper adjustment in scale. It was like half of a soap bubble, five or ten miles in diameter, sitting on the earth. Its curvature was perfect. It was obviously not a natural formation. The road pointed toward it and Tony followed the road. What it was he could not guess.

As they flew, they shouted conjectures to each other, meaningless guesses. Tony said: "It looks like some kind of giant greenhouse." And Eliot James hazarded a notion: "Perhaps the people of Bronson Beta lived under those things when they began to drift out in Space."

The bubble stretched out laterally before them as they flew, and quite suddenly they were able to see in the opalescent glitters of its surface what was within it. It was about six miles in width and more than a mile in height at its center. Inside it, completely contained by it, was a city—a city laid out in a circular geometrical pattern, a city which had at regular intervals gigantic terraced metal skyscrapers—a city with countless layers of roads and streets leading from one group of buildings to the next—a city around the outer edge of which ran a huge trestled railroad.

It was so perfect a city that it might have been a model made by some inspired artist who was handicapped by no structural materials and who allowed his orderly invention no limitations commensurate with logic. Architecturally the plan of the city within that bubble was perfect. The materials of its composition harmonized with each other in a pattern of shimmering beauty.

Tony flew directly to the bubble and circled it at a short distance from its perimeter. The men looked down in stunned silence as the ship wheeled slowly round the great transparent bubble. Both observers realized that the city had been enclosed for some such reason as to keep out cold or to keep its internal temperature unchanged.

Dimly Tony heard James shouting: "It's magnificent!" And in an almost choked voice he replied: "They must have been amazing." In the majestic streets beneath that dome no living thing moved. No lights glowed in those streets where the setting sun allowed shadows to fall; no smoke, no steam, no fire showed anywhere, and although their motor made hearing impossible, they knew instinctively that the colossal, triumphant metropolis below them was as silent as the grave.

Eliot James spoke: "Guess we'd better have a look-see."

Tony nodded. He had already noted that several metal roads led up to the bubble which covered the city, and that the bubble itself was penetrated by gateways. He tipped the nose of the ship toward one of the gates and a few moments later rolled up to a stop on the smooth metal roadway which entered through the locked gate. The two men sat for a moment staring at the spectacle before them, and then, arming themselves, they climbed out of the ship to the ground.

When they put their feet on the ground and looked toward the city, one gate of which was now only a few rods from where they stood, its majesty was a thousand times more apparent than it had been from the air.

When the roar of the motor of their plane had died, when the ringing it left in their ears had abated, when they stood finally at the gate of the city in the sunset, their imaginations were staggered, their very souls were confounded with the awful silence and lonesomeness of the place. They looked at each other without speaking, but their words might very well have been:

"Here are we, two men—two members of a race that appeared on a planet which is no longer—untold millions of miles away from their home—the scouts of their expedition, their eyes and ears for the unknown peril which overshadows them. Here are we, facing a city that we do not understand, facing dangers that are nameless—and all we have is four frail hands, two inadequate minds."

However frail their hands might have been in comparison to the task to which they must be set, however weak and inadequate their minds were in comparison to the Titanic problems confronting them, it could be said that they did not lack in resolution. The haunted expressions left their faces. Tony turned to Eliot James and grinned.

"Here we are, pal!"

"Sure. Here we are. What do you suppose this is—their Chicago? New Orleans? Paris, Bombay, Tokyo?"

"Search me," said Tony, trying to down his awe. Suddenly he shouted, yelled; and Eliot James joined in his half-hysterical cry.

Partly it was a reflex from their wonder, partly a confession that their feelings subdued their intelligence. They knew that this was the city of the dead; it must be. But, standing there at its gate, they could not feel it.

Their eyes searched the curved slope of the great glass dome over the geometrical angles of the metal gate. Nothing stirred; nothing sounded. Not even an echo returned.

They looked down at each other; and on their foreheads glistened the cold sweat of their awed excitement.

"Maybe everybody's asleep," said Eliot James, and knew he made no sense. "Maybe everybody's taking a walk."

"We'll find them inside. We must find some of them inside," said Tony.

"Dead, of course," said Eliot.

"Yes," agreed Tony. "Of course, they're dead." But he had never been further from believing it.

The city stood so in order that it seemed its inhabitants *must* be going about within. It seemed that, down the wide road to this gate, some one must be coming.

Tony suddenly spun about, startling Eliot who jerked around, also.

No one and nothing approached. The wide, smooth, hard road remained utterly deserted.

Again they looked at the gate.

"How do you suppose we can get in here?" Eliot asked.

"There's something that looks very much like a knocker right over there." Tony pointed to a heavy metal ring which was apparently fitted in the end of a lever in a slot at the side of the gate. They walked over to it. The gate itself was perhaps thirty feet in width and forty feet high. The ring was about at the level of Tony's eyes. Above it was an inscription in the unknown language of the unknown inhabitants of Bronson Beta. Tony took hold of the ring and pulled it. Much to his astonishment two gates quietly and swiftly separated. Air blew from the city with a gusty sound, air that seemed age-old, and continued to blow as they hesitantly walked through the gate.

Inside, under the mighty glass dome, they were confronted by a stupendous spectacle. Straight through the heart of the circular city ran a highway along the edge of which were two rails, so that by leaning over they ascertained a moment later that underneath this top street were other thoroughfares at lower levels. On both sides of the street, which was wider than the main avenue of any of the earth's cities, towered colossal buildings. The tallest of them, in the center of the city, must have been more than half a mile in height, and they were made of materials which took brilliant colors, which gave back in the sunlight myriad glittering hues. Exquisitely suspended bridges connected these buildings which rose at intervals of about a quarter of a mile. From their airplane the city had looked like a spangled toy town, but from its own streets it looked like the royal city of Titans. There was no sound in it. Except for the air that whispered through the open gates, not a murmur, not a throb, not a tinkle or a pulsation—just silence. Nothing moved.

A few feet from the gate by which they had entered was a big poster in bright red and white material which was covered by the strange writing of the inhabitants of Bronson Beta. They walked forward almost on tiptoe after looking at the runes beside the gate.

They stared down the avenue ahead of them and aside along the ways that crossed it.

"Where are they, Tony?" Eliot James whispered. He meant not, "Where are living beings?" For he knew the people who built this city must be dead; but he expected, at least, their bodies.

Tony, too, had failed to drive away such expectation. If not living, where were the dead? He could not help expecting the streets to be, somehow, like those of Pompeii after the débris and ash of Vesuvius was cleared away; he could not help expecting to see bones of the Beings, fallen in flight from their city.

But conditions here had been the opposite of those in Pompeii. There it was sudden destruction of fiery blasts, and burial from volcanic ash, that had overwhelmed the people and caught and buried them. Here, instead of sudden, consuming heat, had come slow, creeping cold—cold and darkness, of the coming of which they had been warned for generations. Such a death could have caught no one unprepared on the streets of the city.

"Where are they, Tony?" Eliot James whispered again, as his senses reminded him of the situation. "Where did they go to die? Did they stay in their homes, do you think? Will we find them in these buildings?"

"I don't think so," Tony tried to say steadily, improving his tone above a whisper.

"Where will we find them, then?"

"We won't find them—any of them here, I think," Tony said.

"Why? What did they do?"

"What would such people do?" Tony returned. "Such people as could build this city? What would they do against annihilation which they could see coming for a century?"

"They eliminated themselves, of course: they ceased to reproduce themselves; they ceased to have children."

"That," said Tony, "seems certainly the logical thing to do; and these people appear to have been logical. But there must have been some group who were the last. They could scarcely have buried themselves after they died. Somewhere we will find—somebody."

"It's marvelous," said Eliot James, "how they left this city. They'd covered it over and closed it almost as if they meant to preserve it for us."

"How could they dream of us?" challenged Tony.

"Of course they didn't. Shall we move on?"

"All right," agreed Tony, and ended their paralysis of amazement. "This was a store, I suppose," he said, turning from the stupendous vistas of the streets to the building beside him.

The face of the building was glass, streaked but yet remarkably clear over much of its surface. Behind the glass was an empty area which suggested space for display of goods; but none showed behind the huge high window. The ceiling was perhaps twenty feet high; and above, up and up, stretched glass divided by sills and panels of the multicolored metals.

"Did they live up there, do you suppose?" Eliot James appealed to Tony. Staring up, staring about, but keeping close together, they walked on the silent, utterly empty street. "Did they die up there? If we climbed, would we see—them?"

"The street," said Tony, "might have been swept yesterday."

"They swept it before they left—or died in here," Eliot replied. "They drew their gates and shut out the wind. After they left—or died—what else could disturb it? But, my God, they were neat. No rubbish, no litter."

"And everything locked," Tony said, having halted to try a door. The order of everything, and the utter stillness, was getting his nerves again. "Where've they gone? Where'd they go—leaving it like this?"

Eliot James did not answer; he had run ahead.

"Tables!" he called. "Tables and chairs! This was a restaurant!"

His nose was pressed against the glass, and Tony swiftly joined him. Within stood rows of metal tables and what were, unquestionably, chairs of metal. All bare; and all, of course, empty. It resembled nothing so much as a restaurant; and looking in, no one from earth could doubt that that was what it had been.

The place looked immaculate, as if put in order an hour ago—and then deserted.

"Where are they?" Eliot James appealed again. "Oh, Tony, where did they go?"

"What were they?" Tony countered. "That's what I want to know. Were they huge ants? Were they human-brained reptiles? Were they—"

"They sat in chairs," said Eliot James. "They ate at tables. They ran a car that steered by pedals and a wheel. Their equipment would fit us; their floors and steps are on our scale. Let's break in here."

He tried the door, which was fitted with a handle; but this did not turn or budge, however pulled or pressed. There was no keyhole; no locking device was anywhere apparent; but the door was to be moved no more than those that they had tried before.

Tony looked about. A shudder convulsed him. A thousand windows looked down on this stretch of the silent street; a thousand pairs of eyes once had looked down. It seemed to

Tony that they must—they must do it again. Eyes of what? Huge, sentient, intelligent insects? Reptiles of some strange, semihuman sort?

What lay dead by the tens of thousands in those silent rooms overhead?

Tony was pulling at his pistol. Somehow, it reassured him to hold it in his hand. He reversed it, and beat the butt on the great glass pane behind which stood the strange metal tables and chairs.

The glass did not give way. It twanged, not like glass but like sheet metal—metal utterly transparent.

Tony caught the butt in his palm, and he pulled the trigger. The shot roared and reëchoed. But the metal pane was not pierced. The bullet he had fired lay at Tony's feet. Hysterically, he emptied his pistol.

With the last shot, he jerked about again and stared up at the rows and rows of windows. Did something up there stir?

Eliot James jumped and pointed; and Tony stiffened as he stared.

Something fluttered a hundred yards overhead and farther down the street; something light, like a cloth or a paper. One way, now another, it fluttered as it fell in the still air of that strange sealed city. It reached the street and lay there.

Ten thousand eyes gazed down, it seemed to Tony. It seemed to him that if he could look up twice as quick, he would catch *them* at their windows gazing down at him. But he never could catch them. Always, when he looked up, *they* had anticipated him; *they* were gone; *they* had snatched their heads away.

So he never saw anything but glass and metal—and the single fluttering object which had fallen down.

"We'll go see what that is," he said to Eliot James, wetting his dry lips so he could speak.

But before they gained the object, they forgot it. A window, evidently the vitrine of a gallery of art, confronted them; within the glass was a portrait.

Simultaneously, Tony and Eliot saw it. They stopped as if they were struck; and their breath left them. Breath of relief, and wonder!

They looked at the likeness of a woman!

She was a young woman, strange and fascinating. She was not fair; nor was she dark of skin. Her hair and brows were black—hair arranged with an air that might be individual but which, these discoverers of her felt, was racial.

And of what race?

Not the Caucasian, not the Mongolian; not the Ethiopian, surely; not the Indian. She was of no race upon earth; but she was human.

More than that, she had been sensitive, eager, filled with the joy of living. Her bosom and body were like that of a lovely woman on earth, slight and graceful. Her eyes were wide apart and gray; her cheek-bones were very far apart; and her lips, which were bright red, perhaps because they had been rouged, were pleasant and amiable.

"So," said Eliot James, who first succeeded in speaking, "so they were human! By God, you feel you'd like to know her."

Tony relaxed his hands, which had clenched. "Where did she live, do you suppose, Eliot? Did she live up behind one of these windows?"

"She had a name," said Eliot James. "And surely she had lovers. Where are they?"

"Dead," said Tony. "Dead with her—maybe a million years ago. Let's go on."

"Why go on?" demanded Eliot James. "Why? To pick up a scarf on the street? We've got to get into one of these buildings somewhere. We can break in somehow—with nobody to stop us. We might as well begin here."

So together they attacked the door, which, like those they had pushed and pulled at before, showed no lock, yet was secure.

The door, like the walls of the buildings, was of metal and glass. Indeed, it was difficult to distinguish by texture between the glass and the metal. The panes appeared to be transparent metal. Jeremiah Post had spoken conservatively when, after the examination of the wrecked vehicle discovered near camp, he had said that the People of Bronson Beta had far surpassed any people on earth in metallurgy.

This door evidently was designed to lift; it should rise and slip into the metal wall overhanging it; but no pushing or straining at it, no hammering and pounding, could cause it to budge. And the glass in it—the panel of transparent metal—was not to be broken.

Weary and sweating from their straining at it, Tony and Eliot stepped back.

Their own blows, their own thudding and their gasping for breath, had made the only sound in the silent city.

Repeatedly, while they had worked at the door, each of them had spun about for a glance over his shoulder. The metal seemed so new—some one *must* be about this city standing all in such order.

Tony kept trying his game of looking up quickly, without warning, to catch the heads of the people behind the upper windows who always—so he felt—had jerked back in time.

Now, as the two men from earth stood side by side staring about them, the slightest of sounds reached them; and a door—not the door at which they had pushed and pounded, but a door some twenty steps beyond—began rising.

Tony and Eliot shrank closer together. They pulled out their pistols, which they had reloaded. Up, up steadily, slowly, the metal door was lifted.

"Counterbalanced!" exclaimed Tony to his companion; but his voice was husky. "It was counterbalanced, of course! Our pounding affected some mechanism inside!"

It was the reasonable, rational explanation. For the people of this city could not be alive; it was impossible that they had survived! Yet, here in their city, you could not believe that.

"They're human, anyway," whispered Eliot James.

"Yes," said Tony, his eyes fastened on the aperture under the rising door. "See—anything?"

"Say it, Tony," returned Eliot James. "Or I will."

"All right," said Tony hoarsely. "See—*any one?*"

"There's nobody there," argued Eliot, with himself as much as with his comrade. "They all died—they all died a million years ago."

"Yes," agreed Tony. The door was ceasing to rise; it had reached its limit and stopped, leaving the way into the great metal building open. "They all died a million years ago. But where did they go to die?"

"Who cares?" Eliot continued his argument. "Can a ghost live a million years? I don't believe they can. Come on in, Tony. They can't even haunt us."

"A minute," said Tony.

"Why?"

"I want to look around once more." He was doing it. "All right now!" They approached the open doorway together; and together, neither in advance or in the rear of the other, they entered it, pistols in hands. That was wholly irrational; and both knew it; but neither could help himself.

So, side by side, revolvers ready, they entered the door of the Million Years Dead.

The walls of the hall in which they found themselves were vemilion. It did not appear to be paint. Like the colors of the exteriors, the hue was a quality of the metal. Vermilion surrounded Tony and Eliot—vermilion and gray, in vigorous, pronounced patterns.

There was no furniture in the hall; no covering upon the floor. Perhaps there never had been one; the floor was smooth and even and of agreeable texture. It was not wood nor metal, but of some composition. It might have been meant to be a dance-floor or for a meeting-hall. Nothing declared its use. An open doorway invited to an apartment beyond; and side by side, but with their pistols less at alert, Eliot and Tony stepped into this.

It was blue—ultramarine, they would have called it on earth, with slashes of silver. Great long-beaked, long-legged birds, suggestive of cranes, flew across a marsh—a decoration done by some superlative artist.

61

But this room also was empty.

Tony and Eliot James went on.

"How do you feel?" demanded Tony, after they had entered the fifth great room in gay colors, with marvelous decoration, but empty.

"Feel?" repeated Eliot. "It feels to me that we're in a building that never was used, into which they never moved."

"Perhaps," said Tony, "that goes for the whole city."

"Too soon to say, much too soon to say. How do you go up, d'you suppose?"

"Elevators behind one of these doors, probably. No sign of stairs."

"How do you open the doors?"

"Pound on one of the others, probably," suggested Tony, "judging from recent experience."

"How about the one we opened?" said Eliot. "Is it still up, d'you suppose?"

"What'd lower it?"

"What lifted it?" returned Eliot. "I'll go back and look. Want to go with me?"

"No: I'll stay here and try some of these."

But he had accomplished nothing with any of them when Eliot came back.

"That closed, Tony," he reported soberly.

Tony started. "You didn't close it?"

"No."

"All right!" Tony almost yelled. "Go ahead. Say it!"

"Say what?"

"What you're thinking. Remote control of some sort! Somebody saw us, opened the door, let us walk in, closed it again."

"Somebody!" said Eliot. "Let's be sensible, Tony."

"All right," said Tony, jittering. "You be! . . . Damn it, look at that door. Look at it! That's opening now!"

For a door at the farther edge of this room now slowly was rising.

"Were you working at it?" Eliot whispered.

"Yes."

"Then, that's it. You started another counterbalance working."

"Sure," said Tony. "Sure."

They stepped to the opening. Utter darkness dropped below them. There was a shaft, there—a shaft which, under other circumstances, might have showed machinery. Now it was empty.

Tony and Eliot James knelt side by side at its edge. They shouted, and no voice came back to them.

Tony took a cartridge and dropped it. For so long did it fall silently that they were sure, as they listened, that it must have struck something which gave no sound; then they heard it strike. Tony dropped another, and they timed it. One more they timed, and they stepped back from the shaft carefully.

"Half a mile below!" said Eliot. "They went down almost as far as up; perhaps farther. Why?"

They stepped back from the shaft's threshold carefully.

"There's some control to these damn doors," said Tony, "that probably made it utterly painless to operate them when everything was working. You maybe merely had to stand before them, and some electric gadget would work that's jammed now because the power isn't on. These doors can't all be to shafts."

About fifteen minutes later, they had opened another that exposed a circular passage, leading both upward and downward.

"Ah!" said Eliot. "This is the stuff. No machinery. They probably had it for emergencies."

Tony, awakening, stretched, rubbed his eyes and gazed up at the ceiling. His eyes followed mechanically, forgetfully, the graceful, tenuous lines of decoration which traced down over the walls of the pleasant, beautiful chamber.

He still did not fully recollect where he was, but he realized that he was lying on a couch of soft, agreeable material. Then he saw Eliot James, in trousers and shirt but without his coat, seated at a table, writing. And Tony remembered.

Eliot and he were in the Sealed City—the amazing, stupendous metropolis of the Other People, the People a Million Years Dead.

The light diffused through this chamber, so pleasantly and evenly—it seemed to be spread and intensified somehow by its refraction through the peculiar metal-glass of one wall—was the light of the dawn of the third long Bronson Beta day since Eliot James and Tony Drake, refugees from earth, had discovered and entered the Sealed City.

The amazements of their two days of exploration passed through Tony's mind like reviewing a dream; but they remained reality; for instead of becoming dimmer and dimmer as he sought to recall them, they became only sharper and clearer. Moreover, here before him in a heap upon one of the tables of the Other People, and piled also on the floor, were the proofs of the actuality of what Eliot and he had done. Here were the objects—some of them understandable, more of them utterly incomprehensible as to their purpose or utility—which they had collected to carry with them back to Cole Hendron and the camp.

Eliot was writing so intently and absorbedly that he did not know that Tony was awake. They were in utter stillness; not a sound nor a stir in the Sealed City; and Tony lay quiet watching his companion attempting to deal through words with the wonders they had encountered.

What could a man say that would be adequate?

Tony fingered the stuff of the couch upon which he lay—material not wool, not cotton, not silk. It was soft, pliant fiber, unidentifiable. How old? A million years old, perhaps, in rigidly reckoned time; but not five years old, probably, in the practical period of its use.

It might have been new a million years ago, just before Bronson Beta was torn from its sun; thereafter the time that passed merely preserved it. It was in the utter cold and dark of space. Not even air brushed it. The air was frozen solid. Then this planet found our sun; and time which aged materials, was resumed.

So it was with all the stuff which Eliot and he had collected; those objects might be a million years old, and yet new!

Eliot halted his writing and arose; and glancing at Tony, saw he was awake.

"Hello."

"Hello. How long you been up?"

"Quite a while."

"You would be," complained Tony admiringly. It had been late in the long night, and both had been utterly exhausted, when they lay down to sleep. "It's the third day, isn't it?"

"That's right."

"We ought to go back now."

"Yes," agreed Eliot, "I suppose so. But how can we?"

Tony was sitting up. "How can we leave?" he agreed. "But also, how can we stay—without letting Cole Hendron and the rest of them know?"

"We can come back, of course," Eliot James reluctantly assented.

"Or we may find another city or something else."

"By 'something else,' do you mean the place where 'they' all went, Tony? God, Tony, doesn't it get you? Where did they go? Not one of them—nor the bones of one of them! And all this left in order."

He stood at the table and sifted in his fingers the kernels of a strange grain. Not wheat, not corn, not rice nor barley nor rye; but a starchy kernel. They both had tasted it.

"There's millions of bushels of this, Tony. Should we say 'bushels' or, like the Bible, 'measures'? Well, we know there's millions of measures of this that we've already found. If it's food—and what else could it be?—we've solved our problem of provender indefinitely. And it's foolish to have our people improvising shelter and equipment when all we have to do is to move into—this. Here's equipment we never dreamed of!"

"Yes," said Tony. "Yes." But he remembered that contest

that already had divided the camp. Did the emigrants from the earth dare to move into the city when found? Also, could the people from the earth sustain themselves on this grain or other supplies left by the vanished people? Though the kernels might have been preserved through the epoch of utter cold, had the vitamins—essential to life—remained?

But that was a matter for the experts of the camp to test and to decide. Tony could not doubt his duty to report the tremendous discovery.

"We'll leave to-day, Tony," Eliot pleaded, "but not until later. Let's look about once more."

And Tony agreed; for he too could not bear yet to abandon the amazements of the Sealed City.

It was later than they had planned, when at last they had loaded their ship with the objects—comprehensible and incomprehensible—which they had chosen to carry back to Hendron and his comrades. The sun—the old sun of the shattered world, the new sun of Bronson Beta—was low when Tony drew down once more the great metal ring which closed again the gate of the Sealed City.

"Let's not fly back to the camp by the path we came," said Eliot James.

"No," agreed Tony. "Let's loop to the south before we cut back to the seacoast."

They were in the air again, supported on the rushing golden stream of fire that emerged from their rocket-tubes. They flew through the darkness, occasionally casting upon the ground underneath the bright ray of their searchlight, and still more often thrusting it ahead of them into the gloom. There were no lights anywhere beneath them to indicate that people lived or moved or had their being there.

Long after midnight they flew across what they judged to be either a huge lake or a great inland arm of the sea.

Toward morning they were planning to alight and rest before continuing their adventures, when suddenly they were transfixed. Not in the east, where the first gray bars of the rising sun might be expected to appear, but ahead of them, to the south, a single finger of light pointed upward to the sky—the only light except their own, and except the weird inhuman illumination of the great domed city, which they had seen on the surface of the planet.

CHAPTER VI

SALVATION

THEY were approaching the vertical beam of light at a high speed, but no sooner had its unnatural appearance made a mark in Tony's consciousness than his hands leaped for the controls, and the plane slowed as much as was possible—he'd cut down its elevation.

He turned to James: "What do you think it is?"

"It looks like a searchlight pointed straight up in the air."

"There seems to be a ridge between us and where it comes from."

"Right," James shouted back to him. Tony made a gesture which outlined the process of landing the plane, and James nodded.

When they had come upon the great bubble that covered the city, it had been daylight, and there had been no sign of life about it; but light implied an intelligent agency, and besides, it was night, and their sense of caution was stirred by the very primordial influence of darkness.

Now the plane was skimming low over the empty desert, and in the light of their abruptly switched-on beacon, they could make out racing beneath them a flat aridity.

There was no choice of spots on which to land. The thunder of the tubes had been cut off as Tony turned a switch, and his voice sounded very loud when he said: "How about it?"

"Let 'er go!" James answered, and an instant later they were racing over the ground, stirring up a cloud of dust that had been undisturbed for millennia.

They stopped. They stepped out.

The night around them was warm and clear. Its distant darknesses were weaving with the perpetual aurora of Bronson Beta. Far ahead of the waste in which the plane lay, the single finger of light pointed unwavering toward the stars.

"Shall we wait for day?" Tony asked.

Eliot James looked at the illuminated dial of his wristwatch. "It'll be several hours in coming yet," he said after a pause. He grinned. "I've learned how to tell time by this watch in a mathematical process as complicated as the theory of relativity."

Tony did not smile at James' whimsy. He was staring at the light. "I should say, from the way it spreads, it must come together in some sort of a lens or reflector a couple of hundred feet below the other side of the ridge. If there's anybody around the base of it, I don't think they saw or heard us coming. If they saw anything, it could easily be mistaken for a meteor." He was silent.

James spoke his thoughts in the quiet of the desert night. "It may be four miles away—it may be six. The walking's pretty good; but the point is—shall we leave our ship?"

"I wonder—have we got time to get there and back before it's light?"

"Meaning the top of the ridge?"

"Exactly."

James squinted at the barren black edge of land traced upon the brief width of the light beam. "Plenty."

Tony made no further comment, but started walking through the night. They walked steadily and rapidly. The ground was sandy, and there were no large stones in it, although once or twice their ankles were nearly turned by large pebbles. They said no more. It might have been interesting to their biographers to note also that neither of them had mentioned their safe landing in the hazards of darkness and unknown terrain. That was like each of them. When you had to take a chance, you took it. When you made it, there was nothing more to be said.

They walked for half an hour before the flat plain, the arid waste, began to rise. In the dark they noticed the inclination more by the increase of their breathing than by the change in the strain on their muscles. Presently, however, the upward pitch became steep, and they realized that they were traversing a series of bare undulant ledges. They went more cautiously then, in their imaginings and their fears, not daring to use flashlights, but feeling for each step—sometimes even moving upward with the aid of their hands.

They knew for several minutes precisely when they would reach the top, and they slowed their pace to a crawl.

A breeze fanned their faces. They stepped up over the last rocky surface, and unconsciously moving on tiptoe, crossed it so they could look into the valley beyond.

Because neither of them was conventionally religious, because both of them were thunderstruck by what they saw, they cursed, fluently and sibilantly, in the night on the ridge.

At their feet, not more than a mile away—so close that the purring of machinery was faintly audible—a single searchlight turned its unwinking eye upon the heavens. In the diffused light around the great lamp they were able to see many things. A huge cylinder, a cylinder like their own Ark but larger, lay toppled upon its side, crippled and riven. Near the cylinder was an orderly group of shelters. Standing beside the searchlight, apparently talking to each other, were doll-like figures of human beings.

"It's our Other People!" Tony said, and his voice choked.

Eliot James gripped his arm. "Maybe not."

"But it must be!"

"It's about the same size, but how can you be sure? Those people who flew over a few nights ago and didn't like us, may have come up in it. All the ships that were built to attempt this flight have looked more or less alike."

"Come on," Tony said.

"Quietly, then."

The minutes were like hours. Both men found themselves slipping down the opposite side of the ridge, holding their breath lest their panting might be overheard in the distance, and trembling whenever a fragment of rock fell. Their thoughts were identical. If the space ship which lay wrecked beyond the searchlight was the carrier of enemies, their presence must never be known. But if it was the ship which had embarked from Michigan with themselves—if that beacon stabbing the night was a signal of distress—and what else could it be?—then—

Then they dared not think any further. They were on level ground now, sluicing through the blackness like Indians, alert, ready to run, ready to throw themselves on the ground. They were half a mile from the two figures at the light. Both of them were men; both of them had their backs turned.

At that distance Tony and Eliot could see how horribly the space ship had been mangled when it descended. There was a great scar on the earth where it must have struck first and tipped over. Its forward end had plowed into the ground, cutting a prodigious furrow and piling at its nose a small mountain of earth and stone. The metal of which it had been made was cracked back in accordion-like pleats. Whether they were friends or enemies, their arrival on Bronson Beta had been disastrous.

That quarter-mile was cut to three hundred yards. They could see each other's faces shining palely in the radiance of the searchlight. They crept forward; the three hundred yards became two.

Suddenly, to the astonishment of Eliot James, Tony emitted a wild bellow which woke echoes from every corner of the night, rose to his feet and rushed across the earth toward the light. Eliot James followed him—and presently understood.

Tony's first shout had been inarticulate, but as he ran now, he called: "Ransdell! *Ransdell!* Oh, my God! It's me—Tony! Tony Drake! We've found you at last!"

And Eliot James, running like a deer, saw one of the men at the light turn around, lift his hand, try to say something, fall forward in a faint.

Ten minutes later, only ten minutes, and yet to three hundred and eighteen human souls that ten minutes had marked the beginning of salvation. They were all out now on the bare earth of Bronson Beta. Everyone was awake—all the lights were shining. The cheers still rose sporadically. Ransdell had come to, and was still rocking in the arms of Tony when he did not unclasp him long enough to embrace Eliot James. The crowd of people, delirious with joy, was trying to touch them and talk to them. All the crowd, that is, except those who had not yet recovered from the terrible smash-up of the landing— and those who would never recover.

Ransdell had fainted for the first time in his life out of pure joy, pure ecstasy, and out of cosmic fatigue. He had scrambled to his feet in time to meet Tony's rush toward him. They had not exchanged many coherent words as yet— just, "Glad to see you," "Great!" "Are you all right?" Things like that. Ransdell had managed to say, "Hendron?" Tony had been able to answer, jubilantly: "Made it all right. Everybody well and safe."

Then Ransdell succeeded in reducing his command to a momentary quiet. He said: "Tony has told me that the Ark made the trip and landed safely."

Again the cheering rose and echoed in the night. Again people rushed forward by the score to shake Tony's hand. Jack Little was there, bandaged and grinning. Peter Vanderbilt, apparently calm but blowing his nose in a suspicious manner. Jack Taylor was there too, and Smith and Greve and a hundred other people whose faces had become the faces of friends for Tony and Eliot James in the past two years. Somebody brought from the mêlée of dunnage that had spilled out of the split-open space ship two tubs. Upon them Tony and Ransdell stood.

By waving their arms and smiling in the flood of light which had been turned on over the encampment, they made it plain the whole night could not be spent in cheering and crying. They made it plain by shouting through their dialogue that they had better trade information.

CHAPTER VII

REUNION

Tony felt it utterly useless to attempt to speak to the throng; the people were too hysterical. More than three hundred of them were able-bodied, though many of these still bore bandages that testified to the injuries from which they were recovering. They had thought themselves recuperated from shock; but this intense excitement betrayed them.

Ransdell, restored from his faintness, proved the superior quality of his nerves by attaining composure first. He went to Tony and drew him away from the excited throng which continued to clamor about them.

"Eliot!" shouted Tony to his companion in this flight of exploration. "You try to tell them—as soon as they give you a chance."

"O. K.!" Eliot yelled, and he stepped up on the tub which Tony had quitted. He shouted and made gestures and caught the crowd's attention. Only a few trailed after Tony and their own leader, Ransdell.

Tony could not yet quiet his own inner tumult. He felt an arm about his shoulder, and found Jack Taylor beside him; and he thought how he had traveled on a train along the Hudson, back on the earth, on his way to Cornell University to meet this young man and ask him to become a member of Hendron's party.

On the other side of him walked Peter Vanderbilt; and Tony thought of Fifth Avenue, and its clubs and mansions, so staid, so secure! Or they had felt themselves so. Now where were they?

Reveries of some similar sort were running through Vanderbilt's head. His eyes met Tony's, and he smiled.

"Tony, I woke up laughing, a night or so ago," Peter Vanderbilt said.

"Laughing at what?" Tony inquired. They had passed from the noise of the crowd.

"At my dream. I dreamed, you see, Tony, that I was back on earth. Not only that, but I was on earth before the time these delectable Bronson Bodies were reported in the night skies. I was attending the ceremonies of installation of somebody's statue—for the life of me, I can't say whose—in the Hall of the Immortals! After I woke up, a meteor crossed this sky. I couldn't help wondering if it mightn't have been part of that statue! . . . Well, why not sit here? You can tell us a little more of what happened to you."

So the four friends sat down on the ground close together, seeing each other in the distant radiance of the lights in the camp; and interrupting each other as they told, they traded their experiences in the flight from earth.

The account that Tony heard was far more tragic, of course, than that which he had to tell. The technicians under command of David Ransdell had made their calculations accurately, and the journey through space had been little more eventful than that of the ship in which Tony and his comrades had traveled. However, the second Ark had been built more hastily, and its greater size increased its difficulties; as it approached Bronson Beta, it become evident to its navigators that the lining of its propulsion-tubes was being rapidly fused. It approached the planet safely, however; and like its sister ship, found itself over the surface of a sea. Fortunately, the coast was not far away, or the great vessel would have dropped into the water and all aboard perished.

The coast which the second Ark approached—the coast upon which it now lay—was fog-bound. "In spite of the fog," Ransdell said to Tony, "we had to land at once. Of course, the jets cleared away the fog below us, but only replaced it with a brilliant cloud of gases. We were flying 'blind,' and had to land by instrument. I ordered everybody to be strapped to the floor, and gave the command to set down the ship under the added pressure of the blast required for the delicate business of landing. Three of our tubes fused almost simultaneously. The ship careened and almost tipped over. In trying to right it, we rose perhaps fifty feet above this desert." He swept his hand toward the surrounding darkness. "And then we crashed."

Tony nodded. Ransdell went on: "Every bit of apparatus that was in the least fragile was, of course, demolished. On top of the crash, one of the jet-tubes burst, and its blast penetrated the storeroom. That might have been much worse; it might have annihilated half our party. Perhaps it did so, indirectly—it fused or destroyed more than half our stores and equipment. Since landing, we have not found it possible to construct even a radio. That is why you have heard no signals from us. We had more than we could do, for the first weeks, taking care of our injured and burying the dead—and salvaging and making usable what supplies were spared, in part. The searchlight you saw to-night was the best effort we accomplished."

Suddenly Ransdell's voice failed him. He cleared his throat and continued very quietly: "To tell the truth, Tony, we wondered whether we should try to communicate with Hendron's party—assuming you had come through safe. We are so without supplies or resources, that we could only be a burden to you. We knew that at best you could barely manage for yourselves. It was that, as much as anything else, which stopped us from making efforts to find you. We decided not to drag you down and perhaps cause you, as well as ourselves, to perish."

"You would," said Tony. "You would decide that—Vanderbilt and Taylor and you, Dave. But thank God, that point's past. I haven't told you half the news. Eliot James and I didn't come from our camp to you. We came from a city!"

"City?"

"Of the Other People, Dave!"

"Other People? . . . What Other People? . . . Where?"

"I mean a city of the old inhabitants of this planet!" Tony cried. "For it was inhabited, as we thought. And by what people! Eliot and I spent three days in one of their cities!"

"But not—with Them?"

"No," agreed Tony. "Not with them! They're gone! They're dead, I suppose—for a million years. But wait till you hear what they left behind them! And what the cold and the dark of space saved for us! Food, for one thing. Dave! Peter! Jack!" In their excitement, they were all standing up again, and Tony was beating each of them in turn upon the back. "Food—grain and other things saved for us by Space's wonderful refrigerator of absolute cold. Cheer up! Food—something to fill you—no longer's one of our troubles. Their food—if it doesn't kill us all. And it hasn't killed Eliot or me yet. . . . Listen! What's that?"

For there was shouting in the camp.

"I suspect," said Peter Vanderbilt, "that James has got to that point too. He's been telling them of the food you found. Perhaps now we better rejoin our comrades and—the ladies."

Eliot James *had* reached that point; and it started a new hysteria; for they believed him, and had faith in the food-supplies he reported. The immediate effect was instinctive and practical; they ordered their own sparse supplies distributed more satisfyingly than on any occasion since the terrible landing on this earth.

It was indeed salvation which Tony Drake and Eliot James had brought out of the night—salvation and the end of some of the hardships heroically borne. Tony did not realize then the extent of those hardships; but when half an hour later coffee was served for all of them in the improvised dining-hall, he was made to realize it by a simple statement of Ransdell's. "This is the first ration of coffee we have served, except to those in most desperate condition, since the day after we landed."

It was a hilarious midnight picnic in the impromptu dining-hall, where the men and women dared to eat as much as they wanted for the first time since their epochal journey—where they sang hymns, shouted snatches of gay songs from lost days on the vanished earth, wept and laughed again, over-hilariously. Tony found himself compelled to repeat again and again details of the city which Eliot James and he had found; again and again he had to iterate how Hendron and Eve and all their people had fared; and now he told how the three had died from the strange disease.

In return he gained other items from this and that of his companions, who enabled him gradually to piece together a more coherent account of the experience of the second band of Argonauts. Each detail was made vivid by the various narrators. The horrible day of the landing as the fog cleared away, revealing moment by moment the magnitude of the disaster which had overtaken them; the groans of the wounded; the crushed and mangled bodies of the dead; the desperate efforts of the doctors and surgeons among them to save those who were not beyond hope. Hastily constructed operating-tables under a sun which had once shone on the earth, and which now cast its radiance into the greenish-blue skies of Bronson Beta. The gradual emergence of order. The tallying of the lists of stores and tools. The shocking discovery that every one of the seeds so carefully stored on the ship had been burned by the unleashed atomic blast. The necessary destruction of the animals ·which had survived the crash, and the utilization of them for food. Rationing, then, and hunger. Long and weary expeditions on foot in search of sustenance. Efforts to find vegetation on Bronson Beta for food—efforts which in more than one case had led to illness, and twice had brought about death. The erection of the searchlight. The nights and days of waiting and hoping, complicated by fear to be found, because of the burden their discovery might constitute to those who discovered them.

"For a while," said Jack Taylor, "we believed that nobody else—no other ship from earth—got over. We felt that, desperate as our situation was, yet we were the luckiest."

"But two weeks ago—two weeks of these peculiarly prolonged days, not to mention the similarly protracted nights," put in Peter Vanderbilt, "two weeks ago, we began to believe differently."

"Why?" asked Tony.

"Airplane," replied Vanderbilt succinctly.

"Where?"

"Where would it be?"

"I mean," said Tony, "it didn't land?"

"Not it. Nor too plainly appear."

"Neither did ours," said Tony.

"You mean you sent it? It was your machine?" Ransdell swiftly demanded.

"Not two weeks ago," Tony denied. "We had nothing in

the air then. I mean, an airplane visited us too; and it didn't too plainly appear."

"But you saw it?"

"We got a glimpse of it— a glint of light on a wing through the clouds," explained Tony. "Did you see more here?"

"Yes," said Ransdell. "We got a shape—a silhouette. Queer type; we couldn't identify it. Long, back-pointing wings. Like larks' wings, somebody said. It looked like a giant lark in the sky."

Tony looked up from Ransdell to Eliot James, who had joined the circle.

Eliot softly whistled.

"Well," said Tony to Eliot.

"Well yourself!" Eliot James retorted. "You say it."

"Say what?" demanded Ransdell impatiently. "You know whose plane it was? What party brought that type over?"

"No party," said Tony bluntly.

"What do you mean?"

"What I say. No party from earth brought that ship with them. It wasn't brought over."

He had gone a little pale, as he spoke; and he wiped his forehead and then his hands with his handkerchief.

"What—the—hell!" whispered Jack Taylor with awed deliberation.

"I said," iterated Tony solemnly, "it wasn't brought over. On the edge of the city of the Other People, of which we've been telling you—under the great glass dome, but near an edge where they could be run out, easily—was a sort of hangar of those things. We saw a—a hundred of them. Like larks, they'd look in the sky—all-metal larks of marvelous design. They had engines. Did you tell them of the engine in that car we found wrecked before we went off to find the city?" He appealed to Eliot James.

Eliot nodded; and several voices urged Tony on with: "Yes; he told us. . . . We know."

"Well," said Tony, "they had engines of that same small, powerful type. We recognized it; but we couldn't get one going. We tried to."

He stopped, wet his lips.

"Go on! For God's sake, go on!"

"All right," said Tony. "But where do I go from there? What am I to tell you? I can tell you this; for I know it. I saw it. I saw the machines; and I felt them with my hands; and as I told you, I tried to make the engine work, but Eliot and I couldn't."

"The Other People—the People a Million Years Dead— the inhabitants of Bronson Beta—had aircraft that would look, in the air, like nothing we had on earth but a lark. They had small, economical and evidently exceedingly powerful engines that propelled them by a motive-power we haven't learned to employ."

"I believe it was one of those machines which flew over you—and over us."

"Flew?" repeated Peter Vanderbilt calmly. "Of itself? No pilot?"

Tony shook his head.

"A pilot perhaps," pronounced Vanderbilt softly, *"a million years dead?"*

Tony nodded; the inclination of his head in this affirmative made them jump.

"You don't believe it!" Peter Vanderbilt rebuked him.

"You," said Tony, "haven't been in their city. We were there three days, and never ceased to expect them to walk out any door!"

"After a million years dead?"

"How do we know how it might have been?"

"We know," Jack Taylor reminded him, "how long it must have been at the very shortest. Less than a million years, to be sure; but—plenty long in the dark and absolute zero. They never could have survived it."

Tony looked at him. "Why?"

"Because they couldn't, Tony."

"You mean, because we couldn't have. But we're not— They."

Peter Vanderbilt flicked a speck from his sleeve. "We have no need to be metaphysical," he suggested. "The machine could have come from one source, the pilot from another. The machine could have survived the million years cold; we know that some did. You saw them. But the pilot need have survived no more than a passage from earth—which some three hundred of us here have survived, and a hundred in your camp also."

"Of course," accepted Eliot James practically. "Another party could have got across—several parties; the Germans, the Russians, the Japanese or some others. Two weeks or more ago they may have found another Sealed City with the Other People's aircraft."

"And they," said Tony, "may have got one of the engines going."

"Exactly!"

"All right," said Tony, "that's that. Then let's all sit down again. Why did the pilot, whoever he is, look us over and leave without message or signal? Why—"

They sat down, but drew closer, talking together: "If some of the Other People survived, what would be their attitude to us, would you say? . . . Would they know who we were, and where we came from?"

Tony led a dozen men to the ship in which Eliot and he

had flown; and they bore to the camp the amazing articles from the Sealed City.

Nobody tired. There was no end to their speculations and questions. Tony, seated on the ground and leaning on his hand beside him, felt a queer, soft constriction of his forefinger. He drew his hand up, and the constriction clamped tighter, and he felt a little weight. Some small, living thing had clasped him.

It let go and leaped onto his shoulder.

"Hello!" cried Tony, as two tiny soft hands and two tiny-toed feet clung to him. "Hello! Hello!" It was a monkey.

"Her name's Clara," said Ransdell.

"Yours?" asked Tony. "You brought her over?"

"Nobody brought her over," Ransdell replied. "You know the regulations before leaving earth. I tried to enforce them; but Clara was too good for us. She stowed away."

"Stowed away?"

"We discovered her after things got calm in space," Ransdell said, smiling. "When we were well away from the earth and had good equilibrium. Everybody denied they had anything to do with her being on board. In fact, nobody seemed able to account for her; nobody would even admit having seen her before; but there she was. And she survived the passage; and even our landing. Of course we kept her afterward."

"Of course," said Tony. "Good work, Clara." He extended his finger, which Clara clasped solemnly, and "shook hands" by keeping her clasp as he waved his finger.

"Since we're checking up," added Ransdell, "you might as well know that we brought over one more passenger not on the last lists we made back there in Michigan. —Marian!" he called to the group about them. "You here?"

"Where would I be?" A girl of about twenty-three stood up and walked toward him. Her eyes were gray; her chin was firm; her hair was darkly red. Tony noticed that she carried herself with a boldness different from the others.

"Her name," Ransdell murmured as she approached, "is Marian Jackson. Lived in St. Louis. An acrobatic dancer. Kept her head during the chaos before the destruction. Read about our plans. Crawled into camp the night before we took off. Lived in the woods for three weeks before that—nobody knows what on."

The girl reached the table and took Tony's hand. "I've heard about you," she said. "Often. You don't look anything like I supposed you would."

"I'm glad to meet you," Tony replied.

Unabashed, she studied him. "You look shot," she said finally.

Tony grinned. "I am a little tired."

"You're all in. But then, everybody's tired around here always."

"You better go back to your place," Ransdell said.

"Sure," the girl answered. She smiled buoyantly and returned.

Ransdell looked at her thoughtfully, sipped his coffee, and shook his head. Then he continued privately to Tony: "She's really a moron, I suppose. I doubt if Hendron will approve of having a moron in our company; but her empty-headedness, her astonishment at everything, even her ignorance, which is pretty naïve, have delighted everybody. And she did a big thing for us."

Tony looked thoughtfully at the red-headed girl as she sat down and resumed conversation with those beside her.

"What did she do?" he asked, returning his attention to Ransdell.

"The second night we were here, Eberville went mad. He decided early in the evening that it was against the will of God for us to be here, and that we should all be destroyed. But he quieted down, and he was left alone. Later he got up, got into the ship, started the only generator that would work, and turned on one of the lateral tubes. In the morning you can see a big black patch about four hundred yards to the left of where we were camped. He'd have wiped us out in ten seconds, but Marian jumped on him. She's strong. So was Eberville, insanely strong. But she has teeth and nails. That is why we all escaped annihilation a second time."

Tony shook his head slowly and thoughtfully, without speaking.

The little monkey, Clara, returned to him and squatted before him, peering up at him with its queerly humanlike, puzzled gaze.

She had no business here, Tony recollected. Monkeys were not on the list of necessary or useful creatures to be taken on the terrible transfer from earth to this planet; and a single representative of the tiny monkey clan was particularly impractical and useless. But Tony was glad that Clara was here.

Among the crowd he saw Marian Jackson's red head moving; and he thought: "She had not been selected, either; but all these girls here of higher intelligence, and all the men too, would have been wiped out, but for her."

He did not blame Hendron for the narrowness of the selections more than he blamed himself. He thought: "We must all have become a bit mad in those last days on earth—mad or at least fanatic. We could hope to save so few and became too intent on certain types."

Suddenly Tony got up. Hendron, he remembered, knew none of their discoveries and events. He could delay no longer his return to Hendron.

But when he suggested to Eliot James that they return, others would not allow it.

"Not both of you! . . . You haven't both got to go!"

There was altogether too much yet to tell, and to hear.

"Let Eliot stay here, Tony," Dave Ransdell said. "I'll go to Hendron with you. I ought to report to him; and I want so much to see him."

"Just right," Tony accepted this plan.

"That's the thing to do."

They were in the air, Tony Drake and Dave Ransdell together. In the plane with them, they freighted a fair half of the objects intelligible and unintelligible, which Tony and Eliot had brought from the Sealed City. With them was also Eliot James' record, which he had read to the people in Ransdell's camp.

It was dawn; the slow sunrise of Bronson Beta was spreading its first faint shafts across the sky; and the ground below was beginning to be etched in its pattern of plain and hill and river and estuary from the sea.

The veinlike tracery of roads appeared—the lines left by the Vanished People. Tony gazed far ahead and to each side, searching for another or others of such marvelous, gigantic bubbles which would become, upon approach, other cities. But nothing of the sort came in sight. They spied smears and blotches below which became, when they turned the glass upon them, rows of ruins. They did not stop for these. Already they had much to report; already they were long overdue.

They sighted, far ahead, columns of smoke lifted lazily into the sky. Ransdell pointed and Tony, leaning to his ear, shouted: "Our camp-fires! Our camp!"

He could make out now, in the early morning light, that these were indeed camp-fires ending their duty of lessening the chill of the long night, perhaps, starting their services of cooking. The camp seemed unchanged; it was safe.

Tony compared its crudeness and rudeness with the marvelously proportioned perfections of the Sealed City; and a pang of nostalgia for this encampment suddenly assailed him. Here were his own; here was home.

He glanced aside and surprised his comrade Dave Ransdell, as he stared down. What thousand shattering fragments of thoughts must fill Ransdell's mind! One—and Tony plainly could see it—overwhelmed all the rest. Here, below, was Eve Hendron.

For it was a sudden softness and yearning that was in the eyes of the broad-shouldered, Herculean man at Tony's side. What would be in Eve's eyes when she saw him?

Tony's nostaglia of the moment before was replaced by a jerk of jealousy. Eve always had admired Dave and liked him—and more. More, yes, more than liked him, during those last desperate days on earth. Now he was here; and he had done well.

Yes; any one would say—Hendron himself would declare —that Dave Ransdell had done well indeed to have brought across space the ship intrusted to him with loss of less than half the party. Ransdell would be greeted ecstatically as a hero.

Tony caught his lip between his teeth and tried to establish better control of his inward tumult. If Eve preferred Dave to himself, let her!

He busied himself grimly with his throttles, putting down the ship on the bare soil more than a mile from camp.

They had been seen in the air and recognized; and the camp was outpouring toward them. The tractor was leading, piled with passengers.

Tony and Dave started to run toward them; then they halted. The people from the camp began to see that one figure was not that of Eliot James.

"Who is it? Who's with you?" came the cry from the tractor which was ahead of the runners.

"Ransdell! Dave Ransdell!" Tony yelled; and Dave stopped and lifted high his arms.

"Ransdell! *Ransdell?*" came back.

"Yes! They got over! *The second ship got over!*"

Then the welcome began.

"Tony," said Ransdell later, when for an instant they had a few words together, "how Hendron's changed!"

"Yes," said Tony, "of course he has." But he realized that to Ransdell, who had not seen their leader since the last day on earth, the alteration in Hendron's appearance and manner was more tragic. Indeed, it seemed to Tony that in the few days he had been gone, Hendron had become whiter and weaker.

Never had Tony heard Hendron's voice shake as now it did; and his hand, which clung to the list which Ransdell had given him, quivered as if with palsy.

It was the list of the survivors and of the dead from the second Ark, with which Hendron had insisted that he be supplied.

He had read it several times; but again and again, like a very old man, he went over it.

"It was the tubes, you say, David?" he kept reviewing the disaster at landing, with Ransdell. "Three of the tubes fused! That was the fault of the design—my fault," he blamed himself morbidly.

"Father!" whispered his daughter to him. "Father, you ought to be happier than any other man in the world."

"In the world!" repeated Hendron.

"In all the universe!" Eve quickly corrected. "You brought all the people in our ship over safely; and more than three hundred in the other Ark! Oh, Father, Father, no man in the universe could have done more!"

Hendron shook his head. "These people here, of whom Tony has told us. What metallurgists! They would have made a ship. Ah! Ah! Aha! Tony—David—Higgins! The rest of you! What do you think of this? The People of this planet are not here because they made good their escape through space! They made their own space-ships and better ones and more of them; and escaped when they were passing some habitable sphere as they scraped some star!"

"No, Father!"

"How do you know? I tell you, they probably did it; and accomplished it so much better than I, with my bungling, that I am an amateur—a murderer. How many did I kill, David? How many did you say? . . . What rows of names!"

"Father, you didn't kill them!"

"I tell you I did! The tubes fused—the tubes I figured and designed myself. The human factor did not fail. They piloted it properly. The tubes fused!"

No one could quiet him. His daughter had to lead him away with Tony and Ransdell both helping her. The excitement of Ransdell's news and, on top of it, Tony's had snapped his nerves, drawn too long to extreme tension. It was perfectly plain to all the company whom he had led that his day, as a man of resource, was done.

Tony, thoroughly realizing this, trembled himself as he helped lead his friend to his cabin. Partly it was from pity and compassion; for no one knew better than Tony with what mercilessness Hendron had driven himself and how he had borne so long his enormous burden. But partly this trembling was from an emotion far less worthy. It was jealousy again of Dave Ransdell.

Jealousy more bitter and hard than that which had possessed him when they both were on earth—and rivals. For here they were rivals again and with the conflict between them accentuated.

How Eve had hugged Dave and held to him and kissed him!

To be sure, they had all embraced him—men and girls. Every girl in the camp hysterically had kissed him. But Eve had not been hysterical, Tony knew. Eve—Eve— Well, it had changed this world for her that Dave Ransdell had reached it.

Then there was the talk which Tony had heard: the talk already to-night of Ransdell as the new leader of both camps; the leader of the survivors of earth to replace and follow Hendron.

Tony tingled alternately with hate of Dave, and with shame at himself, as he thought of this talk. He had quieted the talk of himself as leader and he honestly had not wanted it a few days ago; he would not permit himself to be considered a candidate against Hendron; but now that Hendron was surely done, he wanted his people—*his* people, he thought them—to want him for their leader. And some still did; but more, he thought miserably, to-night turned to Dave Ransdell.

This was unworthy; this was childish, this jealousy and hate of his strong, courageous comrade! So Tony told himself; but he could not conquer it.

Now they had come to Hendron's cabin; and Tony felt himself becoming officious in the endeavor to be of more use to Hendron and to Eve than Dave might be.

Ransdell felt this and drew back.

"Thank you, Tony," said Eve, in her gentle voice. "Now you go back to the people."

"All right," said Tony. "Come along, Dave."

"Let him stay here, Tony," said Eve.

"Him—and not me?" Tony stared.

"What more can he tell them?" Eve asked patiently. "He's given them his news, who're living and who"—she lowered her voice carefully so her father could not hear—"who are dead. He has no more to tell. You—you haven't begun to tell them what you must have to tell of the strange city!"

"Don't *you* want to hear it?" Tony persisted.

"I'm staying with Father now," said Eve.

Rebelliously—and yet ashamed of himself for his feeling—Tony turned away and left her with Ransdell.

CHAPTER VIII

THE CITY OF VANISHED PEOPLE

"THE best way to give you some idea of the city," Tony said, facing the entire company except Hendron and Eve, "is to read you extracts from the record made, on the spot and at the time, by Eliot James. Before I begin, however, I ask you to think of a city made of many colored metals built like the spokes of a wheel around a vast central building. Think of a dome of transparent metal over it. And then remember particularly, while I read, that every street, every building, every object in the whole metropolis was in an amazing state of preservation.

"Remember that there was not a single sign of human habitation. I have already told you that the people were human—very much like ourselves—but there was not a sign of them or any remains of them except for statues and paintings and representations which we called photographic for lack of a better word and for record on their remarkable visual machines. Bear all that in mind. Here, for example, is what Eliot wrote on the evening of our first day there. It was the fifty-first day on Bronson Beta. I will skip the part that describes the city in general."

He began to read: "Tony and I are now seated in a bedroom of an apartment in one of the large buildings. The night of Bronson Beta has descended, but we have light. In fact, the adventure of light is the most bizarre which has befallen us since we penetrated this spectacular and silent city. As twilight descended we were about to return to our airplane. We were at the time on the street. We had visited one or two buildings, and the effect of the silence combined with the oncoming darkness was more than we could bear. I know that my scalp was tingling, the palms of my hands were clammy, and when I stood still I could feel my muscles shaking. We could not rid ourselves of the feeling that the city was inhabited; we could not cease looking quickly over our shoulders in the hope or the fear of seeing somebody. As we stood uncertainly on the street the sun vanished altogether, its orange light reflected by low-lying cumulus clouds. The sky took on a deeper green and at a word from Tony I would have run from the place. Suddenly, to our utter confoundation, the city was bathed in light. The light came on without a sound. Its source, or rather, its sources, were invisible. It shone down on the streets from behind cornices. It burst luminously upon the walls of the giant buildings.

"The interiors of many of them were also filled with radiance. All this, suddenly, silently, in the gathering gloom. I shall never forget the expression on Tony's face as he turned to me and whispered: 'It's too much!' My own mind, appalled at this new, marvelous manifestation of the genius of the Other People, was very close to lapsing into unconsciousness for a second. Then I found myself with my hands clenched, saying over and over to myself, 'It's light, just light. It was getting dark, so they turned on the lights.' Then I amended that to—'The lights come on here when it's dark.' Immediately Tony and I fell into an altercation. 'It's just the lights coming on,' I said.

" 'But that's impossible!'

" 'Nevertheless, they're on.'

"Tony, searching frantically for the shreds of his sanity, replied, 'But if the lights come on every night in this city, we'd have seen it through telescopes.'

" 'Maybe we didn't happen to catch it.'

" 'It can't be.'

"Both of us thought of the same thing simultaneously: the lights had come on because the city had been entered. It was true that if the cities of Bronson Beta had been illuminated at night the fact would have been observed before their passing. And a new and utterly irrational feeling struck us. The people were dead, dead a million years—a hundred million years. But in this startling gesture of turning on the lights there was more than mechanical magic. There was hospitality. That was crazy, but it was the way we felt.

" 'It was arranged,' Tony said. 'Arranged for somebody, sometime—so arranged that when they should come here everything would be ready for them. Consequently, unless we do something very stupid, nothing can happen to us.' I repeat that it was utterly irrational; but that was the way it made us feel.

"I was inclined to agree with him, and as my eyes traveled along the brilliant and magnificent streets of this metropolis, I too for the first time felt that the artificial light pouring indirectly upon us had lent to it a humanity that had been hitherto absent.

" 'Let's stay,' Tony said. 'Maybe we can find a place to sleep. We really ought to know more about it before we go back.'

"And so we stayed. We picked a building which we thought contained residences and after some experimenting succeeded in entering it. The ground floor was a hall, or lobby, which was decorated by statuary and bas-reliefs, of animals more fantastic and ferocious-looking than could be contrived in the wildest nightmare. And yet their presentation had a gay note, as if

83

the sculptor had set them as humorous, rather than savage, embellishments in that lobby. At one side of the lobby was another large room which contained the apparatus for what we presently realized was a variety of games. They were like no games on our earth. One of them was played with large metal-like balls, which were extremely light and yet very hard, and with magnets. Another was played over a pool, evidently with jets of water, but we could not turn on the jets and the pool was empty. We did not take the time to puzzle out the technique of these sports, but proceeded by a large staircase to the floor above. There, as we had hoped, we found apartments. One of them, which faced the street from which we had entered the building, was open—and this we have made our own."

As Tony turned a page, his listeners waited almost breathlessly. He continued from the record:

"It is an apartment of indescribable beauty. The living room is more than twenty feet in height. Its walls are decorated with metal figures in various colors. There is no rug on the floor, but the floor is of a texture not unlike that of a very fine, deep rug. There are mirrors on many faces of the walls—the Other People must have enjoyed looking at themselves, or else they must have liked the added effect of distance lent by the mirrors, for large reflecting panels seem to be an important part of their interior decoration. We have also found beds. There were two bedrooms. The beds are very low. We had, I imagine, assumed that they would be of a luxurious softness, but they are rather hard, so that in spite of their comforts the Other People must have been Spartans in some measure. Apparently there are closets and bureaus set in the walls, but we have not been able to get open the panels which cover them. We have also found a bathroom, but we cannot make anything of it. It is a beautiful chamber of all bright metals, the colors of which are gold and azure, but it is filled with fixtures and other gadgets of great intricacy as well as beauty.

"We are leaving the problem of deciphering the Bronson Betans' bathing and toilet-making for experts.

"However, we are quite comfortable in that part of our quarters which we have had the courage to occupy. . . . It is now moderately late in the Bronson Beta night and we have decided to try to sleep. To be sure, we have placed a chair in the door to the hall so it will not magically close upon us, for although we are only one story above the street it is impossible to break these windows. We have also planned to keep our pistols at our sides, although a glance at this world of the Other People makes us quite sure that if there were any survivors and they were bent on our destruction, a revolver would be an extremely useless weapon. However, nobody has survived; of that we are convinced."

Tony looked up and regarded his fascinated audience. They were packed about him, crowding close, eager for his next words. But Eve was not there; nor Ransdell. He tried to dismiss thought of this as he proceeded to read:

"We did sleep, and we slept very well. However, we woke before the actual return of daylight, and feeling sufficiently refreshed, we decided to continue our explorations in the remarkable radiance of the artificial illumination which was so useful though so puzzling to us. You can scarcely understand how this affected us with the conviction that the place must be inhabited, and that around the next corner, beyond the next door, we must find some of the people. But we found no living thing."

Tony looked up again. "I find here a number of pages of notes of the most sober sort. They are Eliot James' attempt to describe and analyze some of the remarkable objects and implements which we examined. Of course neither he nor I are physicists, chemists or engineers, so our notions are probably valueless; those of you who are more expert than either of us will undoubtedly soon have a chance to inspect the engines and implements of the Other People.

"Along with such notes, I find the trivial record of what Eliot and I ate on that amazing morning. I will read that because it will show to you something of our state of mind. We seem to have been so stunned by what we had seen that it never occurred to Eliot that it was ridiculous to describe, along with the wonders of the Sealed City, our breakfast!"

His gaze returned to the notes.

"We got up in what we call the morning," Tony read, "although it was still dark, and we had a breakfast consisting of one bar of chocolate and a rather crumbled piece of hardtack which I had in my pocket, for what reason nobody will ever know. Then an extremely funny thing happened—at least we thought it was funny. We finished the last crumb of the hardtack—for our real food supply was in our ship outside the city —when I, looking for chance provender, felt in a pocket, and produced—to our mutual amazement—a stick of chewing-gum! This we broke evenly in half, and we embarked again on the streets of Bronson Beta chewing gum—a practice which I dare say was unknown on the planet in its earlier days.

"Well, the first thing we investigated that morning was a store. It was a department store in the sense that it contained a great many kinds of things; but it did not contain, for example, clothes or, as far as we could discover, food. It had house-furnishings, and furniture and kitchen appliances—and by the way, cooking must have been a cinch for the Other People, because apparently they cooked things by induced heat and under high pressure with steam, so that it only took a few minutes. The store also exhibited some of those automobile-like vehicles like the one we found wrecked.

"In the store," he continued, "we also found a large department of games and sports, and one of children's toys. The children had very peculiar blocks. Wires extend from their sides and corners so that they look like cockleburs and can be stuck together to make variously shaped figures in which the differently colored blocks are held apart by wires. It was Tony who solved the enigma of those blocks. 'Molecules,' he said, as we stood staring at them. And then I realized that each block was designed to represent an atom and that the children were taught by playing with the blocks the atomic structure of various elements.

"I can give you no idea of the superlative order in which everything in it was arranged. It would be hopeless for me to try to tell you the skill with which those people combined use with beauty. Beauty and use with imaginative intelligence. I can only say two things—first, that you will all see it yourselves, and second, that while the streets, and the buildings, and the apartments of the city of the Other People fascinated us, we had intended to leave that morning."

Again Tony ceased to read. "We appreciated, of course," he observed to his hearers, "that we ought to communicate with you; and after our breakfast, and a brief journey through some of the strange streets, we went out of the city by the way we had entered and returned to our ship where we tried to call you by radio. We failed utterly because of some puzzling interference.

"We argued, then, whether we should return to you with what we had learned or whether we should first try to learn much more. The second argument was overwhelming in its appeal to us. We returned to the city; and on the second day, we discovered that it was not quite so intact as we had supposed. In no less than six places which we observed, the huge transparent dome was pierced and showed great jagged tears or holes and below were marks of demolition exhibiting great violence. Meteors had torn through. But except for the wreckage caused by these, I tell you we found almost nothing out of order in that remarkable city. *They* left it in order, we believe; the meteors probably were met after the city was deserted and during this sphere's long journey through space.

"Now I will give you a few more random details from Eliot's diary:

"One thing we noted on our return to the stores—if they were stores," Tony read, "was that in none of them did there seem to have been a system for collecting money, or a medium of exchange, or of keeping books. Seemingly the Other People just came in and took what they wanted—or individuals must have kept their own books—or some system which we couldn't imagine was used. For at the end of our three days' stay we were pretty certain that they had no medium of exchange to correspond to money.

"A department of that store was given over to musical instruments. Their chromatic scale is different from ours, and their way of writing music entirely different. They had a few stringed instruments, no wind instruments, many percussion instruments, but they had developed a vast variety of instruments which seem to have been operated by the transference of electrical impulses to sound. Unquestionably, music and the science of electricity had existed side by side for so long that the art had developed a science for its expression.

"We found in profusion the small, light vehicles of the type which we first discovered wrecked on the road near our camp. It is plain these were operated by some sort of electric impulse; but we could do nothing with them."

Tony skipped more pages. "Imagine us with the sun rising and the flood of indirect illumination dimming away. Imagine us under that vast transparent bubble in the early morning, having a long look at one marvel after another. We went across bridges and up and down streets. We tramped along ramps and on a dozen levels. We visited civic centers and museums and theaters and recreation-grounds and central kitchens and other places of assembly, the purpose of which was not clear. All we lacked was some one to explain at frequent intervals just what the devil we were seeing, because while we were interested we often could only guess, and sometimes none of our explanations made sense. We never found that some one. One thing was very clear, however: the Other People liked to spend a lot of time together. They had privacy in their own apartments, to be sure, but there were so many things and so many kinds of things for people to do in crowds that we became convinced that they were very gregarious. We felt too that their crowds were not comprised of mobs of unfriendly, unsympathetic, unacquainted individuals—like the crowds that once thronged the streets of New York—but were crowds of people who were associated in a most friendly and coöperative spirit with each other.

"We followed a gallery underground where we found more great machines—engines—which we could not at all understand. We saw further descents into depths we decided not to explore. But we did come upon some of their stores of food —particularly grain."

"Samples of this grain," Tony reminded them, looking up, "already you have examined for yourselves. Eliot and I tasted it; we ate it. It was starchy and not unpleasant. Whether or not it still contains vitamins, at least it has the starch base for nutrition. In the afternoon, we found one other thing of far greater importance to us than any other discovery, if I may except the food supply. This was a school."

"A school?" several voices cried.

"We believe it was a school for their children from their early years up. Can you imagine the benefit of such a discovery to you? We have brought back some of the objects from that school. Some of them seem to be books—books of a different type, to be sure, than our volumes; yet they can be described as books. Other objects, which we believe to have been materials of instruction, are harder to describe. Neither Eliot nor I were able to operate them, but we formed the theory that they probably were mechanisms giving instruction visually or by sound.

"Then we found a sphere. It was in the lobby of the school. It was a sphere about fifty feet in diameter upon which was a relief map which we must assume to be of this planet. Eliot James made a most painstaking sketch of that sphere. There were other maps."

"In short," said Tony, closing Eliot James' book of notes, "we have awaiting us not only an equipment beyond anything dreamed of on earth, but a means of acquiring the secrets of the use of the engines and implements and other knowledge of this planet which we could not have obtained, by ourselves, at all.

"A little study by ourselves as children in those amazing classrooms, a little skill and a little luck in setting in operation their mechanisms of instruction; and their secrets are ours!"

CHAPTER IX

THE MYSTERIOUS ATTACK

LUNCH was very late that day; it was long before the company of the camp could be satisfied that they had heard everything of importance that Tony had to tell them. This included, of course, the report on the finding of the lark-like aircraft of which he had made report to the other camp.

Now Tony sat alone. Many, at first, tried to sit beside him and to talk to him. But he had told them that he was weary and wished to be alone for a little while. When the children came running up to him, however, he talked to them cheerfully. . . . Now they too had left.

Tony had seen meals being sent to Hendron's cabin-like house—watched them being carried past the Ark and the workshop and the lumber-piles. He had stared often at the door of the house. But no one had emerged—and Eve had not sent for him.

He sat alone, on a mound of chips and sawdust. Was Hendron turning over the command to Ransdell, in there now? Was Hendron asleep from exhaustion and were Eve and Ransdell taking advantage of the resultant solitude to express fresh love for each other? His heart was heavy; heavier still because he realized that the torrent of dreads and despairs it held were unworthy of him.

He ached, and stared at his plate. His eyes felt salty and hot. He tried to clamp his mind on present necessities. They should move to the miracle city: they should study the food and machinery there. They should tend their own crops for fresh food. They should learn to run the Other People's vehicles—so that they could all be transported to the new city as rapidly as possible. They should prepare defenses for themselves against the possibility that the people who had flown the lark-like ships might some day attack them. People from earth? Or cautious scouts of the Other People?

His mind jumped incessantly back to Eve—Eve and Ransdell, his two closest friends. They seemed both on the point of deserting him. Ransdell was, of course, a great man. Stronger in character, perhaps. Tony felt the crushing weight of the responsibilities he himself had endured. Still, Ransdell had taken greater risks—held a higher office. And Ransdell had been a new and different sort of man for Eve. She had known plenty of Yale graduates with social position and wealth and superficial culture—plenty—even if the Yale graduates now left alive could be numbered on the fingers of one hand. . . .

"Mr. Drake?" said a voice.

Tony started. "Oh, Kyto!" Suddenly Tony did not want to be alone any longer. The smiling face of the little Japanese was familiar and good. "Sit down here, Kyto."

Kyto hesitated.

"You're not—working for me—any longer!" Tony grinned.

Kyto seated himself with a precise and smooth motion. "That's true," he said slowly. "I'd forgotten for an instant."

Tony was astonished. "You've certainly learned a lot of English in the last few months."

"I always knew more than I pretended to know," the Japanese answered coolly.

Tony smiled. "Really, Kyto? Then why did you pretend not to? Is that one of those things that makes people say the Japs are subtle and dangerous?"

"In a way," Kyto answered. "I pretended not to know much English while I was in your employ, because I was a spy."

"What!"

"It is true."

"But good God, Kyto, what use was my service—to a spy? I didn't know where there was a fort, or a gun—"

"It gave me a respectable character."

"And what did you spy on?"

"It doesn't matter now. I shall tell you some day. You see, I used to be,"—there was scarcely a trace of accent in his words,—"long ago in Tokyo, a professor of foreign languages. I spoke English when I was a baby. Missionaries taught me. I was a patriot. I volunteered for espionage. While I was in America, my ideas changed. I became—before the Bronson Bodies appeared—a pacifist. I had sent in my resignation and offered to give myself up—at the time of the discovery of the approaching planets. My letters were ignored in the subsequent frantic days. So, during those days, I endeavored to reshape my life. You Americans—some of you, at least—stood for the things I desired: A world run by sense and science; a world of peace and fraternity. I wished to go on your ship. But my wish was not exclusively a selfish one. I continued to mingle with my associates in espionage—as one of them. I learned much."

Tony had never been more astonished. As he looked at his former servant he realized that his jaw had literally sagged. "I'll be damned," he murmured.

"You find it amusing?"

"Astounding."

"You were right before." Kyto laughed in a high key. "It is amusing. Delicious! And I was a fool. A blind, patriotic fool."

"I'm glad you told me," Tony said suddenly. "You're a man, Kyto. And we need you here. Need the things your race possesses."

"Thank you," Kyto said solemnly. "You are also a man."

Involuntarily Tony glanced at Hendron's cabin and shook his head.

The Japanese understood perfectly. "I hope you will not mind an expression of my sympathies?"

Tony looked at him—his valet, expressing sympathies on a most personal matter! No—a friend—a professor—a savant. A man who had heroically offered to give up his life for the beliefs that he had gained. "No, Kyto."

"You will need courage," Kyto said. "Courage, restraint. You have both in sufficient quantities."

"I have rats eating my soul," Tony answered stonily.

"It is too big for all the rats on earth."

Tony stared at the little man and said in a curious tone, "Funny."

There was a silence between them.

"I have more to say." Kyto picked up a chip and opened a pocket-knife. He began to whittle as expertly as any country-store porch loafer.

"More?"

"You know that other ships for the trip to this planet were being prepared?"

"Sure. But none of them—"

Kyto shrugged. "Did you know that' in what had been Manchuria the most fanatical Japanese, the Russians, and certain Germans combined to build such a ship?"

"No."

"They were mostly extreme communists. But owing to their need of scientific experts, they took into their group many non-communists."

"So?"

"Great men. They were as likely to succeed as you."

Tony stared at his companion. "And you believe they did? You think they are the people who have been flying here—"

"I know." Kyto drew an object from his pocket—a tightly folded piece of paper. On it were drawn Japanese characters. "I found this a few hours ago. I had been walking from camp. It was blowing along in the wind. It was not mine."

"What is it?"

"A prayer—a written prayer. They are in common use in Japan."

"It might have come on the Ark."

"Yes. But it might not. There is no such thing in the catalogue."

"Anybody who had traveled in Japan might have had one—in a pocketbook—and lost it."

"Again, yes. But I know intuitively."

"If they were Russians and Germans and Japanese—why didn't they land, then?"

"My point in telling this! They do not want company here. They came to set up a Soviet. I have the information in detail. They were sworn, if they reached here, to set up their own government—to wipe out all who might oppose them. It is not even a government like that of Russia. It is ruthless, inhuman—a travesty of socialism, a sort of scientific fanaticism. Most of those men and women believe in nothingness of the individual. They believe that love is really only breeding."

Tony shook his head unbelievingly. "Why didn't they wipe us out, then?"

"Your ray-projectors were good protection. They may find a means of making them powerless. They are manifestly ahead of us here in studying the civilization of the Other People—they use their ships already."

"I mean, the first time. Why didn't they annihilate us that first night? It would have been easy. A bomb or two—"

"I have wondered. There must have been a reason—for they are wholly ruthless. And I can find only one explanation: They wish to found a new state—to be alone on the planet—to make it theirs. To found a state takes people; and for people, one needs women. The more the better—the quicker. They will not strike until they can be selective in their killing—so they wipe out all who may oppose them, but preserve all whom they may convert—especially the women."

"Good God!" Tony stood up. "You mean to tell me you think there is a gang of men or people on Bronson Beta planning that?"

"I am positive."

"It's—it's crazy!"

Kyto shook his head. "Conquest was like that, only two thousand years ago—a short time. And there is no more world. Is there anything that can be said to be crazy now—anything we cannot expect?"

"Then why didn't you tell us sooner?"

Kyto fumbled the paper. "I wanted to be sure. This made me sure."

"It's the worst evidence I ever saw. The thing's fantastic!"

"I have warned you as best I can." He bowed his head, and walked away.

Oddly enough, this scene with Kyto had brought back to Tony some of the strength that had ebbed from him. The thought that his new information would be a good excuse to break in on Hendron and Ransdell and Eve occurred to him, but he thrust it aside without effort.

He walked into the group of people who had finished their midday meal. He touched several on the shoulder. "Duquesne, I want to talk to you privately. Von Beitz! Williamson!"

Fifteen minutes later he had explained his command to a dozen picked men.

"I'll have to tell Ransdell and Hendron later," Tony said. "First, we'll double the guard. Second, we'll put out some sentries—far enough out to give a warning of approaching planes. Third, we'll run off a blast on our projectors to make sure they are in order."

Von Beitz scowled. "I can't believe it. Germans? Maybe—some Germans, Heitbrat, for example. But wouldn't it be better if we said nothing to the women? They might get hysterical."

"These women don't get hysterical," Tony answered succinctly.

He had scarcely finished his instructions when a message was brought to him to report at Hendron's house.

He went in. Eve was in the living room—the room that had been headquarters for the camp since the building of the house. She was sitting at her father's desk, and Ransdell stood at a little distance from her. Dodson was there. The faces of all three were serious.

"Hendron has collapsed," Dodson said to Tony. "Whether he will recover or not, I cannot say."

Tony shook his head sadly.

Eve spoke. "The camp must have a leader."

"Yes," Tony answered.

"Election might be unsatisfactory," she continued. "And it would take time."

"Yes."

"Father appointed no second-in-command. Whoever is in charge while he is ill must remain here. You and Eliot James alone can fly our single plane. We'll need it constantly now. A radio must be taken down to the other camp at once, for example."

Tony looked at her with as little sign of emotion as he could show. This was a new Eve to him—a stern, impartial Eve. Grief and need had combined to make her so. "The static we've been having makes a radio useless," he said.

"That static occurs only at night," she answered. "Sundown to sunup."

"The lights in the city—" Tony murmured. He squared his shoulders. "I'll take a radio down at once."

Eve rose and gestured Ransdell into her father's chair. She shook his hand. Dodson shook his hand. Tony shook his hand

—Tony whose soul was at that moment in exquisite torment.

Ransdell looked drawn and bleak.

"One other thing," Tony said, his voice steady. "We may be in a new and to me fantastic danger." Like a soldier making a report, he detailed the knowledge Kyto had given him and told Ransdell what precautions he had already taken. Even as he spoke the air was filled with a hissing thunder and they waited to continue the conversation until tests of the blast tubes had been finished.

"I'll get outposts established at once," Ransdell said. "I scarcely believe that such a thing could be—but we can take no chances."

"I'd like to talk with Kyto," Eve said. She left the room even as Tony turned to bid her good-by.

"That radio—" said Ransdell. Tony could not make his senses believe that the man who spoke to him now was the man with whom he had spent the latter part of the previous night in deep exultation. Rivalry over leadership—rivalry over Eve —they seemed inadequate things intellectually for the breaking of a friendship. Tony remembered the pact he and Ransdell had reached in Michigan, long ago. Now—it seemed broken!

"I'll take it immediately, Dave," he answered.

The use of his first name startled Ransdell somewhat from his barren mood. He rose and held out his hand.

Tony shook it. "So long," he said.

"Good luck."

Tony opened the throttle regulating the supply of minute quantities of fuel to the atomic blast of his plane. The increase of speed as he fled southward took some of the strain from his nerves. His ears roared to the tune of the jets. The ground underneath moved in a steady blur. Beside him on the extra seat was the radio—a set taken from the ark of the air, and still crated.

Tony had lost his hope of being leader. He had lost Eve. Ransdell came first in the hearts of his companions. Tony wondered how other men in the camp would adjust their philosophies to this double catastrophe. Duquesne would shrug: "C'est la vie." Vanderbilt would have an epigram. Eliot James would tell him to hope and to wait and to be courageous.

Far ahead he saw the cantonment.

He lost altitude, dropped in a tight spiral, straightened out, and landed at an unnecessarily furious speed.

A few minutes later he was surrounded, and the radio was being carried from the plane by experts.

James was at his side. "Lord, you look tired! I've got a bunk for you."

"Thanks."

Questions were being asked. "Got to sleep," Tony said, trying to smile. "Tell you later. Every one's all right—Hendron's somewhat ill—Ransdell's commanding up there. See you after I have a nap." They let him go.

He stretched out under one of the shelters. James, after a private question or two, thoughtfully left him. He could not sleep, however. He did not even want to be alone. Then—some one entered the room where he lay. He turned. It was the girl Marian Jackson.

"You're not asleep," she said easily.

"No."

She sat down on the side of his bed. "Want anything?"

"Guess not."

"Mind if I sit here?"

"No."

She brushed back the hair from his forehead and suddenly exclaimed. "You're all chapped and wind-burned!"

He smiled. "Sure. Flying."

"Wait." She was gone.

A moron, Tony reflected. But she was very sweet. Thoughtful! A woman, just brushing back your hair when you were weary, could do strange things in the way of giving comfort. She returned.

"Shut your eyes. This is salve. Make you feel better. You're shot; I can tell. I'll stay here while you sleep, so you won't need to worry about anything."

He felt her hands—delicate, tender. Then he was asleep.

He woke slowly. He was being shaken. Waking was like falling up a long, black hill.

Light hit his eyes. James stood there.

"Tony! Wake up!"

He sat up, shook himself.

"We got that radio working. Were talking to Hendron's camp. Suddenly the man at the other end coughed and yelled 'Help!'—and now we can't raise any one."

Tony was up again—outdoors—running toward the plane. James was running behind him.

"Give me Vanderbilt and Taylor. We'll go."

"But—"

"What else can we do?"

As Tony descended upon Hendron's encampment, three men peered tensely through the glass windows of the ship: Taylor, Vanderbilt, and Tony himself. Nothing seemed disturbed; the buildings were intact.

"Not a person in sight!" Taylor yelled suddenly.

They slid down the air.

Tony cut the motors so that their descent became a soft whistle.

Then they saw clearly.

Far below were human figures, the people of the cantonment, and all of them lay on the ground, oddly collapsed, utterly motionless.

CHAPTER X

WAR

TONY circled above the stricken camp of the colony from earth. He could count some sixty men and women lying on the ground.

They looked as if they were dead; and Tony thought they were dead. So did Jack Taylor at his side; and Peter Vanderbilt, his saturnine face pressed against the quartz windows of the plane, believed he was witnessing catastrophe to Hendron's attempt to preserve humanity.

The Death spread below them might already have struck, also, the other camp—the camp from which these three had just flown. They might be the last survivors; and the Death might reach them now, at any instant, within their ship.

Tony thought of the illness which had come over the camp after the first finding of the wrecked vehicle of the Other People—the illness that had proved fatal to three of the earth people. He thought: "This might be some more deadly disease of the Other People which they caught." He thought: "I might have brought the virus of it to them myself from the Sealed City. It might have been in or on some of the objects they examined after I left."

This flashed through his mind; but he did not believe it. He believed that the Death so visible below was a result of an attack.

He looked at his companions, and read the same conviction in their faces. He pointed toward the earth, and raised his eyebrows in a question he could not make audible above a spurt from the plane's jets.

Taylor shook his head negatively. The people below them were dead. Descent would doubtless mean their own death.

Vanderbilt shrugged and gestured to Tony, as if to say that the decision was up to him.

Tony cut the propulsive stream and slid down the air in sudden quiet. "Well?"

"Maybe we should take a look," said Vanderbilt.

"What got them," Taylor said slowly, "will get us. We'd better take back a warning to the other camp."

Tony felt the responsibility of deciding. Ransdell was down there—dead. And Eve?

He lost altitude and turned on power as he reached the edge of the landing-field.

Neither of his companions had been in the Hendron encampment; but this was no time for attention to the equipment of the place. The plane bumped to a stop and rested in silence.

No one appeared from the direction of the camp. Nothing in sight there stirred. There was a bit of breeze blowing, and a speck of cloth flapped; but its motion was utterly meaningless. It was the wind fluttering a cloak or a cape of some one who was dead.

Tony put his hand on the lever that opened the hood of the cockpit.

"I'll yank it open and jump out. Looks like gas. Slam it after I go, and see what happens to me."

Either of his companions would have undertaken that terrifying assignment—would have insisted upon undertaking it; but Tony put his words into execution before they could speak. The hatch grated open. Tony leaped out on the fuselage; there was a clang, and almost none of the outer air had entered the plane.

Taylor's knuckles on the hatch-handle were white.

Vanderbilt peered through the glass at Tony, his face unmoving. But he whispered, "Guts!" as if to himself.

Tony slipped to earth. The two men watching expected at any moment to see him stagger or shudder or fall writhing to the earth. But he did not. There was no fright on his face—his expression was locked and blank. He sweated. He sniffed in the air cautiously after expelling the breath he had held. Then he drew in a lungful, deeply, courageously. A light wind from the sea beyond the cliffs fanned him. He stood still—waiting, presumably, to die. He looked at the two men who were watching him, and hunched his shoulders as if to say that nothing had happened so far.

A minute passed.

The men inside the plane sat tensely. Taylor was panting.

Two minutes. . . . Five. Tony stood and breathed and shrugged again.

"Gas or no gas," Taylor said with an almost furious expression, "I'm going out there with Tony."

He went.

Vanderbilt followed in a manner both leisurely and calm.

The three stood outside together watching each other for effects, each waiting for some spasm of illness to attack himself.

"Doesn't seem to be gas," said Tony.

"What, then?" asked Taylor.

"Who knows? Some plague from the Other People? Some death-wave from the sky? Let's look at them."

The first person they approached, as they went slowly toward the camp and its motionless figures, was Jeremiah Post, the metallurgist. He it was, Tony remembered, who first was affected by the illness that followed the finding of the Other People's car. There was no proof that Post was the first to have been affected by this prostration. They happened upon him first; that was all.

The metallurgist lay on his side with his arms over his head. There was no blood or mark of violence upon him.

"Not wounded, anyway," Vanderbilt muttered.

Taylor turned him over; and all three men started. Post's breast heaved.

"Good God!" Tony knelt beside him and opened his shirt. "Breathing! Heart's beating—regularly. He's—"

"Only unconscious!" Taylor exclaimed.

"I was going to say," Tony replied, "it's as if he was drugged."

"Or like anesthesia," observed Vanderbilt.

"Is he coming out of it?"

"He's far under now," Vanderbilt commented. "If he's been further under, who can say?"

"Let's look at the next!"

Near by lay two women; the three men examined them together. They were limp like Jeremiah Post, and like him, lying in a strange, profound stupor—like anesthesia, as Vanderbilt had said. The sleep of one of them seemed, somehow, less deep than that which held Post insensible; but neither of the women could be roused from it more than he.

"Feel anything funny yourself?" Tony challenged Taylor across the form of the girl over whom they worked.

"No; do you?"

"No. . . . It was gas, I believe; but now it's dissipated—but left its effect on everybody that breathed it."

"Gas," said Vanderbilt calmly, "from where?"

Tony's mind flamed with the warning of Kyto's words. A third Ark from the earth had reached Bonson Beta bearing a band of fanatic, ruthless men who would have the planet for their own, completely. They had brought with them some women, but they wished for many more in order to populate it with children of their own bodies and of their own fanatic faiths. These men already had obtained the Lark planes of the Other People, and mastered the secrets of their operation. These men long ago had entered some other Sealed City and had begun an exploration into the science of Dead People. Perhaps they had found some fomula for a gas that stupefied, but was harmless otherwise.

Their plan and their purpose, then, would be plain. They would spread the gas and render Hendron's people helpless; then they would return to the camp and control it, doing whatever they wished with the people, as they awoke.

Tony scanned the sky, the surrounding hills. There was nothing in sight.

Yet he leaped up. "Peter! Jack! They'll be coming back! We'll be ready for them!"

"Who? Who are they?"

"The men who did this! Come on!"

"Where?"

"To the tubes!" And Tony pointed to them, aimed like cannon into the air—the huge propulsion-tubes from the Ark, which Hendron and he had mounted on their swivels at the edges of the camp. From them could be shot into the air the awful blast that had propelled the Ark through space, and which melted every metal except the single substance with which they were lined.

The nearest of these engines of flight, so expediently made into machines of defense, was a couple of hundred yards away; and now as the three made hastily for it, they noticed a grouping of the limp, unconscious forms that told its own significant story.

Several of the men seemed to have been on the way to the great tube when they had collapsed.

"You see?" gasped Tony; for the three now were running. "It was an attack! They saw it, and tried to get the tube going!"

Two men, indeed, lay almost below the tube. Tony stared down at them as his hands moved the controls, and felt them in order.

"Dead?" Tony asked of Taylor, who bent over the men.

Jack shook his head. "Nobody's dead. They're all the same—they're sleeping."

"Do you see Dodson? Have you seen Dodson anywhere?"

"No; you want Dodson, especially?"

"He might be able to tell us what to do."

Tony threw a switch, and a faint corona glowed along a heavy cable. The air crackled softly. "Our power-station's working," he said with satisfaction. "We can give this tube the 'gun' when we want to. You know how to give it the gun, Peter?"

"I know," said Vanderbilt calmly.

"Then you stand by; and give it the gun, if anything appears overhead! Jack, see what you can do with that tube!" Tony pointed to the north corner of the camp. "I'll look over some more of the people; and see what happened to Hendron—and Eve—and Ransdell and Dodson. Dodson's the one to help us, if we can bring him to."

He had caught command again—command over himself and his companions; Taylor already was obeying him; and Vanderbilt took his place at the tube.

Tony moved back into the camp alone. At his feet lay men

100

and girls and women motionless, sightless, deaf—utterly insensible in their stupor. He could do nothing for them but recognize them; and he went, bending over them, whispering their names to himself and to them, as if by his whispering he might exorcise away this sleep.

He repeated to himself Eve's name; but he did not find Eve. Where was she, and how? Had this sleep dropped into death for some? He wanted to find Eve, to assure himself that she at least breathed as did these others; but he realized that he should first of all locate Dodson. . . . Dodson, if he could be aroused, would be worth a thousand laymen. Then he recollected that he had last seen Dodson in Hendron's dwelling.

Tony rushed to it and flung open the door; but what lay beyond it halted him.

He found Eve. She lay where she had fallen, face forward on the desk; and Ransdell lay slumped beside her. His left hand clasped her right hand; they had been overcome together. Both of them breathed slowly; but they were completely insensible. Dodson had crumpled over a table. There was a pen in his hand, a paper in front of him. Cloth—Tony saw that the cloth was from dresses—had been stuffed around the door. In a bedroom lay Hendron, the rise and fall of his chest almost imperceptible. Tony shook Dodson.

Suddenly he realized that his head was spinning.

He plunged to the door and staggered into the fresh air. He breathed hard. But his head cleared so slowly that his thoughts ran slow as minutes. Gas, after all. The people in Hendron's house had seen it strike the others, and attempted to barricade themselves. They thought it was death. There were still fumes in there.

Dodson—he must get Dodson.

He ran back, and dragged the huge man into the open.

He stood over him, panting. Then he remembered that Dodson had been writing. A note—a record. Tony went for it. So strong had been the poison in the air that he found it hard to read.

"We've been gassed," Dodson had scrawled. *"People falling everywhere. No attack visible. We're going to try to seal this room. They're all unconscious out there. I got a smell of it, closing a window. Nothing familiar. I think—"*

Tony shook Dodson. He brought water and doused him. He found Dodson's medical kit and tried to make him swallow aromatic spirits of ammonia, then whisky. Dodson could not swallow.

Tony jerked about, as he heard some one move. It was Vanderbilt, who had left his post at the tube.

"Nothing's in sight out there," Vanderbilt said calmly. "Taylor stays on watch. I ought to be more use in here."

101

"What can you do?" Tony demanded.

"I'm two-thirds of a doctor—for first aid, anyway," Vanderbilt said. "I used to spend a lot of time at hospitals. Morbid, maybe." While he spoke his slow, casual words, he had taken Dodson's kit and had been working over the physician. . . . "I gave him a hypo of caffeine and strychnine and digitalis that would have roused a dead elephant. He's still out, though."

"Will any of them come to?"

"Only one thing will tell."

"What?"

"Time, of course," Peter Vanderbilt said. "Then, if it proves my treatment may have helped Dodson,—and not killed him, —we might try it on others."

Tony bent again over Eve and Ransdell; their respirations and their pulses seemed the same; and Hendron's, though much weaker than theirs, had not further deteriorated.

"They don't seem to be slipping," Tony said.

"No. Anything in sight outside?"

"No," said Tony, but he went out for a better inspection, and for another patrol past those that lay senseless on the ground.

He returned to Peter Vanderbilt and waited with him. They pulled Dodson and Eve and Ransdell out into the open air and laid them on the ground; they carried out Hendron too, and stretched him upon his mattress in the breeze and the sunlight.

Nothing remained to do; so they sat watching the forms that breathed but otherwise did not move, and watching the sky. Three hundred yards away, Jack Taylor stood at his tube watching them and the sky, and the scattered, senseless, sleeping people.

"Our other camp!" said Vanderbilt. "What do you suppose is happening there?"

"I've been thinking of that, of course," said Tony. "We ought to warn them by radio; but if we did, we'd warn the enemy too. He's listening in, we may be sure; he'd know we were laying for him here; our chance to surprise him would be gone. No; I think our best plan is to lie low."

Vanderbilt nodded thoughtfully. "I agree. In all likelihood our enemy is taking on only one of our camps at a time. Having started here, he'll probably finish here before beginning on the other."

"We've no idea what forces they have."

"No."

"There might be enough to take on both our camps at once."

"Yes."

Tony and Peter Vanderbilt moved toward their radio-station; and they were debating there what to do, when their dilemma was solved for them: The sound of a plane came dimly to his ears. Both stepped out of the radio-room and lay down on the ground where vision in every direction was unhampered. Tony saw Taylor slumping into an attitude of unconsciousness.

Then his eye caught the glint of the plane. A speck far away. He lay motionless, like the others, and the speck rapidly enlarged.

It was one of the Bronson Betan ships. It flew fast and with a purring roar which was caused not by its motor but by the sound of its propellers thwacking the air.

It came low, slowed down, circled.

Tony's heart banged as he saw that one of the faces peering over was broad, bearded, strongly Slavic. Another of its occupants had close-cropped hair and spectacles. The slip-stream of the plane fanned him furiously and raised dust around him. People from earth! They completed their inspection, and rushed out of sight toward the northwest.

Tony and Vanderbilt jumped up and ran toward Jack Taylor. The three men met for a frantic moment. "They'll be back." Tony shook with rage. "The swine! They'll be back to take over this camp. I wonder if they'd kill the men. We'll be ready. I'll take the west tube. Wait till they're all here. Wait till the first ship lands—I can rake hell out of that field. Then get 'em all! We can't fool. We can't do anything else."

They went to their positions again.

An hour later a large armada flew from the northwest. They did not fly in formation, like battle-planes. Their maneuvers were not overskillful. Some of the ships were even flown badly, as if their pilots were not well versed in their manipulation.

Tony counted. There were seventeen ships—and some of them were very large.

The three defenders acted on a prearranged plan: They did not follow the fleet with their tubes. They did not even move them from their original angles. They could be swung fast enough. They hid themselves carefully.

The ship circled the camp and the unconscious victims beneath. Then the leading ship prepared to land.

Tony fired his tube. The crackling sound rose as the blast began.

The enemy plane was almost on the ground. He could see lines of rivets in its bright metal body. He could see, through a small peephole, the taut face of the pilot. The wheels touched.

Tony heaved, and the counter-balanced weapon described an arc. There was a noise like the opening of a door to hell. The landing-field became a volcano. The plane vanished in a blistering, tumultuous core of light. The beam swung up, left the ground instantaneously molten.

It curved along the air, and broken and molten things

dropped from the sky. Into that armada probed two other orange fingers of annihilation; and it melted, dissolved, vanished.

It was not a fair fight. . . . It was not a fight.

The blasts yawed wide. They were fed by the horrible energy which had carried the Ark through space. Their voices shook the earth. They were more terrible than death itself, more majestic than lightning or volcanic eruption. They were forces stolen from the awful center of the sun itself.

In less than a minutes they were stilled. The enemy was no more.

Tony did not run, now. He walked back to the center of the camp. There he met Vanderbilt and Taylor.

No one spoke; they sat down, white, trembling, horrified.

Around them lay their unconscious comrades.

Here and there on the ground over and beyond the landing-place, great fragments of twisted metal glowed and blistered.

The sun shone. It warmed them from the green-blue sky of Bronson Beta.

Jack Taylor, student, oarsman, not long ago a carefree college boy—Jack Taylor sucked in a tremulous breath and whispered: *"God! Oh, God!"*

Vanderbilt rose and smiled a ghastly smile. He took a battered package of cigarettes from his pocket—tenderly, and as if he touched something rare and valuable. They knew he had been cherishing those cigarettes. He opened the package; four cigarettes were left. He passed them. He found a match, and they smoked. Still they did not speak.

They looked at the people who lay where they had fallen—the people who had come through that hideous destruction without being aware of it.

One of those people moved. It was Dodson.

They rushed to his side.

Dodson was stirring and mumbling. Vanderbilt opened his medical kit again and poured something into a cup. Tony held the Doctor's head. After several attempts, they managed to make him swallow the stuff.

He began a long, painful struggle toward consciousness. He would open his eyes, and nod and mutter, and go off to sleep for an instant, only to jerk and writhe and try to sit. Finally his fuddled voice enunciated Tony's name. *"Drake!"* he said. "Gas!" Then a meaningless jumble of syllables. Then "Caffeine! Stick it in me. Gimme pills. Caffalooaloclooaloo. Gas. Rum, rum, rum, rum, rum—headache. I'm sick."

Then, quite abruptly, he came to.

He looked at them. He looked at the sleeping forms around him. He squinted toward the field, and saw what was there. He rubbed his head and winced.

104

"Aches," he said. "Aches like sin. You—you came back in time, eh?"

"We laid for them," Tony answered solemnly. "We got them."

"All of them," Jack Taylor added.

Dodson pointed at the sleepers. "Dead?"

"All beathing. We wanted to get you around first—if anybody could be revived."

Dodson's head slumped and then he sat up again. "Right. What'd you use?"

"I gave you a shot of caffeine and strychnine and digitalis about an hour ago," Vanderbilt said.

Dodson grinned feebly. "Wake the dead, eh? Adrenalin might be better. Di-nitro-phenol might help. I've got a clue to this stuff. Last thing I thought of." He looked at the sky. "It just rained down on us—out of nothing."

"Rained?" Tony repeated.

"Yes. Rained—a falling mist. The people it touched never saw or smelled it—went out too fast. But I did both. Inside—we had a minute's grace." He struggled and finally rose to his feet. "Obviously something to knock us out. Nothing fatal. Let's see what we can do about rousing somebody else. Probably'd sleep it off in time—a day, maybe. I want to make some tests."

He was very feeble as he rose, and they supported him.

"I'll put a shot in Runciman and Best and Isaacs first, I guess. They can help with the others." Tony located Runciman, the brain-specialist. Dodson made a thorough examination of the man. "In good shape. Make a fine anesthetic—except for the headache." He filled a hypodermic syringe, then methodically swabbed the surgeon's arm with alcohol, squeezed out a drop of fluid to be sure no air was in the instrument, and pricked deftly. They moved on, looking for Best and Isaacs.

As they worked, Dodson's violent headache began to be dissipated. And the persons they treated presently commenced to writhe and mutter.

Hendron was among the first after the medical men. Dodson lingered over him and shook his head.

"Heart's laboring—bad condition, anyway. I'm afraid—"

Vanderbilt and Taylor and Tony knew what Dodson feared.

In two hours a number of pale and miserable human beings were moving uncertainly around the camp. Best entered the Ark and brought other drugs to alleviate their discomfort. Tony had sent a warning to the southern camp. They replied that they had seen nothing, and were safe.

The three men who were heroes of the raid went together to the landing-field. They walked from place to place examining the wreckage. They collected a host of trifles—buttons, a notebook, a fountain pen made in Germany, a pistol half melted, part of a man's coat, fire-warped pfennig pieces—and found more grisly items which they did not touch.

After they had made their telltale harvest among the still-hot débris, they stood together staring toward the northwest. An expedition in that direction would be necessary at once. It would not be a safe voyage.

NIGHT came on with its long, deliberate twilight; and with this night came cold.

The sentinels outside stood in little groups together, listening, and watching the sky. No lights showed. Wherever they were necessary within the offices and dwellings of the camp, they were screened or covered. The encampment could not risk an air-attack by night.

Tony found himself continued in command; for Hendron held to his bed and made no attempt to give directions. Ransdell was quite himself again, but like all the others but Tony and Tayor and Vanderbilt, he had lain insensible through the attack and the savage, successful defense the three had made.

Everybody came to Tony for advice and orders. Eve, like all the rest, put herself under his direction.

"You'd better stay with your father," Tony said to her. "Keep him quiet as you can. Tell him I'll keep him informed of further developments; but I really expect no more to-night."

Eve disappeared into the darkness which was all but complete. In the north, toward Bronson Beta's pole, hung a faint aurora, and above it shone some stars; but most of the sky was obscured. There was no moon, of course. Strange, still to expect the moon—a moon gone "with yesterday's sev'n thousand years."

Another girl joined the group of men standing and shivering near the great cannon-like tube aimed heavenward.

"Anything stirring?" asked Shirley Cotton's voice.

"Not now," replied Tony.

"It's cold," said Shirley. "It's surely coming on cold, these nights."

"Nothing to what it will be," observed a man's voice gloomily. It was Williamson, who had been insensible all through the fight, like the rest of the camp. Now he had completely recovered, but his spirits, like those of many of the others, seemed low.

"How cold will it be—soon?" asked Shirley.

"Do you want to know?" Williamson challenged. "Or are you just asking?"

"I've heard," said Shirley, taking no offense, "an awful lot of things. I know we're going out toward Mars. But how cold is it out there?"

"That's been figured out a long time," Williamson returned. "They taught that back in school on earth. The surface temperature of a planet like the earth at sixty-seven millions miles' distance from the sun—the distance of Venus—would be one hundred and fifty-one degrees Fahrenheit. The mean temperature of the earth, at ninety-three million miles from the sun—where we used to be—was sixty degrees. The mean temperature of the earth, if it were a hundred and forty-one million miles from the sun—the distance of Mars—would be minus thirty-eight—thirty-eight degrees below zero, Fahrenheit.

"The earth went round the sun almost in a circle—it never got nearer to the sun than ninety-one million miles, and never got farther away than about ninety-four million; so our temperatures there never varied, by season, beyond comfortable limits for most of the surface of the earth.

"But riding this planet, we aren't going around the sun in any such circle; our orbit now is an ellipse, with the sun in a focus but not in the center. So we'll have a very hot summer when we go close to Venus, where the surface temperature averages a hundred and fifty-one; but before we get that summer, we go into winter out by Mars where normal temperatures average about forty below zero—a hundred degrees less than we're used to. We're headed there now."

"Didn't—didn't *they* know that, too?" Shirley gestured a white-clad arm toward the landing-field where the attackers of the camp had been annihilated.

"They must have."

"Then why—why—"

Peter Vanderbilt's urbane voice finished for her: "Why didn't they spend the last of the good weather trying to capture or kill us? Because they also came from that pugnacious planet Earth."

The reality of what had happened, while they were sunk in stupor, still puzzled some of Hendron's people.

"Why weren't they content to let us alone? There's room enough on Bronson Beta. . . . Good God! Imagine two groups of human beings as stranded as ourselves, as forlorn in the universe, as needful of peace and coöperation—fighting!"

"Men never fought for room," Walters, a biologist, objected. "That was just an excuse they gave when civilization advanced to the point when men felt they ought to give explanations for fighting. There surely was plenty of room in the North American continent in pre-Columbian times, with a total population of perhaps three million Indians in all the continent north of Mexico; but the principal occupation—or pastime or whatever you call it—was war. One tribe would sneak a hundred miles through empty forest to attack another. It wasn't room that

108

men wanted in ancient America—or in medieval Europe, for that matter."

"What was it, then?" asked Shirley.

"Domination!" said Walters. "It's an essentially human instinct—the fundamental one which sets man off from all other animals. Did you ever know of any other creature which, by nature, has to dominate? Not even the king of the beasts, the lion. To realize how much more ruthless men are than lions were, imagine a man with the physical equipment of a lion, among other beasts, and imagine him letting all the weaker ones go their own way and killing only what he needed for food.

"You might imagine one lion-man doing that, but you couldn't imagine all lion-men so restrained. You know they would have cleaned up the neighborhood, just to show they could, and then fought among themselves to the finish of many of them.

"That is the nature we brought with us from the world; it is too much to expect it to desert us all here. It couldn't; it didn't."

"That's certainly clear," Williamson agreed.

"That element in our nature," the biologist proceeded, "scarcely had opportunity to reassert itself because of our difficulties in merely maintaining ourselves. The enemy—the party that attacked us—solved their difficulties, evidently, by moving into one of the Other People's cities. From what Tony told us of the city he examined, their city probably supplied them with everything they lacked, and with more equipment and appliances of various sorts than they dreamed existed.

"They found themselves with nothing-to do; they found already built for them dwellings, offices and palaces; they found machinery—even substances for food. They were first in possession of the amazing powers of the original people of this planet. They learned of our presence, and decided to dominate us.

"I have come to believe that probably they would not have killed us; but they wanted us all under their control."

Eve returned to the group. She did not speak, and in the dim light of the stars she was indistinguishable from the other girls; yet Tony knew, as she approached him, that it was Eve.

She halted a few steps away, and he went to her.

"Father asks for you, Tony," she said in a voice so constrained that he prickled with fear.

"He's weaker?" said Tony.

"Come and see," she whispered; and he seized her hand, and she his at the same time, and together through the dark they went to the cabin where lay the stricken leader.

A cloth covered the doorway so when the door opened it

let out no shaft of light to betray the camp to any hovering airman of the enemy. Tony closed the door behind him and Eve, thrust aside the cloth and faced Hendron, who was seated upright in bed, his hair white as the cover of his pillow.

His eyes, large and restless, gazed at his daughter and at his lieutenant; and his thin white hands plucked at the blanket over him.

"Have they come again, Tony?" he challenged. "Have they come again?"

"No, sir."

"Those that came, they are all dead?"

"Yes, sir."

"And none of us?"

"No, sir."

"Arm some of yourselves unto the war, Tony."

"What, sir?"

" 'Arm some of yourselves unto the war,' Tony! 'For the Lord spake unto Moses, saying:

" 'Avenge the children of Israel of the Midianites; afterwards shalt thou be gathered unto thy people.

" 'And Moses spake unto the people, saying, Arm some of yourselves unto the war, and let them go against the Midianites.'

"How many of the Midianites have you slain, Tony?"

"More than fifty, sir," said Tony.

"There might be five hundred more. We don't know the size of their ship; we don't know how many came. It's clear they have taken possession of one of the cities of the Other People."

"Yes, sir."

"Then we must move into another. You must lead my people into the city you found, Tony—the city I shall never see."

"You shall see it, sir!" Tony cried.

"Don't speak to me as if to a child!" Hendron rebuked him. "I know better. I shall see the city; but I shall never enter it. I am like Moses, Tony; I can lead you to the wilderness of this world, but not to its promised places. Do you remember your Bible, Tony? Or did you never learn it?

"I learned whole chapters of it, Tony, when I was a boy, nearly sixty years ago, in a little white house beside a little white church in Iowa. My father was a minister. So I knew the fate of the leader.

" 'And the Lord said unto Moses, Behold, thy days approach that thou must die: call Joshua'—that is you, Tony—'and present yourselves, that I may give him a charge.

" 'Charge Joshua and encourage him, and strengthen him; for he shall go over before this people, and he shall cause them to inherit the land which thou shalt see.' Joshua—my

110

Joshua, Tony, we must move, move, move to-night. Move into one of their cities. 'Thou art to pass over Jordan this day,' Tony, 'to cities great and fenced up to heaven.'"

Hendron stopped speaking and fell back on his pillow. His eyes closed.

"Yes, sir," Tony said softly.

"The cities I shall never see!" Hendron murmured with infinite regret.

"But, Father—" Eve whispered.

The old man leaned forward again. "Go, Tony! I throw the torch to you. Your place is the place I occupied. Lead my people. Fight! Live! Become glorious!"

"You'd better leave," Eve said. "I'll watch here."

Tony went out into the darkness. He whispered to a few people whom he encountered.

Presently he stood inside the circular room that was all that remained of the Ark. No vent or porthole allowed light to filter into the cold and black night. With him were Ransdell and Vanderbilt and Jack Taylor, Dodson and Williamson, Shirley Cotton and Von Beitz, and many others.

Tony stood in front of them: "We're going to embark for one of the Other People's cities—at once. The night is long, fortunately—"

Williamson, who had once openly suggested that Tony should not become their leader, and who had welcomed the reappearance of Ransdell, now spoke dubiously.

"I'm not in favor of that policy. We have the blast tubes—"

"I cannot question it," Tony answered. "Hendron decided."

"Then why isn't he here?"

There was silence in the room. Tony looked from face to face. His own countenance was stone-like. His eyes stopped on the eyes of Ransdell. His voice was low.

"Hendron turned over the command to me."

"Great!" Ransdell was the first to grasp Tony's hand. "I'm in no shape for the responsibility like that I had for a while."

Tony looked at him with gratitude burning in his eyes.

"Orders, then?" Ransdell asked, grinning.

That was better for Tony; action was his forte in life. He pulled a map from his pocket.

"Copy of the globe James and I found in the Other People's city," he said.

They crowded around it: a rough projection of imaginary parallels and meridians marked two circles.

"Here," said Tony, pointing with a pencil, "is where we are. To the south, Ransdell's camp. West, the city we explored. The Midianites—" He smiled. "That's Hendron's term for the Asiatics and Japs and Germans; it comes from the Bible—the Midianites are camped somewhere to the north-

111

west. You note a city at this point. They doubtless occupy that city. Now—"

His pencil moved south and west of the position where they were camped. "You see that there's another city here. It's west of a line between here and Ransdell's camp, and about equidistant from both. I suggest we go to that city—to-night, by the Other People's road—and occupy it. The distance can't be too great. We'll use the tractors."

He then addressed those who could not see the map: "Imagine that we are camped in New York, Ransdell in Washington, the Midianites in Utica—then this other city is about fifty miles west of where Philadelphia would be, while the city James and I explored is say a hundred miles north of Pittsburgh. That's about correct."

"We'll move?" Vanderbilt asked. "Everything?"

"No. People—necessities. Come back for the rest."

Williamson stepped forward. "Congratulate you, Tony. Glad."

Others congratulated Tony. Then he began to issue orders.

The exiles from earth prepared to march at last from the wilderness. They prepared hastily and in the dark. Around them in the impenetrable night were the alarms of danger. They hurried, packing their private goods, loading them onto the lumber-trucks, and gathering together food-supplies and those items of equipment and apparatus most valuable to the hearts of the scientific men who composed the personnel.

An hour after issuing his orders, Tony stepped into Hendron's house. Eve was there.

"How is he?"

She shook her head. "Delirious."

Tony stared at the girl. "I wonder—"

She seized his hand. "I'm glad you said that!"

"Why?"

"I don't know. Perhaps because I'm half-hysterical with fatigue and anxiety. Perhaps because I want to justify him. But possibly because I believe—"

"In God?"

"In some kind of God."

"I do also, Eve. Have your father ready in half an hour."

"It'll be dangerous to move him."

"I know—"

Their voices had unconsciously risen—and now from the other room came the voice of Hendron: " 'And ten thousand at thy right hand: but it shall not come nigh thee.' "

They whispered then. "I'll have him ready," Eve said.

"Right. I'm going out again."

"Tony!" It was Hendron again. "I know you are there! Hurry them. For surely the Midianites are preparing against you."

"Yes, Cole. We'll go soon."

In the night and the cold again, Tony looked toward the aurora-veiled stars, as if he expected almost to catch sight of God there. To his ears came the subdued clatter of the preparation for departure.

Vanderbilt called him, called softly. It was perhaps foolish to try to be quiet as well as to work in the dark—but the darkness somehow gave rise to an impulse toward the stealth.

"Tony!"

"Here, Peter!"

The New Yorker approached, a figure dimly walking. "The first truck is ready."

"Dispatch it."

"Right. And the second will start in thirty minutes?"

"Exactly."

"Which will you take?"

"Second."

"And who commands the first?"

"Ransdell."

Vanderbilt went away.

Tony watched the first truck with its two trailers—one piled full of goods, the other jammed with people. They were like soldiers going to war, or like refugees being evacuated from an endangered position. They lumbered through the dark and out of sight—silhouettes against the stars. . . . Motor sounds. . . . Silence.

When the second convoy was ready, Tony and Williamson carried Hendron aboard on a litter. The old man seemed to be sleeping. Eve walked beside him.

The motor ahead emitted a muffled din. Wheels turned; the three sections bumbled into the blackness toward the Other People's road. When they had reached it, travel became smooth; a single ray of light, a feeble glow, showed the way to the driver.

The people in the trailer wrapped themselves in an assortment of garments and blankets which they had snatched up against the somber chill of this early autumn night on Bronson Beta. Tony did not recognize a shawled figure who crowded through the others to his side until he heard his voice.

"It is a shame to be driven out like this!"

"It is, Duquesne."

"But by whom—and for what?"

"I don't know."

The Frenchman shook his fist toward the northwest. "Pigs!" he muttered. "Beasts! Dogs!"

For an hour they traveled.

They crossed through the valley where they had cut lumber, and they went over the bridge of the Other People. They reached a fork in the road among foothills of the western range. It was a fork hidden by a deep cut, so that Tony and Eliot James had not seen it on their flight of exploration. Then, suddenly, the light of the truck-tractor went out, and word came back in the form of a soft human shushing that made all of them silent.

CHAPTER XII

TONY leaped over the side of the trailer in which he had been standing near Hendron's litter.

He ran forward. "What is it?"

The driver of the truck—Von Beitz—leaned out in the Stygian dark.

"We saw a light ahead!" he whispered.

"Light?"

"Light. . . . Light ahead!" The word ran among the passengers.

"Where?" Tony asked.

"Over the hills."

Tony strained his eyes; and against the aurora and the stars he saw a series of summits. He could even see the metal road that wound over the hills, gleaming faintly. But there was no light.

Not a sound emerged from the fifty human beings packed in the caravan behind.

The wind blew—a raw wind. Then there was a soft, sighing ululation.

Tony gripped Von Beitz' arm. "What was that?"

"God knows."

They strained their eyes.

Tony saw it, then: a shape—a lightless and incomprehensible shape, moving slowly on the gleaming surface of the road—toward them.

"See!" His voice shook.

Von Beitz jumped from his seat behind the wheel. He stood beside Tony.

"Don't see anything."

Tony pointed ahead. "Something. Dipped into a valley. There!"

Again the soft moaning sound. Again the meaningless shape topped a rise and slithered along the road toward them. Its course was crooked, and suggested the motion of an animal that was sniffing its way along.

"Mein Gott!" Von Beitz had seen it.

"It looks"—Duquesne had come up behind them—"like a snuffing dog."

"A dog—as big as that?"

Duquesne shrugged, and murmured to Tony: "It comes this

115

way on the road. We must meet it. Perhaps it is an infernal machine. An enemy scout."

Tony reached into the front compartment of the truck and brought out two rifles. Then he stuffed three grenades into his pocket. He turned to the trailer.

"Vanderbilt!" he whispered.

"Yes, Tony!"

"Something's coming toward us on the road. We're going up to meet it. You're in charge here. If I fire—one, two, one—that means try to rush through on full power—without stopping for us."

"Right. *Bing—bing-bing—bing*—and we lunge."

Tony, Duquesne and Von Beitz began to hurry along the road.

They went to a point about three hundred yards from the trailers. There they waited. The ululation was louder now.

"Sounds like an animal," Von Beitz whispered nervously.

"I hope to God it is!" Duquesne murmured reverently.

Then it topped a nearer hill. It was a bulk in the dark. It wavered along the road at the pace of a man running.

"Machinery!" Tony said softly.

"An engine!" Duquesne murmured simultaneously.

"Ready!" Tony said. "I'll challenge it when its gets near. If it goes on, we'll bomb it."

They waited.

Slowly, along the road toward them, the thing came. They knew presently that it was a vehicle—a vehicle slowly and crazily driven. It loomed out of the night, and Tony stood up at the roadside.

"Stop or we'll blow you up!"

He yelled the words.

At the same time he took the pin of a bomb between his teeth.

The bulk slewed, swerved, slowed. There was a click, and the curious engine-sound ceased.

"I'll give up!" It was a woman's voice.

Tony shot a flashlight-beam at the object. It was one of the large vans the Bronson Betans had used in their cities. Its strange sound was explained by its condenser-battery-run motor.

From it stepped a girl.

Duquesne switched on another light. There was no one else in the van.

"Sacré nom!" he said.

The girl was in breeches and a leather coat. She began to speak.

"You can't blame me for trying—anyway."

"Trying what?" Tony asked, in an odd and mystified tone.

"Are you Rodonover?" she asked.

Tony's skin prickled. He stepped up to the girl. "Who are you, and where did you come from?"

"You're not Rodonover! You're—*oh, God!* You're the Other People!" she said. Tony noticed now that her accent was British. And he was suddenly sure that she did not belong to Hendron's camp, or to Ransdell's. She had not been in Michigan. She had not come to Bronson Beta with them. But her use of the phrase *Other People* startled him.

"We come from earth," he said. "We're Americans."

She swayed dazedly, and Williamson took her arm.

"Better duck the lights," Tony said.

They were in the dark again.

The girl sniffled and shook herself in a little shuddering way, and suddenly poured out a babble of words to which they listened with astonishment.

"I've been a prisoner—or something like it—since—the destruction of earth. To-day I escaped in this van. I'd been running it. That was my job. I knew you were somewhere out here, and I wanted to tell you about us."

"We'll walk back," Tony said. "Can we pass that thing?"

Von Beitz looked. "*Ja,*" he said. He had never spoken German to them before, but now in his intense excitement, he was using his mother tongue.

Tony took the girl's arm. "We're Americans. You seem to know about us. Please try to explain yourself."

"I will." She paused, and thought. They walked toward the silent, waiting train. "You know that other space-ships left earth besides yours?"

Tony said grimly: "We do."

"You've been attacked. Of course. One ship left from Eastern Asia. Its crew were mixed nationalities."

"We know that."

"They're living in a city—a city that belonged to the original inhabitants of this place—north of here."

"And we know that too."

"Good. A ship also left the Alps. An English ship."

"So—"

"I was on that ship. The Eastern Asiatic expedition came through safely. We came down in a fog. We fell into a lake. Half of us, nearly, were drowned. The Russians and Japs—and the others—found us the next day. They fought us. Since then—they've made us work for them. Whoever wouldn't—they killed."

"Good God! How many—"

"There were three hundred and sixty-seven of us left," she said. "Now—there are about three hundred and ten."

The truck loomed up ahead. Tony spoke rapidly. "We are moving from our camp at night. We intend to occupy a city

117

before morning. You'll come with us. My name, by the way, is Tony Drake."

He felt her hand grasp his own.

"Mine is—or was—Lady Cynthia Cruikshank."

"Peter!"

Vanderbilt sprang from the trailer and ran up the road. "You safe, Tony?"

"Safe. This is Lady Cynthia Cruikshank. She'll tell you her story. I think we'd better move."

"Right."

Von Beitz was already in his seat. Tony vaulted aboard. The train started.

Lady Cynthia began a detailed account of the landing of the English ship. Tony moved over beside Eve.

"How's your father?"

"You can't tell. Oh—Tony—I was terrified!"

He took her hand.

"We could see it—up there in the dark, wabbling toward where we knew you were waiting."

He nodded. "It was pretty sour. Listen to her, though—she's got a story."

They listened. When she had finished, long and dark miles had been put behind. The uncomfortable passengers had stood spellbound, chilly, swaying, listening to her narrative. Now they questioned her.

"Why did the Midianites seize you?" one asked.

"Midianites?"

"That's what we call the 'Asiatic Expedition.' "

The Englishwoman laughed softly. "Oh, Oh, I see. Joshua! Not inapt. Why—because they want to run everything and rule everything on this planet. And because their men greatly outnumber their women." She spoke bitterly. "We'd chosen the pride of England. And pretty faces—"

"Why," some one else asked, "did you wabble so horribly?"

"Wabble?"

"Weave, then. In that Bronson Beta van you drove?"

"Bronson Beta? Oh—you used the astronomical name for this planet. Why—I wabbled because I had to turn my lights out when I saw you coming, and I could only stay on the road by driving very slowly and letting the front wheels run off the edge. When they did, I yanked the car back onto the pavement."

Several people laughed. The van bumbled on toward the promised land. Some one else asked: "What did you call this planet?"

Lady Cynthia replied: "We in our ship—thought— just Britannia. But the people who captured us called it Asiatica. You must realize that when I say captured, I don't mean that in the sense that we were jailed. We lived among them—

were part of them. Only—we weren't allowed arms—and we were forced to live by their laws."

"What laws?"

"German was to be their universal language. We had to learn it. Every woman was to be married. We had been given three months to choose mates. We were to bear children. There was no property. No God. No amusements or sports. No art—except for education—propaganda, you might call it. No love, no sentiment. We were being told to consider ourselves as ants, part of a colony. The colony was all-important, the individual ants—nothing."

"Swell," said one of the younger men from the dark.

Lady Cynthia nodded.

"How did you escape?"

"I'd elected to marry a leader. I was considering—seriously —jumping from a building in one of the cities. But I had a little more freedom than most. I was assigned to truck-driving. I went out every day to the gardens for vegetables. I befriended one of the guards there—I made rather deceitful promises to him; and he let me enjoy what I had told him was a craving of mine—going for a spin alone. I went—and I didn't come back."

Duquesne asked: "You knew where to find us?"

"Vaguely. In our city—the city was called Bergrad, by them—there had been discussions of you. Our captors called you American rabble. They are determined to subdue you."

"Sweet!" said Williamson.

"Of course—in the last days on earth—I'd read about you. I knew two or three of your party. I knew Eliot James. He'd stayed once at our castle. Is he——"

"Very much so," said Tony happily.

"That will be marvelous! And how many of you——"

Tony explained. "We have two camps."

"So I heard."

"A van has gone ahead of us. It will deposit its stores and passengers at the new city, and then start at once to the other camp. We did not dare radio."

"They listen for you all day," said Lady Cynthia. "And at night. But my other friends: Nesbit Darrington? Is he here?"

There was silence.

"I see," she said slowly. "And Hawley Tubbs?"

Again there was silence.

The Englishwoman sighed heavily. "So many people! Ah, God, so many! Why was I spared? Why do I stand here this night with you on this foreign world? . . . I'm sorry!"

Tony jumped. Von Beitz was rapping on the window of his driver's compartment. Tony peered through the window. Von Beitz was pointing ahead.

Tony's eyes followed the German's arm. Far away on the

horizon the night sky was pinkly radiant. At first he thought that it was the aurora. Then he knew. He turned to the others.

"There are the lights of our new home!"

A murmur rose, a prayer, a hushed thanksgiving. . . .

The tractor-truck and its two huge trailers rumbled toward the distant illumination.

Tony bent over Eve. "We'll be safe soon, dear."

"Yes, Tony."

They descended into a long and shadowed cut. At the end was a slow curve.

Then they came out on a valley floor.

In the valley's center was the bubble of the new city. It was not as large as the first one they had seen. But its transparent cover was identical; and like the first, it was radiant with light. Did the lights go on all over Bronson Beta every night? Had Ransdell turned them on? They did not know. They only saw out on the valley floor the resplendent glory of a Bronson Betan city at night, and because none there save Tony and Lady Cynthia had seen the sight before, their emotions were ineffable.

There, under its dome, stood the city, its multi-colored metal minarets and terraces, its spiral set-backs and its network of bridges and viaducts, shining, strong, incredibly beautiful.

"Surpassing a dream of heaven!" Duquesne murmured.

"Magnificent!" Williamson whispered. There were tears on almost every enraptured countenance.

Then a strange thing happened:

Cole Hendron stirred.

Eve dropped a tear on his face as she bent over him. She let go of Tony's hand to adjust the blankets over her father. But Hendron put her hand aside and slowly, majestically, sat up in his improvised cot.

"Father!" she said.

He was staring at the city.

"Cole!" Tony whispered.

The others in the trailer sensed what was happening. They looked at their old leader. And the caravan moved forward so that in the light of the city, faces became visible.

Cole Hendron stood now.

"Tony, my son!" His words rang like iron.

"Yes—"

The greatest scientist earth had ever produced stretched out his two hands toward the city. "The promised land!" Now his voice was thunder.

Eve sobbed. Tony felt a lump swelling in his throat.

Hendron looked up to the cold stars—to Arcturus and Sirius and Vega.

"Father!" he said in a mighty voice. "We thank Thee!"

Then he pitched forward.

Tony caught him, or he would have fallen to the earth. He lifted him back on his pallet and opened his coat. Dodson pushed through the herded people.

The head of the physician bent over the old man's chest. He looked up.

"His brain imagined this," said Dodson. "He brought us here in his two hands, and with his courage as our spiritual flame we shall remain!"

It was an epitaph.

Eve wept silently. Tony stood behind her with his hands on her shoulders—mute consolation and strength.

"Hendron's dead," was whispered through the throng.

The city was now looming in front of them, the buildings inside visible in detail and rising high over the heads of the travelers.

Von Beitz was driving rapidly. This was the most dangerous part of the trip, this dash across the lighted exterior of the city, without protection of any kind.

They could see presently that the great gate was open. Figures stood beside it, motionlessly watching their approach.

Light poured over them. They were inside the city. They slowed to a stop at the mighty portals boomed shut behind them.

Ransdell had been one of those waiting. Tony leaped out, and Ransdell smiled.

"Welcome!"

"Hendron's dead."

"Oh!"

The people began to alight—but they were quiet and made no attempt to celebrate their security.

Others came up.

"We'll take his body into one of these buildings," said Tony. "In the morning we'll bury him—out there, under the sun and the stars—in the bare earth of Bronson Beta."

Behind the voyagers through the night was a wide avenue, and at its center in the city stood a magnificent building. Some one of those who came in the first caravan had brought a large American flag and fixed it on an improvised pole. It was hanging there when they entered the gates. Tony noticed it presently as it was being drawn down to half-mast.

No other symbol of the death of their leader was made that night. There were too many important things to do, things upon which their existence depended.

Dodson, Duquesne and Eve sat in a room with Hendron's body—a room of weird and gorgeous decoration, a room of august dimensions, a room indirectly illuminated. If they had but known, they would have been glad that Cole Hendron lay in the hall of the edifice that had been home of the greatest

121

scientists of Bronson Beta some incalculable age before them.

Tony left the watchers reluctantly and sought Ransdell. The former South African was in a smaller chamber in the building where the Stars and Stripes hung at half-mast.

"He died," said Tony to Ransdell and the other people with him, "standing in the trailer, thanking God, and staring at the city."

"Like Moses," said Ransdell. "A single glimpse of the Promised Land."

"Like Moses." Tony looked with astonishment at the man. He had not imagined Ransdell as a reader of the Scriptures.

"We must go on. He'd want it," said Williamson.

Tony nodded. "The first van has left for your camp?"

"Yes."

"And the second?"

"Fifteen minutes ago."

"It is about four miles from the road to your camp. But I think those tractors can pull all the way in. They'll bring nothing but people—and they'll be able to accommodate every one." He looked at his watch and pondered. "They should be here before daybreak. Now—I don't know about the power and light in these cities. Von Beitz, suppose you take another man and start an investigation of its source. We'll want to know that. The other city I investigated had enormous subterranean granaries and storehouses. Williamson—you search for them. Jack—you take care of housing."

"We've been working on that," said Ransdell. "There's ample room already available—for your people and mine."

"Good. Water?"

"We've located the main conduits. They're full. The water's apparently fresh. We've turned it on in this building. We're running a set of fountains in the rear court and filling a swimming-pool to be sure it is fresh."

"Right.—Shirley, find Kyto and arrange for a meal at daybreak. Prepare for five hundred—we're almost that many."

Shirley left.

Hastily Tony dispatched others from his improvised headquarters. Soon he was alone with Ransdell.

"I got your signal," he said. "You wanted every one cleared out but me. Why?"

Ransdell glanced at the door. "For a good reason, Tony. I've got something important to tell you."

"What?"

"There's somebody else in this city."

Tony smiled. "I know that feeling. James and I had it. You get used to it."

Ransdell shrugged. "I'm not queasy—you know. I don't get those feelings. Here's my evidence: I drove the first caravan. When I reached the gates, I saw something whisk

122

around a distant building. It might have been a man—it might have been the end of one of these little automobiles. . . . Then, after I'd started things going, I took a walk. I found this."

He handed Tony a half of a sandwich. A bite had been taken out of it—a big bite. The other half and the filling were missing. But the bread was fresh.

Tony stared at it. "Good Lord!"

"That bread would be stale in twelve hours, lying as it was on the street."

"Anything else?"

"This building was open. The others were shut. We used your instructions for getting into them. But in here, things were—disturbed. Chairs, tables. There was a ball of paper on the floor of this room. Nothing on it." Ransdell produced a crumpled sheet of paper.

"The Other People had paper," Tony said.

"Not paper watermarked in English."

Tony walked around the room, pondering this. "Well?"

"There can't be many people. Since we arrived, ever since I found the sandwich, I've been conducting a search. So have five other small posses. Nothing was discovered, however."

"I see." Tony sat down. "The Midianites have foreseen our scheme, then, and put watchers here."

"I think so."

"Do you believe that we can find them to-night?"

"You know better than I."

"I doubt it," Tony answered. "It would take months to cover every room, every subterranean chamber."

"Of course," said Ransdell, "it might be some one else. The Midianites might have explored here—and left. The Other People had bread—like ours more or less; and this isn't familiar—exactly. It looks like whole wheat—"

Tony grinned. "You aren't seriously suggesting that the Other People may be alive here?"

"Why not?"

"Well—why not? Anyway—some one is. Spies—ghosts—some one."

It was growing light when the trucks came back from the other camp. They were crowded with cheering people, who grew silent when they heard of Hendron's death. Tony and Ransdell went to greet them. Breakfast was ready; it was served from caldrons borrowed from the Other People's kitchens.

Tony was busy with hot soup when Peter Vanderbilt approached him. "Where's Von Beitz?"

"I don't know."

"Didn't he see you?"

"No."

Vanderbilt scowled. "Funny! Quarter of an hour ago I saw him a few streets from the square here. He was on his way to tell you something about the power. He turned a corner. I thought I heard the first faint part of a yell—choked off. I hustled around the same corner, but he was out of sight. It seemed odd—he'd have had to run pretty fast to make the next corner. So I jammed along looking for him. No sign of him. Thought he was reporting to you. But I went back. Nothing to see at the spot where he'd left me. I—"

Tony was calling. "Taylor—Williamson—Smith—Alexander—look for Von Beitz. Arm yourselves."

But two hours later Von Beitz had not been found.

CHAPTER XIII

DAY broke with its long, deliberate dawn, while the strange, eerie glow of the night light that illumined the city faded. There was no sound in the streets but the scuffing feet of the sentinels whom Tony had posted, and the echo of their voices as they made occasional reports to each other or called a challenge.

Now the night watch was relieved; and with the brightening day, searching parties set out again under strict order not to separate into squads of less than six, and to make communication, at regular intervals, with the Central Authority.

This was set up in the offices near the great hall in which Hendron lay dead—the Hall of Sciences of the Other People.

So the enormous chamber manifested itself. It had been, one time, a meeting-place of august, noble-minded Beings. The dimensions and proportions of the great hall, its modeling and decorations, declared their character. It was most fitting that the greatest scientist from Earth—he who attempted and triumphed in the flight through space—lie here in this hall.

Thus Hendron lay in state, his face stern and yet peaceful; and his people, whom he had saved from the cataclysm, slowly filed past.

Eve, his daughter, stood at his side.

Dodson had begun the vigil with her, but he had retired to a couch at the end of the great hall, where he had dropped down, meaning to rest for a few moments. Exhaustion had overcome him, and he slept, his huge chest rising and falling, the coat-sleeve of his armless shoulder moving on the floor with the rhythm of his breathing.

As the people filed from the hall, they passed Dodson, gazing at him but never disturbing him. His empty sleeve brought keenly to mind the savage battle in Michigan in the horrible hours when the mob there assailed the camp near the end of the waiting for the escape from earth. Where was Michigan? Where was the earth now?

The people passed more slowly for gazing back again at the catafalque of the Bronson Betans, whereon Hendron lay. . . .

Maltby, the electrical engineer, together with four others was exploring behind the walls of the building. Power was "on." Impulses, electrical in character, were perceptible; and Maltby was studying the problem of them.

Their manifestations were most conspicuous in the glow

which illumined the dome over the city at night, and which so agreeably lighted certain interiors by night and by day. These manifestations resembled those which Tony and Eliot James had reported from the first Sealed City which they had entered.

Maltby and his assistants discovered many other proofs of power impulses.

The source of the power they could not locate; but Lady Cynthia's account of the activities of the "Midianites" suggested to Maltby a key to the secret.

"I believe," Maltby said, "that the Bronson Betans undoubtedly solved the problem of obtaining power from the inner heat of the planet, and probably learned to utilize the radium-bearing strata under the outer crust. They must have perfected some apparatus to make practical use of that power. It is possible, but highly improbable, that the apparatus came through the passage of cold and darkness in such state that when the air thawed out and the crust-conditions approached normal, it set itself in operation automatically.

"What is far more probable is that the Midianites have discovered one installation of the apparatus. We know from Lady Cynthia that they are months ahead of us in experimenting with Bronson Betan machinery. I believe that they have put in order and set going the power-impulse machinery connected with the city which they have occupied.

"The impulses from that installation may be carried by cables under the ground; more probably, however, they are disseminated as some sort of radio-waves. Consequently they reach this city, as they reached the city that Tony and James entered, and we benefit from them."

Behind the wall at the end of the hall, near the couch upon which Dodson slept, one of Maltby's men came upon a mechanism connected with what was, plainly, a huge metal diaphragm. He called his chief, and the entire party of engineers worked over the mechanism.

Suddenly sound burst forth. Voices! Singing! And the thunder of a tremendous chorus filled the hall! Men's voices, and women's! How triumphant, sublime, the chant of this chorus!

No syllable was of itself understandable; the very scale and notes of the music were strange. Strange but magnificent!

It caught all the people in the hall and awed them into stillness. They stood staring up, agape; not frightened at all, only uplifted in their wonder!

Voices—voices of men and women a million years dead—resounded about them, singing this strange, enthralling requiem.

Eve, beside the body of her father, straightened and stood,

with her head raised, her eyes dry, her pulses pounding full again.

Tony, outside in the street, heard the chorus, and he came running in—to be checked at the entrance of the hall as though caught there in a spell. Only slowly, and as if he had to struggle through an invisible interference, could he advance; for the singing continued.

It suggested somehow, though its notes were not like, the Pilgrims' Chorus in "Tannhäuser." It was now like the "Fire Music"—now an exalted frenzy like the "Ride of the Valkyries." Some great Wagner had lived a million years ago when this planet pursued its accustomed course about its distant star!

The chorus ceased.

Tony caught Eve in his arms, lest she collapse in the reaction from her ecstasy.

"Tony! Tony, what a requiem for him! It leaves us nothing now to do for him! Oh, Tony, that was his requiem!"

Down the sunlit streets of the city the children of the earth, Dan and Dorothy, walked hand in hand, staring at the wonders about them, crying out, pointing, and flattening their noses against the show panes.

Though they plainly remembered the thrills and terrors of the Flight, they could not completely understand that the world was gone, that they had left it forever. This was to them merely another, more magic domain—an enthralling land of Oz, with especially splendid sights, with all the buildings strange in shape and resplendent in colors, with tiers of streets and breath-taking bridges. Behind the children, Shirley Cotton and Lady Cynthia strolled and stared; and along with them went Eliot James, who could not—and who did not attempt—to conceal his continued astonishments.

"Isn't this like the other city?" Shirley asked him.

"In general, but not in details," Eliot answered; and he asked Lady Cynthia: "Is it like the city where you were?"

"In general, as you say," the Englishwoman agreed. "But in detail these people certainly were capable of infinite variety. And what artisans they were!"

"And architects!" added Shirley.

"And engineers—and everything else!" said Eliot James.

"Where," demanded Dan, turning to his older companions, "where are all the people?"

"Where?" echoed Eliot to himself, below his breath, while Shirley answered the child: "They went away, Danny."

"Where did they go? . . . Are they coming back? . . . Why did they all go away? . . . What for?"

The questions of the child were the perplexities also of the scientists, which no one yet could resolve.

"Don't run too far ahead of us," Shirley bade the children

in a tone to avoid frightening them. For danger dangled over these splendid silent thoroughfares apparently untenanted, yet capable of catching away and keeping Van Beitz. Was it conceivable that survivors of the builders—the Other People—haunted these unruined remains of their own creation? Or was it that the ruthless men from earth—the "Midianites"—had sent their spies ahead to hide in this metropolis before its occupation by Hendron's people?

Tony called a council of the Central Authority to consider, especially, this problem. The Committee of Authority assembled in what had clearly been a council-chamber near to the great quiet secluded room, and yet illumined by the sunlight reflected down and disseminated agreeably and without glare.

Ten men chosen more or less arbitrarily by Tony himself composed the Committee of the Central Authority—four from the survivors of the hundred who had come from Hendron's camp, six from Ransdell's greater group; and these, of course, included Ransdell himself.

Such was the Central Authority improvised by Tony and accepted by his followers to deal with the strange and immediate emergencies arising from the occupation of this great empty city by five hundred people ignorant of it.

The searching-parties, as they returned or sent back couriers with reports, appeared before this committee.

Jack Taylor, haggard and hungry, made the first report.

"I'm back only to suggest a better search organization," Taylor said excitedly. "I took a truck and toured the widest streets at the lower levels; and some of them at the upper levels. At every corner my driver and I stopped, and yelled for Von Beitz. We didn't see a sign of life or get any reply."

"Did you see any evidence of recent—occupation?" Higgins, of the Authority, asked.

"Nothing."

Kyto brought food for Taylor, and he talked as he ate. "I've been over miles of streets, and covered only a little of the central section. The city's too damned big. If five hundred people had moved into New York when it was emptied—and nobody else was there except maybe three or four people, or a dozen who wanted to keep in hiding—what chance would the five hundred have of finding the dozen?"

"Of course there may be no dozen, or even four or five hiding people to find," Tony responded. "We can't be sure that Von Beitz fails to return because he was captured. He might have fallen when exploring somewhere; or something might have toppled on him; or he might have got himself locked in a building."

Taylor shrugged. "In that case, he'd be harder to find than the dozen who, we think, are hiding from us."

"You feel surer, I see," Tony observed, "that some people, unknown to us, are here hiding from us."

"Yes, I do."

"But without any further proof of it?"

Jack Taylor nodded. "I tell you, there are people here. I can feel it."

Duquesne came in. He had returned from a search in another section of the city.

"Rien!" he made his report explosively. "Nozzing. Except —perhaps I saw a face peering from a window—very high! It was gone—*pouf!* I entered the building. I climbed to the room where the window was. Again—*rien!* Only—as I stood there—I said: 'Duquesne, people have been in this room not long ago.' With the sixth sensation, I smell it." He was excited; but he could add nothing more positive to the account.

He also began to eat, and soon reported himself ready to go out for more investigation.

Ransdell quietly arose. "I'd like to go out again too. You don't need us, Tony," he continued, speaking for the rest of the committee as well as for himself. "It's nice of you to pretend we're necessary; but we know we're not—though we'll be glad to try to be useful when you really want us. We'll all obey you as we would have obeyed Hendron."

"You're going to join the search?" Tony asked.

Ransdell shook his head. "There's enough of us searching now. I want to join Maltby and Williamson and their men, who are working on the Bronson Beta machines and techniques."

Duquesne gestured emphatically, unable to speak for a moment because of the food crammed in his mouth.

"They are mad—mad—all but mad, our technicians! I have seen them!" he presently exclaimed. "It is the problem of the charging the batteries of the Bronson Betans that eludes them—those marvelous, amazing batteries which first we saw in the vehicle wrecked beside the road; and one of which Lady Cynthia herself operated in the vehicle that carried her to us.

"To operate the vehicle, once the charged battery is installed —that is nothing. But the secret of putting power into the battery!

"The Midianites have discovered it, my friends; but they have guarded it so that Lady Cynthia could not even suspect what it is. But if they conquered it, so may we! Ransdell is right," Duquesne ended his declamation. "That secret is far more important than further search. I too will join our technicians!"

Tony found himself alone in the great council-chamber. Now and then some one else arrived to report; but all reports, which had to do with the search for Von Beitz and for the unknown people who might have captured him, were negative. The couriers returned to their exploring squads; and the others scattered in their wondering examination of the marvels of the city.

There proved to be eight gates to this city, and four great central highways which met and crossed in the Place before the Hall of the Sciences, in which Hendron lay, and before also the splendid structure housing the council-chamber.

From right to left, before the Hall, ran a wide roadway, and another equally splendid cut across it at right angles, while obliquely, so that seen from above they must have made a pattern like the Cross of St. George, were two other highways only slightly less majestic. Each of these roads ran straight to the edge of the city, where the huge transparent dome joined the ground; at the eight points where these four roads penetrated were the gates; and at each of these gates stood a squad on watch.

High toward the top of the dome, on towers attained by arduous climbing, others of the men whom Hendron had brought from earth stood on watch, scanning the sky.

Tony strode out into the sunlight of the wide square, and he halted and lifted his head in awe.

He was in command in this city!

He had had nothing to do with creating it. A million years, perhaps, before he was born, this city had been built; and then the light which fell upon it was from some sun to which the sun of the world—the sun which now shone upon it—was a distant twinkling star. Quadrillions and quintillions of miles of space—distances indescribable in terms that the mind could comprehend—separated this city from Tony Drake, who would not be born for a million years. But it had traveled the tremendous reaches of space after it lost its sun until it found the star—the sun—that lighted the earth! So Tony Drake to-day stood here in its central square—in command.

He glanced up toward the orb of the sun; and he saw how small it was; and in spite of himself his shoulders jerked in a convulsive shiver.

"Tony!"

He heard his name, and turned. Eve had come out to the square, and she approached him, quietly and calmly.

"We must—proceed now, Tony," she said.

"Proceed? Of course," he assured her gently. He had ceased to be a commander of a city built a million years before his birth and endowed with marvels which men of his time—if they had remained on earth—might not have made for themselves for another millennium. He became again Tony Drake, recently—not three earthly years ago—a young broker in Wall Street, and friend of Eve Hendron, whose father was a scientist. On earth, Tony Drake had wanted her for his wife; here he wanted her also, and especially in her grief he longed to be her close comforter.

"Your mind doesn't help you much, does it, Tony?" she said.

"At a time like this, you mean. No."

"I went once with Father and with a friend of his, Professor Rior, through the Pyramids, Tony—when we were back on earth."

"Of course," said Tony.

"It was before ever the Bronson Bodies were seen, Tony; when the earth seemed practically eternal. How out of fashion it had become to look to the end of the earth, Tony! Though once it was not. . . . I was saying that Professor Rior was showing us through the Pyramids, and he read us some of the Pyramid Texts. Did you know, Tony, that in all the Pyramid Texts the word *death* never occurs except in the negative, or applied to a foe? How the old Egyptians tried to defeat death by denying! Of course, the Pyramids themselves were their most tremendous attempt to deny death."

"Yes," said Tony.

"Over and over again, I remember, Tony, they declared that he, whom they put away, lived. I remember the words: *'King Teti has not died the death; he has become a glorious one in the horizon!'* And, *'Ho! King Unis! Thou didst not depart dead; thou didst depart living! Thou diest not!'* And *'This King Pepi dies not; this King Pepi lives forever! This King Pepi has escaped his day of death!'*

"Tony, how pitiful those protests seemed to me to be! Yet now I myself am making them.

" '*Men fall; their name is not*,' the Egyptian psalmist of the Pyramid Texts sang, Tony:

> *"Men fall;*
> *Their name is not.*
> *Seize thou King Teti by his arm*
> *Take thou King Teti to the sky,*
> *That he die not on earth,*
> *Among men."*

Tony reminded her, very gently: "Your father did not die on earth."

"No; he escaped to the sky, bringing us all with him. . . . There's the sun. How small the sun has become, Tony."

"We are farther from the sun, Eve, than men of earth have ever been."

"But we're going farther away, yet."

"Yes."

"We're swinging away from the sun; but they say—Father

131

said, and so did M. Duquesne and the rest of the scientists—
we shall swing back again when we have reached almost to
the orbit of Mars. But shall we, Tony?"

"Reach almost to the orbit of Mars?"

"Shall we swing back then, I mean. Or shall we keep on out
and out into the utter cold?"

"You don't believe your father—or Duquesne?" Tony asked.

"Yes; I believe they believed it. Yet like the old Egyptians,
they may have been declaring denials of a fact they could not
face."

"But your father and Duquesne and the rest faced the end
of the world, Eve."

"That's true; but when they faced it,—and admitted it,—
they already had schemed their escape, and ours. For this
end, if Bronson Beta drifts out into the cold without return,
there is no escape."

"No," said Tony, and combated the chill within him.

"And could they *know?*" Eve persisted. "They could calculate—and undoubtedly they did—that the path of this planet
has become an ellipse, that it will turn back again toward
the sun; but it never *has* turned back toward the sun, Tony.
Not once! This planet appeared out of space, approached the
sun and swung about it, and now is going away from the sun.
That we *know;* and that is all we do know; the rest we can
merely calculate."

"You mean," questioned Tony, "that your father said something privately, during those days he was dying, to make you
believe he was deceiving us?"

"No," said Eve. "Yet I wonder, I cannot help wondering.
But if we keep on away from the sun, don't think, Tony,
I'm—"

"What?" he demanded as she faltered and stopped.

"Unprepared," she said; and she recited:

" *'Thy seats among the Gods abide; Re leans upon thee
with his shoulder.*
" *'Thy odor is as their odor, thy sweat is as the sweat of
the Eighteen Gods.'* "

"What's that?" asked Tony.

"Something else I remembered from earth, from the Pyramid Texts, Tony. " *'Sail thou with the Imperishable Stars, sail
thou with the Unwearied Stars!'* "

She returned to the great Hall of Science of the men a million years dead, the hall wherein lay her father.

Several people crossed the square, some obviously on errands, others curiously wandering. Tony returned the hails of
those who spoke to him, but encouraged no one to linger
with him; he remained before the great hall, alone.

He had taken completely on faith the assurance which Hendron and Duquesne had given him, together with the rest of the people, that the path of this planet had ceased to follow the pattern of a parabola, but had become closed to an ellipse, and that therefore Bronson Beta, bearing these few Emigrants from Earth, would circle the sun. Tony still believed that; he had to believe it; but the death of Eve's father seemed to have shaken her from such a necessity.

He gazed about at the magnificent façades of the City of the Vanished People—his city, where he had come to the command perhaps only to die in it, with all his refugees from Earth's doomsday, as they drifted out into the coldness and darkness of space.

As this strange world had done once before with its own indigenous people! Where had they gone when the deadly drift began? Where lay the last builders of Bronson Beta?

"Hello! How's every little thing?" said a cheerful voice at his side.

Tony faced about, and confronted the red-haired girl whom he had met in Ransdell's camp, and who had not been selected for the voyage from earth; her name had not been on the lists in Michigan.

Tony remembered her name, however—Marian Jackson. She had been an acrobatic dancer in St. Louis.

She carried on her shoulder the animal stowaway of the second Ark, the little monkey, Clara.

"Can you beat this place? Can you tie it?" Marian challenged Tony cheerfully. "Gay but not gaudy, I'd call it. D'you agree?"

"I agree," acquiesced Tony, grateful for the letdown. The girl might be mentally a moron; but morons, he was discovering, had their points. This girl simply could not take anything seriously.

"But the taxi-service here is terrible," objected Marian.

"We hope to improve it," offered Tony.

The girl walked away. "Don't go into any of the buildings alone!" Tony reminded. "And even on the streets, keep close to other people!"

Marian halted, looking up. "Hello! Hello!" she cried out softly. "Look at the taxies!" And she pointed to one of the wide spiral ramps to the right.

Down the ramp Tony saw descending two Bronson Beta vehicles of the type discovered wrecked beside the first-found roadway, and duplicates of which were stored by the hundred in the first Sealed City. Here there were hundreds or thousands more of the machines.

The two that appeared were followed by two more, and these by two larger and heavier vehicles not of the passenger type, but of truck design.

"By God," cried Marian, "they got 'em going.—Hey! Hey!" she hailed them.

Tony thrilled too, but tempered his triumph by realization that, since the cars came in sight they had been descending, so that they might not be under power at all, but having been pushed to the incline of the ramp, were coasting.

The drivers seemed aware of this flaw in their demonstration, or else they could not yet be content to stop; for when they gained the ground in rapid procession, instantly they steered up the ascending spiral on the other side, and putting on power, climbed even faster than they had dropped.

That ended any doubt of their means of propulsion. Tony felt his scalp tingling. One more secret of the mechanics of these people a million years dead was in possession of his own people!

Now the vehicles, having vanished briefly, swept into sight again, still climbing; then they whirled down, sped into the square, and though braked somewhat raggedly, halted in line before Tony.

Eliot James stepped from the first with a flourish.

"Your car, sir!" He doffed his battered felt hat.

From the second car stepped the English girl Lady Cynthia. Williamson piloted the third; Maltby, Jack Taylor and Peter Vanderbilt were the other drivers.

Williamson, the electrical engineer, made his report to Tony as a hundred others gathered around.

"We discovered the technique of charging the batteries, which are beyond anything we had on earth," he said with envious admiration, "both in simplicity and in economy of power application. There is a station underground which They used. We are using it. All the batteries which we have discovered were discharged or had discharged themselves, naturally, in the tremendous time that the planet was drifting through space; but two out of three batteries proved capable of receiving a charge when placed in sockets of the charging station."

"You mean you found the charging station with its power on?" Tony asked.

Williamson looked at Maltby as if to enlist his support when replying: "We found the power on."

"What sort of power?"

"Something between the electrical impulses with which we were familiar on earth, and radio-activity. We believe the Bronson Beta scientists, before they died—or disappeared—learned to blend the two."

"Blend?" asked Tony.

Maltby took up the task of explanation. "You remember that on earth we didn't even know what electricity was; but we knew how to use it for some of our purposes. Still less

134

did we understand the exact nature of radio-activity; but we used that too. Here we have come upon impulses which exhibit some of the phenomena of electricity, and others of radio-activity. We do not understand it; but we do find ourselves able to use it."

"But the power-station below ground in order and in operation!" objected Tony.

"I think," said Maltby, "it should not have been described as a power-station, but rather as a mere distributing station. The power, I believe, does not originate in the station which we discovered, and in which we charged the batteries of these machines. Our station is, I think, merely a terminus for the generating station."

"The generating station—where?"

At this, Maltby and Williamson, the technicians, both gazed at the English girl; but she, without making direct reply, nodded to Maltby to proceed.

"She believes that the chief generating station is under the city of our Midianites. It is a far larger city than this, and was probably the metropolis of the planet—or at least of this continent. She knows that the technicians with the Asiatic party got much of the machinery of the city going weeks ago.

"We believe that their technicians are employing the power-generators of the ancient civilization here without thoroughly understanding it—or without understanding it at all beyond having learned how it works, and what they can do with the power impulses.

"We believe that we get the power here because they cannot use it themselves without giving us some of it. Probably much of the power is disseminated without wires or cables. Undoubtedly the light-impulses are—those that light this city at night and illuminate interior apartments by day.

"These impulses probably are spread in a manner similar to radio waves. Williamson feels sure that power in the charging station cannot be so explained. He feels sure that the charging station below this city must have a cable connection—underground, undoubtedly—with the generating station.

"Now, if that generating station is under the city of the Midianites, either they know they are sending us that power—or they don't know it. If they know it, they may be unable to cut off our power without also cutting off their own; but if they don't know they are now giving us power, they may find it out at any moment—and cut us off. Duquesne thinks the latter; so he has remained below with all the men he needs to keep all the charging sockets busy, while we"—Maltby smiled deprecatingly—"allowed ourselves this celebration before busying ourselves above."

"At what?" asked Tony, half stupidly, half dazedly. "At

135

what here above?" Too much was being told him at once; too much—if one had to think about it.

Marian Jackson, who had remained beside him, had heard it all; but it had not confused her. It had merely amused her. She went to Eliot James and teased him to show her the controls of his machine; and she sat in it and started it.

"Easy! Easy!" Eliot yelled, and running beside her, shut off the power. "It's perfectly easy and obvious in its steering and controls. Anybody can run it; but from the little I've seen, it must do over two hundred miles an hour, or three hundred, if you open it up. *So don't open it up!*"

The other drivers argued only less emphatically with other experimenters, and the crowd followed the machines.

"You see," Maltby was explaining to Tony, "now we know how to use their power, we ought to get other things going besides the vehicles; we ought to get a part of the city, at least, in some sort of operation."

"Of course," Tony comprehended. "Of course." And he led Lady Cynthia aside, with Williamson and Maltby. "When we have power," he challenged the English girl, "how much of its use can you show us?"

"I know how to get in and out of the buildings which have doors operated by electricity—or whatever it is. I know how they run the kitchens and the lights and baths, and things like that."

Tony said: "Then you had better take these men through a few buildings. Show them everything you've seen in operation —how it seemed to work. . . . Williamson,—Maltby,—you choose the party to go with her. When you're through with her, please ask her to come back to the Council Hall."

As Tony turned away, Jack Taylor approached him.

"You don't want a ride," he tempted his friend, "in one of the new million-year-old machines through the city?"

"Not yet," Tony said.

"Why not yet?"

"You," said Tony, "you take it for me, Jack."

"All right," said Jack, staring at him almost understandingly. "Sure. I'll take the ride for you!"

Tony retired to his deserted Hall of the Central Authority. He would have liked nothing better than to feel free to ride the ramps to the highest pinnacles as, in the square below him, others—many of them no younger than he—were preparing to do. Those allowed to experiment with the vehicles were as eager and excited as children with their first velocipedes. Tony watched them for a time enviously. No one but himself stopped him from rejoining them and claiming his right to ride the amazing highroads of this city. But not yet!

"Why?"

He glanced up toward the sun, the small, distant sun, warm

enough yet when the sky was clear, warm enough especially under the splendid shield spread over the city.

He dropped back from the window and slumped down before the beautiful desk which had served its original purpose countless years ago when this world whirled about some other star. He still was alone.

Two tiny images of men—men not of the world, but of this planet—decorated the desk, one standing at each of the far corners of the desk-top. They were not secured to the metal top, but could be plucked from their fastening without breaking. Tony toyed with them; they reminded him of little images brought from Egypt. There had been a name for them in the world. *"Ush—ushab—"* He could not quite recall it.

Some one entered. It was Eve; and he arose, awaiting her. His mood had returned to readiness for her; and she was calmer than before, and quite collected.

"What are those, Tony?" She gazed at the exquisite little images in his hand.

"You tell me, Eve."

"Why, they look like *ushabtin*, Tony."

"That's it! The *'answerers,'* weren't they? The *Respondents.*"

"Yes," she said. "The *Answerers,* the *Respondents for the Dead.* For when a man died, the Egyptians could not believe that he would not be called upon to continue his tasks as always he had done them in his life. So they placed in his tomb the *'Answerer'* to respond when he was called to perform a task after he was dead. *'O Answerer!'* the soul appealed to the statuette: *'If I am called, if I am counted upon to do any work that is to be done by the Dead . . . thou shalt substitute thyself for me at all times, to cultivate the field, to water the shores, to transport sand of the east to the west, and say "Here am I; I am here to do it!" ' "*

"I see," said Tony. "Thank you. I remember. I hope your father can feel I am his *Answerer,* Eve."

He knew, then, why he had not left the Hall of Authority to ride the ramps of the city: Cole Hendron would not have done it.

CHAPTER XIV

"WHAT weapons did the Midianites find in their city?"

"Practically none. None at all, that I know of," Lady Cynthia corrected.

She had returned from her tour with the technicians, having demonstrated all she had learned of the manner of manipulating electric locks, taps, pumping-apparatus and other mechanisms which now were capable of being operated.

Duquesne had delegated to other competent hands the continuous charging of the batteries; and he sat with Tony, as did also Eliot James in the office of the Hall of the Central Authority. So the three men listened to the girl and questioned her—to learn, with least delay, of the discoveries of the Midianites.

"We found no weapons in the city we entered," Eliot James reminded Tony. "We have come on nothing like a weapon—except some implements in what must have been a museum—here."

"The people of Bronson Beta," pronounced Duquesne, "seem to have had no need of war in their later development. Why? Because morally they had passed beyond it? I do not believe it. Other causes and conditions intervened. No greater authority upon human development than Flinders Petrie lived on earth; and what did he say?

" 'There is no advance without strife. Man must strive with Nature or with man, if he is not to fall back and degenerate.' Certainly these people did not degenerate; there is no sign in this city but of a struggle, *magnifique*—epic. But not of man against man. It was, of course, of man against Nature—even against the drift into the darkness of doom which they saw before them.

"In comparison with this struggle, strife between themselves became puny—imbecile. Long ago, long before the drift into the dark, they ceased to wage war; and so they left to our enemies none of their weapons."

"They left material, however, which could be used as weapons," the English girl corrected.

"Most certainly; the gas—gas that was merciful anesthetic for the Vanished People, probably."

"How much progress," Tony asked the girl who had been a prisoner in the other city, "did your captors make in reading the records of the Vanished People?"

"Very considerable, I am sure. They brought over from earth an especially strong staff of linguists. They seemed to have realized, even better than did our party—or perhaps than did you," the English girl said, "the importance of solving quickly the secrets of the original civilization. And they went right at it."

"How did they learn?"

"From repairing and putting into operation what seems to have been instruction-machines for the children of this planet—machines which in form are very unlike but in effect are like talking motion pictures. The machines illustrate an object, and print and pronounce a word at the same time. I have shown M. Duquesne similar machines found here."

"Maltby and Williamson together," said Duquesne to Tony, "are working on them now."

Tony arose. Again the implications of what he heard were so tremendous that he could not think of them without confusion. He put them aside for the moment.

He paced up and down. "What was on that lake where your space-ship fell?" he asked the English girl.

"Nothing. It seemed to have been burned over all around the border. The water was fresh."

"Half of you, you said, were drowned?"

"Nearly half."

"All the survivors of the crash were captured?"

"Yes; and when I escaped, I figured that three hundred and ten of us were living." She repeated the figure she had given in her first account.

"And how many were *they*—your captors—our 'Midianites'?"

"More than our number, considerably. They never said how many they were, nor gave us a chance to count them. They were always on the move."

"Where to?"

"Everywhere."

"You mean they visited several other cities?"

"Oh, yes."

"How many?"

"As many as they could find and reach. And I believe they could have found all within reach. For they had a globe of this planet. I heard about it; but they never let any of us slaves see it."

"Every city of course has a globe—or several," Tony said to himself, aloud, and asked her: "What did you pick up from them as to their opinion of the different cities?"

"They believed they had the best one."

"Did they say why they believed it the best?"

"No."

"What else could you pick up?"

"They said that one city was a good example of every other. They're all complete, and all similar in a general way."

Tony gazed out of the window. More and more of the vehicles of the Vanished People were appearing on the ramps and the streets. The sun, the small clear sun, shone down through the huge transparent dome. He swung back.

"Did they find how the air was kept fresh in the cities when they were fully—populated?"

"Yes; and they even operated some of the ventilators, though it was not necessary with so few people in the city, of course. The Original People had huge apparatus for what we would call air-conditioning, and for heating the air. The Asiatics of course were especially interested in that."

"The heating, eh? Did they think the planet was drifting again into the cold?"

"That," said Lady Cynthia, "surely worried them. They had their own computations, but they repeatedly asked what ours were. They were—and are, I am sure—especially careful with our scientists. They aren't sure, you see, that this planet will stay livably near the sun."

"Were your scientists—the English, I mean—sure?" asked Tony.

"They said they were. We'd go out into the cold nearly as far as Mars—and then come back."

"Yes," said Tony.

"That's what you think here, isn't it?" the girl appealed.

Intentionally Tony waited until Duquesne replied. "It is upon that," said the Frenchman, "that we rely. Now may I ask something? Did these people—your captors, these Midianites —find any trace as to where the builders of these *magnifique* cities and the other inhabitants went?"

"No! Constantly they talked about it. Where were they? Where did they go? And did any—survive?"

"Precisely," said Duquesne.

"We shall name this city," said Tony suddenly, "Hendron. *Hendron.* I am sure no one objects. . . . I thank you," he said to the English girl, "for all you have told us. Of course we will have much more to ask; but not now."

He left them and went out. Now he had need, as he had not before, for an inspection of the city.

Jack Taylor, seeing him, stopped one of the cars and took Tony in with him. Dizzily they spun up a twisting ramp and shot out upon a wide boulevard. They pulled up after a couple of miles, which had been coursed in barely a minute, beside a building at one of the guarded gates. On the far side of its entrance-lobby was a dining-room where a score of women were setting out upon tables the square metal plates upon which the Other People had dined perhaps a million years before.

140

Tony got out and went in. He smelled the aroma from a caldron of stew, but he was not hungry.

Higgins was there eating—excited to be sure, but eating.

"Tony!" Higgins called. "Tony!" he beckoned, rising.

Tony sat beside him. "I've been two miles underground!" Higgins reported. "Two miles! Maltby got the lifts working. I took a chance on one. Two miles down. Wonderful. Temperature rises all the way."

Tony whipped his thoughts to this problem. "Temperature rises? How could it? Didn't this planet cool—ages ago?"

"Not to the core. Only the crust. Two miles down, it was a hundred and six degrees Fahrenheit. I brought back—well, you will see."

"What?"

"Samples of what they tried to preserve below, or store for themselves. Some of it preserved, some of it not; some sealed in naked rock close to the surface and allowed to get terribly cold; some stored in metal containers and placed at strata where some heat would have endured—and did. There is enough stuff under this city to feed a Chicago for years—generations. I can't estimate how long—that is, if the stuff remained edible. The meat must be decidedly questionable."

"Meat!"

"From what animals I can't say; the vegetables from what plants I am unable to guess. Some of it may not be digestible by us. Some may be poison, we'll discover. But some must be edible, for I've eaten some and I still feel fine."

Tony went down the staircase to the hall with Higgins. In the hall a half-dozen square glasslike containers, each about two feet high and a foot in its other dimensions, had been set on tables. Covers sealed them hermetically. Their contents were visible; meat indeed—a reddish lean meat not unlike beef, and a lighter meat in small fragments; and vegetables—one appeared as long yellow cylinders, another as pink balls not unlike radishes, a third streaked with yellow and green and of an indeterminate lumpy shape.

Tony regarded the exhibit thoughtfully. "They covered their cities. They stored food-supplies for a prodigious time. They must have prepared for the journey into space."

"Of course," said Higgins.

"But where are they?"

"I do not know."

"And the heat increased with depth?"

"Exactly."

"Probably the same system that lights the cities heated the storerooms, so the precious food there would not at first freeze, crack its containers and spoil."

"Possibly." said Higgins. "I am a plant biologist, not an engineer. But I would venture to disagree, even so."

"Why?"

"I saw no evidence of heating-mechanisms. Ventilation—yes. Heat—no."

"But the air—it's warmed," Tony persisted.

"It wasn't. Observation showed the air on Bronson Beta was frozen solid—as it approached."

"We couldn't make observation under the domes."

"True. But you will find ample evidence in fractures and wash-marks to show that the air in the city was frozen. Yes— it is not heated air from the domed city which has kept these immense subterranean warehouses warm." Higgins shook his head. "Radium."

"Radium?" Tony repeated.

"Radium. Deep in this planet. Only radio-active minerals could maintain heat inside a planet during untold ages of drift through frigid space. So we may conclude that the interior of Bronson Beta is rich in such minerals."

"Then it must be dangerous—"

Higgins shrugged. "The presence of heat does not mean that rays are also present. They are doubtless absorbed by miles of rock. Hundreds of miles, maybe. But the heat is there, the activity of radium; and the rocks carry the heat almost to the surface."

There was silence in the group. Tony addressed a bystander. "Jim, get Duquesne. Tell him to turn the power-station over to Klein, and investigate this. Take Higgins with you." Then: "If the interior of Bronson Beta is warm still—then it is quite possible—"

"That the original inhabitants still persist somewhere? How? They melted air from the frozen lightless desert above them on the surface, and lived down in the radium-warmed bowels of their planet? I found no living quarters underground. But —who can say!"

Tony squared his chin against his imagination. "They are all dead," he said.

Higgins started away with Jim Turnsey, talking excitedly.

Before noon, people began to collect for their next meal. No one brought any information about Von Beitz. He had vanished. But another clew to the possible existence of living people in Hendron had been discovered. Williamson, exploring with a searching-party, had found three beds that had been slept in. He had been led to the find by an open window in a building on the northern edge of the city. Whether the beds had afforded resting-places for the Other People after the city was built, or for scouts from the Midianite camp, he could not be sure.

Three beds, with synthetic bed-covers rumpled upon them. No more.

The vast dining-room was filled as the sun came directly

overhead. Twenty of the women waited on table. Plates of stew were served, then coffee in stemmed receptacles which had handles for five fingers—five fingers a little different from human fingers, evidently, for they were awkward to use.

After that, Tony rose and spoke.

"My friends," he said, "we are safe. Our security is due to the courage and intelligence of our dead leader. No praise is adequate for him. I shall not attempt to reduce what is in your hearts to words. Prodigious labors, great dangers, even the dangers of battle and peril of annihilation at the perihelion of our orbit, lie ahead of us. Unknown conditions, diseases, poisons, threaten us. Enemies may lurk among us. An evil and powerful aggregation of fellowmen is striving and planning now to conquer us. Mysteries of the most appalling sort surround us. Still—Cole Hendron faced calmly both hazards and enigmas as awesome. We must endeavor to emulate him. And on this afternoon we shall pay a last homage to him.

"I have prepared the earth to receive him. I have named this city for him. I shall ask you to remain inside the protecting dome of this city—standing on the ramp of the western skyscraper—while Cole Hendron is buried. I do not dare to expose you all. The following will accompany me to the grave." He read from a paper: "Eve Hendron, David Ransdell, Pierre Duquesne, Eliot James and Doctor Dodson. His pall-bearers to the gate will be the men whose names I have just read, and also Taylor, Williamson, Smith, Higgins and Wycherley.

"We will march from here to the gate. You will follow; Eve will open the gate."

Once more, before Cole Hendron—Conqueror of Space—was borne from the Hall of Science, the music of Bronson Beta burst forth. Maltby once more made rise the tremendous tones from the throats a million years silent to sing Cole Hendron's requiem. Then the bearers of the body descended the staircase of the majestic building.

Cole Hendron had no coffin. Over the body was an immense black tapestry—a hanging taken from the great Hall in which he had lain.

The procession reached the street, amid muffled sobs and the sound of feet.

At the gate, Eve pulled the control lever. Hendron's closest friends and his daughter marched into the open.

It was cold.

The mourners filed up a great spiral ramp and stood watching.

Tony beside Ransdell, at the head of the bier, walked with his head down. Eve came last, a lone regal figure.

They surmounted the knoll. The body was lowered. They stood around the grave, shivering a little in the cold.

"The greatest American," Tony said at last.

"The greatest man," said Duquesne, weeping openly.

Dodson, a person of expletives rather than of eloquence, looked down at the dark-swathed and pathetic bundle. "I doubt if ever before so much has depended upon one man. A race, maybe—or a religion—or a nation; but never a species."

Eliot James spoke last. "He did not make mere history. He made a mark across cosmos and infinity. Only in memory can adequate honor be paid to him. . . . Good-by, Cole Hendron!"

Then, from the city, came suddenly the sound of earth's voices raised in Rudyard Kipling's "Recessional":

> *God of our fathers, known of old. . . .*
> *The tumult and the shouting dies,*
> *The captains and the kings depart. . . .*

Earth's voices singing to the skies, where never earth people had been before.

Tony sprinkled earth upon Hendron—earth not of the earth, but of the planet that had come from the edges of infinity to replace it. The grave was filled.

At the last Eve and Tony stood side by side, while the others rolled a great bowlder over the spot as a temporary marker.

Tony heard Eve whispering to herself. "What is it?" he said. "Tell me!"

"Only the Tenth Psalm, Tony," she whispered: *"Why standest thou afar off, O Lord? Why hidest thou thyself in times of trouble?"*

And in the far sky a speck passed and vanished beyond the hill, an abrupt and vivid reminder of the exigencies of the present.

CHAPTER XV

ELIOT JAMES sat in the apartment which he had chosen for his residence, and looked from its unornamented gray walls out over the city of Hendron. Presently he began to write. In a cabinet at his side were drawers filled with notebooks upon which was scribbled the history of the migration from earth.

"In summary," he began, "since there has been no time for detail, I will set down an outline of our conditions since our perilous removal to this city of the ancient people.

"We have shelter, the gorgeous shelter of these buildings rising in a hundred hues under their transparent dome. We have warmth, for although we are moving out into the cold at a prodigious speed, the air sucked into the city is heated. Around the rim of the dome are situated eight tremendous ventilating and air-conditioning plants. We have light in abundance—our city in the long dark of night is like day. Underground is food enough for us for unmeasured generations. Some of that food disagrees with us. Some is indigestible. In some there is no nourishment which our gastric juices can extract. Two varieties of vegetables are definitely poisonous to us. But the vast bulk of the stored produce is edible, delicious and healthful.

"We have a plethora of tools and machines. In the development of electricity the Other People have far outstripped us. Also in the extension of what we called 'robot-control.' They manufactured almost no machinery which needed human attention. A technique of photo-electric cell inspection and auxiliary engines makes every continuous mechanical process self-operating. The vast generators which run underground to supply light, the powerful motors of the ventilators, and the pumps which supply processed water from the river for our consumption, not only run by themselves but repair themselves.

"The northwest ventilator cracked a bearing last week—and in the presence of Tony and Ransdell it stopped itself, took itself apart, removed the cracked metal, put on a new bearing, reassembled itself and went into operation again. They said that the thing reminded them of the operation of one of those earthly phonographs which stops automatically and has a moving arm to take off played records and put on new ones. Only —the ventilator motor was thirty feet in height and proportionately broad and long.

"We have clothing. In our first camp there is still much clothing from earth, but we have not reclaimed it. The Bronson

145

Betans wore very light and very little clothing. We know so much about them now, that we can follow their clothing trends over ages of their history. With domed cities, always warm, they needed clothes only for ornament—as do we—in reality. But they left behind not only vast stores of garments and goods, but the mills in which the materials were fabricated. We are using the materials now. No one has yet appeared, except for amusement, in a Bronson Betan costume. Their shoes, of soft materials, are all too wide for us. Their garments were like sweaters and shorts,—both for men and women,—although the women also wore flowing robes not unlike negligees. However, we do wear portions of their garments, and we use their materials—all intermingled with the remains of the clothes we brought from earth, so that we are a motley mob.

"All Bronson Betan clothes were of the most brilliant colors —they must have loved color to live in a paradise of it. I saw Tony yesterday, for example, in a pair of old brogans, old corduroy trousers and a shirt (made by Shirley Cotton, who is now in charge of textiles) crimson in color, ornamented with green birds about a foot high—by all odds a more strident and stunning garment than I've ever seen on one of New York's four hundred. Ransdell has been running around in jade green Bronson Beta shorts, and Lady Cynthia has remodeled one of the 'negligees' I mentioned into a short metallic gold dress.

"We have baths of every temperature—private and public. The Bronson Betans were great swimmers. Jack Taylor made a study of their athletic records—and found them superior in almost every kind of event to ourselves. We have ray baths— ultra-violet and infra-red, and others we cannot use until they have been more thoroughly studied.

"We—and when I say we, I mean a score of our number— have mastered the language and much of the science of the Other People. Of course, we have not delved into their history deeply as yet, or into their fiction, or their philosophy or their arts—into their biography or their music. And their poetry is still quite incomprehensible to us.

"We fly their planes now. We run their machines."

Here Eliot James paused before continuing:

"Our personal relations are interesting at this point. I have given them little time in my diary hitherto, because of the pressure of my activities.

"Our most notable romance—the love of Tony and Dave Ransdell for Eve Hendron—has reached a culmination.

"Tony is going to marry Eve.

"There was a period shortly before our desertion of our original camp when it appeared for a little while that Eve would marry Ransdell. That was immediately after his dramatic return to our midst. Eve indubitably still holds Ransdell in high esteem, and even has a place of sorts for him in her heart. But

Tony is her kind of man. Tony is nearer her age. Tony is our leader—and she was the daughter of the greatest leader of all time. Tony worships her. They announced that they would celebrate the first wedding on Bronson Beta in the near future. And it will be the first. The Asiatics have, according to Lady Cynthia, made a complete mockery of marriage—and marriage was apparently unknown to the Other People.

"Ransdell, I think, knew always that Eve was not for him. He is a silent person, usually; but I believe that occasionally his love for Eve must have been very nearly indomitable—that he was more than once on the verge of asserting it wildly and insisting on it. He has that kind of passion—but I believe it will never be seen uncontrolled. Now he is resigned—or at least calm. And he has been not only one of Tony's ablest men, but one of his closest friends—if not his closest.

"Shirley Cotton, the siren of the city, is still in love with Tony. She talks about it in public, and tells Eve that when the biologists eventually decide that because of the larger number of women than men, two women will have to marry one man, she is going to be Tony's second wife. An odd situation—because some day that may be a necessity—or a common practice. There are now nearly ninety more women than men in our city. Eve is so brave and so broad-minded and so fond of Shirley, that if the situation ever became actual, I almost think that she would not mind. We have passed through too much to stoop now to jealousy. And all of us feel, I think, that we belong not to ourselves but to the future of man. The emotion rises from the spirit of self-sacrifice that has marked our whole adventure—rather than from such a cold, cruel and inhuman law as that which attempts to set up the identical feeling among the Midianites.

"Dan and Dorothy, under Westerley, are going to Bronson Beta school—learning the language by the talking-picture machines, just as the Other People's children did. And they are the only ones who are beginning to be able to speak it naturally. In two or three years they would be able to pass as Bronson Betan—except for their minor physiological differences.

"Dodson is having trouble with the language. He goes about the city talking to friends, eating in the central dining-room and mumbling that 'you can't teach an old dog new tricks.' He never was a good linguist—as Duquesne has proved by talking in French with him for the amused benefit of all who spoke the language. But Dodson is frantic to learn, because from illustrations in the metal books and in the screened lectures on the subject, he has found that surgery on this planet was a science far beyond terrestrial dreams. Working with him are five women and eleven men doctors.

"Jack Taylor is the sheik and Romeo of Hendron. About

147

twenty of our handsome girls and women (they are handsome again, the long strain of our first rugged months having ended) are wildly vying for his attention. The tall red-headed oarsman takes his popularity with delight—and he is seldom seen without a beautiful lady companion. When he was absent on a mission for Tony, the number of blue damsels was appalling. They could not even write to him, which seemed to distress them enormously.

"Duquesne has moved next door to the German actress who joined us in Michigan. He is working on the mystery of our power source—and 'cementing the bonds of international amity,' he says.

"Higgins has found some carefully preserved seeds in the radium-warmed cellars of the city, and he has planted them. He keeps digging them up to see if they have sprouted—which, so far, they have not; and he goes about in a perpetual daze."

Again Eliot James paused. Again he wrote:

"All those factors are on the pleasant side of our ledger. We are a civilization again. Love and clothes and cosmetics and fancy desserts and gossip and apartment-decoration have returned to us. Our animals have been collected from the encampments, and they are installed in a 'barn' made from a very elaborate theater. We have harvested and dried a quantity of the spore vegetation as hay for them. They thrive. We are wakened by a cock's crow in the morning, and we serve fresh eggs as a badge of honor with great ceremony at the rate of four or five a day. Dan and Dorothy have milk. We've made butter to go with the eggs. We should be perfectly happy, perfectly content. But—

"Where is Von Beitz?

"He vanished the day Cole Hendron died—the day we arrived here. That was sixty Bronson Beta days ago. And nothing has been seen of him or learned about him since then.

"And—

"Who dwells secretly in our city? Who stole one of our three roosters? Who stole Hibb's translation of a book on electricity? Who screamed on the street in the dead of night three days ago—turning out the people in Dormitory A to find—no one? Do the Other People still live here—watching us, waiting to strike against us? Do the Midianites have spies here?

"We are virtually agreed upon that theory. Yet we cannot find where they hide. But we do know—to our sorrow—that they have spies in other cities.

"After learning to fly the planes, we armed them. Then Tony dispatched a fleet of six to make a thorough inspection of the surrounding country and the neighboring cities. He wanted full information on the Midianites, and on the territory around us.

148

"There are two cities south of where Ransdell landed his ship. There are several inland. All were entered and explored. In the southernmost city the crew of a plane commanded by Jack Taylor was sniped upon, and two of his men were killed.

"In the nearest vacant western city Ransdell fought hand-to-hand with twelve or fourteen Midianites, who attacked his party as it came through the gate. Ransdell is a deadly shot. His five men took cover, and in a battle that lasted for three-quarters of an hour, one was wounded. Six Midianites were killed. I should say—three Japs and three Russians.

"A third plane did not return. It was subsequently sighted near the northern city occupied by the main Midianite colony —shot down and wrecked completely.

"We have been spied upon several times by planes flying over the city. A request for surrender to the Dominion of Asian Realists' was dropped twice, and our failure to reply brought one tremendous bomb—which, however, did not penetrate our tough, transparent envelope, although it was unquestionably intended for that purpose.

"It is not safe to leave the city. Twice parties on foot exploring the geology and flora outside the gates have been fired at by the enemy planes which appeared from the north and dived at them.

"It is evident that the Midianites are engaged in a war of attrition. They mean to conquer us. They mean to have Bronson Beta for themselves—or at least to insure that all human beings upon the planet will be governed by them and will live by their precepts. And Lady Cynthia has left no doubt in our minds about their desire for our women. They need what they call 'breeding females.' I think that 'need' in itself would be sufficient to cause every man and woman here to fight to the death.

"Yes, we could and should be happy here now. But—

"More than three hundred Englishmen and Englishwomen are living in subjugation, and we are unable to set them free. They are our own blood and kin. They are living under conditions at best odious, at worst horrible to them. We cannot be happy while they are virtually slaves.

"And also—Bronson Beta moves ever into cold. Bitter cold! Sixty days ago the surface of the planet was chilly. Then, for a while, it warmed again, so that we enjoyed a long fall or Indian summer. But now the chill is returning. Our seasons are due not to an inclination of our axis, as on earth, but to our eccentric orbit. The earth in winter was actually nearer to the sun than in the summer, but in winter the earth's axis caused the sun's rays to fall obliquely. Here on Bronson Beta we move from a point close to the orbit of

149

Venus to a point near that of Mars—and the change in distance from the sun will bring extremes of temperature.

"That is not all. That is not the only problem—anxious problem—which faces us in these autumn days. Shall we turn back toward the sun? Our scientists say so; but shall we? This planet has not done it yet. Its specialty seems to be a drift out into space.

"Our astrophysicists and mathematicians burn their lights far into the night of this new planet in order to anticipate the possibilities in our state. They are not romantic men.

"Meanwhile as we move out into space toward Mars, that red world increases in size and brilliance. Already it is a more vivid body than was Venus from the earth, and its color is malevolent and ominous.

"So the days and nights pass.

"Yes, our colony is returning to the happy human pursuits of love and knowledge and social relationships. But we are surrounded by mysteries, terrors, spies within our city, enemies who would conquer us; and always the red planet draws nearer—as not long ago the two bodies from cosmos drew toward the condemned and terrified earth."

As Eliot James finished that entry in his diary, he was interrupted by a knock on his door.

"Come in!" he called.

Shirley Cotton entered. She said something that sounded like *"Hopayiato!"*

"*Hopayiato* yourself," Eliot James answered.

"That's a Bronson Beta word," she said. "It means, 'How the devil are you?'—or something like that."

"Sit," said the writer. "I'm fine. What's news?"

Shirley grinned. "Want a nice mauve-and-yellow shirt? Want a pair of red-and-silver shorts?"

"Any rags? Any old iron? What's the trouble? Your clothing-department running out of orders?"

"Nope. And when we do, we'll revive fashions—so you'll have to patronize Shirley Cotton's mills, whether you want to or not."

"My God," said James with mock anger, "you'd think that after managing to abolish styles for a couple of years, people would be glad enough to give them up forever!"

She shook her head. "This year we're going in for light clothing with animal designs. Next year I plan flowers. Higgins is going to present some patterns—"

"He never will, I trust."

"I'll bribe him with a waistcoat in Bronson Beta orchids and mushrooms. By the way—how long have you been sitting in this cramped hole?"

"All morning. Why?"

"Then you haven't heard about the green rain."

150

James looked at her with surprise. "Green rain?"

"Sure. Outdoors. Didn't amount to anything—but for about ten minutes it rained green."

"I'll be damned! What was it?"

Shirley shrugged. "Search me. A green sky is bad enough. But a green rain—well, anything can happen. Higgins has bottles full of whatever it was—more like snow than rain—only not frozen. It misted the dome a little. And then—you probably haven't heard the rumor about Von Beitz that was going around."

"News?"

"Not news. A rumor. Scandal, I'd call it. People have been saying this morning that the spies hiding here are undoubtedly from the Midianite gang. Some of them are Germans. Von Beitz was a German. So they say that he wasn't kidnaped, but that he had always belonged to them, and merely joined them at the first opportunity."

Eliot James swore. "That's a lousy libel. Why—Von Beitz is one of the whitest men I know. A great brain. And nerve! I fought side by side with that guy in Michigan, and—why—hell! He's practically a brother of mine. Why do you think I went out scouring the other cities last month, and why do you think I've been in every corner of this burg looking? Because Von Beitz wouldn't turn us in for his life—that's why."

The handsome Shirley Cotton nodded. "I agree. But everybody's nervous these days."

"The Lord knows there's enough to make them nervous—"

They were interrupted by a banging on the door.

"Come in!" James called.

The door swung inward automatically. On the threshold stood Duquesne. He was ordinarily of ruddy complexion, but now his face was white. "Have you seen Tony?" he asked.

"No. What's the trouble?"

The Frenchman stepped into the room, and the door closed behind him. "I have searched everywhere."

James leaped to his feet. "You don't mean that Tony—"

"Oh—no, not lost. Just busy somewhere." Duquesne regarded the man and woman for a moment. "I was in a hurry to find him, because I have some very interesting information. I shall tell you. It is for the moment confidential."

"Sit," said the writer, as he had to his previous guest. "What's it about?"

"The source of our power."

James leaned forward. "You found it?"

"Not specifically. I have clung to the theory that power was generated under the city. When we learned that the interior of the planet was still warm, it seemed plausible that the power was generated from that heat—deep in the earth.

151

So I explored. It was difficult. All the electrical connections are built into the very foundation of the city. They cannot be traced. My assistants meanwhile studied the plans of the city—we found many. The clew in them pointed always toward a place in the earth. We finally—this morning—located that place. It is far underground. But it is not a generating plant. No."

"What is it, then?" James asked.

"A relay-station. A mere series of transformers. Stupendous in size and capacity. From it lead the great conduits—out, underground, deep down—toward the north. The station for this city is not here. It is as we suspected, in some other city —or place. And all the cities near here derive their power from that place. That is the explanation of why, when the lights came in one city, they came in all. It was a central plant which had been turned on—and which supplied every city."

"That's a very interesting confirmation," James said.

Duquesne snorted. "My dear young man! Can't you think of more to say than that it is interesting?"

James leaned back. "I see. You mean that now it is sure that they have control of our power."

"Exactly."

"And they can shut it off whenever they wish."

"Precisely."

"So that—when it gets colder—they can cut our power and not only put out our lights, but stop our heat."

"Right."

James tapped on his desk with the pencil he had been using.

"How much chance," he asked, "have we of setting up a power-station of our own—a station big enough to heat a couple of buildings, and light them, all winter?"

Duquesne shrugged. "What do we use for fuel?"

"Not coal—we've seen none. Or oil. How about wood? Those forests?"

"And how do we get wood here?"

"Trucks."

"And if our enemies are trying to freeze us into submission, would they let us save ourselves by running trucks day and night to distant forests for fuel? No. They would blow up the roads and bomb the trucks. It would take much wood to keep us warm. We could not run any sort of blockade—or cut wood under fire from an enemy. No."

"The river, then?"

Duquesne spread his hands. "You have imagination, my boy. But already it is too cold. And to build a dam and a hydro-electric plant takes months. I have thought of those things."

"In other words," Shirley said slowly, "if you are right about the Midianites being in possession of the power-plant, we'll have to take it way from them—or beat them somehow. Or else—"

James grinned bitterly. "Why not just leave it at, 'or else'?"

The Frenchman rose. "That is told in confidence. I may be mistaken in my conjectures. I shall now search for Tony further. He will in any case appear for luncheon." He left them, and they heard the nervous click of his heels as his short legs carried his large body down the hall.

"Not so good," said Shirley Cotton.

James went to the window. Down on the street below, people moved hither and thither. A few of the Bronson Beta automobiles shot back and forth on their roadways, and wound the spiral ramps of buildings. Overhead in the green sky the sun shone, brightening the city, touching with splendor its many-colored facets.

Then a mighty bell sent a rolling reverberation over the district. James turned from the window. "Lunch," he said.

He went with the girl to the dining-room. The five-hundred-odd inhabitants of Hendron were gathering. They came together on the street outside the dining-hall in twos and threes, and moved through the wide doorway to their appointed places. They talked and laughed and joked with each other, and on the faces only of a minority was an expression of unalterable apprehension. The rest were at least calm.

In ten minutes the hall was a bedlam of voices and clatterings, and the women on duty as waitresses hurried from the kitchens with huge trays.

Higgins invaded this peaceful and commonplace scene in great excitement. Instead of taking his place, he went to Tony —who was engaged in earnest private conversation with Duquesne—and spoke for a moment. Tony stood, then, and struck a note on a gong. Immediate silence was the response to the sound.

"Doctor Higgins," said Tony, "has made a discovery."

Higgins stood. This ritual had been followed in the announcement of hundreds of discoveries relative to Bronson Beta, and the life, arts and sciences of its original inhabitants.

"It concerns the greenness of the sky," Higgins said. "We have all remarked upon it. We have agreed that normal light polarization would always produce blue. We have agreed that any gases which would cause a green tint in atmosphere— halogens, for example—would also be poisonous.

"This morning at seven-eighty, Bronson Beta time, we had a green rain of nine and a half Bronson Beta minutes' duration. I collected the precipitated substance. It proved to be the explanation of our atmospheric color." He took a vial from his pocket and held it up. Its contents were green. "The color is caused by this. A new form of life—a type of plant unknown on earth. You are all familiar with the algæ in the sea—minute plants which floated in the oceans of earth in such numbers as to change the color in many places. Very well. The higher atmosphere of Bronson Beta is crowded by plants in some ways similar. These plants are in effect tiny balloons. They germinate on the surface of the earth apparently, in the spring. As they grow (the ground everywhere must be covered by them), they manufacture within themselves hydrogen gas. They swell with it until, like small balloons, they rise. Their hydrogen holds them suspended high in the atmosphere during the summer and fall—trillions upon countless trillions of them. They make a level of thin, greenish fog overhead. Examined microscopically, they reveal their secret at once.

"There is sufficient carbon dioxide and moisture to nourish them. They live by simple photosynthesis; and it is the chlorophyll they contain which makes them green—a characteristic of all terrestrial plants except the parasites. These plants reproduce from spores."

Higgins sat down.

His brief description was greeted by applause in which the botanists and biologists were most vehement.

Carter stood up. "About their precipitation, Higgins?"

Again Higgins took the floor. "I have only a theory to offer. Temperature. I believe that, although they are resistant to cold, an adequate drop in temperature will cause them to crack and lose their hydrogen. Then, naturally, they fall to earth."

"So you anticipate more green rain?"

"I do—a tremendous volume of it. And I may add that these plants fix nitrogen, so that their dead bodies, so to speak, will constitute a fine fertilizer, laid annually upon the soil of the entire planet."

Carter nodded. "Excellent, Higgins! Have you made calculations relative to the possible and probable depth of 'green rain' we may expect?"

"Only the roughest sort. I shall work on that at once, of course."

Again there was applause. Other questions were asked. The bottle began to pass from hand to hand. The meal was resumed. It did not continue long without interruption, however. While the five hundred people saved by Hendron dined in the city named for him, they were guarded by a perpetual watch. Not since the first glimpse of a strange plane flying over the original camp, had vigilance been relaxed. In Hendron, day and night, men and women stood guard—at the gates, in the top of the tallest building, and underground in the central chambers.

154

During that noonday meal the guards on the north gate saw one of the Midianite planes moving toward the city.

It was not uncommon for an enemy plane to pass across their range of vision. This plane, however, was evidently headed for the city of Hendron. When that fact became assured, the alarm was sounded.

In the dining-hall there was an orderly stampede.

A swift car from the north gate brought news of the danger.

Arms were taken from racks, and at vantage-points near the gates, men and women—some still carrying hastily snatched bits of food—took their posts.

The plane, meanwhile, had reached the dome of the city. It did not fly over, however. It did not drop bombs, or a message. Instead, it circled twice to lose altitude, and from a hatch in its fuselage a white flag was run up on a miniature mast.

Then it landed.

By the time it touched the ground, more than two hundred persons were on hand to see. The transparent cover of their city gave them a feeling of security. However, the flag of truce upon the plane did not encourage them to any careless maneuver.

The ship was expertly brought down to the ground, but afterward it behaved badly. It slewed and skidded. Its engine died and then picked up as it started to taxi toward the gate. It did not cover the intervening stretch of ground. Instead, it lurched crazily, hit a rock, smashed a wheel, dragged a wing —and its motor was cut. Then, half wrecked, it stopped.

There it stood, like a bird shot down, for five full minutes. No one moved inside it. No one made an effort to descend.

By that time every one in the city had rushed to its edge.

Tony gathered his lieutenants and advisers together.

"Ruse to get the gate open," Williams said.

"I think so," Tony agreed.

They waited.

Dodson, standing near Tony, murmured: "The Trojan-horse gag."

Tony nodded. . . .

Ten minutes.

"Let me go out there," Jack Taylor said finally. "Just open one gate a crack. They can't get a wedge in at that distance. It's some sort of booby trap—but I'll spring it."

Tony said no. They sat.

A thought moved through the mind of Eliot James. He went to Tony. "It might be Von Beitz. He might be hurt—"

Tony lifted a pair of powerful glasses to his eye. He saw several areas of holes on the plane's side. Machine-gun bullet-holes.

"Open the gate a crack—and lock it behind me," he commanded. He stalked to the portal. It yawned for an instant. He went out. Jack Taylor, winking at the men who manipulated the gate, followed close behind Tony.

Tony turned after the gate clanged, and saw Jack. He grinned. The people inside the city who watched, were deeply moved. Tony's decision to accept the danger—Jack's pursuit of his leader into peril—those were the things of which the saga of Hendron's hundreds were made.

They went cautiously toward the broken ship. No sound came from it. They were ready to throw themselves to the earth at the first stirring.

There was none.

The crowd watching held its breath. The two men were under the shattered wing. . . . Now they were climbing the fuselage.

Tony looked cautiously through a window.

Inside the plane, alone, on its floor, in a pool of blood, lay Von Beitz.

Tony yanked the door open. Taylor followed him inside.

Von Beitz was badly wounded, but still breathing. They lifted him a little. He opened his eyes. A stern smile came upon his Teutonic face.

"Good!" he mumbled. "I escaped. They have the power city. They plan to cut you off as soon as it is cold enough to freeze you to terms. I do not know where the power city is—it is not like the other cities."

He closed his eyes.

"Did they kidnap you here?" Tony asked.

He thought that Von Beitz nodded an affirmative.

From the outside came a yell of warning from many throats. Tony looked. The gate was open. People were pointing. In the north was a fleet of enemy planes winging toward the spot.

"Hurry!" Tony said to Taylor. "Take his feet. Gently—and fast! They're going to try to bomb us before we get Von Beitz' information back to the others!"

As he spoke, he and Taylor were carrying the inert man to the door of the shattered ship.

CHAPTER XVI

HISTORY

THE watchers at the gate of the city ceased to be mere spectators, and poured out. Many were useless; they merely endangered themselves to no purpose. Eliot James, who had the local command, shouted for all but one other, besides himself, to keep under the shield of the city; and he and that other ran forward as Tony and Jack Taylor emerged from the half-wrecked plane and pulled out the limp form of Von Beitz.

The two uninjured men, bearing Von Beitz, began to run across the open space between the city and the ship; and Eliot with his companion, Waterman, ran toward them.

From the north the swarm of pursuing planes approached —the planes of the Other People, of the Vanished People of this planet, which had been appropriated by the "Midianites."

At least, that was what Eliot believed as he glanced up and saw the great metal larks in the sky. It must be men from the earth who piloted them; yet deep in his thoughts clung the fantastic idea that it might be Bronson Betan hands which piloted these splendid planes, even as Bronson Betan hands and brains had built them a million years ago before the Other People began their frightful drift into the cold and darkness of space between the stars.

Bullets, or some sort of projectiles, splashed up dirt before him and left Eliot 'no illusions as to the attitude of these pilots, whoever they might be. But he was unhurt; his comrade also was unhurt, and neither Tony nor Jack Taylor stumbled.

The attack from the air ceased; the planes veered away and dispersed so suddenly that it seemed to Eliot that they must have been signaled.

Waterman and he reached Tony and Taylor, and the four bore Von Beitz within the gate, which swiftly was shut behind them.

Women, as well as men, surrounded them. Tony turned at Eve's touch, and he stared at her dazedly.

"Tony," she implored him, "are you hurt too? Did they hit you?"

He shook his head; he was panting so violently that any expression of his feelings, as she held to him, was impossible. For a brief moment he caught her hand and held it, but gasped only: "Get Dodson—for—Von Beitz."

The command was unnecessary. Dodson was already kneeling over the German.

Eliot pressed back the people who crowded too close. The surgeon opened his kit, which had never been far from his hand during the perilous months on this planet. He began to administer drugs. "Half starved," he muttered. "No bones broken. Exhaustion. In terrible fight. Fists. Knife—at least some one had one in the fight. Wait!"

The German opened his eyes and sat up. *"Danke schöne,"* he said.

"Not yet!" Dodson warned, pushing his patient back into a reclining position.

"Take your time," Tony begged him, though he himself jerked with impatience for Von Beitz' report. He gazed up through the shield over the city into the sky, for the airplanes which had pursued, and which so suddenly had abandoned attack.

"Where are they?" he said to Eliot James.

"Gone."

"What scared them off?"

"What happened to their other planes before, I guess," said Eliot.

"Would they all have remembered it together just at the same second?" Tony asked.

Eliot shook his head; the planes were gone, whatever had turned them back; thought of them could engage neither Eliot nor Tony—nor Eve, since they had spared Tony.

She clung close to him in tender concern. They were in the inner edge of the circle, watching the German, who lay now with eyes shut and a scowl on his face.

The spasm of pain appeared to pass; he opened his eyes, and looking up at Tony, he winked.

It was the most reassuring thing he could have done. "Good stuff!" Tony whispered to Eve.

"Where was he, Tony?"

The German seemed to have heard; he spoke to the Doctor. "I should not sit up, eh?"

Dodson reminded: "You've had a terrible beating, Von Beitz. You're half starved. When you've had some hot soup, and when I've dressed your various cuts and bruises, you'll be able to talk."

"Pooh!" said the man on the ground. "You've been searching for me, eh? And now you want to know why I come dramatically in a ship from the north? Well—I will tell you. I can eat later. But I lie down. You must know at once.

"I rounded a corner in this city as you know; and to you, I vanished. To myself—four men seized me. A cord about the neck, a sack over the head. It gave me no fear that my assailants might have been men from Bronson Beta," Von

Beitz added sardonically. "The technique was too much of our world as we have known it. I was down and helpless, knowing no more of my attackers than that they must be men from earth.

"We spent I do not know how long hiding high in a building in this city. My eyes were taped shut. I was gagged much of the time, but I was given food, and—except on occasions which I will come to—I was not badly treated.

"At first they spoke between themselves in tongues I could not understand, but it was not language of another planet. It was speech from our old world—Russian sometimes, I am sure; sometimes, I think, Japanese."

Von Beitz rested a moment.

"Did you discover how many they were?"

"Here in this city watching us," Von Beitz proceeded after a moment, "there were four at least. I am sure I heard four different voices speak. Sometimes it seemed to me that more moved back and forth; but I cannot be certain that more than four actually were here."

"Men?" asked Tony.

"They were all men. I heard no woman speak; it was never a woman's hand that touched me. But they talked a great deal about women as they watched us," Von Beitz said.

"You mean, you heard them talking about our women? They talked in some language you understood?"

"No; not then. They talked about our women in their own tongues. But I did not need to understand the words to know they were talking about—women."

"I see," said Tony.

"They did talk to me in English later—two of them did."

He stopped again.

"What did they tell you?"

"Tell me?" repeated Von Beitz. "Nothing. They asked me."

"Asked you what?"

"About you—about us. They wanted to know what we knew, how far we had progressed in mastering the secrets of the Old People."

"Ah!" said Tony.

"They were here—those four—before we moved into this city. They were sent here as similar squads of them were sent to every other city accessible to them. You see, they moved into their city—which apparently was the old capital of this planet or at least of this continent—long before we made any move at all."

"Yes," said Tony. "That's clear."

"Our delay," breathed Von Beitz, "laid on us a great handicap." He did not continue that criticism, but observed: "For *they* grasped the essentials of the situation almost at once. It lay, of course, in mastery of the mechanics of the ancient civilization. So they seized at once and occupied the key city; and they dispatched a squad to each of the other cities, to explore and bring back to them whatever might be useful."

Again he had to rest, and the others waited.

"Particularly diagrams."

"Diagrams?"

"The working plans of the cities, and the machinery and of the passages which, without the diagrams, you could not suspect."

"Underground passages?"

"Precisely. That is how they took me out of the city. They laughed at us guarding all the gates! When they decided to take me away, two of them escorted me underground and led me on foot to a door that was opened only after some special ceremony, and which communicated with a conduit."

"Conduit for what?"

"I could only suppose what. My eyes were taped, and during this journey, even my ears were muffled; but I am sure from my sensations during the journey that I was underground, and carried through a long, close conduit like a great pipe."

"Carried?" repeated Tony, as the others in the group excitedly crowded closer to catch the weak word. "How did they carry you?"

"In a car. They sat me up in some sort of small car which ran very rapidly—and, I am sure, underground. I could feel enough of it with my hands to be sure it was not what we would call a passenger-car. I am sure now, from what I felt at the time, and what I learned later, that it was a work-car, built by the Old People for their workmen in the conduit. I was taken into a power tunnel, I believe, and transported in a work-car through the conduit to the other city. Certainly when, after a time I can only estimate as hours, I was brought up to daylight, it was in the city occupied by Russians and Japanese, and with them, on the same terms, some Germans. There are also English there, men and women; but not on the same terms as the others."

"Go on!" begged several voices.

"They let me see the city—and themselves," said Von Beitz. "It is a great city—greater than this, and very beautiful. It offers them everything that they could have dreamed of—and more! It makes them, as they succeed in mastering its secrets, like gods! Or they think so!"

"Like gods!"

"Yes," said Von Beitz, "that is our great danger. They feel like gods; they must be like gods; and how can they be gods, without mortals to make them obeisance and do them reverence? So they will be the gods; and we will be the mortals to do their bidding. Already they have taken the English and

160

set themselves above them, as you have heard. They tried to take us—as you know. We killed some of them—some of the most ruthless and dangerous; but others remain. They know they need not endanger themselves. They wait for us confidently."

"Wait for us? How?"

"To come to them."

"But if we don't come?"

"We must."

"Why?"

"We have no help for ourselves—and they know it. For the truth is as we feared. For all these great cities of the eastern section of this continent," the German declared solemnly and slowly, "there is a single power city—or station. It is located deep underground—not directly beneath their city, but near it. Of course they control it, and control, therefore, light and power— and heat. Any of these we can enjoy only as they ration it to us.

"We move out, as we know, toward the cold orbit of Mars where heat will mean life in our long dark nights. They wait for that moment for us to admit their godship, and come and bow down before them."

Tony stared silently at Von Beitz, biting his lip and clenching his hands. He remembered the exaltation which he had felt—which he could not help feeling—when he realized that he was in command in this single city. *They* felt themselves in command—in absolute power—over this planet. He could comprehend their believing themselves almost gods.

The weakened man went on: "In the cavern city where are the engines which draw power from the hot center of this planet, a guard of the 'gods' stands watch. It is the citadel of their authority, the palladium of their power. I have not seen the station; but yesterday I learned its location. I stole a diagram and traced it before I was discovered. I escaped my guards. I fought my way into a ship this morning."

"You have the tracing?" Dodson whispered.

The German smiled. "I have it."

He shut his eyes and gave a sigh that was partly a groan. Dodson leaned over him. "We'll carry you to the center of the city now. You've taken a terrible beating."

Von Beitz opened one eye, then, and a grin overspread his battered features. "My dear Dodson," he replied spiritedly, although in a low tone, "if you think I've taken a terrible beating, you ought to see the other fellows. Three of them! One I left without so many teeth as he had had. The one who had the knife, I robbed of his weapon, and I put it between his ribs—where, I fear, it will take mortal effect. The third— alas, his own mother would neither recognize nor receive him!"

With those words the courageous Von Beitz quietly fainted.

Tony told Jack Taylor to post a call for a meeting, in the evening, of the Council of the Central Authority; and he himself accompanied those who bore Von Beitz to Dodson's hospital.

It was, of course, really a hospital of the Other People which Dodson had preëmpted. The plan of the place and its equipment delighted Dodson and at the same time drove him to despair trying to imagine the right uses of some of the implements of the surgery, and the procedures of those Vanished People.

Von Beitz' case was, however, a simple one; and Tony left, fully assured that the German would completely recover.

Tony went home—to the splendid, graceful apartment where he knew he would find Eve, and which they called their home because they occupied it. But they could never be free from consciousness that it was not theirs—that minds and emotions immensely distant from them had designed this place of repose.

Minds far in the future, Tony always felt, though he knew that the Other People actually pertained to the epochal past; but though they had lived a million years ago, yet they had passed beyond the people of earth before they came to gaze on the dawn of their day of extinction. So, strangely, Tony knew he was living in an apartment of the past, but felt it to be like one of the future. Time had become completely confusing.

What were years? What had they been? A year had been the measure of an interval in which the earth circled the sun. But the earth, except in fragments, no longer went around the sun. This planet had taken its place; and earthly time ceased to have significance. You lived in the time of this strange planet; its eons and epochs were behind you; and the incalculable accomplishments of its people.

The soft illumination of interiors, to which he had now become accustomed, glowed in the hallway. It was agreeable, soothing, never harsh; and the soft pastel colors of the walls showed patterns pleasing to the eyes, though they were eyes from earth, and earth never had seen anything similar.

Taste, thought Tony, reached through the universe; and beauty; and happiness—and peace. And cruelty also? When had these Other People been cruel? Had they cast it off only at last?

He was very tired, but excited too; he was glad to find Eve alone, awaiting him.

He kissed her, and held her, and for a moment let himself forget all else but the softness of her in his arms, and the warmth of her lips on his.

"Lord of my love," she whispered, in her own ecstasy. "Lord of my love," she repeated; and holding him, went on:

> *"To whom in vassalage,*
> *Thy merit hath my duty strongly knit."*

"Oh," said Tony.

"I memorized it as a child, Tony, never guessing at its meaning till now. How could Shakespeare have found words, dear, for so many feelings? . . . This place was planned for love, Tony."

"Yes."

"*They* loved here, Tony; some couple very young—a million years ago. We lie on their couch. . . . Where are they?"

"Where we, sometime, shall probably be; but why think of that? *'From fairest creatures'*—finish that for me, Eve, can you?"

"The first sonnet, you mean?"

"I don't know the number; but I knew it once—at Groton. I had to learn it to get into Harvard for the college board examinations. Wait: I've got more of it:

> *'From fairest creatures we desire increase,*
> *That thereby beauty's rose might never die.'*

"Where are Harvard, and Groton, now, Tony?"

"With Nineveh and Tyre; but you're here—and beauty's rose shall never die. . . . And by God, no one will take you from me—or freeze you in the cold, if I don't let you go."

"You've the diagram that Von Beitz brought?"

"I've seen it—studied it. He did well; but not enough. We know now where is the great central power-station; but we don't know how to get to it. We don't know even how they get in and out of this city."

"You think they still do?"

"We can't say that they don't. Undoubtedly Von Beitz was right; he was taken out by way of some conduit. We'll have to find that first, and stop it up or guard it; and then there may be a dozen underground doors leading anywhere, for purposes we've not progressed enough to guess. We've got to catch up on the old records of this place—though it's plain that some of them have been removed by the men who captured Von Beitz. Yet we've an awful lot to learn that we can learn."

"Tony, it's perfectly fascinating—and terrible, some of it. I met Professor Philbin when I was coming here. I never saw him so excited. He didn't know anything about what had just happened; he didn't even know that Von Beitz had returned. When I told him, he only stared at me; he wondered why I'd mentioned it. He was living in something far more exciting. He'd found the record, Tony, of the Other People when they first discovered the star of their doom approaching! He was looking for you; he wants to report to you what happened here, Tony, a million years ago!"

But Tony not yet could leave her. "If it's waited a million years, it can wait," he said, "ten minutes more."

TONY found Philbin with Duquesne, to whom the linguist had brought his version of the records he had decoded.

The French astronomer strode about the table in his excitement.

"We may picture now, with some confidence," he proclaimed to Tony, "the original situation of this planet—the place which it occupied in the universe when the people, who have provided these cities for us, lived.

"Its star—its sun—was, as we know, in the south. Eleven planets, of which this was one, circled that sun. This planet, and the one which we called Bronson Alpha, were the fifth and sixth in order of distance away from their sun. They were more closely associated than any other two planets; in fact, this planet revolved about Bronson Alpha almost like a moon. But it was not like our moon, which was always a dead world. It was Bronson Alpha, the greater planet, which bore no life; it was this planet—the smaller of the two—which bore life. And what a splendid order of life it bore at the end of its time!

"It seems to have been about two hundred years before the end that the people on this planet began to appreciate that a star was approaching which was to tear them away from their sun and cast them out into utter darkness and cold. There appear to have been living on this world, at that time, about one billion people."

"One billion people!" Tony exclaimed.

Philbin nodded. "One thousand million—about two-thirds of the population of our earth before our destruction began. I have found reference to earlier conditions of this planet which indicates that at one time the total population here might have been similar to ours. They had solved sanitation problems, and health and nutrition difficulties, at least a thousand years earlier; and for centuries their population grew rapidly; yet I believe that they never had quite the total population of our earth.

"After they became scientific and gained control of their living conditions,—and the conditions of birth,—they seem to have reduced their total number to about a billion. They seem to have stabilized at that figure.

"For centuries there seems to have been little change, except locally; they kept their birth-rate approximately level with their death rate. The thousand millions of people were spread fairly evenly, in cities, towns and villages, over the best parts of this planet. Civilization seems to have spread and been established everywhere, though the people were not everywhere homogeneous. It is perfectly plain that they had developed at least six different races of men, with some forty or fifty subdivisions distinguished by what we called 'national' characteristics. I have not yet been able to make out the form of their government at the time prior to the approach of the destroying star; but it is clear that war either was very rare or had been completely abandoned.

"They had come to provide for themselves a very high quality of life; they seemed to have established throughout their globe both peace and comfort—when their scientists saw their fatal star approaching."

"Go on," said Tony, when Philbin halted. "Or can't you?"

"Yes. I know a little more of what they did at that time— or at least how they felt—that billion people who used to live on this earth."

Yet he halted again while he gazed about the hall at their handicraft, their lovely sensitive art and decorations. They were gone—the billion of them—but they had been people who strived and struggled, and who had undergone an ordeal surpassing, in its prolonged torture, the agonies of the end of the earth. Philbin, the linguist and translator, tried to put some of this into words.

"You will pardon me, my friends," he said to Tony and Duquesne, "and understand that I can give you facts in fragmentary manner only, at this moment. My source is an autobiography of a man called Lagon—Lagon Itol. Lagon was what we would consider his surname. He was an artist and an architect of the time I speak of—the period of their discovery of, or their realization of, their threatened extinction from the approach of the star.

"With this autobiography of Lagon Itol, I found a volume about him by one of his contemporaries—one Jerad Kan. Lagon was a genius; he was, I think, the Michelangelo of this planet; and with this enormous artistic and architectural ability, he had an insatiable curiosity and interest in personalities. He kept a most careful diary, which is like nothing so much as Samuel Pepys'. Think of this remarkable man—Lagon Itol —as an amazingly vital, vigorous blending of our Michelangelo and Samuel Pepys.

"He records on this page,"—Philbin spread it before Tony and Duquesne,—"his first fear, if you will call it that, of the star.

"This is how I translate his words:

" 'Colk called to-day. He says the star Borak will certainly disturb us—or rather the great-grandchildren of our great-grandchildren. It presents us a pretty problem for survival.'

"Now the inspiring, and the exciting thing," exclaimed Philbin, "is to follow how this Lagon Itol immediately set to work to plan a scheme of survival for these people—though the need for that scheme would not come until the time of his great-grandchildren's grandchildren."

Duquesne, with Tony, was staring at the page, the words of which they could not read; but there was a sketch there which fascinated them.

"It looks," cried Duquesne, "like a first imagination of this city!"

"That's what it was," said Philbin. "It is perfectly clear that cities of this type were Wend, Strahl, Gorfulu, Danot and Khorlu.

"None of these names appear anywhere in the records of the time of which I am speaking; no such cities existed. Here Lagon Itol first began to dream of them, and he and his friend Jerad Kan began to write, educating the people to plan for what lay ahead of their grandchildren's grandchildren.

"For what happened to them—what, at that time, was threatened and had not yet occurred—was a widely different doom from that of our earth. When we discovered our destroyers, we knew that we ourselves must face the destruction, and that very soon."

"Precisely!" Duquesne had to exclaim. "Time for us was more merciful! For them—for two hundred years, at least, they must have looked at their doom! Tell me—tell me, friend, how a mind like Michelangelo's—this Lagon Itol—met it."

"In the most inevasive way. It is plain from his diary that, in his time, there was doubt—or at least the best scientists were divided—over the point as to whether the approaching star would tear this planet completely away from its sun, or would merely alter its orbit so as to make the climate, for part of the year, very much colder. Lagon Itol considered both of those possibilities. He made a plan for survival under colder conditions; he also speculated on the possibilities of survival even in the dark and cold of space.

"Lagon Itol himself did not believe that was the probability. The approach of the star was not to be a near passing, except in astronomical terms; it would not come within a billion miles of the sun of Bronson Beta. It was certain to effect the orbit of this planet; but would it make that orbit wholly unstable?

"Lagon Itol seems to have proceeded on the assumption it would not. On this day, on this page, he discusses that. On this next page, he is discussing the effects of the uses of *klul*."

"*Klul?*" asked Tony.

"Apparently it was a drug they used to make the air more exhilarating—or intoxicating. It seems to have been one of the dearest vices, or indulgences, of the Other People. They let *klul* evaporate in a room; then they came in and breathed it. It appears to have been extraordinarily pleasant; both sexes indulged in it, but it was forbidden to children. Lagon Itol records the formula, as he did all things that interested him."

"But," said Tony, "you found no actual diagram of the engineering arrangements under the cities?"

"At the time in which I now find myself," said Philbin, "these cities existed only in Lagon Itol's fancy. His diary either was missed by our friends the Midianites, when they tried to remove all diagrams that would have been useful to us; or else they considered this book harmless."

No one found more useful diagrams, during the days which swiftly were becoming colder.

Steadily the sun diminished in size; blue shadows stole across the plains of the adopted planet as the long, late afternoons dwindled to dark, and in the night, the outer temperature dropped far below zero.

Under the shield of the city, heat remained, and was renewed from the huge transformers fed from impulses far away.

By mercy of the Midianites!

By mercy, or by policy?

They argued this under the great glass shield of the city of Hendron—known to its builders long ago as Khorlu—while their world slipped farther and farther from the sun.

Hourly they argued this, especially at night, when the needed lights burned bright, and the ventilators spun, circulating the warmed currents of air to combat the bitter cold that settled on the shield. And machinery moved, because the power impulses sent from the station in control of the Midianites continued.

The enemy made no attack. Indeed, only at a distance did they reappear at all; and then it was in the sky. Larks hovered but far away—watching; that was all. And Tony told his pilots, who also were flying larks, not to molest them, or even appear to attack them.

What if they sent down a few flyers from the sky? Attack upon the city with a few planes would be absurd; attack from the ground would be fantastic. The defense, established in any of these great metal cities, must be impregnable; the advantage of cover was overwhelming. The Midianites themselves appreciated this. After the pursuit of Von Beitz, they made no move which even suggested an attack upon Hendron. To the contrary, they continued to send through the conduits under the ground the power-impulses which kept lighted and warm the city of Hendron, much as it had been when it was Khorlu, a million years ago.

Khorlu, Wend, Strahl, Gorfulu, and *Danot*—so the Other People had named the five cities they had built in defiance of the destruction stealing upon them—the five cities forecast in the sketches of Lagon Itol.

Wend was the great shielded metropolis which Tony and Eliot James first had visited; *Strahl* and *Danot* were the two similar cities seen, and mapped, to the south.

Gorfulu was the greatest; and not only that—it was the control-city of the group; for it dominated the underground works which generated the power for the entire group of cities. It was *Gorfulu* that the Midianites had seized for themselves, and to which they had brought the survivors of the English space-ship, as captives.

It had been easy enough to promise to the English girl who had escaped—Lady Cynthia, met on the road to Hendron-Khorlu—that Hendron's people would rescue the English from the Midianites. But that promise appeared only more and more wild and fantastic as the new inhabitants of Hendron-Khorlu became more familiar with the peculiar strength of the shielded cities.

Attack upon the city, with the weapons at hand and transportable, would be folly; every feature and material of construction of the cities gave overwhelming advantage to the defense.

No one offered any scheme of attack that suggested any chance of success.

Jack Taylor and Ransdell, and Tony and Eliot James and Peter Vanderbilt (for though he was not of the younger men, he remained of the boldest) met often and planned attack; but while they talked, they knew they were helpless.

"The fact is," said Eliot James once, putting frankly in open words what they all were feeling, "so far from being able to conquer *them,* we're at their mercy this minute; and they know it."

Peter Vanderbilt nodded. "And as regards them, I have little illusion that the quality of mercy is much strained. Let us adjourn for a walk in the square, or—what have you?"

"Tony, did you know that the portrait bust near the north gate is of Lagon Itol? Philbin assured me of it, quite positively, yesterday. He looked a good deal like Goethe, don't you think?"

"I'll take another look at it," said Tony; but he did not go out with the others. He sought Eve in the delightful apartment fitted for other lovers a million years ago, and lighted by the small distant sun whose heat was reinforced by warmth from power-impulses from machines engineered and prepared by the minds and hands of a million years ago, which had been repaired and were operated by the Midianites.

For the power-impulses continued to come; and this fact persuaded many, in the city of Hendron-Khorlu, that a change of heart must have affected the party of men from earth who held control of the capitol of the Vanished People.

They had come to their senses, some were sure as they worked, under the shield of the city of Hendron-Khorlu, at the emergency measures which the council of the Central Authority had ordered.

But if some believed in the mercy of the men who had taken over the capital that controlled the conditions in all the cities, others did not become so credulous.

"When are *they* going to shut us off?" they asked each other; and when they did not utter the words, they wanted to. The waiting had become an obsession.

They felt themselves teased and tantalized by this unceasing, silent provision of light and heat and power which kept them comfortable—indeed in luxury—under the dome of the great transparent shield when the world without was frozen.

The long rivers had turned to ice; the lake became a sheet of ice which the sun at noonday scarcely affected. Floes filled the seas, the pilots of the larks reported. Frequently at noonday, when the small sun stood nearly overhead, surfaces thawed, but when the world began to turn away, and long before the darkness, it was bitter cold again.

It was at night that It came—at dinner-time.

The company under Tony's command were assembled in the great hall where meals were served. A few of the men stood at salient posts, always on watch. There was a watch at the top of the tallest towers, and at the eight gates. Guards were posted also at the passages to the chief channels below the city. . . .

The lights went out. Later it was realized that, simultaneously, the movement of the currents of warmed air ceased; but at first this was appreciated only by those stationed near the fans, which whirred to a stop in a humming diminuendo.

Not only the great halls were blackened, but the streets became tombs.

It was an overcast night; and no single star showed even to the watchers on the towers. Light died and was buried; and all in silence.

In the unbreathing, Stygian oppressiveness of the dining-hall, Tony arose—an invisible figure. He felt blotted out. He wondered whether his voice, when he spoke, could be heard.

"They've done it, my friends. This is no accident, no failure which they will repair. They have shut off our power-source. So immediately we put into effect our plans for this emergency! we go under the power-loss orders which you all already know."

Matches were struck and applied to torches previously fixed on brackets about the hall. Everybody pretended to like it; everybody sat down again. Dinner went on in a medieval gloom.

Ransdell, charged with the security of the streets, went out and inspected the guard positions where he was challenged by his sentries, who examined him in the glare of flashlights attached to condenser batteries; but the stored electricity was to be used but sparingly. The company had charged the batteries by the thousand; but what were they against the darkness and cold to come?

Combustible substances must be used for light wherever possible, and always for heat.

"It's begun," said Dodson, the surgeon, to Eliot James.

"I won't worry about putting it down in my book to-night," the diarist replied. "I'll not forget it before to-morrow!"

He was aware of an anger within him which had no parallel in his experience—a smoldering anger that grew and grew.

"*They're* doing this," he said, scarcely more to Dodson than to himself. "They're doing this deliberately to freeze us out to them—to take their terms."

"What terms exactly, d'you suppose?" some one inquired calmly.

Eliot turned, and in the flickering glow of a flare, he faced Peter Vanderbilt.

"We'll hear soon enough, I'd say."

CHAPTER XVIII

THE FATE OF THE OTHER PEOPLE

BUT no terms came.

No proclamation, no communication at all, arrived from those in control of the capital city—and in control, therefore, of the five shielded cities.

Gorfulu maintained its illumination, as Eliot James and Ransdell ascertained by flying at dawn and sighting the great glowing dome of the ancient capital. Light pervaded that city as before; and beyond question, heat was there.

Ransdell circled the city and turned back, as larks, piloted by the Midianites, rose into the sky. Ransdell had promised Tony neither to seem to offer attack, nor to provoke it. He flew directly home.

Other pilots inspected the three other cities—Wend, Strahl and Danot, the shields of which, like the dome of the capital, remained aglow; and these pilots flew back also to Hendron-Khorlu, which alone of the five cities lay lightless and cold in the winter morning.

In the great Hall of the Council, these pilots joined James and Ransdell and completed their reports:

"They've cut us off—and us alone."

"Why not, then," some one said, "move to another city? To Wend?"

"Then wouldn't they cut us off there?" countered Ransdell practically. "The only reason those cities aren't cut off is because we aren't there."

"But they're not occupied, are they?"

"Not in force," replied Ransdell. "But they've an observation group in each of the other cities—as they had here."

"Then how about some other cities—elsewhere?"

"Where else?" questioned Ransdell; for he had done much observation flying.

"On some other continent—perhaps in the other hemisphere."

"There are no other cities suitable."

"Nowhere else in this world?"

"None. The old globes which we found do not show them; and we have never found any others."

"But why were there only these five?"

"Well," said Ransdell, "why were there even as many as five cities at the end?"

172

"But we have been told that the old population of the planet was one billion people!"

"Not at the end, however!"

"What happened?"

Dave Ransdell, for reply, turned about to Tony.

"We can give to-day at least a partial answer to that," Tony said, looking about the little group of his Council. "And I think it can be considered pertinent to our discussion of our own emergency, for we are dealing with a mechanism of living —or of dying—created not by ourselves but by the original people of this planet. It certainly can only be of help to us to understand what they did. Professor Philbin," he said, "please tell us."

The little linguist arose.

"You have all heard, I may assume, something of the state of this planet at the time when the studies of the star approaching convinced the scientists of this planet that it was certain to disturb life here greatly."

Peter Vanderbilt arose quietly; when Philbin stopped, Vanderbilt suggested:

"Should not every one hear this?"

"Certainly," said Tony. "Open the doors." And into the great room hundreds came and stood. For the halls without had been crowded. Nearly everybody was there, except men on watch or detailed to definite errands. Men, women and girls crowded as close as they could to the council-table; even the children came—the two children saved from the doom of earth on the first space-ship.

"I can assume," the little linguist repeated, "that you all have learned what we, who have been interpreting the books, learned and reported some days ago of the time of Lagon Itol, which was approximately two hundred years before this planet was torn from its sun.

"Lagon Itol—who was certainly a very great man, one of enormous perceptions and imagination—considers in his diary the fate facing one billion people; so we may put that as a rough figure for the population of this planet in his time. But he astutely observes that there would be nothing like that number finally to face their fate; and he was right. From his time, the people of this planet rapidly reduced themselves in number by diminishing births. In fact, before he died, he observed it and recorded it; he even speculated on the probable number who would be alive to face the catastrophe.

"I have now discovered an official record of their year 16,584, Ecliptic."

"Ecliptic?" a woman, close to the table, questioned.

"Ecliptic—reckoned, I mean, from the first eclipse. The old people here," Philbin explained, "had a very accurate and rational way of reckoning. For thousands of years, their determinations of time were exceedingly precise; but as on earth, of course their history went back through ages of rough record and without record into oral traditions. Undoubtedly they once had scores or hundreds of arbitrary points from which they reckoned the years locally—as our Egyptians reckoned years from the start of the reigns of each Pharaoh. As we all recollect, most of our civilized world finally agreed upon a year which we called the Year of Our Lord, from which we reckoned backward and forward.

"The people of Bronson Beta chose a year of a famous eclipse. For this planet, and its huge companion Bronson Alpha, circled their sun in such a way that eclipses sometimes— though rarely—occurred. They were not so frequent as with the earth; they happened, on the average, about once in fifty years. Each was, therefore, more notable; and early in the history of man on this planet, there was a special eclipse which was noted by many nations of the primitive people. Later civilized ages could identify that eclipse with certainty and assign it a definite date. It offered itself as a very convenient and logical point from which to reckon the start of rational processes— the first recorded eclipse.

"Lagon Itol first mentions the disturbing star in the year 16,481, Ecliptic. He died in the year 16,504—before which time, as I have told you, he saw the population of the planet rapidly being reduced.

"For the year 16,584 I have, I say, the official census figures; they total slightly over two hundred millions of people—a reduction of four-fifths in approximately a century, or a loss of eight hundred millions of people."

Many gasped aloud. "What happened?" voices asked. "A world plague? The Black Death?"

"No plague, no unusual death," the little linguist continued. "Merely a cessation of births—or what must have been, for a time, almost a cessation. Would we have done differently? Who of us brought babies into the world, in our last two years, only to be destroyed? How many of us would have wanted children against a destruction if it was still a hundred years away?

"What happened to this planet was one of the things that might have happened to our earth—"

Duquesne broke in: "In fact, my friends, what happened here was the commoner occurrence in the cosmos. The fate of our earth was one of the ends of existence which always was possible, but yet exceedingly rare. The fate of this planet was much more typical of the ends of the earths which have been happening, and must continue to happen, until the termination of time. What is the first state of a star? Loneliness. At last another star approaches; and from its own substance, streamers are torn forth. The disturbing star passes on; but it has begot—planets. For it is from the substance that streamed from the sun, when another sun came close, that worlds are born.

"They circle their solitary parent, the sun; they cool and grow old; and upon one or two, not too large or too small, or too near or too far away from the sun, life begins—and grows and changes, and becomes man.

"Through millions of years!

"And what saves him, through all these ages? Nothing but the solitary situation of his sun; it is the loneliness of the Life-giver—the loneliness of his sun in space—that permits man and his world to endure.

"But at last the sun suffers it no longer; once more, it must speak to another star; and at last—for always sometime it must be so, even in the loneliness of the sky—another sun approaches; and before fresh material is sucked out to start another set of worlds, the spheres already old are drawn away and cast out into space. Such is the circle of life—and death—of worlds, to which all must, in the end, submit. Sometime one of those cast-off worlds may find another sun, as this has done."

The Frenchman bowed to Philbin. "You were, monsieur, in the year of this planet the sixteenth thousand, five hundred and eighty-fourth, Ecliptic. I return you to it."

"It was a remarkable year," said the little linquist, thrillingly, "if for no other reason, because of the production of the tremendous pessimistic poem 'Talon.'

"I translate the original title—*Talon*, a claw. The Talon of Time was meant. The people here understood the awful circle of the life, and death, of worlds as M. Duquesne has just sketched it. The poet of 'Talon' was the Omar Khayyám of their days of facing their fate. So in a poem of marvelous power he pictures man pursued by Time—a great tantalizing, merciless bird of prey which waits for him through the ages while he rises from a clod without soul to feel and brain to know, until he can appreciate and apperceive the awful irony of his fate; then the bird reaches out its great talon and tears him to pieces.

"I despair adequately to render in our words the ironic tragedy of this poem; but Fitzgerald, translating our Omar, has rendered two lines like two of these:

> 'And lo!—the phantom Caravan has reach'd
> The nothing it set out from. Oh, make haste!'

"Like Omar, the poet preached pleasure; and he laughed at the ghastly futility of those who defied and fought the fated drift of their world into eternal darkness and cold.

"Clearly he presented the prevailing mood of the period; but clearly, also, there was another mood. The spiritual and in-

tellectual heirs of Lagon Itol had proceeded with his plans for
these cities.

"There was yet no complete agreement among the scientists
that this world must be torn away from its sun. Its orbit was
on the edge of the critical area of disturbance. Every one agreed
that the five outer planets would surely be torn away; they
agreed that the next planet inferior—that is, nearer its sun
than this one—probably would not be torn away.

"The name of that planet was Ocron; and by the way, these
people knew that it was inhabited.

"They agreed that this world on which we now stand would
be severely altered in its orbit; yet they considered there was a
chance it would not be torn away.

"Yet that chance did not appeal to many. By the year
16,675 Ecliptic—which is the last year for which I can find
a census—the total population was under twelve million, and
many of them very old. The number of children under ten
years is given separately; they were less than a hundred and
fifty thousand. At the rate they were allowing themselves to die,
probably there were barely ten millions of people of all ages
when the disturbing star—which they called Borak—came its
closest and cast them off into space.

"The best of the energies of the dwindling millions had been
put, for two generations, into these five cities which were
planned, located and created and equipped for the final defiance
of extinction. They abandoned all older habitations and adopted
these."

"But where did they go, in the end?"

A dozen demanded it, together.

"Of that mystery, we have not yet," Philbin confessed, "a
trace. They had reduced themselves, we know, from a billion
in number at the time of Lagon Itol—two hundred years
before—to about ten millions. Barely one per cent of them,
therefore, were spared up to the time of the catastrophe to attempt the tremendous task of further survival.

"Throughout at least the last five thousand years of their
history, cremation of the dead was universal among them. We
will find no cemeteries or entombments, except perhaps a very
few archaic barrows from a very early age. The people throughout their civilized period disposed of their dead in a systematic,
orderly and decent way.

"Now, did the last ten million also die, and as they went,
were they also cremated by their survivors, so that we will find,
at the end, only the bones of some small group who, enduring
to the last, had disposed of those immediately before them? Or
somehow, did some of them—escape?"

The great chamber of the Council was tensely silent, close-
crowded as it was.

It was Tony, presiding, and having the advantage of having heard most of these facts before, who first found voice:

"Returning to our present problem," he recalled them to that which had gathered them together, "it is clear that we can find no other cities of the shielded type, and equipped to combat the cold, except the five we know; for no others ever were built. We know also that there is no other generating station providing light and heat and power, except that close to Gorfulu; for no other ever was planned or built."

CHAPTER XIX

THE PIONEERS PLAN REPRISALS

JACK TAYLOR'S post, when on watch, was the northern gate.

"The Porte de Gorfulu," Duquesne had dubbed it, recalling the fashion in Paris of naming the gate after the city to which, and from which, its road ran.

There was not at this gate, or at any of the seven others, any actual guard station. What Philbin had read had made certain, if it had been doubtful before, that the builders of these cities had acted in complete coöperation and unison; they had been banded together in their desperate attempt to defy their fate of dark and cold.

However, the structural scheme and the materials chosen had made each gate exceedingly strong. It would have required artillery to reduce it; and artillery here did not exist, except perhaps in some museum of archæology of the Vanished People.

The blast of the atomic tubes, which had transported the Arks through space, of course could reduce any of the gates; but first they must be brought to the vicinity and placed in position; and if this could be done without danger, there was the problem of the lining of the tubes. Those in the second space-ship from Michigan, commanded by Ransdell, actually had burnt out at the end of the passage, and had contributed to the disaster which overtook that party.

Little, indeed, had been left of the lining in the tubes of the Ark which Hendron himself, more successfully, had piloted. So it was fairly certain that the propulsion tubes in the possession of the Midianites must be in similar state.

"What they have left of the lining, they'll save for their own defense—as we used ours," Jack expressed his opinion to Eliot James, who to-day was standing watch with him.

Eliot nodded. "I think so. At least, I'm sure they'll not attack us with the tubes; they'll not think it necessary. They figure, of course, we've got to come to them."

"Well," challenged Jack, "haven't we?"

Eliot gazed out the gate along the road where the shadow of a post placed by the Ancient People lay long and faint upon the ground.

"There goes the sun," he said. "And gosh, it's cold already! But we can burn things to keep warm. It's humiliating as hell; but we can burn old wood or grain, or a thousand things, and keep warm for a while, anyway. Physically, we're not forced to go to *them;* but can we be men—and stay away?"

"That's it," Jack commended his friend. "That's it exactly."

"I know," said Eliot. "I was never so mad in my life as the night when they cut off our light and heat. I could have done anything—if I could have got to them, for it. It was the most infuriating thing I ever felt."

"Are you telling me?" said Jack. "You thought you were alone in that feeling?"

"Of course not; but I can't laugh at it yet. Can you?"

"No; and I never expect to—until I can fix that feeling."

"But how can we fix it?"

"Exactly. How can we? How in the world—how on Bronson Beta, Jack, are we going to be able to get at *them?"*

"Tony'd like to know; but it's got to be without too great a risk. He won't have us killed—not too many, anyway."

"Well, how many of us would he think it worth while to lose, if we took Gorfulu?"

"Do you think you know how to do it? . . . Whew, that chill certainly comes on."

"Sun's gone; and damn' little of it there was to go. We simply weren't made to be this far away from the sun."

"Half a year from now, you'll be saying we weren't made to be as near the sun as we'll be."

"If we live till then."

"Yes; and if this cock-eyed world decides to do a decent orbit really around the sun, and not go sliding off into space, as it's done before."

"What makes you say that? Do you think Duquesne and Eiffenstein are giving us a run-around? They say we're coming back, and too close to the old sun for comfort."

"Yes," agreed Jack. "But do they *know?* Does anybody know until the old apple does it—or doesn't do it? Somebody certainly must have told the people who built these cities that they were going to stay in sight, at least, of some sun; and they certainly took a long ride in the dark. . . . Hello, here's our relief." And Jack hailed the pair who appeared in the twilight of the street; he passed them his report, *"Everything quiet,"* and he started up the street with Eliot toward his quarters.

"What's the hurry, soldiers?" some one softly hailed from the darkness of a hooded doorway. It was a girl's voice, teasing, provocative.

Both halted. "Who are you?"

"Please, soldiers, we're only friends caught out in the dark and needing protection."

Jack laughed, and knew her before he turned on his flashlight. "Marian," he demanded, "what are you doing here, and who's with you?"

Then her companion, Shirley Cotton, made herself known.

179

"We were hoping," Marian Jackson said, as the two girls walked along with the two young men, "for somebody to come by who knows how to turn on the heat again, not to speak of the lights."

"Were you in that building?" Eliot asked her.

"We were; and I tell you, it's hard to open doors now that the power's off. They stick terribly."

"What were you doing in that building? You know you shouldn't have gone in from the street alone."

"Sure I know," agreed Marian blandly. "But where have we got by obeying all your nice orders?"

"What were you doing, Marian?"

"Shall we tell them, Shirley?"

"Why not?"

"Well," said Marian, speaking carefully as though she might be overheard, "we decided we'd see what we could do as baits."

"Baits?"

"Baits. The chunks of meat trappers used to put in traps, and like minnows on hooks—baits, you know. My idea."

"Then," said Jack generously, "it must have been a pippin. Baits. I've got the general underlying scheme of you girls now; go on."

"But there's nothing to go on to; nothing happened."

"The fish didn't come?"

"No nibble. No. But give us time, boy. There's some way, we know, by which somebody still gets in and out of this city. The idea is, we hope he—or they, if they're two of 'em—will try to grab us. We'll go along."

"Sabine-women stuff, Eliot," Shirley put in.

"What?" asked Marian Jackson.

"I'll tell you later, dear," Shirley offered.

"Oh," sniffed Marian. "Deep stuff! Well, anything they didn't teach in the first six grades of the St. Louis grammar schools is lost on me. Still, you got me curious. What did the Sabine women do, Shirley?"

"They went along," Shirley told her, "with the men from the other city that grabbed them."

"And then what did they do, darling?"

"They stayed with them as willing little wives."

"No stabbing after they found the way in and out?"

"No," said Shirley. "That's where the Sabine women were different."

Jack Taylor whistled softly. "So that's what you little girls were up to?" he said. "Perhaps it's just as well we came along. But they rather show us up, eh, Eliot?"

Dinner was a moody meal in the evening of that prolonged day. The natures of the people from earth had not adjusted themselves to the increased length of both day and night; most of the people still slept, or at least went to bed, for eight hours of each twenty-four, so they dozed by day and were awake, on the average, sixteen hours of each period of darkness.

Philbin had learned that this had not been the custom among the ancient people; they had passed through the stages of evolution adapted to the long day and night; but it appeared impossible for the people from earth to acquire this adaptation.

Accordingly, after dark, there were long, restless periods; and to-night Eliot James, Jack Taylor and Peter Vanderbilt, with two more of the younger men—Crosby and Whittington —met for a midnight discussion.

Tony was not called to this informal council of his friends; nor was Ransdell; for Tony, though personally the same with all of them, yet was Chief of the Central Authority; he bore the responsibility; and if he forbade the enterprise on foot, his friends could scarcely proceed. So it was agreed not to let him know. And Ransdell, too—being charged with the security of the city—had better learn about the plan much later.

The five gathered in Vanderbilt's quarters, which were not cramped, to say the least. There was no need in that city, constructed on its splendid scale for some two millions of people, for any one now to be niggardly of room. Each of the emigrants from earth could choose his own dwelling-place, so long as it was approved for its security.

Peter Vanderbilt had chosen what would have been called, on earth, a penthouse—a roof-dwelling, built, he was sure, by some connoisseur of living.

The place delighted Peter; it was on a roof but near an edge of the city where the shield sloped steeply down; so the roof there was not high, and was easily reached by foot, after the power failed.

Also it was especially well adapted for habitation in the present emergency when the heating apparatus prepared for the city had failed or rather, had been cut off. For the original builders had allowed for no such emergency; they had been dealing with elements in respect to which they had no reason to figure on that factor of failure—the internal heat and radioactivity of the core of the planet. Stoppage of that was unthinkable; and so, to them, was the cutting of the power-conduits to any of the cities. Therefore they had supplied no alternative heating arrangement.

As a consequence the present tenants had to employ the most primitive methods of keeping themselves warm in these lovely supercivilized chambers. They were driven to build bonfires in some of the great halls; but they spared those of exceptional splendor.

Peter Vanderbilt, being on the roof in his "penthouse," had contrived a chimney and a fireplace which gave him heat without much smoke or soot.

181

It was before this fire that the five gathered.

"Wonderful place you have, Peter," said Whittington, looking around. He had not visited it before, and he went about examining the metal panels of mountain, woodland, marsh and sea, all splendid in the colors of enamel paints baked on.

Peter asked him: "Are you complimenting me? All I've done is to choose it. . . . Do you know, not a thing was flecked or rubbed, not a thing was worn. The man who made it never used it."

"It seems so with most of the buildings," said Whittington. "It seems they must have gone on building them to complete their plan, after they knew they themselves would never fill them."

"What else could they do," asked Eliot, who had thought much about this, "while they waited? Could they just wait—for slow annihilation?"

"Philbin," said Vanderbilt, "rendered a couple of lines of his poem 'Talon.' He says it gives no idea of the enormous melancholy of the original; but as he said modestly, it is better than no translation at all:

" 'And now the winds flow liquid,
  The sole cascades to seek the sea.
  At last these awful streams themselves are hardened.
  The air that once was breath is metal, frozen.
  Where, then, are we?' "

Nobody spoke until Taylor, after a moment, put wood on the fire.

"Did you hear, Peter," he questioned, "what those girls—Marian and Shirley—were out to do?"

"Yes," said Vanderbilt; and the five got immediately at the problem of how to gain entrance and control of Gorfulu.

"Seidel is in command, Von Beitz is sure," Eliot James said. "Cynthia agrees that is most probable. He was pushing aside Morkev, who was nominally chief Commissar—he called himself that—when Lady Cynthia escaped.

"Von Beitz says that Seidel supplanted Morkev but did not kill him, Morkev had too many friends. It is perfectly certain that there are two factions among our friends the Midianites, which is complicated, of course, by their racial mixture. Their position is further complicated by the English, who obey them only because they must.

"Cynthia has told us, and Von Beitz has confirmed it, that the mixture on top is constantly afraid of what they call 'a rising of the serfs'—that is, the English. They guard against it. The English are allowed to gather—even for work—only in very small groups, and always under supervision."

"It looks like a set-up," observed Whittington, optimistically, "if once we get in."

Vanderbilt shook his head. "Eliot specialized, in that speech, on their elements of weakness. Their strength is utter ruthlessness. I believe that, when they attacked your camp," he said to Eliot James, "you killed a good many of them, and some of the most violent fell. But enough were left. Von Beitz says that Seidel keeps himself surrounded by them. He has no use for the milder men. He has a despotism which he completely controls by intimidation; and no form of government is more merciless and efficient—at least at first. And this is very early in the life of this particular despotism."

"There is a building which they call the Citadel," Jack Taylor said, as if he had heard none of this. "It held the offices of administration of the Old People. Seidel occupies it with his inner ring.

"If three of us could get in—or two of us—and kill ten of them,—the ten top men, including Seidel,—we'd—"

"What?"

"We'd at least be able to start something," Jack ended somewhat weakly.

"But the two of you would have to kill the ten of them and the top ten—before you could really begin," said Peter Vanderbilt quietly. "How simple you make it seem!"

Taylor swore, then laughed. "We don't know what we could do; or what we'd have to do. But we do know this: some of us, somehow, have got to get into that city, and that Citadel of that city. Then we can trust to God and what chances He may offer us. But first, and whatever's before us, we're going to get in! Agreed?"

"Agreed!" said all voices, and Vanderbilt's was distinct among them.

"Now how? We've no chance to advance against them by air or on the ground—or under the ground from the direction of this city. We know they've got guarded all the conduits and passages which we've discovered; and probably some we don't know about. But would they guard the conduits from the other cities?"

"That's something, Jack! Say—"

"See here. There's Danot—on the other side of them from us. They've a guard in there; we've nobody. They'd never look for us to come from that quarter. We get into Danot and go underground! We—"

That night was long, but not long enough for the five conspirators.

CHAPTER XX

RANSDELL, on the evening of the third day later, reported to Tony:

"Five men have not returned—three of our best friends, Tony," he said, dropping formality. "Eliot, Jack Taylor and Peter Vanderbilt—and Whittington and Crosby with them. They left, you know, in two 'larks' about two hours before dusk yesterday. They said they were only going to have a look around. I thought it was a good idea; I told them to go."

"No word from them at all since?" Tony asked.

"Not a syllable. Marian Jackson is missing too."

"She went with them?"

"No. Entirely separately; and she went on the ground, not in the air. The gate watch who let her go out—it was Cluett—was ashamed of himself and did not report it promptly. It appears that she drove to the gate in one of the small cars, and wheedled Cluett into letting her take a turn outside. It was near noon, and the sun was shining. He saw no harm and let her pass. Then she turned the battery on full, and streaked away.

"Still he thought she was just fooling with him, and would return, probably by another gate; so he sent no one after her. But as far as we're concerned, that was the end of her."

"Which gate?" asked Tony briefly.

"The northern gate. Duquesne's Porte de Gorfulu."

"She disappeared down that road?"

"Yes. And the only word she left behind with the girls she knew was that she was tired of being cold; she thought she'd try being warm again. She commented, further, that she sees now she pried herself into the wrong party."

Tony nodded; he knew what that meant. Marian frequently reminded everybody that she hadn't been selected among the original company for either Hendron's or Ransdell's spaceships; she had pried herself into the party. Obviously, she meant she wished she had chosen the ship of the Asian Realists who now held the capital city, Gorfulu.

"Have you searched for her?" asked Tony.

"I've flown myself," Dave said, "along the road more than halfway, to be sure she wasn't wrecked by the road."

"Probably," said Tony, "she went right on. But do you think the others were up to anything foolish?"

"I'm sure of it," Ransdell answered.

"Why? Did they tell you?"

"Not me—Higgins. And he's just told me. Tony, they're dead now; or they're trying to get into Gorfulu from Danot. From what they told Higgins,—who swore to keep it until to-night,—we can't possibly help them now, except by being ready to respond to their signal that they're in Gorfulu and will have a gate open for us."

Tony rose excitedly.

"From what they told Higgins, and he told you, is the signal—overdue?"

"It is, Tony; that's the trouble. I don't know in detail what those—those glorious idiots tried to do; but the signal, Tony, is overdue!"

Four of them, at that moment, were alive. Crosby was dead; they had his body with them. Of the four alive, not one was unwounded; and they were lying in the dark in the tube of the power-conduit between Danot and Gorfulu, and with both ends of the tube closed against them.

They had taken Danot; at least, they had surprised one gate and got in. For they had grounded their larks in the valley beyond Danot, and accomplished this in the twilight, unseen. Then they had crept to the western gate, surprised the guard and got in.

Two of the other side fell in this fight; and Crosby and Taylor were shot. Jack still could walk, but the others had to drag Crosby with them.

Once inside, they met their bit of luck—or they thought it that. Four men had been at the gate they surprised; and the two that fled separated. James and Whittington took after one of them, leaving Vanderbilt with the wounded men. The luck was that the man they pursued fled to the conduit-tube which supplied Danot from Gorfulu.

They caught that man in the tube, overpowered him; and Whittington went back to guide Taylor and Vanderbilt and help him with Crosby. Meanwhile, Eliot had found the work-car which traveled in the tube beside the great cables to the transformers. It was part of the equipment made by the Other People which the Midianites were using when they traveled back and forth.

The five had hardly got into the tube; and Vanderbilt was helping Crosby to the car, when the man who had escaped led another group of the guard underground. Eliot and Whittington turned back to fight them; and Vanderbilt and Taylor turned too.

It was revolvers and knives and iron bars—anything was a weapon at close quarters.

Everybody was wounded; but the five got away on the car, with Crosby dying. Power was on; and lights were on. The whole tunnel was illuminated; and the track of the car in the huge conduit was clear.

Eliot James put on the power, full. He saw the chance to surprise Gorfulu; he saw the probability, too, that some signal might be sent ahead by the survivors of the fight in the tube.

But there was a chance—a chance!

So Eliot opened it wide, and they sped on—the four living men wounded, and one dead, on the car to catch by surprise the city that controlled the continent and which the enemy from earth held. For two hours thus they traveled.

Then—the lights were extinguished; the car rushed on in a Stygian cave. But the car's speed was slowing; the power that propelled it was shut off.

It did no good for Eliot to thump the control; the power was gone; the car slid to a stop.

So there they lay underground in the tube, without light or food or water; one dead, four wounded. It seemed senseless; yet the only thing left to do was for the wounded to crawl the rest of the way to the chief city held by the enemy.

Marian Jackson's situation was not in the least like theirs. Marian had driven by broad daylight to the chief gate, and shown herself and begged admittance.

Marian was exceedingly good-looking; and the guard who parleyed with her had the good sense to take her at once to his superior, who knew that his business was to show her to Seidel.

Seidel spoke English; Marian's "line," as well as her appearance, pleased him.

She pointed out that the American parties—both of them from both ships—were composed of fools. She congratulated herself that she had not been chosen by them to join them; she had made them take her.

This was true; and Seidel had learned that it was true, from his spies in the city. Marian was tired, she said, of ninnies from America who had chosen themselves to people this planet. They couldn't even keep themselves warm!

Seidel had Marian assigned to quarters close to his in the Citadel.

During the second day, she got a good view of the local situation, learning, among other things, that Seidel had taken very clever measures to protect himself against the always-feared uprising of the serfs: All the other rooms surrounding his suite were equipped with sprays which, upon pressing a lever, spread stupefying and paralyzing gas—the same gas which the Midianites had used in the attack on Hendron's camp.

186

Also, Seidel had learned the use of *klul*. Indeed, he was addicted to *klul*, but he had let no one but the chemist who supplied him with the drug, know it.

However, he let Marian know.

Marian pretended she had never heard of it before. How would she, among the Americans, who were only fools? The fact was, Marian had tried it out pretty thoroughly, and was proud of the fact that she had a pretty good "head" for it.

Seidel thought it would be very amusing to induct Marian into the uses of *klul*. It was most pleasant and effective, he had found, when breathed in a warm, almost steamy atmosphere. He liked to let it evaporate beside the bath, then to lie in the bath, breathing the *klul*-drenched air. He had a marvelous bath in his suite in the Citadel. The Ancient People had built a pool which could be heated to any temperature—a beautiful, enamel-tiled pool with gay decorations.

Seidel insisted that Marian swim with him alone in the lovely pool and breathe *klul*. He dismissed his attendants and led her in.

The *klul*, in its big basin, was rapidly evaporating in the warm, steamy air. Marian kept herself covered with a single garment like a kimono.

He ordered her to throw it off and bathe with him. She asked, first, to breathe more *klul;* and she pretended that she was very intoxicated.

She danced and delighted Seidel, who ordered her to throw off her garment and dive into the water with him.

"Why do you keep it clutched about you?" he demanded.

In a moment, she showed him; for he tried to tear off her kimono, and she let go with her hand, which had been holding, under the cloth, a knife.

She stabbed him as he reached for her. She left the dagger in him as he staggered back. He cursed her, and found his alarm signal before he pulled out the knife, threw it at her—and died.

Marian heard them at the door. For a moment she was dizzy; perhaps the *klul* was affecting her. She picked up the knife, with which she had killed him, and armed herself with it again. Then she remembered the protection he had prepared for himself against the uprising of the serfs.

She pulled the lever that sprayed all the outer rooms with the stupefying gas—the rooms filled with his friends, the most dependable and trustworthy of those who had supported him.

The signal promised by the five—if they succeeded—did not come to Hendron-Khorlu. It was longer and longer overdue.

At dawn Ransdell set out to fly toward the capital city and toward Danot beyond it; but on the way he met another plane.

A lark, it was—one of the machines of the Vanished People flown by another pilot from earth; and Ransdell, not seeking encounter, was avoiding it when he saw that the passenger—or observer—in that plane was standing, waving to him.

Ransdell swung about, and curiously, yet keeping a cautious distance, pursued the plane, which was making straight for Hendron.

It landed on the field outside the city; and Dave followed it down.

Two men stepped out; and it was evident that the passenger was watching the pilot; the passenger was armed; the pilot was not.

Ransdell and Waterman, who was with him, approached the pair; and the passenger, forgetting his watch of the pilot, hurried to them.

"You're the Americans?" he hailed them in English; more, he spoke like an Englishman.

"Yes!" called Ransdell. "Who are you?"

"Griggsby-Cook! Once Major Griggsby-Cook, of the Royal Air Forces!"

"Where from?" challenged Ransdell wonderingly.

"Where from?" repeated the Englishman. "Out of slavery, I'd say! I came to tell you. We've taken over the city, since that girl of yours stabbed Seidel and gassed the rest of the ring! We've taken over the city!"

"Who?" demanded Ransdell; and answered himself: "Oh, you mean the English! Then Taylor and James and Vanderbilt and the five of them got in!"

"The five?" repeated Griggsby-Cook. "It was a girl that got in! She did for Seidel in his bath—like Charlotte Corday with Marat!

"Then she gassed a lot more. . . . There was nothing to it when we got wind of that, and rose against them. I say, we've quite taken over the city! I buzzed off to tell you chaps. Didn't take time to learn the trick of this plane myself; so I pistoled one of their pilots into taking me. But he's good now, isn't he?"

Ransdell nodded; for the pilot was meekly waiting.

"Oh, they'll all be good!" said Griggsby-Cook confidently. "They'll have to be."

"But the five—the five men that went from here?" Ransdell persisted.

"Know nothing of them!" said the Englishman. "Sorry."

Then no one spoke; but the four of them stared, as in the dim gray dawn, the great dome of Khorlu began glowing, and illumination showed in the streets too.

"The lights are coming on!" Ransdell exclaimed incredulously.

"Yes," said the Englishman. "We were working at that; they hoped to get the power to you before I got here!"

It was only a little later that the same English engineers restored the power-supply to Danot, which had been cut off for reasons unguessed, until they had searched the tunnel and found one dead and four wounded Americans.

Tony Drake, on entering the capital city, went first to the hospital rooms where Eliot and Jack Taylor and Whittington and Peter Vanderbilt lay. They would all "pull through," the English surgeon promised; but he could not say so much of others under his care; for the uprising had cost, on both sides, thirty lives; and ten more of the wounded would not recover.

But battle on Bronson Beta was over—at least for the present. Further contest was unthinkable; yet it was prevented only by the overpowering numbers of the Americans and English together, when compared to the still defiant few of the "Asian Realists." Some score of these had to be confined; but all the rest were reconciled to the government that was being arranged by the Americans and the English.

They were gathered all together in Gorfulu; and they were going to have a great meeting to discuss and agree upon the form of government.

Marian Jackson sat with the men on the committee; for surely she had earned the right; but she had not, as she herself proclaimed, "the first ghost of a glimpse of government."

What was it to be?

Some suggested an alternate dictatorship, like the consuls of Roman republic, with an American consul alternating in power with an English. Others declared as positively that all rivalries and jealousies of the shattered earth should be forever banished and denied.

There were a score of other schemes.

And more debate than ever before on manners and morals—especially about marriage. Should there be laws for love? Cast off conventions and taboos! All right; try to get along without any. . . .

Tony retired to the lovely apartment provided in the capital city for Eve and himself; he was very tired. The day had been dark and long, and outside the shield of the city, very cold.

It was neither dark nor cold within; for the power-plant more than supplied needed heat and light. The people were provided with every material thing.

"And to-day," said Tony to his wife, "we ascertained beyond possible question that this planet stays with the sun. To-day we passed aphelion, and have definitely begun to approach the sun again. Life here will go on."

"Our life together, Tony!"

He kissed her more tenderly for his child within her.

"I've not dared think too much of—our son, Eve. But now it seems certain he'll come into a world where he can live. But what strange, strange things, my dear, he is sure to see!"

THE END

In the Bison Frontiers of Imagination series

To order or obtain more information on these or other University of Nebraska Press titles, visit www.nebraskapress.unl.edu.